Thrice Blest

M. L. Greer

ISBN: 1543000207
ISBN-13: 978-1543000207

DEDICATION

This book is dedicated to my great-grandfather, Harry, who had the courage late in his life to come to a new land, "not for himself, but for future generations". It is also dedicated to my father, Michael, who was a storyteller to the very end of his days.

CONTENTS

ACKNOWLEDGMENTS

This book would not have been possible if my great-grandfather hadn't made the difficult decision to immigrate to Canada for the sake of future generations. Nor could it have been if not for my diedo and baba, whose unshakable faith laid the foundation for a good life for themselves and their descendants in a new land. It could not have been if not for my father, a storyteller to the very end and for all the storytellers, who have shaped our understanding of other times, peoples, and places. So, to all great-grandfathers, grandfathers and grandmothers, fathers and storytellers, those who inspire and encourage storytelling, and all who have brought us to where we are today – thank you!

I am grateful to all who encouraged and supported my efforts to write this book. I am especially grateful to my husband, for reading and re-reading the manuscript and providing input and technical support. I thank my mother, ever the teacher, for helping to proof the manuscript. I am also grateful to a beloved aunt, who supported this book up to her final days. It was she who first heard the initial chapter read aloud. Her involuntary reactions to the characters and what they were doing was the most rewarding experience I had during the writing process. Finally, I am grateful to my sister, a historian and member of the Sister Servants of Mary Immaculate.

Ivan's Family Galicia

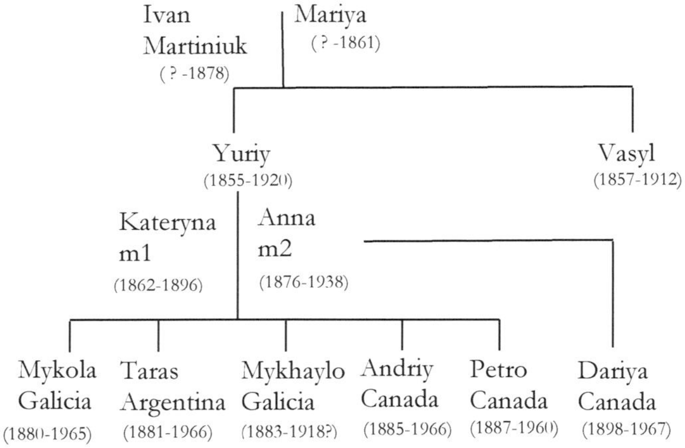

Yuriy's Family in Canada

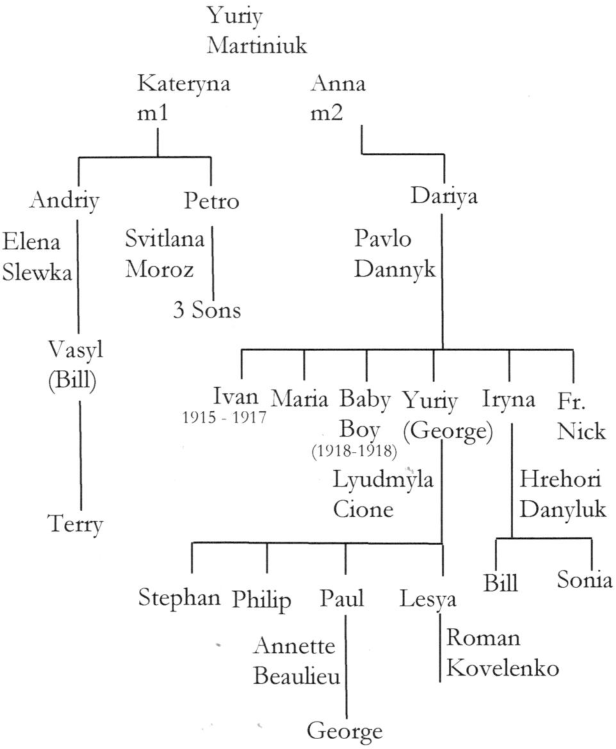

Mykola's Family Ukraine

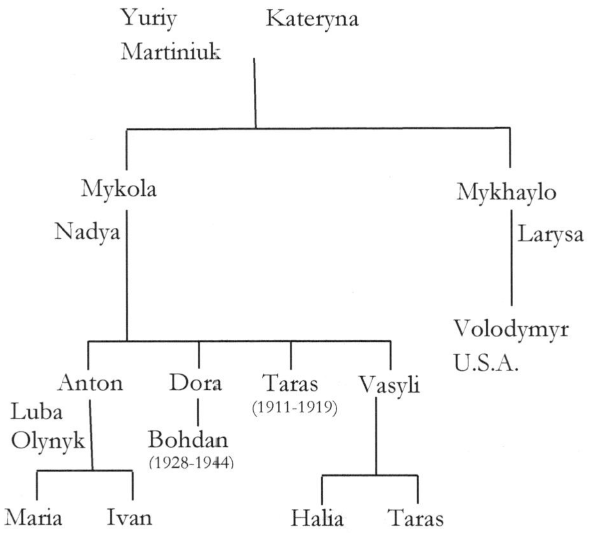

Taras' Family Argentina

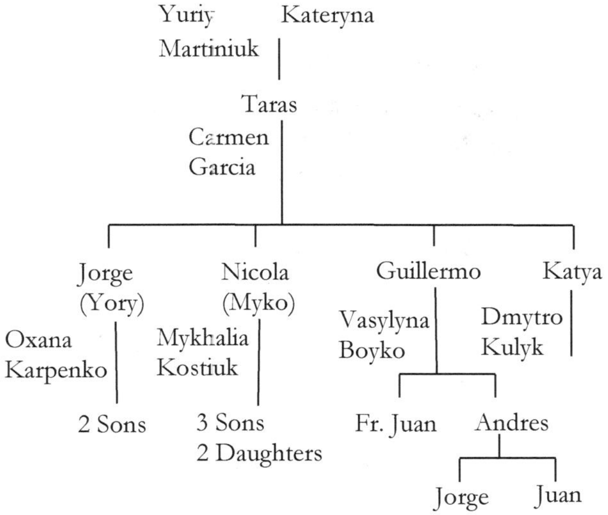

LIST OF CHARACTERS

Annette (Beaulieu) Dannyk – wife of Paul, mother of George

Andres Martiniuk – son of Guillermo & Vasylyna (Boyko)

Andriy Martiniuk – fourth son of Yuriy & Kateryna, husband of Elena (Slewka), father of Vasyl (Bill), grandfather of Terry

Anna (?) Martiniuk – second wife of Yuriy, mother of Dariya

Anton Martiniuk – first son of Mykola & Nadya, husband of Luba (Olynyk), father of Maria & Ivan

Baba Cione – Stephan's mother; Lena, Pylyp, Miroslav & Lyudmyla's grandmother

Baba Ditka – Lesya (Bastiuk) Cione's maternal grandmother

Baba Pelik – Pavlo's maternal grandmother

Bill Danyluk – son of Hrehori & Iryna (Dannyk)

Bohdan (?) – son of Dora, grandson of Mykola & Nadya

Carmen (Garcia) Martiniuk – wife of Taras, mother of Yory, Myko, Guillermo & Katya

Dariya (Martiniuk) Dannyk – daughter of Yuriy & Anna, wife of Pavlo, mother of Ivan, Maria, Baby Boy Dannyk, George, Iryna & Fr. Nick

Dmytro Kulyk – husband of Katya (Martiniuk)

Dora (Martiniuk) (?) – daughter of Mykola & Nadya, mother of Bohdan

Elena (Slewka) Martiniuk – wife of Andriy, mother of Vasyl (Bill), grandmother of Terry

Esperanza (?) Boyko – wife of Ivan, mother of Vasylyna & two sons

Fr. Borys – old parish priest in Galicia

Fr. Juan Martiniuk - son of Guillermo & Vasylyna (Boyko)

Fr. Mykhaylo – young parish priest in Galicia, father of Luba Olynyk

Fr. Nick Dannyk – son of Pavlo & Dariya (Martiniuk)

George Dannyk – son of Pavlo & Dariya (Martiniuk), husband of Lyudmyla (Cione), father of Stephan, Philip, Paul & Lesya

Guillermo Martiniuk – third son of Taras & Carmen (Garcia), husband of Vasylyna (Boyko), father of Fr. Juan & Andres

Iryna (Dannyk) Danyluk – daughter of Pavlo & Dariya (Martiniuk), wife of Hrehori, mother of Bill & Sonia

Ivan Boyko – Taras Martiniuk's partner, husband of Esperanza, father of Vasylyna & two sons

Ivan Dannyk – first son of Pavlo and Dariya, died at age two

Ivan Martiniuk – husband of Mariya, father of Yuriy & Vasyl

Ivan Martiniuk – son of Anton & Luba (Olynyk), grandson of Mykola & Nadya

Jorge (Yory) Martiniuk (Martin) – first son of Taras & Carmen, husband of Oxana (Karpenko), father of two sons

Jorge Martiniuk – son of Andres, grandson of Guillermo & Vasylyna

Juan Martiniuk – son of Andres, grandson of Guillermo & Vasylyna

Kateryna (?) Martiniuk – first wife of Yuriy, mother of Mykola, Taras, Mykhaylo, Andriy & Petro

Katya (Martiniuk) Kulyk – daughter of Taras & Carmen, wife of Dmytro

Larysa (Melnyk) Martiniuk – wife of Mykhaylo, mother of Volodymyr

Lena (Cione) Prytula – daughter of Stephan & Lesya (Bastiuk), sister of Pylyp, Miroslav, & Lyudmyla

Lesya (Bastiuk) Cione – wife of Stephan Cione, mother of Lena, Pylyp, Miroslav & Lyudmyla

Lesya (Dannyk) – daughter of George & Lyudmyla (Cione)

Luba (Olynyk) Martiniuk – wife of Anton, daughter of Fr. Mykhaylo, mother of Maria and Ivan

Lyudmyla (Cione) Dannyk – daughter of Stephan & Lesya (Bastiuk), sister of Lena, Pylyp, & Miroslav, wife of George, mother of Stephan, Philip, Paul & Lesya

Mariya (?) Martiniuk – wife of Ivan, mother of Yuriy & Vasyl

Miroslav Cione – second son of Stephan & Lesya (Bastiuk), died at age four

Mykhalia (Kostiuk) Martiniuk – wife of Nicola (Myko)

Mykhaylo Martiniuk – third son of Yuriy & Kateryna, husband of Larysa (Melnyk), father of Volodymyr

Mykola Martiniuk – first son of Yuriy & Kateryna, husband of Nadya, father of Anton, Dora, Taras & Vasyli

Nadya (?) Martiniuk – wife of Mykola, mother of Anton, Dora, Taras & Vasyli

Nicola (Myko) Martiniuk – second son of Taras & Carmen, husband of Mykhalia (Kostiuk), father of three sons & two daughters

Oxana (Karpenko) Martiniuk – wife of Jorge (Yory) (Martin), mother of two sons

Paul Dannyk – third son of George & Lyudmyla (Cione), husband of Annette (Beaulieu), father of George

Pavlo Dannyk – husband of Dariya (Martiniuk), father of Ivan, Maria, Baby Boy Dannyk, George, Iryna & Fr. Nick

Petro Martiniuk – fifth son of Yuriy & Kateryna, husband of Svitlana (Moroz), father of three sons

Philip Dannyk – second son of George & Lyudmyla (Cione)

Mr. Prytula – husband of Lena Cione

Pylyp Cione – first son of Stephan & Lesya (Bastiuk), husband of Ulianna (Hryniuk)

Roman Kovelenko – husband of Lesya Dannyk

Stephan Cione – husband of Lesya (Bastiuk), father of Lena, Pylyp, Miroslav & Lyudmyla

Stephan Dannyk – first son of George & Lyudmyla (Bastiuk)

Svitlana (Moroz) Martiniuk – wife of Petro, mother of three sons

Taras Martiniuk – second son of Yuriy & Kateryna, husband of Carmen (Garcia), father of Yory, Myko, Guillermo & Katya

Taras Martiniuk – second son of Mykola & Nadya, died at age eight

Taras Martiniuk – son of Vasyli, grandson of Mykola & Nadya

Terry Martiniuk – son of Vasyl (Bill), grandson of Andriy & Elena (Slewka)

Ulianna (Hryniuk) Cione – wife of Pylyp

Vasyl (Bill) Martiniuk – son of Andriy & Elena (Slewka)

Vasyl Martiniuk – second son of Ivan & Mariya, brother of Yuriy

Vasyli Martiniuk – third son of Mykola & Nadya

Vasylyna (Boyko) Martiniuk – daughter of Ivan & Esperanza, wife of Guillermo, mother of Andres & Fr. Juan

Volodymyr Martiniuk – son of Mykhaylo & Larysa (Melnyk)

Yuriy Martiniuk – first son of Ivan & Mariya, brother of Vasyl, husband of Kateryna (m1) & Anna (m2), father of Mykola, Taras, Mykhaylo, Andriy, Petro & Dariya

PREFACE

Like many people, I have been long fascinated by the family stories I grew up with. I had a sense that my family had lived through extraordinary times and my generation was especially blessed, largely because of the lives lived and the momentous decisions taken by those who went before.

This book was inspired by my family's story. Some of the events bear a resemblance to family tales and legends but I have embellished, extended, adapted, and incorporated them into the overall narrative, largely because they were just too good not to share.

People I have known or known about form the basis of some of the characters in this novel. However, I caution the reader that none of the characters are intended to be representative of any one, specific person. As with the family tales, I have taken artistic license to create, what I hope will be, memorable characters. I hope that readers, especially those who may have heard some of our family stories and may be tempted to try to match the characters in this book with the individuals who inspired the tales, will take this book for what it is – historical fiction – rather than a family history. Tempting though it may be, I truly hope no one will tell me, "but that is not how it was" or "that must have been uncle so-and-so."

As I began to think seriously about writing this book, it was necessary to research many historical locations and events. It was during this process when I became aware of the fact that many of the issues and circumstances, which affected my forebearers were not unique to them. It is my hope that this work of historical fiction will ignite and fan the cherished family memories of all who read it.

The surname, Pelik, of the kindly baba who took in her five orphaned grandchildren, is not a typical Ukrainian name. It was selected as the short form of the word for pelican, because in mythology the mother pelican is said to have fed her chicks with her own blood. This self-sacrificing mother bird exemplifies the baba, who gives all she has for her grandchildren. Such a situation was not uncommon in an era when many children were orphaned and would have been lucky to have a grandparent to care for them. My own grandfather was one of several orphaned siblings and cousins, raised by his widowed baba.

Similarly, the surname selected for Pavlo, the young man who is sent to Canada by a kindly, young priest, is a Ukrainian word for tributary, 'dannyk'. This story begins in a Southeastern Galician Village, where two streams meet to form a tributary of the Dniester River. This important geographical feature shapes the lives of all the villagers, including those who emigrate.

The surname of the main family in this story, Martiniuk, was selected because in its many forms it is relatively common in several cultures and languages.

Other surnames used in this novel are common Ukrainian names and not intended to be indicative of anyone who may share them.

The towns and villages inhabited by the characters of this book are a compilation of my own memories of small-town Saskatchewan, along with pictures and satellite images of actual villages in Western Ukraine and Misiones, Argentina.

1 THE OLD COUNTRY

1904

She couldn't sleep. She was tired enough. Even at six years of age, she had worked hard with Mama all day in the garden and then in the kitchen, preparing and storing food. Fall was always such a busy time.

They were talking about it again. She could hear their hushed voices. Not that they didn't want her to hear them – she knew all about 'The Plan'. They had been discussing it for months. But whenever they talked about it - it was always in hushed tones. She thought that Tato spoke of 'The Plan' in this way to hide his excitement. Mama spoke softly when they discussed 'The Plan' because she was afraid. Andriy shared his father's enthusiasm for 'The Plan', but only occasionally added a comment of support, especially when Mama became stubborn or emotional.

Dariya rolled over in her narrow cot to face the wall. She still couldn't sleep. She let the murmur of soft voices in the next room fade into the background of her consciousness and began to daydream. Dariya had a good imagination and she often used it to amuse herself, especially as she worked long hours alongside her mother but also in her limited free time or to help her to fall asleep at night. She always had trouble falling asleep.

What would the new world look like? Where would they live? What would it be like to be on a big ship, crossing the ocean? She had imagined these things many times, sometimes, it seemed to her they had already happened and she was just remembering them.

The ship would be bigger than anything she had ever seen. The letters from Taras, who had left for Argentina two years ago, told her so. They would be on the ship for weeks, with nothing around them but the sea. Dariya had never seen the sea. She tried hard to imagine what it would be like to see nothing on the horizon but water.

She began imagining the other children she would meet on the ship. There would be another girl her age to play with. She had imagined her before and had even given her a name, Maria. They would share secrets and play games all day long on the ship. They would feed scraps to the birds, which Taras said followed ships.... and they would ....

The sun was shining through the small window in the room where she slept. Mama and Tato were already up and gone. So were the boys. The house was empty. She wondered why Mama had not called her.

Yuriy and Vasyl

Yuriy Martiniuk was born on a chilly November day in 1855, the first-born son of Ivan and his young wife Mariya. Ivan owned a small plot of land of about five morgs (approximately seven and a half acres) on the edge of a village in the foothills of the Carpathian Mountains. At this time the region was called Galicia and was part of the Austrian Empire. Less than a decade before, in 1848, Emperor Ferdinand I had abolished serfdom or the corvee (panshchyna).

The village was located at the confluence of two streams, which joined to form one tributary of the great Dniester River. One stream flowed from the west, while its sister flowed from the southwest. Where the two streams joined forces had been an attractive location for human settlement for millennia. The location had been convenient for gathering trade goods from the surrounding foothills, for transporting these down the tributary and on to the larger river several kilometers away and eventually to the Black Sea. Over time, this gentle, Y-shaped valley drew more and more people and the homes and fields spread back up the valleys of the two sister streams and along the larger tributary, which combined their waters. By the time Ivan and Mariya were married, the village was home to about three thousand souls.

The fertile area west of the Dniester River had drawn many human civilizations since prehistoric times. It is thought that people of Slavic origin had lived there for thousands of years. The economic and political control of the area had shifted many, many times - most recently it had been a part of the Polish-Lithuanian Commonwealth and, then in 1772, after the First Partition of Poland, the Habsburg Austrian Empire. Under Polish rule, the local peasants, as serfs, had been the virtual slaves of the Polish nobles and there had been considerable pressure to convert to Roman Catholicism.

Ivan was not overburdened by the political struggles that raged around the village, which comprised his entire world. He had more pressing matters to attend to, such as providing for his family. Most of his neighbours had descended from people who had lived on this land for generations, regardless of the political control of the region. Most of the people in the village shared the same customs, traditions, religion, and language. Ivan knew who and what he was, he did not need a king or an emperor to tell him.

Each house in the village had a bit of land surrounding it – enough for a garden and sheds for a cow or goat, a few pigs, and chickens or ducks. Long thin fields within a kilometer or two of the village were considered 'rustical' lands, which the peasants had traditionally farmed, providing a subsistence living. The fields had the characteristic long, narrow shape because of the tradition of dividing land holdings equally among the sons of each family.

During feudal times, all the land had belonged to nobles for whom the peasant-serfs laboured. These lords had considerable power over the peasants, even to the extent that serfs needed the lord's permission to marry, change occupation, or leave the land. The serfs were tied to the lord and his land. In essence, the lord owned the serfs.

In 1781, Emperor Joseph II removed many of the lord's powers over the serfs and divided the land into two types: estates, owned by the landlord, or rustical lands, worked by the peasants. By 1844, much of the meadows and pastures were classified as rustical lands, although the vast majority of the forests remained part of the landlords' estates. In exchange for the rustical holdings, peasants were obligated to pay heavy taxes and provide long-term military service. The landlords were responsible for collecting taxes and ensuring that military service requirements were fulfilled. The peasants saw the landlords as the reason for these heavy burdens rather than blaming the Emperor, who was often perceived to be a good and caring 'father' figure.

In 1848, serfdom, that is, all previous labour obligations owed by the peasants to the landowners, was eliminated in the Austrian Empire. The rustical lands, along with some of the landlords' holdings, were distributed to the newly freed peasants. Originally, compensation to the former, feudal landlords for the loss of some of their land, as well as for the loss of their serfs, was to be made from Vienna but ultimately the new peasant landowners were taxed. In addition, the former feudal landlords would eventually be granted ownership of the forests and pasturelands. So now, the new peasant landowners had to pay, not only for pasturing their cattle and sheep, but also for wood for fuel and building. But they owned their land. And with land ownership came the right to participate in governance - the right to vote.

While the little plot of land did not make Ivan and Mariya wealthy, by any means, if they were very careful and diligent, it could afford them a living. They did not have to work for a landowner, as in the days before the abolishment of serfdom but they did have to pay taxes.

Ivan's house was the home in which he had been born. As an only son, Ivan had continued to live in the family hut, while his parents were still alive. It was only after they had both died in an epidemic that Ivan had decided to marry.

The house to which Ivan had brought his bride, Mariya, was typical for that time and place. It was a rectangular-shaped, two-roomed hut, with a central hallway used for storage. Because there were forests covering the hilly countryside, logs were used to build the home. In regions further east, houses may have looked similar but they were built of sod, rather than logs. In both areas, the cracks between the logs or sod were filled with a mixture of clay, water, cow dung, and dry straw. The walls, inside and out, were covered with several coats of this mixture. Then the walls were white washed with a mixture of slaked lime and water to produce the 'little, white houses' so loved by Schevchenko. The roof was high-pitched, four-sided, and thatched, with extensive overhangs to protect the walls and provide shade. This high-pitched roof provided an attic for storage and additional sleeping space. The floor was hard-packed clay.

The only door in the house faced south. There were also two small windows on this same wall, one for each of the two interior rooms. From the door, one entered the central hallway, which was adorned with a row of pegs, upon which coats and other clothing could be hung. From the hallway, one could enter either the smaller eastern room or the larger, western room. The larger room served as the main family gathering space.

The prominent feature in the larger room was a peitch (clay oven), which had been built into one corner. A second, similarly constructed peitch was situated in the yard, primarily for baking bread and for cooking in the heat of summer. The interior peitch was used to cook food, as well as to heat the home. It sat on a wooden bench, beneath which firewood was stored. To one side of the clay oven was a firebox, which, when the oven had been heated, provided a hot surface for boiling or frying food. The oven itself was used for baking and roasting. A hood above and in front of the oven door was designed to catch the smoke from the fire in the peitch and funnel it through a chimney and up into the attic. When the fire had died down and only hot coals remained, the food was arranged inside and the oven door was closed. The temperature in the oven could be regulated only by opening the door by degrees.

Above the oven was a ledge of planks, which made a cozy place for children to sleep. Benches could also be transformed into beds, with planks laid across them and straw mattresses placed on top. Other furniture in the room included a table, chairs, a stool, and a cupboard, all made by Ivan or his father before him.

The smaller, eastern room contained a bed frame with a straw mattress and a pyryna (duvet), which had been part of Mariya's dowry. The only other furniture in the small room was Mariya's dowry chest. Her father had made the chest and it contained all her worldly possessions, most of which she had made herself.

The only decorative item gracing the walls, although no one at that time would have thought of it as decorative, was a small icon. The holy relic hung in a place of honor, on the eastern wall. The icon was the sacred image of the Mother of God and had been a part of the blessing (blahoslovenia) ritual prior to their marriage. Before the icon stood a small stand upon which were an embroidered cloth and candles. The candles would be lit daily as the couple gathered in adoration before the icon, in order to say their evening prayers.

Ivan was a careful man. He was proud of the fact that he owned his land and was determined to keep it. As a result, he did not drink in the local taverns, where many of the other peasants spent their hard-earned income. He knew that the landlords had a monopoly on alcohol production and they encouraged peasants to drink away their small earnings, so they would have to return to working on the estates. In this way, the landlords won three times – they made a profit on the alcohol sold, they bought back the land from the ruined peasants, and they re-gained workers for their estates.

Ivan also vowed he would never borrow money, for that path also led to ruin. He knew moneylenders often charged one hundred and twenty-five per cent per year on loans. Once borrowed, it was nearly impossible to repay a debt. And so, the careful Ivan always had a little put aside for hard times, which he knew would come to him, as they did to everyone. Mariya was a great help, as she was very resourceful and frugal.

And so it was with great joy that the young couple welcomed the first of their two sons, Yuriy, on that grey November day in 1855. In fewer than two years, Mariya gave birth to their second son, Vasyl. The birth had been very difficult; so much so that the midwife warned Ivan they must not have another child. Ivan loved his wife very much. He thanked God she was safe and that they had two healthy sons. He was content with his little family.

As Yuriy and Vasyl grew, they helped Ivan farm the small plot of land. They learned from their father how to prepare the soil, plant the seed, care for the growing plants, and harvest the crops. They helped take care of their milk cow, pigs, chickens, and ducks. They also helped their mother tend the large vegetable garden next to the house.

Some years were better than others. Some years the crops were good and Ivan might even have a bit of surplus to store or trade. Mariya's garden and their animals usually provided them with the bulk of their dietary needs.

She was adept at growing vegetables to produce the best yields even in poor years. Then she would preserve what she had grown for the winter. As a resourceful housewife, she knew how to use what she had on hand to make practical, nutritious meals.

In some years, the crops were poor, so poor one might say they had failed altogether. In those years, Ivan, and later the boys, would find work among the villagers to supplement the food they had grown. Only when it was absolutely necessary, in order to save his family from starvation, would Ivan use any of his hard earned savings. Starvation was a very real threat and in those lean years, many peasants did starve to death. As soon as a better crop was harvested, Ivan never failed to replenish any savings he had used.

It was not only Ivan and Mariya's prudence that saved them from famine. They fervently believed it was the Grace of God, which kept them from ruin and starvation. They were devout Greek Catholics, but more than mere religious devotion their lives were immersed in spirituality.

The Greek Catholic religion came into existence when, in 1596, under pressure from the then ruling Roman Catholic Poles, a group of Orthodox bishops approached Pope Clement VIII. He recognized the union of the church, which these bishops represented, with that of Rome, under the conditions that the traditional liturgy and rites, as well as the right of priests to marry, would be guaranteed. So the Greek Catholic Church retained the look and feel of the Orthodox Church, with the exception that it recognized the Pope in Rome as its supreme leader, rather than the Orthodox Metropolitan in Kiev. The Greek Catholic religion had been established in this region for nearly three centuries, despite constant pressure from Polish overlords to Polonize the people and convert them to Roman Catholicism. At the time of Ivan and Mariya's marriage, the Greek Catholic Church used the Julian calendar, as did the Orthodox Church.

Like all devout peasants, Ivan and Mariya's lives revolved around the village church and the church calendar, which prescribed much of their day-to-day observances. The little family worked, ate, and prayed together. They also talked and laughed, as both Ivan and Mariya were content with their lot in life and expressed this by thanking God for all they had, especially for their two fine sons.

Ivan pondered using his savings to buy more land, as some of the other peasants had done. After all, when he was gone, his two sons would have to provide for their mother and share his small plot of land. It wasn't much. But Ivan was cautious. He did not want to gamble what he had for what he might have and so he hesitated and then ignored the whole idea.

When Yuriy was just six years old, his mother, Mariya, died in an epidemic, which had swept the village. She had been frail since the difficult birth of her second son - never quite recovering from the strain it had put on her body. When her own mother had fallen ill, Mariya had left her family to nurse her. In so doing she had contracted the same illness and never returned to her home. The unexpectedness and speed with which she had been taken from them was a great shock to Ivan and his sons.

From then on, it was just the three of them, his father, his little brother, and Yuriy. His world had changed forever. Ivan never remarried. When Ivan died in the spring of 1878, the small narrow plot of land was divided between Yuriy and his brother, Vasyl. Because he was the eldest son, Yuriy inherited the part of the plot on which the family home stood. Vasyl continued to live and work with Yuriy. Besides the land, there was a small leather bag with a few coins, Ivan's precious savings. The brothers agreed that their father's savings would only be used for extreme emergencies and that, whoever needed it most would have use of the savings.

Yuriy was a very good man. He was quiet but when he spoke everyone knew to listen to what he had to say. Although he had not been to school, he was intelligent. He could fix anything and could create innovative solutions to almost any problem. Many of his neighbours came to him for help and advice.

Yuriy also had a very strong sense of 'what was right'. He saw a lot of injustice in the world and this always troubled him greatly. He knew there would always be people, who were ready to take advantage of others but he tried to be just in all his own dealings. If he saw someone being treated unfairly, Yuriy would do whatever he could to rectify the situation, if it were at all possible.

Life for a Ukrainian (or Ruthenian, as they were commonly called then) peasant in the Austrian Empire may have been better than in other parts of the world, but injustice was never far away. For generations, the Polish nobles had considered the Austrian province of Galicia as still a part of Poland, even though it had been ruled by Austria since the First Partition in 1772. The Austrian rulers initially relied on local authority through the existing nobles and landowners, the majority of whom were Polish. Meanwhile, the Galician serfs, many of whom were Ukrainian, were allowed to preserve their religion and customs. Over the years, Austria had played the Polish nobility off against the Ukrainian peasantry, resulting in periods of social gain for one group, followed by periods of gain for the other, in a sort of tug-of-war. Ukrainians were granted schools, in which their children were taught in the vernacular and then those schools would be converted to Polish instruction, then back again, depending on the political whims of the Emperor in Vienna.

As a result of this 'to and fro', political tug-of-war, Ukrainian peasants often felt themselves to be the victims of injustice, the blame for which was often placed at the feet of the Polish nationalists, who worked tirelessly to Polonize the entire population of Galicia. Through it all, however, the majority of Ukrainians developed a deep sense of loyalty to the Austrian rulers. This loyalty was heightened with the abolishment of serfdom, which brought with it the ownership of land, the right to vote, and the obligations of paying taxes and compulsory military service.

In order to help ensure that military recruits would report for service, the population was carefully monitored by a process involving numbering each house in every settlement. This house number was then cross-referenced to birth records, so that men of recruitment age could be identified and located should they fail to report for duty.

During the years when Yuriy was growing up, the viceroy of Galicia was a Polish count, Agenor Goluchowski. He had become a close advisor to Emperor Franz Joseph. His aim was to achieve complete Polish autonomy and authority in all of Galicia. This extended to the language of instruction in secondary schools, which became exclusively Polish, and to the restriction of the growth of Ukrainian schools. After the constitution of the empire was revised in 1867, to create the Habsburg Dual Monarchy of Austria-Hungary, the Polish nobility demanded political autonomy in Galicia, similar what the Hungarians had achieved. While this was not granted, huge strides were made in favour of the Polish faction, primarily in the form of further Polonization of the schools and administration of the region.

Yuriy served three years of compulsory military service, then, at the age of twenty-four, he married Kateryna. As was the custom of the day, dictated by the rigors of agricultural life, the wedding took place during the winter months - after the celebration of Christmas and before the beginning of the Lenten Season.

Yuriy and Kateryna had practically grown up together, since she was one of five daughters of a neighbouring farmer. They knew each other very well and suited one another. They loved each other and together they had built a comfortable home on Yuriy's share (two and a half morgs, about three and a quarter acres) of his father's land.

By that time, Vasyl had built himself a small hut, adjacent to Yuriy's home. Vasyl had always looked up to his brother, who had been his main source of support and comfort since the loss of their mother, so many years before. Vasyl had been only four years old when their mother had died. Their father had been devastated. Yuriy grieved deeply, as well, but he sensed that both his father and young brother needed him to be strong. He prayed daily that God grant him the strength to help them. And so it was that Vasyl grew up with a deep admiration and love for his older brother.

Vasyl was the quieter of the two boys. He enjoyed spending time alone in the garden, the fields, and the woods, which surrounded the village. At an early age he discovered he had a talent for woodcarving. He could often be found sitting in the doorway of the shed at the back of the yard, amidst a pile of wood chips and shavings. At first he concentrated on carving simple utensils, like spoons and combs. But his love of nature soon saw the awakening of a deep desire to represent the loveliness of God's creations. He kept much of his work to himself, only occasionally showing a piece he was particularly proud of to Yuriy. Yuriy was always amazed by his brother's talents and encouraged him to continue his efforts.

As Vasyl grew, he came to believe that God had a higher purpose for him. At first, he thought perhaps he had been meant to serve God as a priest. However, when he went to speak to Father Borys, the village priest, he was assured that to be a priest a young man needed an education and education cost money. God did not want poor peasants, who could not afford to study His rites and laws. Undeterred, Vasyl decided to serve God in any way he could, which at that time meant using his God-given gift to copy the glories of creation with his carvings and to support his father and his older brother. This dedication to his little family continued after their father's death and was transferred, whole-heartedly, to his brother's growing family.

As the years unfolded, Yuriy and Kateryna had five healthy sons, the first two born in rapid succession. Mykola (Nicholas), named after Kateryna's father, was born in October of 1880, only ten months after their wedding. Then, less than a year later, came Taras (Terrance). Mykhaylo (Michael), the third son, was born two years later and, at roughly two-year intervals, Andriy (Andrew), and Petro (Peter) completed the family.

Vasyl loved spending time with his brother's family. When he wasn't working with Yuriy, he liked nothing more than to spend time with his five nephews. He was godfather to the eldest, Mykola, so of course he had a special fondness for this nephew but he was always careful not to let the other boys see it. Uncle Vasyl always had a special gift, a lovely carved creation, for each boy on his birthday and at Christmas. The boys cherished these wonders, which were really their only toys, and looked forward, with great anticipation, to the next gift from Uncle Vasyl.

Mykola and Taras

Mykola was the first-born son of Yuriy and Kateryna. He had been born within a year of their marriage and, because his mother had been only eighteen when he was born, mother and son were relatively close in age. They were close in many other ways as well. Mykola had the same warm, good humor as his mother. From his father he had inherited intelligence and patience. Yuriy often thought his first-born son had inherited the best from his two parents.

But Mykola was only the beginning of his parents' great joy, for within a year of his birth, a second son, Taras, was born. Mykola and Taras were inseparable. Although, they did not look alike, the brothers loved each other and did everything together. Mykola looked more like his mother, with her tall, slim build; fine, sandy hair; and soft grey eyes; while Taras looked more like his father, a bit stocky, with a shock of dark hair and hazel eyes. They were a handsome pair of boys and their parents were very proud of them.

Mykola, the quieter and more serious of the two, depended on Taras, as his constant companion and confidant. Taras always looked to what Mykola had done before him, in order to emulate his older brother. Mykola enjoyed the role of older brother and patiently taught Taras any new skill he had mastered. Taras relied on Mykola to support and help him with his latest, new idea or scheme.

From a very early age, Taras was the one who would come up with amazing ideas for things the two brothers could do. He would get an idea and get entirely caught up with enthusiastic plans for bringing the idea to reality.

Taras was the one who invented new games for the village children to play. He would have an idea and then develop the rules and teach the children to play his latest game. Many of the village children anticipated Taras' next new game and were always ready to participate.

Once, Taras thought the brothers should learn to make wooden carvings, like Uncle Vasyl. Uncle Vasyl had always carved useful items, beautiful toys and images of nature, but only for his own use or as gifts. He had never sold what he carved in the village market. Taras was sure the brothers could make carvings like Uncle Vasyl's and sell them to the townsfolk for a small profit. After all, pieces of wood could be scavenged for free, so it would only be their time, which would determine how many items could be made for sale.

Uncle Vasyl, unaware of Taras' latest scheme, was very pleased that his young nephews had suddenly taken an interest in the avocation, which had brought him so much joy throughout his lifetime. He patiently showed the boys how to select a piece of wood and the rudiments of carving.

It wasn't until after several futile attempts, Taras realized he had no talent for carving and the idea was relinquished in favor of the next big idea! Mykola wasn't always so sure about Taras' schemes and plans but he was always supportive of his brother and willing to help in any way he could.

As they grew, Yuriy's two eldest sons learned to work closely with their father. They were respectful and cheerful about helping him to farm their little plot of land. The boys also earned a good reputation among the townsfolk. If anyone ever needed a hand, the brothers were happy to help. People began to say "If you ask for help from one of the Martiniuk boys, you get help from both." Because both boys had a gentle, caring nature, they were liked by everyone they met.

When Mykola turned seven, Yuriy decided he should attend the church school. Yuriy had not gone to school himself, since Emperor Leopold II had abolished compulsory elementary education in 1812 but he wanted his sons to have some education. So Yuriy took young Mykola to see Father Borys, the village priest, who also served as the schoolmaster. Father Borys looked the young boy over, asked him a few questions and, seeing that the boy had some natural intelligence, told Yuriy that Mykola could begin classes the next day. Yuriy was very pleased and, because his father was pleased, so was Mykola.

However, when the next day came and Yuriy again took his son to the school, Taras was devastated. What would he do while Mykola was at school all day? He was obviously affected by the fact that his brother was away and so Yuriy found small extra jobs for Taras to do that morning.

"Your turn to go to school will come soon," he told his second son.

"But when I go to school," Taras thought, "I won't be in the same class as Mykola. We will never be together every day again!"

And so Taras was quiet and withdrawn all day. Both his parents tried very hard to help Taras adjust to days without his brother, but as the days and weeks went by, it was clear that an adjustment would be a long time coming.

For Mykola, it was a similar experience. At first he was very excited about going to school but his shy, quiet ways made it hard for him to make friends. The other boys had been in class together for some time and knew each other well. They were not readily accepting of this new classmate. Mykola tried to focus on his studies but he missed Taras very much.

Every day, when Mykola came home from school the two boys would run off together to talk about what each had seen and done all day long. Taras begged his brother to take him to school with him but Mykola knew he could not do that. Only Tato could ask the schoolmaster for a place for Taras, who was just a bit too young. So instead, Taras asked his brother to teach him what he learned each day.

And so it was that Mykola studied very hard all day at school, so he could teach what he had learned to Taras each evening. Both parents were completely unaware of what the boys were doing. Yuriy was very busy working. He had not realized how much more help the two boys together had been. Sometimes, as in the old days, he would call on Vasyl for help as well but he knew Vasyl, who had never married and had no sons of his own, had plenty of his own work to do. Kateryna had her hands full with four-year old Mykhaylo, two-year old Andriy, and a newborn baby, Petro.

One day, several weeks after Mykola had started school, Taras was sitting quietly at the table. He was not eating and it was clear he was very unhappy. Yuriy asked him what was troubling him and Taras broke down in tears.

"I miss Mykola. I want to go to school with him."

"But Taras," his father replied, "you are too young. You will go to school next year."

"But Tato, next year I won't be at the same level as Mykola in school!"

Yuriy and Kateryna talked long into the night about how much their two boys had changed since Mykola had started going to school.

"But what can we do?" Kateryna asked.

"Tomorrow, I take Taras to see the schoolmaster."

And so, the next day, Father Borys had a second Martiniuk boy to consider for classes. He asked him a few questions and was surprised to learn that Taras actually knew almost everything Mykola had been studying. The schoolmaster was impressed and told Yuriy that the next day, both of his sons could come to school.

"You can't get just one Martiniuk boy," the villagers said.

From that day on, Mykola and Taras were inseparable again.

And, because Vasyl was so fond of his nephews and really wanted to see them educated, he proposed that he and Yuriy continue to work their father's land together, as they had most of their lives.

The two older boys went to school for several years. They learned the basics of reading and writing, taught in the church language of Old Slavonic. They also learned some rudimentary mathematics and history.

Both Yuriy and Uncle Vasyl were getting older and so it eventually became necessary for Mykola and Taras to leave school, in order to either help farm the small plot of land or work for neighbours in the village.

Then disaster struck the family. Another epidemic swept through the region. First little Andriy fell ill and then Petro. Kateryna nursed them day and night. Eventually the two boys began to recover but Kateryna was now growing ill, weakened by her efforts to save her sons. Kateryna succumbed in the fall of 1896, at the age of thirty-four. Yuriy, at the age of forty-one, was left with five sons, aged nine, eleven, thirteen, fifteen, and sixteen.

Yuriy was broken hearted. Vasyl spent long hours comforting his older brother. "How strange it is," he thought, "that Yuriy was here to help me when our mother died and now I can do the same for him, God truly does work in mysterious ways!"

Yuriy, despite his own grief, knew he had to think of his boys. He knew all too well from his own experience of losing his mother at an early age, that he had to re-marry. He had no delusions about ever finding someone as perfect for him as his Kateryna had been but he hoped to find someone who would be a surrogate mother to his sons, as well as a companion and helpmate. So, somewhat reluctantly, Yuriy began looking for a second wife.

It wasn't as hard as he thought it would be. The epidemic had left several widows in the village. Yuriy watched many of these women - some younger than himself, some older, some with children, some without children. He made discreet inquiries, but avoided the matchmakers. Soon he settled on a widow who was about fifteen years his junior. She had not been married for long when her husband had taken ill and died. They had no children. Her husband had been an apprentice to a tradesman, so she didn't have a widow's portion of land and would have had to depend on her parents and siblings or work on an estate, if she were not to remarry. Yuriy thought he could offer her a better alternative.

Anna

Anna was the eldest daughter of a shopkeeper's assistant. She had five younger siblings and had had much responsibility caring for her brothers and sisters while she was growing up.

Anna's mother and father had known each other all their lives. Her father had decided to work for a shopkeeper rather than splitting his father's land with his brothers. This suited Anna's mother, who believed her husband would earn a more stable livelihood in this way. The couple married and planned to settle into a comfortable life in the heart of the village. However, the arrival of six children, born in quick succession, had taken its toll. Her husband contracted pneumonia and had been gravely ill. Although he had survived, he continued to suffer reoccurrences of that dreaded disease ever since. Anna's mother thought the comfortable life she had hoped for had slipped away, leaving her bitter and resentful. She lost interest in caring for her family and became pale and thin. She came to rely more and more on her eldest daughter to care for the younger children.

Anna had resented her mother's decline and the extra burden it had placed on her shoulders. Yet she loved her siblings and really made an effort to keep them clean and fed. Anna's father was too busy, trying to earn enough to keep his family fed, to notice the great responsibility Anna had assumed. He worked in the shop, as well as at odd jobs for people in the village. It seemed he couldn't earn enough, no matter what he did, to keep up with the demands of his large family. Anna loved her father but she could see he was frequently not well and all the work he was doing was having its toll on him. Anna felt her mother was not helping the situation and resented her even more.

During this time, Anna's greatest joy was to escape the overwhelming demands on her by running barefoot under the cherry trees, which grew behind their house. This was especially wonderful in the springtime, when the trees were in blossom. She would run round and round the trees, weaving in and out and finally collapsing on the cool, damp earth to watch the clouds high up in the clear blue sky and the cherry blossom petals floating down upon her.

Eventually Anna's sisters began to take on their share of caring for the youngest children in the family. Anna was now a young woman and beginning to think of a home of her own. She promised herself that she would never have more children than she could care for.

There was a young man, whom she had met in the shop where her father worked. He was an apprentice to the shop owner and very charming. He talked to her whenever she came to the shop and she found herself going to the shop often. Eventually, the young man began to tell her of his dreams for the future and Anna began to think of herself as a part of that future.

One day, Anna was surprised to hear from her father that he thought the young man would like to marry her. Anna had secretly hoped this might be so, but had never thought it would actually be possible. Her father asked if he should talk to the young man but Anna was embarrassed and asked him not to. However, a few weeks after her father had made this suggestion, the young man had arrived, along with the shopkeeper, to talk to her father about a marriage. Anna was delighted, although she wondered if her father had suggested the idea to her young suitor.

They were married in the early spring of 1893. Anna was seventeen but she felt she had already lived a lifetime for others. Now she would finally begin her own life. The young couple moved into a room above the shop where her new husband worked. They did not have much but they were young and in love, so they hardly noticed how little they had. They had a warm room, enough food, and each other. Anna felt she had never been happy until then.

It wasn't long before Anna suspected she was pregnant. She was overjoyed and wanted to share the secret with her husband. But, she wanted to be sure before she told him the great news. She knew how much it would please him! Then, just as suddenly as the first symptoms had appeared, something went wrong. And then it was over. She had lost the child she had been so anticipating and longing to tell her husband about. It was a devastating blow but she decided to keep it to herself. They were young. She prayed God would give them another chance.

Then, late in the winter of 1894, her husband came upstairs to their little room early. He was feverish and shaky. Anna put him to bed and kept him covered, while he alternated between sweats and chills. She made him tea and soup but he was not able to eat or drink anything. After three days, she went, in desperation, to the local healer. The old woman gave her some dried herbs and told her to make a tea for her husband to drink, three times a day. Unfortunately, it was too little too late. The young man's condition worsened and, within two weeks, he was dead.

Anna was in shock. She couldn't believe that their dream had vanished into thin air. Her husband was gone. Now what would she do? She could not go back to her father's house. She did not want to put an additional burden on him. She knew his health was failing and he was having a hard time continuing to work. Anna had to find an alternative.

The shopkeeper was as shocked as Anna was that his young apprentice had died so suddenly. Many in the region had succumbed to this latest epidemic but the young man had been so strong and virile. The shopkeeper had liked the young man and his wife and had done what he could to help them get a start in life. Their own, poor parents had not been able to provide much help. He told Anna to stay in the room above the shop until she decided what she would do. He also knew her father was often not well and that Anna would not want to be an additional burden on him.

Anna went to the old woman who had given her the herbs for her husband. She wanted something to help her sleep. The old woman knew that Anna's husband had died and felt sorry for the young woman. She told Anna she was young to be a healer but, if Anna were interested, she would be willing to begin teaching her. Anna was excited about the prospect. She did not see herself as a healer but she knew healers did not share their knowledge with just anyone. She also knew that anything she could learn form the old woman would be useful in her life, no matter what happened in the future.

And so it was that Anna moved from the room above the shop into a room at the back of the old healer's hut and began her training.

It was only a year later that Yuriy Martiniuk approached her with a marriage proposal. She knew who he was, of course, everyone in the village knew Yuriy. He was a kind, gentle fellow who had loved his first wife and had grieved for her loss. He had a large family of boys, so he may not want any more children, which suited Anna well. He didn't have much land, but there was a decent house and a fine vegetable garden. She could see herself planting healing herbs along with vegetables in his garden. She was twenty-one and this would likely be her last chance to marry. Although she had grown fond of the old healer, she could not imagine herself living in the small hut for the rest of her life. But could she imagine herself living with Yuriy and his brood?

Yuriy and Anna

In his gentle, careful way, Yuriy approached the young widow. She seemed pleasant, although she didn't smile much. "She's had a difficult time. What has she got to smile about?" Yuriy thought.

After a cautious initial period, Yuriy asked the young widow if she might re-marry and, if so, would a man such as himself with five sons be someone she might consider. Yuriy was delighted to see one of her rare smiles, as she shyly nodded that she would consider such a proposal.

Before bringing Anna into his home, Yuriy had spent a long night going through the things in Kateryna's chest. His plan was to empty the chest and present it to Anna as a place to store her personal possessions. He did not know if she had such a chest of her own and he wanted her to have some personal space in her new home.

Kateryna's chest had stood at the foot of their bed since the day they had married. Yuriy had not had the strength to even look into the chest after her passing but he knew it was something he had to do before his new wife arrived in his home. And so, late at night after the boys were asleep, Yuriy opened the chest. He carefully lifted out each beautifully embroidered item, remembering a time when Kateryna had made or used it. Just as carefully, he re-folded each item and placed it in another box for storage. Perhaps one day, one of the boys' wives could use these items, although he thought it would be hard for him to ever part with them. Near the bottom of the chest, Yuriy found Kateryna's coral (coraliya) necklace. She had worn it on the day they had wed and every time they went to church. He had not realized just how much emotion this simple personal item could evoke. The tears started before he even realized he was about to cry. Yuriy carefully folded the coral beads in one of Kateryna's embroidered scarves and tucked them into a corner of the storage box. The next morning, after the boys were up and out the door, Yuriy took the box into the attic. Now he was ready to re-marry.

Yuriy took his brother Vasyl and the two of them went to see the young widow's father. The father was very eager to have his daughter re-married. He seemed to believe that she had had bad luck to lose her husband so quickly, before even having a child. He also may not have wanted to take responsibility for her in his own home again. At any rate, the union was easily agreed upon, the banns were read in the church, and they were married in the late summer of 1897.

At first it seemed that Yuriy had made a good decision to marry Anna. She showed an interested in and an affection toward the boys. She was a good cook and worked very hard. She kept the house clean and made a wonderful garden, which included many healing herbs and plants. Anna occasionally lost her temper and spoke sharply but she had had a difficult life and becoming the instant mother of five, rambunctious boys could not have been easy. Yuriy tried to help her in every way he could.

The boys tried to help Anna adjust, as well. Mykola, especially, did whatever he could to make her feel welcome and comfortable in her new home. He was only four years her junior, so they could talk easily. Furthermore, Mykola had a kind and generous spirit, so it was only natural that the two formed a close friendship. As usual, where Mykola went, Taras followed. So Taras also went out of his way to be kind and helpful to Anna. It didn't take long before the two youngest boys accepted her as well. It was only Mykhaylo who kept his distance.

"He is missing his mother," Yuriy said, "it is natural".

But Anna was not so sure. Surely the other boys also missed their mother. Anna never tried to take Kateryna's place, either with the boys or with their father. Yuriy had noted this and, in his quiet way, was grateful. And so the happy home, which Yuriy hoped to re-establish, began to form.

Then only ten months after they had married, their daughter, Dariya was born. Yuriy was delighted. He had always wanted a daughter. Anna seemed less pleased. She seemed distant toward her new baby.

"She's a first-time mother, it will take time," Yuriy thought.

When it came time to have the baby baptized, Yuriy went to the old village priest, Father Borys. The child had been born on the twelfth of June, so according to tradition, her name would come from the saint who was commemorated on that day. The old priest looked carefully for the corresponding saint and proclaimed that the child's name would be Petronilla, after the first century, virgin martyr, possibly the daughter of Saint Peter.

Yuriy was not pleased. He did not like the name. He didn't even tell Anna about the priest's pronouncement. Instead, he borrowed a horse and wagon from a neighbor and took his wife and baby daughter to the next village. There he had a young village priest baptize his daughter with the name he preferred, Dariya.

When Father Borys heard what Yuriy had done he was very angry. He told Yuriy: "You have five sons. Soon they will want to marry and then you will pay for your disobedience and willfulness!"

Yuriy had never thought of himself as being disobedient or willful but perhaps, just this once, he had been. What was done was done. He hoped his actions would not weigh too heavily on the rest of his family.

Unfortunately for Dariya and Yuriy, Anna never was a very warm mother. She seemed to blame the child for its birth and what that had meant, in terms of changes to Anna's life. Anna made it clear she would not have another child. Yuriy was disappointed, but tried to understand his new wife's feelings. Ultimately he accepted her wishes and poured his affections on his daughter, whom he feared would feel the distance and coolness of her mother.

As time went on, Anna became more and more sharp-tongued. Yuriy bore her outbursts with patience but he noticed that sometimes his sons were less obliging. They too were getting older and perhaps less in need of a mother figure. Sometimes Yuriy had to take on the role of peacemaker. Usually it was Mykhaylo who was at the root of the disturbance. As always, Yuriy's patience and good nature were often required to maintain peace in his home.

Mykhaylo

Mykhaylo was very different from his two elder brothers. No doubt they had never intended to exclude him but they had formed such a close bond that they didn't notice how much their younger brother longed to be closer to them and how he had often felt left out. Perhaps it was this feeling of being excluded from their close relationship, perhaps it was just his nature, or perhaps it was the result of being the middle child, but for whatever reason, Mykhaylo grew in time to resent all his siblings.

Early on, he gave up trying to please and tag along with Mykola and Taras. He started to boss his younger brothers. Eventually the bossing turned into bullying and tormenting. His mother, Kateryna, had tried to explain to him that Andriy and Petro were too young to understand what he wanted them to do. His father had sat him down and talked gently to him about treating others the way he would like to be treated. In desperation, Yuriy eventually resorted to disciplining Mykhaylo for his behavior toward his younger brothers. Nothing seemed to help.

When it came time for Mykhaylo to go to school, he stubbornly refused. It was not as if he were much help to his father, for he often disappeared for hours on end just when his help was needed most. Yuriy and Kateryna had been at a loss as what to do with their third son.

As Mykhaylo came of age, he became acutely aware that there was little for him to inherit. Tato's small farm was barely enough to support this family. How could it ever support the families of all five brothers, when Tato was gone and the land divided? Even if Uncle Vasyl never married, and it seemed that he wouldn't, his plot added to Tato's would still not be enough for the five of them. No, as always, Mykhaylo was going to have to find another alternative to make his way in the world.

It all came to a head for him on the night he had gone to visit his friend, Bohdan. Bohdan was not feeling well, so Mykhaylo was returning home. He happened upon some boys from a neighbouring village, who had a crock of horiwka (home brew). They had invited him to share the potent drink as they were talking and laughing. Little did Mykhaylo know that these young ruffians had come to his village to make trouble. It was their intention to get a local fellow drunk, include him in their hi-jinx, and then leave him to take the blame. Mykhaylo was totally oblivious to their scheme.

That evening, it just so happened that old Dmytro had been walking through the village and had seen the young fellows, along with Mykhaylo, drinking from a crock. Dmytro knew the fellows were likely up to no good, so he continued his walk but on a different path than he had originally intended. He walked straight to Yuriy Martiniuk's little hut. He hated to disturb his neighbours but he was sure Mykhaylo was going to get into trouble and he wanted to let Yuriy know before anything happened.

As soon as Yuriy heard Dmytro's story, he set off to find Mykhaylo. When he did, he took him in hand and insisted the boy follow him back home. Mykhaylo was drunk, angry, and embarrassed but he had never disobeyed a direct order from his father before and so he followed Tato home.

The next morning, Mykhaylo was suffering his first hangover. Tato was very tolerant and said nothing about the prior evening. Anna was not so kind. Mykhaylo had never liked his stepmother. He could never understand why his father had married her. He was aware that a growing number of villagers described her a 'sharp tongued' and wondered why his father put up with her.

On that morning, Anna plagued Mykhaylo from the moment he woke up. She scolded him relentlessly for drinking and carousing with young ruffians from the neighbouring village. Mykhaylo just held his head, drank his chai (tea), and suffered in silence.

Later that day, the whole village was buzzing with news of the events of the prior evening. After Yuriy had taken Mykhaylo home, the other youngsters had raided several gardens, not for food but to do damage. They had stolen tools from the blacksmith and broken a window in the church. The whole village was in an uproar. Even this did not ease Mykhaylo's anger toward his father. He was embarrassed that Tato had intervened in his evening.

Mykhaylo vowed he would find a way to leave Tato's house, as soon as possible. From that day on, he looked for every opportunity to create a future for himself.

Andriy

Andriy was the fourth son of Yuriy and Kateryna Martiniuk. He had been only eleven years old when his mother, whom he adored, had succumbed to illness. Andriy was old enough to feel a sense of guilt that his mother had died after saving his life and that of his younger brother, Petro.

Andriy was a sensitive, serious boy. Everything he did was done carefully and to the best of his abilities. He always strove for excellence. When he turned seven and was to start school, he promised himself he would work very hard and learn everything he could. Andriy was a natural student. He loved school. He learned to read and write with ease. He had a little more difficulty with mathematics but persistence paid off and he was usually at the top of his class in all subjects. Andriy read everything he could get his hands on. He learned to speak and write in Polish and Austrian German, as well as his native Ukrainian. He was a veritable sponge for knowledge of any kind. Yuriy sometimes looked at his fourth son and marveled at his thirst for knowledge. God surely had a special purpose for this son.

Uncle Vasyl took note of Andriy's love of learning and encouraged him. He harbored a dream that perhaps this nephew would become the priest he himself had hoped to be. Of course, Vasyl kept his hopes for the boy to himself. So it would have surprised Vasyl greatly to learn that Andriy, while anxious to learn as much as possible, had no desire whatsoever for the priesthood. What Andriy longed for was to write poetry.

As a young boy, Andriy had followed his Uncle Vasyl into the woods for long walks along the streams, which ran through the village. As Uncle Vasyl searched for wood for his carvings, almost without realizing it, he had inspired the boy to appreciate all of God's creations in the natural world.

When Andriy's father had married Anna, at first, he had been rather shy around her. He kept his distance, not because he didn't like her but because he still harbored feelings of grief and guilt over his mother's death. And besides, little Petro who was only ten when Anna came into their home seemed to need her attention more than he did.

Andriy only warmed to Anna over time, when he saw the way Mykhaylo treated her. Mykhaylo had never been kind to anyone, especially his two younger brothers. It was this desire to help Anna cope with Mykhaylo, which made Andriy go out of his way to befriend her. True, she could be harsh in what she said but Andriy suspected the transition into their home had been difficult for her, as well as for them.

And then little Dariya had arrived. Andriy adored his baby sister. He didn't really remembered Petro as a baby, so everything Dariya did amazed him. Because he was so keen to learn, he marveled at how quickly the baby developed and learned to talk, walk, think, and play. Andriy was always willing to help mind little Dariya and loved to carry her around, even after she began to walk on her own. As a result the two developed a close bond, which remained throughout their lives.

When Andriy grew older, whenever he had a spare moment, he would wander the environs of the village. Invariably he would end up on a hill over looking the two streams, composing poetry, inspired by the world in which he felt so privileged to live.

Andriy kept his poetry a secret from his family, especially Mykhaylo. Mykhaylo had never been kind to either Andriy or Petro and Andriy had no intention of giving him any reason for further torment. If it hadn't been for Mykhaylo, Andriy would have thought himself the luckiest person in the world, for everything else about the world around him seemed glorious.

Petro

Petro had been the baby of the family until, at the age of eleven, suddenly he had a baby sister. Petro couldn't understand what all the fuss was about. She was just a baby and a girl at that! Petro resented being asked to help watch the baby and was only too glad to have Andriy take over the task. Petro found every excuse to be scarce whenever he suspected Anna would need help with Dariya.

Petro remembered his mother through the eyes of the nine-year-old he had been when she died. He had been very sick. He remembered lying in bed, too weak to move, while pain wracked his body. He vaguely remembered his mother wiping his forehead and sitting beside him through the night. He had been aware of her praying over him and pleading with God not to take her baby. He had always been her baby. And then, just as he was beginning to get his strength back, it was his father who was sitting with him through the night. And his mother was gone. He was hurt and angry that she had left him. How could she leave her baby?

Petro longed for his mother to return. He spent many nights crying for her. It had broken his father's heart to hear his youngest son weeping through the night. This, in part, was what had determined Yuriy to re-marry. In a way, Petro sensed this new 'mother' was for his benefit. Although he longed for his mama, he had come to accept that she was gone forever and so he 'adopted' Anna.

Of all Yuriy's boys, Anna's heart warmed more to Petro than any of the others. True Mykola was friendly and helpful and it was soon obvious that, wherever Mykola went, Taras followed, so the two eldest sons quickly became her allies in the family. But little Petro – he needed her in a way that no one else she had ever known had needed her. She loved the little boy unconditionally. And he, in turn, grew to love her, as the replacement for his lost mother.

It was only after Dariya's birth that Petro felt a sense of betrayal. Suddenly, he was no longer the baby nor the focus of Anna's attention. He vowed to do as little as possible to help with the new baby. Just as there had developed a strong bond between Andriy and Dariya, there was always a distance between Dariya and the brother who was closest to her in age.

Dariya felt the distance instinctively from a very young age but she had no idea why it was there.

Petro was a mystery to his father. He was not like any of his brothers. He went to school and got by, but did not excel. He was neither kind nor mean. Nothing in particular seemed to ignite his enthusiasm. He didn't have the gentle, kind-heartedness of Mykola, the brilliant scheming of Taras, the resentfulness of Mykhaylo, or the scholarly penchant of Andriy. What on earth did God have planned for this, his youngest son?

Father Borys

Father Borys was born in 1831 in the city of Stanyslaviv (later Ivano-Frankivsk). His father and elder brothers were all priests. Unfortunately as the youngest, Borys had been sent to the small, insignificant village where two streams joined to form a tributary of the mighty Dniester. At first, Father Borys thought this was just a place for him to learn the skills of a parish priest and soon his father would find a better position for him. This was not to be. From his arrival at the age of twenty-one nearly until his death almost fifty years later, Father Borys' entire life was spent as the head of the flock of Greek Catholics of the small village.

Although Father Borys married, he and his wife had not been blessed with children. It was perhaps this misfortune, more than anything else, which shaped both of their lives. In the early years, Father Borys had tried to be a loving 'father' to his flock but he had always seen them as somewhat inferior to his own status and position in life. As a result, it was sometimes difficult for him to empathize with his poor congregation and their basic, worldly, as well as spiritual, needs.

Father Borys remembered well the time when young Vasyl Martiniuk had come, asking if perhaps God was calling him to become a priest. Father Borys had been astonished. How could this uneducated peasant have even thought such a thing? Why his grandfather had been a serf! Father Borys planned to tell the young man to spend his life serving God by using what talents he had been given, but some how as the words were spoken, his own human frailties interceded and he had been rather hash with the young man. Perhaps it had been unfair of him but he could not conceive of this lowly peasant, who had never been to school, as ever becoming a priest. Even with an immediate start, a supreme effort, a private tutor for years, none of these could make up for the lack of an elementary education, let alone prepare the young man to study theology, Latin, etc. at a university. It was impossible. Surely the boy was wrong. God could not have called him.

As Father Borys thought more about the Martiniuk family, he recalled Yuriy's eldest boys as adequate students in the church school he operated. The most memorable thing about them was that they were constantly together in everything they did. The third son had not bothered to improve his mind by attending school. But Andriy Martiniuk, Father Borys remembered him very well. What an excellent student he had been. However, there was nothing much to recall about the youngest Martiniuk boy.

And then there had been the unpleasant affair with Yuriy Martiniuk. Father Borys was not unaware of the fact that some of the village people had occasionally gone to the neighbouring village church, especially for the great Holy Feast Days. They said it was to be with friends and family for those special times but Father Borys suspected some of his flock were less than subservient to his authority. But when Yuriy came about the baptism of his daughter and then took her instead to the next village to be baptized – that had been an unforgivable offence. Father Borys had felt vindicated about his prior dealings with the family. Surely God would not have wanted such as these to serve Him.

Father Borys' wife had been a quiet, stately young woman when he married her. She had been from a good family and the proper wife for a priest. However, because she had never borne children, she grew to be rather self-centered and her natural pride was enhanced by her status as the wife of the village priest. True, she took good care of her husband and supported him in his daily efforts to minister to the people of the village. Also, she took her responsibilities regarding the poor very seriously. She would make the rounds of the poorest homes in the village in order to determine their most urgent needs and then call upon the rest of the village, often through her husband's sermons, to provide the donations, which she, herself, would then graciously bestow upon the needy. In this way, she both fulfilled her role and met her own personal need for recognition.

At the age of sixty-nine, Father Borys was becoming increasingly challenged by his duties. His brother's grandson, a newly ordained priest, Father Mykhaylo, had asked to be sent to the village, in order to assist the aging parish priest. Father Borys thought the young man must be simple for having made such a request. He did not have high hopes for the help this young fellow might offer.

Father Mykhaylo

There had never been a question about Father Mykhaylo becoming a priest. His grandfather and father before him, as well as his brothers, were all priests. But for Father Mykhaylo, it was more than a family occupation or tradition. All his life he had known that God had intended him to serve His people as a parish priest. Father Mykhaylo had no ambitions to be elevated in the church hierarchy – all he wanted was to work among the devout poor in one of the Ukrainian villages scattered throughout Galicia.

After his ordination, there had been a great family discussion about where he would go to start his service. His father and elder brothers all had suggestions. But it was Father Mykhaylo who insisted he be sent to the village where the two streams met to form a tributary of the Dniester. Father Mykhaylo knew Father Borys, he knew the parish priest was getting on in years and could probably use some help. He also knew that many of the villagers were poor. And so he had made up his mind that this was where he would begin his life's work.

Eventually, his father agreed to the plan and the arrangements had been made. The day Father Mykhaylo arrived in the village was a bright, warm day in early summer. Father Borys insisted on taking the young man on a round of visits to meet the most prominent members of his congregation. He hoped to impress the young man with a sense that this congregation, though unimportant in the worldview, had its notables and worthies.

Father Mykhaylo was grateful for the old priest's efforts to introduce him to the great families of the village but the young priest had come to serve the entire congregation, including the less notable. Father Mykhaylo was very devout and took his responsibilities for all of God's children very seriously. He had specifically requested this village because he knew there were many who were much in need of God's loving care and he had pledged himself to help provide it.

As the villagers met and then gradually got to know Father Mykhaylo, it became obvious to them that this man was very different from their current parish priest. It did not take long for the villagers to respond to Father Mykhaylo's goodness and generosity. The church filled whenever he performed the Divine Liturgy. People came to him for help and advice. He was never at a loss for an invitation to a meal. Even the poorest families wanted the young priest to grace their homes for a meager supper. Father Mykhaylo had won the hearts of the villagers, simply by being himself.

One day, old Dmytro had come upon the good Father on one of his walks.

"So, will you be looking for a wife soon?" the old man asked.

Taken aback, Father Mykhaylo hesitated and then responded, "Perhaps in a few years. I have so much to do, I do not have time to think about a wife."

"Oh, but a wife could help you with your work," old Dmytro answered. "And besides," he continued, "you must take a wife soon, so all the village girls will stop dreaming about you!"

It was only half in jest, for Father Mykhaylo was a very good-looking young man. He had been surprised and a bit embarrassed by what the old man had said. He blushed. He had not thought seriously about taking a wife and he had never thought of himself as one whom the village girls would think of as a prospective husband. But this simple conversation had made him aware that perhaps a wife might be helpful. He would have to pray about this.

Pavlo Dannyk

There were many orphans in the village, in fact throughout the region.

Pavlo was among the most unfortunate of these. At the age of seven he had had the misfortune of losing both his parents. He had two younger brothers and, even at this tender age, he felt a strong responsibility for them. After the death of his parents, Pavlo and his brothers were sent to live with their maternal grandmother on the far side of the village, past where the two streams merged. Unfortunately, his baba was already caring for two other grandchildren, Pavlo's cousins, who had suffered the same loss. This family had been very unfortunate indeed.

Baba Pelik was a generous and kindly woman but she had definitely been challenged to her limits. She was a widow. She had lost her husband, daughter, and son, all within the space of three years. She had only a little income from the widow's portion of land, which had been left to her by her husband. If it had been just herself, this might have been enough to keep body and soul together but now she had the responsibility of caring for her five grandchildren….

Her son had been a widower at the time of his death. His own small land holding had to be sold to pay off debts and to provide a small income to care for his two orphaned children. Her daughter and son-in-law had died in rapid succession, leaving only a small hut on a garden-sized plot at the far edge of the village beside the tributary, along with three small boys. Baba Pelik had sold the hut, in the hope that the income would be enough to help raise her daughter's sons. Pavlo, her eldest grandson, only seven years old, could perhaps help a little to support the family but the bulk of the burden had fallen on Baba Pelik

Baba Pelik had encouraged Pavlo to take his cousin, her second eldest grandson, to the stream to try to catch fish. The boys were diligent and, some days, lucky. The younger of the two soon showed a real love and talent for fishing and this became his occupation and family responsibility. Pavlo was neither as lucky nor as enthusiastic a fisherman as his cousin but he soon found another way to contribute to the family's welfare.

Pavlo approached a neighbor who raised geese. He volunteered to herd the geese to the neighbour's hillside plot, just above the village, in order for them to feed on insects and grain seeds left over from the prior harvest. With only a walking stick and a slingshot, which he had made himself, Pavlo became a goose herder. He rose early each day to herd the geese out of their pens and up to the hillside plot. There he would watch them feeding and especially watch for predators that might try to steal a goose for supper. In the evening, Pavlo would herd the geese back to the village and secure them in their pens. For this, he was paid one small coin, a Heller, each month. It wasn't much but it was a help to Baba Pelik in her efforts to feed and care for her grandchildren.

Pavlo had enjoyed this occupation. It wasn't too hard and he had lots of time to himself to think. He loved to sit on the hillside overlooking the village. From there he could see the hut in which he had lived with his mother, father, and brothers. Across the village, he could see the little house in which he now lived with his baba, brothers, and cousins. And between the two, looming large and white, even from this distant hillside, he could see the village church.

He loved the great, white church, built of lumber, rather than logs. It sat atop the prominent hill, just at the spot where the two streams joined to form the tributary. Its door faced west and the window above the altar, at the opposite end, faced east. The church building was in the shape of a cross, with the east-west wing slightly longer than the north-south wing. The three walls - south, east, and north - bowed out with three tall windows in each bow. Over the place where the two wings of the church crossed was a huge dome, set above a drum encircled with tall windows. Each of the four ends of the two wings had a steep, gabled roof, topped with a small bania or onion-shaped copula. The large dome and the four smaller copulas were each crowned with a golden cross. The dome and copulas were painted gold. Pavlo loved to watch the changing sunlight as it fell on the large dome throughout the day. He loved the church for it was, to him as to many of the villagers, the centre of his world. It was a place of light and peace in a world otherwise filled with darkness, pain, sorrow, and hunger.

One day, as Pavlo was bringing the geese home, he came across Father Mykhaylo. Father Mykhaylo often walked around the village. In this way he learned about the needs of the people. When he saw Pavlo, Father Mykhaylo had thought, "Now there's a brave lad. A poor orphan, working all day long to help support his brothers, cousins, and baba." And at that moment Father Mykhaylo had a thought.

"Pavlo," Father Mykhaylo asked, "do you know how to drive a buggy?"

"Yes, Sir" Pavlo answered, although he had never even been in a buggy, let alone driven one. How hard could it be? He had spent some time tending his neighbour's horse after returning the geese to their pens. He had a fondness for horses, which they sensed. So Pavlo was sure he could drive a buggy if he could win the trust of the horses pulling it.

"Well then," Father Mykhaylo continued, "how would you like to give up these geese in order to drive Father Borys' wife. She must make many trips around the village to minister to the poor and she needs someone to drive her."

Pavlo could not believe his good fortune. This would be a dream job.

"Oh yes, I would like that very much! But first, I must teach my brother to herd the geese. I cannot leave them alone."

Father Mykhaylo was very happy with the young boy's dedication to his employer and glad he had thought of the new job for him.

And so it was that Pavlo took his younger brother with him to herd geese for several days. He then asked the owner if his brother might take his place. The owner, having been aware that the two boys had been working together for several days, was happy to turn the job over to the younger boy. It was, after all, a job for a youngster and Pavlo was getting old enough to do something more. "God knows," he thought, "that family needs all the help it can get!"

So Pavlo reported to Father Mykhaylo, who introduced him to Paraska, Father Borys' wife. She of course knew who Pavlo was. Baba Pelik was one of the unfortunates she had often provided for. She looked the boy over, but was not impressed with what she saw. He was not very clean and was dressed in rags. She could not see herself being driven by this urchin. But she knew Father Mykhaylo was set on the plan. And so she said to him, "I am willing to give the boy a trial but he must be washed, thoroughly, and have better clothes … and shoes." She added. Father Mykhaylo agreed that he would help Pavlo get clean and find a more suitable set of clothing. Pavlo was ecstatic!

Next, Father Mykhaylo took Pavlo to the barn to meet the horses. He noticed Pavlo had a gentle, confident way with them and so, he was much relieved, as he had wondered if the boy really had ever driven a buggy. To put his mind at ease, Father Mykhaylo told Pavlo to hitch a horse to the buggy so they could take a ride. Pavlo knew this was a test but he also knew the kindly Father would help him. So the boy started the task and with the good Father's help, got the horse hitched to the buggy. Then they went for a ride. The priest showed Pavlo how to hold the reins and how to guide the horse. Pavlo was a natural and, because the horse liked him, it decided it would work with the boy.

When they got back from their trial tour of the village, Father Mykhaylo gave Pavlo a small bar of soap and told him to go to the stream to wash. When Pavlo returned, the priest had a pair of baggy trousers, a bit too loose and a bit too long; a large, loose-fitting shirt; a cord to use as a belt; and, best of all, a pair of shoes. The shoes were not new and were a bit big but Pavlo had not had shoes for a long time. He was very proud of them. Father Mykhaylo told Pavlo to take care of the new suit of clothing and to keep it clean. He suggested that it be worn only for his new job.

"And for church," Pavlo added.

"Yes," Father Mykhaylo agreed, "and for church".

That night, as Pavlo lay beside his brothers and cousins, he felt himself the luckiest boy in the world!

Pavlo reported the next morning to the rectory, freshly washed and in his new suit of clothing. The dobrodika (priest's wife) greeted him coolly, but asked if he had had anything to eat yet that morning. Pavlo nodded that he had, even though he had been too excited to eat. She then sent him to the barn to hitch a horse to the buggy. Paraska watched the boy carefully. He did seem to know what he was doing. And then a thought crossed her mind. Having this poor urchin drive her might well enhance her reputation as a generous benefactor. Perhaps he would do after all.

And so, Pavlo handed Paraska into the buggy and waited for her to get settled. Then he politely asked where she wanted to go. Her first stop that morning, as Pavlo would soon learn to be her routine, was the church.

There she went to pray for guidance from God for her day's duties. Pavlo tethered the horse across from the church and followed the dobrodika inside. He watched as she prayed and he, too, prayed silently from the back of the church that he would serve her well in her mission. When the dobrodika completed her prayer, Pavlo followed her back to the carriage and they were off.

It might have been a coincidence but Pavlo wondered why, as the very first stop on his first day, the dobrodika had decided to visit Baba Pelik. She took a basket of food and insisted on sitting with Baba to pray. Baba, of course, was a prayerful woman but she had a lot to do that day. She was grateful for the food, but anxious to get on with her tasks. Pavlo could not help wondering whether the dobrodika had chosen to visit his own home on the first day, in order to emphasize that his family was among the poorest in the village and in need of her charity.

But soon, they were off again and Pavlo was enjoying driving the dobrodika to her various destinations.

1901

At first, things went well. Pavlo learned what the dobrodika liked and didn't like. He learned her habits and routine. And he always aimed to please her, even on days when she seemed cross or out of sorts. Then one day, after it had been raining and the roads were rutted and rough, the dobrodika decided she needed to go to a neighbouring village. Pavlo was excited because he had never been outside of his own village. As they drove along the dobrodika kept telling him to slow down – the road was too rough. Pavlo did his best but the road was very rough after the rains.

That evening, old Father Borys heard Paraska's complaints about how the boy had driven her over the roughest parts of the road – it was an unacceptable show of disrespect, both for her and for her venerable husband. Father Borys was determined to teach the boy a lesson.

And so, the next morning when Pavlo arrived at the rectory, he was met, not by the dobrodika Paraska, but by the old priest. First Father Borys scolded and berated Pavlo. Then he marched him to the barn where he beat him with a walking stick. Even though the old priest was seventy years old and Pavlo was thirteen, the beating was a vicious attack on the young boy's body and mind. After the beating, Pavlo was left alone in the barn. He had a blackened eye and blood running down his face from a head wound. His back and legs had been beaten black and blue, as were his arms from his attempts to defend himself. He lay on the straw, whimpering in pain and unable to move.

At some point he must have lost consciousness, because the next thing he knew, he was lying in the bed of the rectory guest room. He was alone but he realized he had been washed and his wounds dressed. He ached all over, but worst of all, he was confused about why the old priest had beaten him so viciously. He drifted off to sleep.

When Pavlo awoke, Father Mykhaylo was sitting next to the bed, head bent in prayer. When the priest saw that Pavlo was awake, he asked him quietly, "How do you feel?"

"I hurt." was all that Pavlo could say.

"I have told your baba that you will stay with us until you are well," the priest said. "Now pray with me, Pavlo, pray that we can both forgive Father Borys as God forgives us for our sins."

And so they prayed. And then Father Mykhaylo went to get Pavlo something to eat.

Pavlo stayed as a guest in the rectory for two days. It was probably longer than was necessary, but Father Mykhaylo wanted to be sure the boy would recover, both in body and in spirit.

Father Mykhaylo had spoken with old Father Borys about the beating. It was clear that the old man had completely lost control. They prayed together and eventually Father Mykhaylo convinced the old man he must relinquish his position as parish priest. Father Mykhaylo would assume that role and old Father Borys would assist him. It was a grave penance for the act of rage, for which he himself was ashamed.

And so it was that Pavlo became the driver for the new parish priest, Father Mykhaylo, instead of the wife of the old parish priest.

Pavlo loved to drive Father Mykhaylo. The two talked of many things on their drives and Pavlo learned a great deal from the young priest. The two became good friends. For Pavlo, it was like having an earthly father. For Father Mykhaylo it was at first, his way of making restitution to the young boy, but soon it had grown into genuine affection.

That fall, old Father Borys died peacefully in his sleep. His wife, feeling that there was nothing left for her in the village, returned to Stanyslaviv to live with her sister. She had given the better part of her life to improve the lot of the miserable villagers and now, finally, she was released from her duties.

Toward the end of that same year, when Mykola turned twenty-one, he reported for military service. It was his duty so he would go. He looked forward to completing the required three years of service because he knew when he came back, he could get married and start a family of his own. He didn't have a particular girl in mind but he knew he wanted to be a husband and a father. He did worry about how he would support a family, since he had no land of his own and his portion of his father's land, when he inherited it, would not be large enough. "Perhaps he could find a wife with land of her own," he thought, and then laughed at himself for even thinking such a thing. Maybe he could make a good connection in the army or learn a skill, which would help him. And so on a bright autumn morning, Mykola and two other young men from the village set off on foot for the military office, situated in the town where the tributary flowed into the mighty Dniester River.

Although the law provided for a universal, three-year military service by twenty-one-year-old males, not all who qualified were actually conscripted. Compared to other European countries of the time, the Austrian Empire actually had a smaller, less well-funded army and conscripted fewer than one third of those eligible. The bulk of the conscripts were relatively poor peasants. Sons of nobles, priests, those in commerce, and only sons, as well as those who could not pass the physical examination were often exempted.

Each house in every village was numbered. In this way the authorities knew from the church records where each eligible conscript lived. After the initial three-year term of service, all conscripts were put on reserve for a further ten years and could be called up if they were needed.

Even though the last fifty years or so had been relatively peaceful times there had been increasing unrest in many regions as the new century began. Quelling this unrest was the main military activity at the time when Mykola began his service. The military authorities were concerned about armed peasants being stationed too near their own homes, so Mykola was sent some distance away for eight weeks of training and then wherever his unit was needed, also far from home.

This was one time that Taras was not anxious to go wherever his brother went. Taras knew he would miss Mykola but he had begun thinking of his own future.

Taras was twenty. He had been popular with the girls but he knew he couldn't get serious about anyone until after he had completed his military service and he was not looking forward to that. He, too, realized that his father's small plot of land, if divided among the five brothers, would not feed any of them for long. No … another solution had to be found.

One day, not long after Mykola had departed, while helping a neighbor, Taras was taken by surprise when he learned that another village family was planning to immigrate to Argentina. Argentina! He had to learn more. Of course there had been other families who had emigrated but he had not known anyone who had gone to Argentina. After he was finished with the job at hand, he went to Mr. Bodnar to ask him why he had chosen Argentina.

"Well," said Mr. Bodnar, "my brother's wife's family went last year. They have written that the government gives land to immigrants and the weather is much better than in Canada. So we are following them."

Taras sat with Mr. Bodnar for some time, quizzing him about the planned trip, how much it would cost, how long it would take, how much land was available … Taras was amazed. The Argentinian government was giving immigrants fifty hectares of land – an astonishing amount, given his father's holding was a mere three and a quarter acres. The place where the Bodnars were heading was called Misiones. It was in the north of Argentina, near the border with Brazil. There were already several Ukrainian families in the region.

For days Taras could think of nothing else. His imagination had been ignited once again. The only drawback was that Mykola was not there to share his excitement!

A few days later, Yuriy asked his second son, "So you are missing Mykola? Do you want to follow him into the army?"

"No Tato," Taras replied, "but I do want to talk with you about something."

And so Taras told his father all he had learned about immigrating to Argentina. At first, Yuriy was concerned that his son would even consider such an idea but both father and son knew that emigration might well be the only way in which Taras could ever have enough land to raise a family.

"So you would really leave us and go half-way around the world to seek your fortune?" Yuriy asked sadly but he already knew what Taras had decided. And he couldn't blame him. "If I were younger," Yuriy thought, "I'd be considering it too."

"So how would you go?" Yuriy asked.

"Well, I could ask Mr. Bodnar to sponsor me. He has no sons, only three daughters. He could probably use the help of another man. And, if I go with him, I can get my own land grant eventually. Imagine fifty hectares of land – unbelievable!"

"Even if Mr. Bodnar agreed to sponsor you, there would still be costs," Yuriy cautioned.

"I know father and I know you cannot afford to help me, so I am hoping to start working for Mr. Bodnar right away. That way he will see I am a good worker and a good investment. I will pay him back whatever it costs to take me with them. I think he will agree. If Argentina is a good place for me, it could be a good place for our whole family. After I get there and see how it really is, I can send word for the rest of you to follow."

Yuriy looked pensive for a moment and then sadly shook his head, "I am too old," he replied.

But the more he thought about his small holding and his large family, about the opportunities in Argentina, about his son's excitement over this new adventure, he began to think perhaps it might be worth considering.

The Bodnars readily agreed to sponsor Taras and to take him with them to Argentina.

Unbeknownst to Yuriy, Vasyl had a small amount of savings of his own. Not long after Taras' failed scheme to make and sell woodcarvings, Vasyl had decided it was not such a bad idea and had begun to sell some of his creations. Between what he earned in this way and the fact that, as a single man, his financial needs were never very great, Vasyl had put aside a bit of money. Perhaps he had inherited his father's penchant for saving. Uncle Vasyl insisted on giving Taras enough money to pay his own passage to Argentina. He felt this was the least he could do for the boy whose idea had resulted in a good portion of the savings. Uncle Vasyl knew that the amount of money he could give to Taras wasn't much but at least Taras would not be completely dependent upon the good will of the Bodnars.

1902

The Bodnars had booked space on a ship leaving from Antwerp in the early spring of 1902. This was in order to arrive in the southern-hemisphere autumn, as advised by their relatives already in Argentina. The timing could not have been better for Taras. If the Bodnars had decided to leave in the fall of 1902, he would have had his twenty-first birthday in September and would have been required to report for military service.

The day that Taras left with the Bodnars was a day filled with mixed emotions. Yuriy was excited for his second son, whom he had always known would find a grand adventure in life but he was saddened by the fact that he might never see him again. He had spent long hours the evening before, talking with Taras about the days when, as young boys, he and

Mykola had been inseparable. It seemed unbelievable to him that the brothers, once so very close, would now be half a world apart possibly for the rest of their lives.

Taras was very excited about his adventure. However, he truly believed Argentina would be so wonderful that soon his whole family would be joining him. In his heart he especially longed to be reunited with his brother Mykola. Taras made a final promise to his father that he would write, as soon as possible, to let them know if they should follow. To himself he promised to save his money and, as soon as he had earned enough, to send for Mykola. Surely by the time Mykola's military service was complete Taras would have saved enough to send for him.

Now that Taras was gone, Yuriy began to plan in earnest to emigrate with his family. The plan consumed his every waking hour and had begun creeping into his dreams, as well. He was hearing more and more about others who had moved their families halfway around the world for large plots of land and a better future. He had seen the advertisements for free land – enough land to farm and raise a family, as well as for each of his sons to raise their own families. He knew he was getting old for such an undertaking but he believed that this was the only way his family could hope to survive and perhaps prosper.

From the information he was collecting, either Canada or Argentina were good prospects; they attracted many immigrants because both offered free land and had lower immigration fees than other countries. Many people from the village had gone to Canada but the Bodnars were the first to go to Argentina. Of course, with Taras already there, perhaps Argentina was the better choice. He knew Anna did not like this plan but the more he thought about it the more he came to believe he had to do something for the future of his children and their children, in turn.

Mykhaylo continued to grudgingly work in the field with Tato and his brothers. He kept his thoughts to himself. As the fall progressed and the harvest was completed Mykhaylo had a little more time to himself. He often went to visit his friend, Bohdan. The two young men spent time sitting in front of one of the village stores, talking and watching the town's people walk by. One evening Mykhaylo noticed a girl who was a bit younger than himself. He knew who she was, of course. Larysa Melnyk was the only daughter of a wealthy Ukrainian landowner.

Mykhaylo made a point of making this young woman aware of him. He smiled, he winked, and he watched her intently. In church on Sunday he stared unashamedly at her. Eventually the young girl succumbed to his attentions and soon believed herself to be in love with him. Mykhaylo had found his way out.

Throughout the long fall and into the winter months Mykhaylo sought every opportunity to meet and talk to Larysa.

Her mother, who was ten years younger than her father, had married him because of the life he could offer her. He owned twenty morgs of land (about thirty acres) and had a fine house, a housekeeper, and field hands. She had been the village beauty and the daughter of a local tradesman. Larysa's father knew why his wife had married him but he had been smitten. A pregnancy swiftly followed the wedding but it had been very difficult. The birth had been more difficult still. For whatever reason, physical or emotional, Larysa was the only child of that union. Her father didn't seem to mind. He loved his daughter unconditionally and knew he could provide her with whatever her heart desired – so he did. As a consequence Larysa had had an amazing childhood.

When Larysa's father first became aware of his daughter's growing interest in the Martiniuk boy he was alarmed. He had hoped she would not be interested in a young man for some time to come and when it happened, he would have some say in whom she might consider. He had hoped she would become the wife of one of the sons of another wealthy landowner ensuring that she would continue to have the means to live the life he had provided for her.

However, as the weeks went by and father and daughter continued to discuss her feelings for Mykhaylo, it became clear that Larysa would have her way – as usual.

Young Martiniuk had some good qualities. He worked hard with his father and uncle. He had not gotten into trouble like some of the young boys in the village. He didn't drink or fight. True, his prospects were not good. His father had five sons and a very small plot of land. But Larysa loved him. So the father began to watch the young man very carefully. Mykhaylo was aware that he was being watched… and judged. His behaviour was flawless. The father discretely asked about Mykhaylo's actions and found nothing distressing. At last the father knew he would have to agree to the union.

Just after the Christmas of 1902, Yuriy Martiniuk accompanied his third son, Mykhaylo, to the wealthy landowner's home to officially ask for Larysa's hand in marriage. The pair were greeted and welcomed into the front room. The light from the fireplace danced over the sinuously carved wooden furniture. Yuriy was uncomfortable but tried hard not to let his feelings show.

Larysa's father led the conversation. He commented on local events in the village and asked Yuriy about the yield on his farm that fall. Yuriy answered all of the wealthy landowner's queries and said little else. Mykhaylo was silent.

They were offered brandy to drink. Mykhaylo declined.

As time passed Mykhaylo began to wonder if Larysa's father had any idea of the purpose of their visit. At a pause in the conversation Mykhaylo stood and quietly and calmly addressed the wealthy landowner.

"I wish to ask for the hand of your precious daughter, Larysa. We are in love. All I have to offer her is my work and myself. She knows this but loves me still. Will you grant your blessing?"

Mykhaylo heard a muffled giggle from behind a door, which was slightly ajar – he suddenly realized Larysa had been watching the proceedings since their arrival.

Larysa's father rose slowly and then put his hand on Mykhaylo's shoulder. "I know how my daughter feels about you and you do have my blessing." Then he turned to Yuriy, who was astonished at both his son's boldness and the wealthy landowner's response.

"So we have a wedding to plan," he said.

Mykhaylo spoke once again: "We hope to marry in spring."

Both Larysa's father and Yuriy were stunned. Most engagements lasted at least a year. Furthermore, the agricultural year often dictated that marriages took place in late fall or during the winter months after the harvest had been completed. But Mykhaylo was determined and more importantly, so was Larysa.

Fleetingly, Yuriy remembered old Father Borys' threat when he had taken Dariya to the next village to be baptized. The poor old priest had not lived long enough to have his revenge for that action. "God rest his soul and Vichnya Pamyat (Grant him Eternal Memory)," Yuriy thought.

When she had been just a small girl Larysa's father had had a beautiful chest made for her. It had always been proudly at the foot of her bed. As she grew and learned how to sew and embroider, Larysa had begun to fill the chest with the items she would someday take to her own home after she was married. During the winter following her engagement, Larysa spent long hours completing projects to fill her chest. Every time she placed a completed object in the chest she thought how proud Mykhaylo would be of her skill and how happy she would be to use the item in her new home.

1903

Larysa's father had sent presents to Yuriy. The money was immediately put aside. He knew exactly how it would be used. Anna received a length of good quality cloth, which would make a new blouse for her and perhaps one for Dariya, as well.

As the wedding day approached, Larysa's family gathered to prepare her for her marriage. A few days before, her baba sent her into the woods to find the myrtle, a symbol of fertility, for her wedding wreath. Larysa took her girlfriends with her. When they returned to the house, Baba, Mama, and her aunts gathered around her and began singing the mournful tunes, which bespoke the loss of a daughter, a custom during the wreath-making ceremony. After a portion of the wreath had been made, Larysa's baba called one of the young girls forward and held the partial wreath to her head. No, it would not do, so the singing and wreath making continued.

This process was repeated until only Larysa had not tried the wreath. When it was finally her turn, lo and behold the wreath fit and it was complete. Larysa's mother took the myrtle wreath, placed it on a Korovai (braided bread decorated with birds), and hid it somewhere in the house. Larysa would not see the wreath again until she was being dressed for her wedding.

And so it was that in the spring of 1903, on the first Sunday of May, Mykhaylo and Larysa were married during the regular Sunday Liturgy. Larysa was sixteen. Mykhaylo was about to turn twenty. Normally, young men were required to serve a mandatory, three-year service in the Austrian army, from age twenty-one to twenty-three, and were not permitted to marry until completing this service. But the landowner had pled his case and Mykhaylo had been allowed to marry. Likely Larysa's father had had to pay someone but Mykhaylo didn't care. True, he might still be called to military service when he turned twenty-one, but by then there might be a child and land to manage for his father-in-law … all might be very different by then. He had managed to achieve his life's goal of freedom from his father's house.

On the morning of the wedding, Larysa's friends and female relatives took special care helping her to get dressed. First there was the long white sheath, which covered her from neck to ankles. Then a beautifully embroidered white blouse, with voluminous sleeves, tucked into a red skirt, also embroidered along the bottom hem. Over this was tied a white, embroidered apron. Finally, on her feet were the softest, red leather boots. Her hair was plaited into a single thick braid, which fell down her back. She and her girlfriends had picked flowers to braid into a 'crown' for her head and the myrtle wreath had been fastened into the crown of flowers. Around her neck were three strands of coral beads (coraliya), which her father had given to her. These beads represented the wealth she brought to the marriage, but would remain hers and hers alone to wear or use as she liked.

Larysa felt like a woman. She was very excited about the wedding. She looked like the princess her father had always thought her to be.

Larysa came before her mother and father, who were seated side-by-side in the front room with a rushnyk (embroidered cloth) over their laps. They held the Korovai and a small bowl of salt. Larysa knelt before her parents to receive the traditional blessing (blahoslovenia). The sarosta (family elder), in this case Larysa's godfather and uncle, held the icon that would be given to the young couple for their new home. He recited the traditional words and led the gathered relatives as they invoked God's blessings on the bride.

This same ritual was being performed by Mykhaylo in his father's home and would then be repeated once more, the third blessing, by the couple before both sets of parents at Larysa's home before leaving for the church.

Mykhaylo had worked hard for a tradesman in the village all winter so he could be properly attired for his wedding. Even Anna had spent long hours during the winter embroidering his wedding shirt.

Anna, keenly aware of the difference in standing and wealth between the two families, was determined her family would be well dressed for the wedding. She picked out the best clothing each family member owned and then set about ensuring that every garment fit properly, was clean, and embellished. A few items of clothing were repaired or replaced; additional embroidery was added here and there. Yuriy was very proud of Anna and the results of her dedication to their family.

That Sunday morning as Mykhaylo, his friends, and family prepared to set out for Larysa's house, Anna sprinkled the group with holy water, which had been blessed in church on the feast of Jordan (Epiphany). She then tossed a few handfuls of grain and some small coins at Mykhaylo, as a symbol of the family's wishes for him for prosperity and good luck. Then the entire group walked through the village. Mykhaylo was going to claim his bride.

When they arrived, Larysa was sitting atop her chest, which had been placed in the yard in front of the house. Since she had no brothers, her male cousins surrounded her. Mykhaylo made a great show, much to the delight of the gathered crowd, of offering these cousins various small gifts in order to ransom his bride.

Larysa's father could not bear to have his daughter move too far away, so he was building a small house next to his own for the young couple. Until the new house was completed, the couple would live in the big house with

Larysa's parents. Larysa was very pleased with the arrangement, as she had dreaded the thought of leaving her father and home. So, after ransoming his bride, Mykhaylo and his friends took the chest back into her father's house.

At last it was time to proceed to the church. When they arrived, Father Mykhaylo met the young couple while the congregation continued to file into the church. The ceremony would begin at the back of the church with the formal betrothal. Here Father Mykhaylo asked the bride and the bridegroom if they had come willingly to be married. They both solemnly replied that they had. He blessed the ring and put it on Larysa's finger and then led the couple to the front of the church. Here, Larysa and Mykhaylo stood before the tetrapod (small table, which stands before the iconostas) during the Liturgy. Instead of a sermon, Father Mykhaylo performed the wedding ceremony. He held crowns above each of their heads, representing their new status as king and queen of their home together. He bound their hands with a rushnyk and then led them three times around the tetrapod. Thus the young couple took their first steps together as a married couple.

A great many of the villagers had been invited to Larysa's father's home to celebrate the wedding. There was food and drink aplenty. There was a band playing music and the guests sang and danced all afternoon and into the night. At one point during the festivities, Baba and Mama unplaited Larysa's braid and re-did it into two braids, which were then fastened around the top of her head. Then they covered her head with an ochipok (scarf), which indicated she was now a married woman.

Many people commented on the young couple. Some whispered that they could not believe Yuriy's third son could have won such a prize! Mykhaylo knew what was being said but he didn't care. He had won his freedom and was on his path to a better life. He was triumphant.

There had been letters from Taras in Argentina. At first they had been excited missives, filled with details of the ocean crossing, their arrival in the new land, and descriptions of all that he had seen and learned. Surprisingly, there had not been the awaited entreaties to for the family to follow. Yuriy had his younger son, Andriy, write a letter to Taras with very specific questions about the availability of land, the climate, the suitability for farming, and the prospects for the rest of the family. Taras' letters had become less frequent and less enthusiastic and not once did he encourage his father to follow. Yuriy began to question his plan to emigrate. But perhaps it was just that Argentina wasn't the place to go.

More and more families from the village were leaving for Canada. The news from those who had gone seemed promising. There was land and lots of it. It really was free – the only cost was a ten-dollar registration fee for the land claim. The winters were bitterly cold. The first years were hard but there was a growing Ukrainian community and neighbours all helped one another. Some families had prospered in a very short time. Yuriy was seriously thinking about taking his family, what was left of it, to Canada.

Whenever he talked of emigrating, Anna would say: "Send for Taras first. Bring him home so we can all go to Canada together." Or "Wait until Mykola returns so he can come too." Mykola was due to return the following autumn. Yuriy knew Anna was just hoping that if they waited long enough they simply would not go.

But now that Mykhaylo was married, Yuriy's thoughts turned more and more toward immigrating to Canada. It would take planning and preparation. Even if they started to prepare immediately, they could not be ready to go before next spring.

Perhaps Anna was right. He would have Andriy write to Taras again and ask him to come home so they could all go to Canada. They would wait until Mykola returned in autumn and then they would all leave together the following spring.

1904

Taras had not returned. Yuriy's letter resulted in no reply. Yuriy was worried about his second son. He inquired of the Bodnars' relatives in the village but there had been no news for several months. Yuriy prayed his son was safe and well and simply out of reach for the present. Communication would be re-established and all would be explained. There could still be time for Taras to return or even to meet them in Canada.

As autumn turned to winter another worry entered Yuriy's life. Mykola had not returned as expected in autumn. Yuriy had walked to the town on the Dniester to inquire at the military office, but could not get any information about his oldest son. It was not unusual for a recruit's return to be delayed. As soon as they heard something they would let the family know. It wasn't as if there was a war. Their son would be fine and would be home before they knew it.

This did not satisfy Yuriy. He had his son, Andriy, write a letter to Mykola. The family was looking forward to seeing him before Christmas. They were planning to immigrate to Canada after Easter. Tato had obtained a passport for Mykola, as well as for the others in the family. When he returned there would be time for him to decide whether he wanted to follow Taras to Argentina or come with the rest of the family to Canada. The letter was sent to Mykola's unit, so it eventually made its way to Sarajevo where Mykola had been stationed. Unfortunately, it was delivered just days after Mykola's unit was sent to a border town near Serbia. Unbeknownst to Yuriy, Mykola would never see this letter.

Yuriy prayed for his eldest sons. Anna would exclaim over and over again, "Bozhe mi, Bozhe mi! (My God, my God!)" It was a very tense time.

Tensions were rising in the wider world as well as in Yuriy's family. There had been student rallies and assassinations. The news from the world was unsettling. Yuriy was convinced he must take his family to Canada and soon. They would have to leave next spring at the latest. He would be fifty years old in the coming year. If they waited any longer he would be much too old to go. His mind was made up. He would start making preparations to leave in spring, come what may.

In addition to the usual preparations for winter, Yuriy and his two youngest sons were busy preparing to emigrate. Yuriy had talked to an immigration agent and knew how much it would cost and on which ship they would sail. There was a sailing from the port of Hamburg, which would leave the week following Easter. The family would celebrate the Great Day (Easter Sunday) on April 10th and leave immediately afterwards to make the sailing. They would arrive in Canada at the end of April or beginning of May and would have the whole summer to get established and ready for their first Canadian winter.

Vasyl wanted Yuriy to use the last of their father's savings but Yuriy insisted Vasyl keep the money for Mykola if he didn't get home before the family left or for Taras if he returned and wanted to join the family in Canada. Yuriy even suggested that Vasyl might use the money to emigrate with them. Vasyl was two years younger than Yuriy but he had no interest in leaving his home. He would stay put and when the two eldest boys returned he would help them in any way he could.

Yuriy had gone through all of their belongings with Andriy, now nineteen, and Petro, seventeen, having them make lists of what they would take and what would be sold. Between the gift of money he had received from Mykhaylo's father-in-law and the sale of anything they would not take to Canada, he thought they could buy their passage and have a small amount of money to get them started in the new country.

It was difficult for him to sell the farmland, which he had inherited from his father but the money was needed to get much more land in Canada. In the end, Vasyl decided he would buy Yuriy's share of the land and the house. He would sell his own small hut and the bit of land it stood upon and move back into the family home where he had grown up. Vasyl said it was because he wanted to keep all of their father's land in the family and to move back into their childhood home but Yuriy suspected he just wanted to help the family have enough money for their trip.

The only disturbance in all these plans came, as usual, from Mykhaylo. He was not happy that his father was selling 'his inheritance' and demanded his father grant him a fifth of the land before selling the rest to Uncle Vasyl. An agreement was finally reached whereby Uncle Vasyl would bequeath to Mykhaylo one fifth of the entire holding, which had been Dido (Grandpa) Ivan's, rather than only one fifth of Yuriy's half. That seemed to satisfy Mykhaylo but it left both Yuriy and Vasyl with a bad feeling about how Mykhaylo had behaved.

Christmas came and went and still there had been no word from Argentina nor had Mykola returned. Yuriy tried hard to think of his eldest sons as healthy and well but it was difficult to remain positive.

That winter Yuriy and his youngest sons worked with a gang of men who were repairing the rail line, which ran past the town along the Dniester River. They saved everything they earned. Every little bit helped. By spring they would have the funds needed to emigrate.

Anna had taken to exclaiming, "Bozhe mi, Bozhe mi (my God, my God), if only we would hear something! How can you be so calm? God is telling us we must wait here for the boys to return."

Maybe she was right. Yuriy could not bear the thought of leaving without hearing the fate of his two eldest sons.

"Dear God" he prayed, "take care of my boys, wherever they are."

Pavlo had been Father Mykhaylo's driver for four years. He also did chores and ran errands for the good Father. He was very happy with his life. So he was extremely surprised when one day, Father Mykhaylo asked him to sit down so that they could talk about his future. Pavlo had come to see his future as remaining in the service of the good Father.

Father Mykhaylo started, "So how are your brothers doing?"

Pavlo, who had not had to worry about food or a place to live while working for Father Mykhaylo, had given everything he earned to Baba Pelik. It had helped a great deal. Since Pavlo was taken care of, his brother was herding geese and his cousin had begun working with a local fisherman, she had only to provide for her two youngest grandchildren. And now these two were old enough to begin contributing to the family's resources as well.

With all this in mind Pavlo answered that all was well with his brothers.

"Dobra (Good)," the priest responded as he already knew the answer to this inquiry. "Pavlo, you are almost a grown man. Your brothers can take care of themselves now. You do not have many prospects in the village."

Pavlo was devastated. Father Mykhaylo no longer needed him.

Father Mykhaylo saw Pavlo's reaction and quickly continued, "I think you could have better opportunities in Canada. If I were a younger man I would consider going myself. But, as it is, the best I can do is to help you to go."

Once more Pavlo was stunned. What could he say? He really didn't want to go anywhere, least of all to Canada. But as Father Mykhaylo continued to talk Pavlo began to see that perhaps the priest had a good idea after all.

"But how could I go?" he asked. "I have no money." The priest was well aware that Pavlo had given up all his earnings for the support of his family.

Here Father Mykhaylo revealed the plan he had been formulating for some time. "I will help you to emigrate and pay for your trip. I ask only two things of you – that you will always remain a devout Greek Catholic and that you pray for me."

"Oh Father, of course I will always be devout and I will pray for you for the rest of my life. I also will pay you back everything it has cost you."

Father Mykhaylo smiled. He didn't care if he ever saw the money. He hoped Pavlo would do well in the new world and that was the best reward he could hope for.

And so it was that Pavlo Dannyk, with Father Mykhaylo's help, began to plan for his trip to Canada.

1905

The long Lenten period was particularly difficult for the Martiniuk family, who began to grieve in their hearts for the two, eldest, lost sons.

The land was sold to Uncle Vasyl in time for spring planting. Extraneous belongings had been sold. Passports were granted. Travel arrangements made. Tickets bought.

Yuriy retrieved Kateryna's coral beads from the storage box in the attic and carefully packed them with the belongings to accompany them. He would give them to Dariya when she wed. He knew Kateryna would have wanted his only daughter to have the precious beads. He did not tell Anna, who might have wanted the necklace for herself.

Vasyl had insisted that Yuriy take the icon, which had hung in the family home since their parents were married. Yuriy had thought to leave it in the hut for Vasyl but Vasyl insisted.

"They will need the protection of the Mother of God in the new land more than I will here," Vasyl had thought.

And so Yuriy carefully packed the precious icon among his most cherished possessions for the trip to their new home. It was then that Yuriy came to the full realization of just how much he would miss his brother.

Yuriy carefully selected what would be taken to the new country, a sickle and scythe, a hammer and saw, a piece of rope, a bag of grain for seed. He also packed his clothing including his big sheepskin coat.

Even Anna began to prepare for their departure. She sorted through her precious store of seeds, both for a kitchen garden and for healing plants and herbs, including hemp and poppy seeds. Since she knew nothing of what grew naturally in Canada or what the climate was really like, she took everything she thought might be needed. And so she packed the spindle and wool carder, threads and needles, cooking pots and utensils, their clothing and feather quilts and pillows. She was bound and determined she would have all her worldly possessions with her in the new country.

Yuriy managed to fit everything that they planned to take with them into two wooden chests, which he and the boys would be able to manage throughout their travels. Anna had sack to carry and even little Dariya had a small sack, which would be her responsibility during the journey.

The family approached Holy Week with a mixture of excitement and dread. Yuriy's daily prayers ended with the appeal, "Dear God, show me a sign that I am doing the right thing!"

As Easter approached Anna had become sullen. She really did not want to leave but she knew she had no choice. She prayed for a miracle that would keep them from going. She knew her miracle would not come. There were times when she wondered why she had ever married Yuriy. He had been a good husband, gentle and caring, but this obsession with emigration had undone her. The children of course were no better than their father. Andriy and Petro were eager for the adventure. Even Dariya, her own daughter, was excited in her childish way. Only Anna saw that this was a disaster from which they would never recover. Her only hope was that Canada would be so bad, they would have to return.

The Great Day of Easter Sunday arrived. The celebration was especially poignant for the family, as it was to be their last Easter in the village church, which had been the center of their spiritual lives.

Had she slept at all? She didn't think so but perhaps she had dozed a bit toward morning. It was very early - still dark. She heard Tato and Mama getting ready for church. Her stomach rumbled - she hadn't eaten much in the last two days. First the Great Fast of Good Friday and then just the barest essentials yesterday on Holy Saturday. Of course, they had been to church several times and had been busy praying … and packing! She knew it would be several hours yet before she would eat.

And then they were all dressed in their best clothing and walking through the village to the church. It was just before sunrise. There was a chill in the air. And she was so excited! Not just because it was the Great Day but also because it was their last day in the village! Tomorrow they would be setting off on their journey. She could barely contain herself.

The church was full. She knew that the first part of the service would be conducted in the dark. Then the candles, which everyone held, would be lit. Then the congregation would form a procession to walk three times around the outside of the church, singing songs about the women going to Christ's tomb early in the morning. And then the priest would stand before the doors of the church and strike them with the golden crucifix. The doors would magically open to reveal that the tomb was empty – the shroud (plaschinetsy) was gone! And then he would pronounce "Christ is risen – Christos Voskras". The priest would sing the Easter anthem and then the people would repeat it and the third time, the priest would sing the first half and the people would respond with the final half. And then, in joyous revelry, the church would be filled with light and song and the ringing of bells! She loved Easter – it truly was a Great Day! She would remember this last Easter in the village all her life.

After the Divine Liturgy, the villagers arrayed their Easter baskets around the entrance to the church for blessing. "Would there be a priest to bless their Easter food in the new country?" Anna wondered.

Instead of rushing home to the traditional breakfast of blessed Easter foods, the family lingered outside the church. Many neighbours stopped to wish them well. There were six families from the village leaving together the next day. There were joyous farewells along with tears. All of this just made it harder for Anna. She couldn't believe this was actually going to happen. She was seeing her family, relatives, friends, and neighbours for probably the last time in her life … unless of course they would return.

At that moment, Anna noticed one of the women who would be travelling with them. She was walking to the cemetery behind the church. Anna watched the woman and her husband who followed a few steps behind her. The woman first knelt to pray at a little grave and then prostrated herself upon it. Anna remembered the funeral of the little girl who was buried there. She had been such a pretty little thing, always clinging to her mother. With three older, rowdy brothers, no wonder she had been shy. The mother had been heart-broken at her loss – it was a very difficult funeral for all who had attended.

"She may never be able to pray at her daughter's graveside again," Anna thought, "thank God I am not leaving behind the grave of a child."

Early on Bright (Easter) Monday, the Martiniuk family loaded the belongings they were taking with them into a cart, which Vasyl had borrowed. He drove them to the railway station in the town where the tributary emptied into the Dniester River. There they boarded the train for their journey, first to Stanyslaviv, then on to Lviv, and then north to Hamburg. They were on their way.

2 CROSSINGS

Taras, 1902

It was early spring in Europe when Taras left the village with the Bodnars. They took a wagon drawn by horses to the town where the tributary emptied into the Dniester. There they boarded a train, which took them to Stanyslaviv, Lviv, Munich, Brussels, and finally to Antwerp. There were immigrant hotels in Antwerp but the Bodnars had been warned that these were teeming with pick-pockets, bandits, and prostitutes, all looking for an opportunity to part the emigrants from their money and valuables. And so, avoiding the immigrant hotels, they carried their bundles further into the town to find a place to stay. They knew on which date, at what time, and from which pier their ship would depart. They had a few days to rest and obtain necessities for the voyage.

Taras assisted Mr. Bodnar to prepare for the voyage while his wife and daughters stayed out of sight with their belongings in a rented room. Mr. Bodnar was grateful to have another man to help him.

At last, it was time to head for the pier and their ship. They arrived in plenty of time. In fact, the ship was not yet ready for passengers to board. As a result the little group huddled together a short distance from the gangplank avoiding hustlers until they could board. It was an uncomfortable time but it passed without incident. Finally they were told they could board the ship. They were shown where to stow their belongings, where they would sleep, and where they would eat. The ship pulled away from the dock in the middle of the afternoon. Taras could not help but be excited. This was the adventure he had been dreaming of and he wanted to savor every minute.

The ship's initial progress was very slow. The passengers watched, first the bustling people on the dock, then the skyline of the receding city, and finally the last signs of land. They were at sea!

The first days out were cold and windy - too unpleasant to be on deck for very long at a time. A few people had become sea sick but Taras was well and grateful for this blessing. The ship made several stops at various ports of call, in order to pick up more passengers. The sleeping spaces would all be filled and there would be little individual space and little or no privacy. The food had been adequate because fresh provisions had been brought on board at each stop. However, after the last stop at the Canary Islands, there would be no more fresh provisions until they reached South America. During the rest of the voyage they would have to rely solely on preserved foods and what could be prepared on board.

The voyage was expected to take three weeks, but a few days out from the Canaries rough seas were encountered. At this point there were very few who were not seasick, including some of the crew. The stench below deck was overwhelming but for those afflicted there was little chance of escaping it. The few who were not sick tried to spend as much time on deck as possible. This is where Taras could be found most of the time. Unfortunately it meant he was exposed to the cold sea spray and sharp winds.

After a few days he knew he could no longer spend time on deck – he had to go below to lie down because he had contracted a nasty head cold. He was feverish. He felt stuffy and congested. His throat felt like it was on fire. His head and everything else ached. He was miserable. He lay in his narrow bunk and tried to sleep, but sleep would not come. So he tried to focus on his dream. He thought of his boyhood days with Mykola. He remembered his father and the rest of the family – anything to keep from thinking about his physical misery.

Others had head colds and worse. Many were coughing violently. Between seasickness and other illnesses there were few passengers in good health.

Then one day the sea calmed; the sharp, cold winds ceased; and a calm fell over the ship. The air temperature warmed with every hour. Taras, weaken by illness, struggled up to the deck. He still wasn't feeling well but he needed fresh air. He found a quiet spot where he could hunker down in the warmth of the sun. And there he sat for hours … perhaps days. He wasn't sure because, finally he was able to sleep.

The dramatic change in the weather as the ship approached and then crossed the equator resulted in all the remaining passengers becoming ill. No one escaped the impact of the change in weather conditions. Those who had been seasick might have become used to the heaving of the sea, only to fall victim to a severe head cold, bronchitis, or pneumonia. Those who had had a mild head cold developed more serious complications. There was a doctor on the ship but he had few remedies that really helped. A few people became so ill that they were quarantined, in order to avoid spreading their illness. Some of these died.

It was after crossing the equator that Taras became acutely aware of Mr. Bodnar's eldest daughter. Her name was Maria. She was short and just a little plump. If her mother were any indication, Maria would become plumper with age. Not that Taras had any objection to plumpness – most of the girls in the village, whom he had liked and teased, had been plump. No that wasn't it. She seemed good-natured enough and Taras had often enjoyed watching her and her sisters giggling over something they had seen or heard. So what was it, then that bothered him about her? There was something but he just couldn't put his finger on it.

Then one day he happened to hear the young woman talking with her sisters. It was clearly a conversation he was not intended to overhear. It seemed Maria had decided Taras would make a wonderful husband and she intended for him to marry her!

Taras was taken aback. He had not been thinking of getting married. All his energies had been focused on his grand adventure.

He wondered if Mr. Bodnar knew of Maria's plans. Then he wondered if Mr. Bodnar had encouraged her. This would not do. He wasn't sure how he felt about Maria but he was sure he didn't want to get married – not just yet. He had big plans for when he got to Argentina and being married didn't figure into them! And besides, when he decided to get married it would be to someone he chose. He clearly remembered his mother and father having been in love and had always wanted the same kind of marriage for himself.

He decided he would have to be very careful not to say or do anything to encourage Maria. He would have a long talk with Mr. Bodnar. He had agreed to work with Mr. Bodnar for the first year in Argentina but after that Taras wanted to obtain land of his own. He could not let anything, especially marriage, get in the way of his dream of becoming a landowner. This last point he would have to make tactfully, but very clearly, just in case Mr. Bodnar had ideas of having Taras as a son-in-law.

It was a full month before the ship docked in Rio de Janeiro, Brazil. While cargo was being unloaded the majority of the immigrants on board, for whom this was their point of departure, were inspected and processed before being allowed to disembark. Those who were continuing to Argentina were ordered to stay in their quarters. Fresh provisions were taken on board along with new cargo and passengers. This process took the better part of a day. Taras would have liked to watch what was happening in the port but instead he busied himself writing a long letter to his father.

Buenos Aries was still several days away. It was during these last days of the voyage that Taras encountered a young man from Galicia. His name was Ivan Boyko. He had actually been to Argentina before. This made Taras very interested in speaking with him, in order to learn what he could of the new land.

It seemed Ivan had several sisters, all of whom were married and settled away from their home village. Since his mother had died, it had been only Ivan and his aging father at home. They had not owned any land, except for a small yard upon which their tiny house sat.

While Ivan had been in the army he had learned that many men from his region walked to Romania to work as seasonal farm labourers. There was good money to be made in that way. As soon as Ivan was released from the army he and a friend had set out for Romania. It was true. He could make enough money during spring, summer, and autumn to feed his father and himself for the whole year. He had done this for two years. Then his father had died.

One of his acquaintances from the Romanian trips was going to Argentina as a farm labourer. A rich, English landowner in Argentina was paying his passage. The fellow was just going for part of the year, then returning to Galicia. Ivan decided to join him.

And so it was that Ivan and his companion had sailed to Argentina and worked for the English landowner. They were able to save enough money to pay for their return passage and to live comfortably for a year. While the companion decided not to return to Argentina, Ivan was going back – this time to stay. He had sold his father's small house and there was nothing more to keep him in the little village.

But there was another reason for Ivan's decision to immigrate to Argentina. He had met a girl. She had been working in the kitchens on the Englishman's estate. Her name was Esperanza and Ivan planned to marry her and take her north with him. He was going to obtain a homestead and farm for himself.

Taras was fascinated by Ivan's story. They spent long hours talking about Argentina. Taras soaked up every detail Ivan had to offer.

Finally the ship docked at Puerto Madero, Darsena Norte (Northern Dock). The immigration officers, medical examiners, and interpreters boarded the ship. Passengers, their documentation, and their belongings were inspected. Passengers who were ill, over eighty years of age, or physically or mentally incapacitated, were not allowed to leave the ship and would be required to return to Europe. Finally after all the inspections were completed, the passengers were taken to the Immigration Hotel. Despite their concerns regarding such establishments, here in Argentina the interpreters told them they had no choice. Their belongings were transported separately to the Immigration Hotel.

No one was sorry to be leaving the ship. Many had thought they would not survive the passage and thanked God for their deliverance. Some parties disembarked without a loved one, who had succumbed to illness during the voyage, making their arrival a solemn and depressing event.

Since the Bodnars were not planning to stay in the city, nor were they in need of assistance to find employment, their stay at the Immigration Hotel would be brief. Because the party was travelling to an agricultural territory to join established relatives, they were provided with the necessary travel documents and rail passes, issued free of charge as part of the Argentine government's commitment to immigrants.

The Argentine Constitution of 1853 contained a commitment to encouraging immigration summed up by the slogan: 'to rule is to populate'. There was a desire to attract immigrants, particularly agricultural workers, to the Northern Province of Misiones, which had become part of Argentina as a consequence of the War of the Triple Alliance (1864-70). This newly acquired region had previously been part of Paraguay. The Argentine government encouraged immigration during the nineteenth century and, as a result, was second only to the United States in terms of welcoming immigrants. The vast majority of immigrants to Argentina during this period were from Europe.

The Bodnar family group spent only one night in the Immigration Hotel. In the large, multistory building, several thousand immigrants could be lodged at one time. Women and children slept in dormitories separated from the men. Immigrants who planned to stay in Buenos Aries or to find work in other parts of the country would be housed in the Immigration Hotel, free of charge, for up to five days. The hotel had kitchens and large dining halls, outdoor spaces, an infirmary, interpreters, and an employment bureau - all designed to help the immigrants begin the process of assimilation.

The mighty Parana River merges with the Uruguay River to form the Rio de la Plata, which empties into the Atlantic Ocean just to the northeast of the city of Buenos Aries. The Parana is navigable far inland. This, combined with the nature of the historical development of railways in Argentina - several different, foreign-backed railway companies - resulted in a patchwork of forms of transportation, which would be used to reach Misiones Territory.

After breakfast in the Immigration Hotel the next morning, the reconstituted Bodnar family group boarded a steamship, which took them up the Parana to the river port of Bajada Grande in the town of Parana, about two hundred and forty miles northwest of Buenos Aries. From here the group transferred to an Entre Rios Line train to travel almost one hundred and seventy miles southeast to Concepcion del Uruguay. Then they transferred to a train of the North-Eastern Rail Line for another one hundred and sixty-five miles northeast to Monte Caseros, then to La Cruz, and finally on the newly constructed rail extension to Santo Tome, another one hundred and seventy miles to the northeast. It had been a long, three-day journey from Buenos Aries and the Immigrant Hotel.

In Santo Tome, the Bodnar family group and their belongings were loaded onto a wooden, four-wheeled cart, locally referred to as a 'carro polaco' (Polish wagon) for the sixty-five-mile journey to the village of Apostoles in Misiones territory. There the Bodnar's relatives would meet them. It was their intention to join their relative's existing agricultural colony.

It had been a grueling journey - a month by sea, three days by train, followed by several days in a jostling carro over rough trails. The party was completely exhausted when it finally arrived in Apostoles. There, the news that several more miles of travel were required to reach their final destination was not greeted with a great deal of enthusiasm. Belongings were transferred from one carro to another and once more the travellers set off.

Even Taras' enthusiasm for the travel portion of his grand adventure had been dampened!

Yuriy, 1905

On the Monday of Bright Week, the week following Easter, Uncle Vasyl drove his brother's family to the train station in the town on the Dniester River. There were long tearful good-byes but soon it was time to load their chests and bundles onto the train and begin their long journey. As they boarded the train, Anna took one long, last look at the countryside she so loved. She said a silent prayer that they would be returning before long.

The train ride was long, bumpy, and dusty. Anna just couldn't get comfortable. Andriy and Petro, of course, had to explore the train but Anna insisted Dariya stay by her side. This was very difficult for the young girl, who was excited and wanted to see and experience everything. She would beg her brothers, whenever they re-joined the family group, to tell her everything they had seen. There were posh cars filled with rich people, four-person compartment cars, a lounge car, and a dining car. The young men had made their way to the very back of the train and had watched the world go by from that vantage point. How Dariya had wanted to go with them!

The train took them to Stanyslaviv, Lviv, and then to Krakow. At Krakow, an agent of the steam ship company, which had arranged their passage to Canada, joined the emigrant families as they boarded a special train for Hamburg. The train stopped at a control station at Ratibor, where the emigrants were medically inspected to ensure they were healthy and free of communicable diseases. The train then continued to Berlin and finally to Hamburg.

When the train arrived in a suburb of Hamburg, the families were taken to the steamship line's emigrant barracks where they received their tickets in exchange for the passes they had been issued at the control station. The emigrant barracks were under the supervision of the local police. A medical officer visited daily to ensure that everyone who was housed there remained healthy prior to sailing. It was several days before their ship was to sail. They could have left the barracks, but there was no need and few did so. Yuriy and some of the men from his village would go off to talk with other emigrant families. Anna was concerned and worried constantly whenever Yuriy was away - she was fearful something would happen to him and she and the rest of the family would be abandoned in this strange place.

The day before their departure they were taken by tender to the passenger halls where their belongings were inspected, disinfected, and labeled as such. Then the people underwent a final medical inspection, which consisted of passing in single file before surgeons and steamship-line officials. This resulted in their documents being stamped as 'Medically Examined'. Then they passed by the local police, who were watching for draft dodgers, criminals, minors, and others who were not bona fide emigrants. After this final inspection they returned to the tenders and directly to the ship. At this point they could no longer go ashore.

The Port of Hamburg was some distance from the mouth of the Elbe River where it emptied into the North Sea. As a result, the ship headed down river into deeper water before taking on the cargo and cabin passengers. At that point the entire ship was inspected once more before it could leave the Elbe River and head for open seas. All of these inspections were intended to ensure only healthy and qualified individuals embarked on the journey to the new land. This was necessary, as the steamship company would be required to return any passengers who were not admitted when they arrived in Canada.

Once on the ship, Anna began to relax a bit. She knew she could not be separated from Yuriy and, while at sea, there was really nothing that could be done but to wait out the voyage and prepare for the next stage of the journey.

Yuriy took his children to the upper deck to watch as the ship pull away from land. Anna stayed in the sleeping quarters with their belongings. She had no wish to watch the land slip over the horizon. She prayed the voyage would be smooth and would pass quickly. If she could, she would have slept through the entire ordeal!

On the first evening everyone gathered in the large dining hall for supper. The food was basic, but good. At the end of the meal a wonderful desert, which many of the emigrant passengers had never seen before, appeared. It was called 'pie'. Andriy and Petro were especially fond of this sweet treat. Because Yuriy had listed Dariya as being six years of age, she travelled for free so there was no place for her at the dining table. She stood between her mother and father and ate from their plates. When the pie came, she ate most of her father's portion and some of her mother's, as well. It was a treat she would remember all her life.

That night, as the ship rocked and rolled, Anna became seasick. She was sorry she had eaten anything for supper for it was all lost! She lay in her bunk in agony all night, occasionally rushing to the pail, which had been placed near their set of bunks for the purpose. A few others were taken ill that night as well. Fortunately Yuriy and Dariya were not affected and slept well. The next day Petro was also feeling queasy so he didn't eat much. Anna ate nothing but drank a little tea. For her the seasickness persisted during the entire trip. Petro was never as ill as she had been but he did not eat much during the voyage. Anna stayed below deck, often in her bunk, alternating between praying, moaning, and weeping. There were times when she wished she were dead.

Dariya was in her element. She met other children her age and ran and played with them all day long on deck. The weather was fine with clear, bright, sunny days but the constant wind was often sharp. Yuriy and his sons spent much of the day visiting with the families from their village and eventually meeting other emigrants. There was so much to learn from what everyone had heard or read about Canada – what to expect when they arrived, what would happen next, how they would get to their new home in the Northwest Territories, how they would obtain their homesteads, what would need to be done to prepare for their first Canadian winter….

The voyage took fifteen days. These were the longest days of Anna's life. They were the greatest adventure of Dariya's life. Both would remember these days of the journey as life-defining.

When the ship docked in Halifax, Nova Scotia on Canada's eastern shore, the families from the little village stuck together. The pier was teeming with ship workers and those trying to sell all manner of things (some useful, some not) to the immigrants. There were photographers from a newspaper sent to take pictures of the people coming off the ship. Yuriy did not want his family to be photographed, so he told them to turn their backs when a photographer came in their direction. Dariya, who had never seen a camera, was very curious about what these people were doing but she obeyed Tato.

The families were herded into the immigration hall where they waited in long lines to be inspected and processed. The medical inspectors watched carefully as the passengers disembarked. Their passports were examined and stamped and then they were asked questions such as: name, country of origin, destination, and available funds. Then the medical officers did a quick physical inspection, which focused on potential communicable diseases, diseases of the eyes, and potential mental health problems.

After their belongings were inspected, Yuriy's family and the others were sent to temporary immigrant lodgings near the train station. The next morning they boarded a long train composed of many 'colonist cars'. These cars had a row of double seats on each side, which were arranged so two double seats faced each other with a small table between them. At night, the table could be lowered to create a 'bed'. Above the seats, on either side of the car, were pull-down sleeping compartments. Each car accommodated about sixty passengers. At one end there was a toilet and at the other, a small stove where passengers could heat water for tea. There were no doors in the cars except at each end where, with care, a person could move from one car to the next or at a stop, leave the train. The train ride was very rough, loud, and dusty.

Once again Anna felt the sickness in her stomach. She dreaded the illness, which had marked the sea voyage. Consequently, she nibbled gingerly on dry bread and took only small sips of water or tea. Between the harrowing sea voyage and the rough train trip, Anna, who had not been a particularly robust woman, had dwindled to a shadow of her former self. Yuriy was worried about the health of his second wife and watched her carefully.

The Martiniuk family would be on the train all the way to Winnipeg, Manitoba. No one really knew how long it would take, so it came as a surprise to the immigrants that day after day the train kept travelling west. They passed through the provinces of Nova Scotia, New Brunswick, Quebec, and then into Ontario. The place names in Canada were all so strange sounding. Dariya and her brothers marveled at what they saw through the windows of the 'colonist cars', especially as the train passed through the big city of Montreal.

The train stopped often along the way, every two hundred miles or so, in order to take on water and fuel for the steam engines. When the train stopped, Yuriy disembarked with the other men to buy food for their families. Whenever this happened Anna prayed: "Please God, don't let him miss the train!" In some towns the train stopped for a longer time and anyone could get off to eat in a railway company-owned restaurant, adjacent to the station. Anna never left the train but constantly worried she would be abandoned on it. It was torture for her.

Sometimes the train would stop on the tracks where there was no town or station and wait, as if for something to happen. The passengers never knew what the train waited for, but eventually it would begin to move again. There were plenty of stories told among the passengers about rockslides, snowdrifts, derailments, and wild animals crossing the tracks, all offered as possible explanations for such stops. All of this only served to make Anna more nervous and anxious.

After Ottawa, the train headed north and west toward the settlements of North Bay and then Sudbury. All that could be seen was scrubby trees, rocks, and lakes. The train passed through North Bay during the night, so it was a surprise to the passengers when they awoke to see the world blanketed in snow. Imagine – snow in early May! The temperature had dropped as well. When the train passed through Marathon, it began following the northern shore of Lake Superior. The scenery was breath taking. In some places the rock cliffs to one side of the train tracks rose high above and even over the train, while on the other side the land dropped dramatically down to the distant lake. At one point, the passengers were awestruck by the fact that they could, at one time, see the long train's engine up front and as the train doubled back on itself the caboose at the other end. Another night passed on the train.

With every mile of the clickety clack train ride Anna thought about how very far away her homeland was and how it was getting further and further away with every day of travel.

Soon the train arrived in Fort William and then on and on through more forest. Not long before the train was expected to arrive in Winnipeg, suddenly the rocks and trees and lakes gave way to wide-open, flat, treeless, countryside. And then by mid-afternoon, they arrived in Winnipeg. Everyone had to get off the train with their belongings. The families who were going on to the Northwest Territories would board another train.

The Canadian Pacific Railway station in Winnipeg had just opened that very month. As the immigrants were ushered into a basement waiting room they could just catch a glimpse of the huge main rotunda with its high, barrel-vaulted ceiling and white marble floors and columns.

The station was filled with the noise of a throng of people, hustling and jostling their way to and fro. There were all manner of folk, from hucksters and hawkers to church groups and bible salesmen. Once again the village families kept close together as they awaited their next train.

Those who planned to stay in Winnipeg or in rural areas in the province of

Manitoba were taken to the immigrant sheds. A new immigrant hall was being constructed next to the train station but it would not be completed for a few months. So the folks on this journey would have to stay in the dilapidated immigration sheds, which had been in use for several decades. For those wishing to stay in the city of Winnipeg, the sheds would be their home until they had found employment. For those who were fortunate enough to be moving further afield from the city, their stay in the immigrant sheds would be of a shorter duration, perhaps a few days or weeks. Once these folks had received their land grants they would be transported from the immigrant sheds to their new homes.

As the new, westward-bound train carrying the Martiniuk family pulled away from the Winnipeg station, it seemed to Anna that they would be travelling forever. When would they finally get to their destination? Everyone was getting tired of travelling. Everyone was anxious to get off the train and stay in one place for a change.

The train travelled through the short night and the family huddled together with their belongings, dreaming of their new life or longing for their old one. The next morning the train stopped in Regina, the capital of the Northwest Territories. In just a few months Regina would be become the capital of the newly constituted province of Saskatchewan. The train car the family had been riding was disconnected from the main train, which would continue heading west. An engine from the Qu'Appelle, Long Lake, and Saskatchewan Railway Company, connecting Regina to Prince Albert (a settlement to the northwest) would take their abbreviated train of colonist cars through Saskatoon, across the South Saskatchewan River, and to the settlement of Rosthern at the end of their train journey.

In Rosthern an official from the local immigration office greeted them. The train ride was finally over. The small settlement seemed to revolve around the train station, which had two components, one for passengers and a shed for freight. The station was a two-story building with passenger facilities on the ground floor and living quarters for the stationmaster above. Next to the station was the two-story, National Hotel. In addition to these buildings the town boasted a recently-constructed town office, a bank, and two churches. A new college was just being built.

Where on God's great earth were they? The landscape surrounding the small settlement seemed expansive and lonely. All that could be seen was bush and rolling hills.

The families disembarked from the train, tired and weary. They had travelled almost five thousand miles from their home village in the space of less than a month. In those days this was almost too much to comprehend.

The local authorities arranged for transportation of the families to places nearer where land was still available. So the families loaded their belongings into the two-wheeled, oxen-drawn wagons, referred to as Carlton or Red River Carts for yet another leg of the journey. That same day they would be within seven miles of another small settlement closer to the available land. Local families, who had established homesteads in the region, would take in the immigrant families until they were able to file their land claims and build their own first shelters. The grand adventure was about to begin in earnest.

Exhausted, physically and mentally, the weary travellers were grateful for the hospitality of the established pioneer families who welcomed them. Some of these families had relatives among the newcomers. Some had been from the same village in the old country. Others were just warm, generous folk, who had been treated well by their forerunners and now were extending their own hospitality to the latest group of immigrants.

"How strange it is to be so very far from home – but this is home now! Mama is so tired, I hope she will get some rest and begin to relax and enjoy this new land. It really is quite beautiful. I love the big open spaces and wide skies. Tato says there are so few people and so much land that we will have to walk over a mile to see our neighbors. What a very big country this is. When I went out to fetch water this afternoon, I couldn't help feeling very, very small and just a little alone. The feeling didn't make me frightened but it is a feeling I have never had before. I must get some sleep now so that I can help Mama tomorrow. She will grow to love this place, I know she will."

Mykola, 1905

After basic training, Mykola's time in the army had been quite uneventful. There had been a posting to Lviv to maintain the peace during a student demonstration but it had not required armed force. For the most part he and his unit had been kept busy patrolling and serving as peacekeepers in various locations to the west of Stanyslaviv.

Mykola had received a few letters from his family. Clearly Andriy had written them for his father. The first came a few months after his enlistment. It was to tell him his brother, Taras, had immigrated to Argentina with the Bodnar family. Mykola was astonished. He knew Taras had not been looking forward to following him into military service but he was not aware Taras had any interest in emigrating. And to Argentina of all places! Mykola was saddened by the idea that he might never again see this dear brother of his. Argentina was half a world away! But then, perhaps to cheer himself up, Mykola smiled and thought: "This is so like Taras! He gets an idea into his head and then it's full steam ahead! Well I am not surprised that he has undertaken such a grand adventure! Good for him! God go with him."

The next letter Mykola received was to inform him of Mykhaylo's marriage to Larysa Melnyk. Now that was news indeed! How on earth had Mykhaylo managed to win such a prize? And furthermore, how did he manage to get married before completing military service. Of course Larysa's father would have arranged that. "Well, good for him," Mykola thought. "I hope he will find happiness and peace at last. Mnohaya Lita - God grant them many years, long and happy years."

There had been so many changes in his family since he had left them. For the first time since he had enlisted, Mykola was overwhelmed by homesickness. "But it won't be too much longer," he thought, "and I will be heading back to the village and my beloved family".

Then in the late summer of 1904, just a few months before his three-year military term was to end, his unit was sent to the southern colony of Bosnia and Herzegovina. After the Russo-Turkish War, the 1878 Congress of Berlin had declared this area to remain nominally in the Ottoman Empire but the Austro-Hungarian Empire would have the right to occupy it.

This was a very troubled region. There were three principal, opposing factions living cheek to jowl in a relatively small area. These factions were roughly classified as the western Catholics, the eastern Orthodox, and the southern Muslims. But religion was not the only dividing factor among these peoples. Although there was a common Bosnian language, the preferred language of each group along with a growing sense of nationalism added to the divisiveness in the region. In general, the majority of Catholics aligned with neighbouring Croatia; the Orthodox, with neighbouring Serbia; and the Muslims, with the Ottoman Empire. In addition to these issues, an overlay of agrarian tradition (near feudalism and large-scale land ownership by Ottomans and Hungarians), a lack of modernization, and low levels of industrialization, added fuel to the many smoldering fires.

Peasants in this region had not been freed from serfdom, as they had in other parts of the Austro-Hungarian Empire and there was a growing demand for such freedom. Education had been used as a reward for loyalty to the Empire but students had been able to circumvent this attempted control by travelling outside to attend universities. As a consequence, students became actively involved in opposing the Emperor's authority.

When the Austrian Empire had moved into the region, serious misconceptions of the colonizers regarding how they would be received and the role they would play added yet another layer of discontent among the populace. In particular, the Emperor had interposed himself between the religious leaders of the three factions and their traditional authorities outside of the region, namely the Pope, the Patriarch of Istanbul, and the Caliph. This paternal colonialism; the imposition of a new, mandatory military conscription; and the growing number of Austrian administrators and militia in the region, were all sore points with the people.

And so it was in the summer of 1904, that Mykola's unit was sent to join the growing number of Austrian militia stationed in Sarajevo. There were large barracks and many soldiers stationed there. It was from this post that units were sent to various parts of the region as protests, strikes, or riots erupted, in order to quell the trouble before it got out of hand.

In between, the soldiers stationed in Sarajevo worked with contractors, who had been sent to help build the administrative infrastructure required to rule the colony in the Austrian manner. Mykola had worked along side locals on several such projects. He found as he began to understand their concerns that he could empathize with them. Mykola was not as good as his younger brother, Andriy, at learning new languages but he made an attempt to learn the basics of Bosnian, as well as a bit of Croatian, Serbian, and Turkish. The people he worked with seemed to appreciate these efforts.

The leader of Mykola's unit noted his efforts and said to his men, "We are here to ease the tensions between and among these peoples, anything you can do to help will be rewarded. You should all follow Martiniuk's example and try to learn as much as you can about the people we are here to help."

In another unit being singled out and praised in this way might have had negative consequences for the soldier but Mykola's unit was different. The leader was an intelligent man who tried to treat his men fairly. He knew his success and that of his unit depended on his men working together for common goals. So unlike many units in the Austrian army at the time, Mykola, as neither an Austrian nor a Pole, was not abused or mistreated. Rather he had been treated as a valued member of the unit - as valuable as every other member. This had made his tour of duty much more pleasant than it could have been and often was for others.

In November, Mykola's unit was sent to a village on the northeastern border with Serbia. There a secret student group had sworn to oppose the Empire even if this required violence. Although there had been no incidents of violence as yet, the unit had been sent to set up a post and keep an eye on the situation. During the long, hot, dry autumn, a few of the men at a time had been sent back to Sarajevo on leave.

In early December, one of Mykola's colleagues had been injured when a glass bottle, converted into a small bomb, was thrown into the barracks. The corpsman of the group had removed the glass fragments and treated the man's leg wounds as best he could, but as there had been damage to blood vessels and muscle, he recommended the man be sent to Sarajevo for further care and recovery. The unit leader was aware that Mykola's three-year term had been up in November and he had not enjoyed a leave since the posting in August.

Consequently, he ordered Mykola to accompany the injured man back to Sarajevo. He gave Mykola a letter to present to the commander on arrival, which contained a recommendation for his discharge. The two soldiers were to take a wagon to the nearest train station and from there travel first north, then change trains and travel south, back-tracking to Sarajevo. The rail system in the region had been constructed for competing interests and, consequently, satisfied few. It was piecemeal at best, but was the only option to move an injured man from the unit's posting back to Sarajevo.

When they arrived at the train station, Mykola helped his comrade get into the passenger car and settled as comfortably as possible. The other people in the passenger car were not pleased to see them board the train and stayed as far away from the two Emperor's soldiers as possible. It would be a long, rough journey back to Sarajevo and, although Mykola was pleased he might be released, he was not looking forward to the ride.

The first stop was at a rail hub town. The main rail line continued northwest from this point, while a secondary rail line headed due north before swinging to the northeast toward the border with Croatia. Many of the people who had been in the same passenger car with the two soldiers got off the train. The stop was brief and soon they were on their way again. Within minutes of the train pulling out of the station there was a loud explosion from up near the front of the train. The car in which Mykola and his comrade were riding was rocked violently. The train stopped suddenly. Everyone on the train was in a panic and trying to get out. Mykola tried to help the people calm down and exit the train in an orderly fashion but no one was interested in the soldier's attempts to maintain order and safety.

Mykola helped his comrade exit the rail car. They looked forward and saw that a freight car near the front of the train was on fire. There was no time to lose; they must get as far away from the train as possible. And so the two soldiers, one supported by the other, walked as hastily as they could back toward the town the train had just left. As they approached the town they met a group of men who did not want them to come any closer.

"It is because of you," they said, "that the train was bombed! Get out of here. We do not want you near our town."

Mykola tried to explain that his comrade was injured and they needed to have a place to rest until the next train came. The town's people were not willing to let the two soldiers enter the community. And so Mykola helped his comrade to walk away from the train and the town. Where they would go he was not sure.

Mykola thought the damage done to the main rail line would mean no trains would be using it until it had been repaired. He considered just finding a place to hole up until the rails were repaired and then continue on their journey as planned. But his comrade was very shaken by recent events and without access to the village this didn't seem like the best plan. In the end Mykola decided it would be better to follow the secondary railway tracks to the north. With the main railway line damaged, trains would likely be diverted to the secondary line so there should be a good chance of catching a train and resuming their journey, albeit via a detour.

But Mykola worried that the town's people may have been right and the train had been bombed because of their presence. Perhaps it would be wiser to take cover in the woods near the tracks. They could find a spot to rest and wait until a train came. He had no idea when that would be or if the town's people would allow them to approach the station and board a train when it did come, but there was little else to do.

That night Mykola and his comrade ate the small amount of food they had with them for the train trip. If the trip had not been interrupted they would have been on a second train heading south toward Sarajevo by now. Mykola noticed his comrade was showing signs of fever. Between his injured leg and the events of the day he was looking ill, haggard, and drawn.

Mykola built a shelter of tree branches against a fallen log and insisted that his comrade rest there. He would stand watch so his friend could rest easily through the night. The bomb had probably been put on the train at the last stop and there was a chance that if the two soldiers had been the intended target or the reason for the bombing, someone was watching or looking for them. Mykola wasn't sure if this was the case but to ease his friend's mind he assured him that he would stand guard.

The next morning Mykola was very worried about his friend. He had slept fitfully and now was drenched in sweat even though the morning air was cool. The fever, which had set in during the previous evening seemed much more serious now. Mykola knew he had to try to find some help for his friend. He considered going back to the town but that seemed too dangerous. He wondered how far it was to the next village. His friend would not be able to travel but perhaps he could go ahead and bring back help. But go where? Where could he find help? In the end he found a nearby spring and filled their canteens with fresh water. He made his friend drink as much water as he would.

Mykola looked at the injured leg. It was red and swollen. He wanted to try to clean the wounds and re-wrap them but the injured man was in too much pain. He used his own uniform jacket to help keep his friend warm. By afternoon the injured soldier was drifting in and out of consciousness. Mykola hoped sleep would cure him. He prayed his friend would have the strength to fight the infection raging in his body.

That night was a very long one. The injured soldier tossed and turned in a restless, half-conscious state. By morning he was quiet but still breathing. Mykola didn't know what he could do so he continued to pray. By mid-afternoon his friend was dead.

Mykola dug a shallow grave and buried the soldier. He covered the grave with the tree branches, which had been their shelter. Now he must move on.

Mykola decided to follow the train tracks at a distance and under cover of the woods and darkness in case someone was watching for him. He had no way of knowing that the bombing of the train had not been an attack directed specifically at the two soldiers. Rather it had been part of a larger, coordinated, series of assaults along the border and in other parts of the country, intended to cripple the railroad and thus prevent further mobilization of the Emperor's troops. So there was no one watching for the two soldiers who had wandered into the woods. Mykola, however, did not know this. Of course if he had been discovered there was no doubt he would have been seen as an enemy and possibly killed. So he was in very real danger. A soldier from a hated army, isolated from his unit, in a region filled with political discontent – Mykola was very much aware of the danger of his situation.

So Mykola spent the rest of the day sleeping – he had slept only a little since the bomb had exploded on the train. When he awoke the moon was high in the sky. He gathered up his few belongings and headed toward the edge of the woods. He walked, remaining just within the woods while keeping the train tracks in sight, until daybreak. Then he would find a hiding place in the woods to sleep the day away.

Fortunately the weather was mild even for December. The last of the berries, nuts, and edible roots were still available to sustain him. Mykola walked all the next night without seeing a village or a train. Finally, he came to a small settlement. It was on the Croatian border. Mykola was hesitant but he knew he had to approach the village. At the very least he needed directions to get back to the main rail line to Sarajevo.

Mykola watched the village for some time before he selected a man to approach. He had singled this man out because he had reminded Mykola of his own father. He walked slowly toward the man and called out in Bosnian, "Hello there, can you help a poor lost soul to find his way to a train station. I need to get to Sarajevo."

The man was alarmed for he recognized Mykola's uniform. He did not want to help the soldier but he did not want trouble either. There could be more soldiers in the woods. So the man, saying nothing, pointed in a northerly direction.

"How far is it?" Mykola asked.

"Two days on foot" was the reply.

Mykola was about to ask if he could get something to eat when the man abruptly turned and quickly walked away.

"Thank you for your help," Mykola called after him.

The man did not acknowledge Mykola's final comment.

"No food then," Mykola thought as he shrugged and set off in the direction the man had indicated.

After walking another two days Mykola found the village with the train station. He was surprised to find he was now deep in Croatia. He was heading in the exact opposite direction of Sarajevo. Either the man who had given him directions had not understood his request or he had just wanted to get the soldier as far away as possible.

As a soldier of the Austrian Army, he would be able to board the train without paying a fare but he approached the ticket window with caution, none-the-less. He had to find out when the next train for Sarajevo would leave.

"Oh you don't want to go to Sarajevo," the ticket master replied. "Haven't you heard? There's been a lot of trouble there. The army has closed the city. No one can go in or out until further notice. More troops have been sent for. It is not a good situation."

Mykola was sure the man must be exaggerating. There had been a large contingent of troops in Sarajevo already. Surely they could have handled any trouble that may have developed.

The ticket master continued with a knowing look, "There has been trouble in a lot of places in the last week." Then eyeing Mykola carefully he added, "You wouldn't be coming from the Serbian border towns would you?"

"Why do you ask?" Mykola responded.

"Well," said the ticket master, "many garrisons along the border towns have been wiped out by rebels. And a lone soldier who has been on the road for a while …"

This really made Mykola think. Could his unit have been overcome after he left it? He wasn't sure at this point what to believe or what to do.

As if reading the young soldier's mind the ticket master suggested, "You might continue going north to Kaposvar in Hungary. From there you can head to Budapest if you want to re-join the troops. Kaposvar is a rail hub so there are many travel options from there. You could even head back to Sarajevo from there – by then things may have settled down. But perhaps you should wear 'traveling clothes' for your journey. A soldier on his own might find it difficult..."

This was good advice. But where would he get 'travelling clothes'. Once again the ticket master anticipated the young soldier's thoughts.

"Do you have any money?" he asked. "For a small coin I can get peasant clothing for you. I will not charge you for a train ticket but I would prefer you not tell anyone that I have helped you."

Mykola wasn't sure whether the man was kind hearted or just wanted to make a little money but he agreed to the plan. A short time later the ticket master presented him with homespun trousers, a baggy shirt, and a cap, so Mykola could dress in 'travelling clothes'. He kept his uniform tied up in a bundle and before he knew it he was on a train heading northeast to Kaposvar.

As he rode Mykola thought about what he would do when he got to Kaposvar. He could report to the military office rather than going either back to Sarajevo or all the way to Budapest. With any luck at all, the letter from his Unit Leader might mean he would be discharged and he could head for home.

This was most likely wishful thinking. He had several concerns. First of all, the Hungarian Army and the Common Army of the Dual Monarchy (Austro-Hungarian Empire) of which Mykola was a part were not always cooperative and sometimes actually competitive or contradictory to one another. If it were true that his unit had been obliterated it might be difficult for anyone to believe how it was that he alone had survived. His Unit Leader had been a kindly man but not all army leaders were. He could easily be charged with desertion.

Furthermore, if Sarajevo was in need of more troops the likelihood of him being discharged was probably slim. Rather it would be more likely he would be attached to another unit and sent back to Sarajevo.

As Mykola was riding north through Croatia he thought of how he was actually getting closer and closer to Galicia and home. He longed to return home. It would be wonderful to rejoin his family for Christmas!

When he finally reached Kaposvar he had almost decided to continue to Budapest, so he checked on the next train to that destination; it would be leaving at eight in the morning.

Mykola found the town market and bought some bread and cheese; this would be his supper. He found a spot near the train station by the river where he planned to spend the night.

All evening he agonized over what to do. Should he take the train to Budapest in the morning in order to attempt reuniting with the army; should he head south, back to Sarajevo; or, as his heart told him, should he continue heading toward Galicia and home. It was a difficult decision. He hadn't actually been discharged but he had served his three-year term and his Unit Leader had recommended his discharge. He wanted to do the right thing but at the same time…. Tato always did what was right. Mykola wished with all his heart that his father were there to help him make his decision.

If he went to Budapest, would his story be believed? Would he be sent to Sarajevo? Would he be discharged and sent home? Or would he be charged as a deserter and jailed or worse? If he travelled south to Sarajevo, should he travel as a soldier or a peasant? If he arrived in Sarajevo the chances of being discharged were not at all likely.

As he sat looking at the river flowing by he suddenly spotted a young fellow wearing an army hat much like his own.

"You there," he called, "where did you get that cap?"

"What's it to you?" the boy answered belligerently.

"It's a fine hat," Mykola answered, "I would like one for myself."

"Well then," the boy responded, "you'll have to kill a soldier!"

Mykola was shocked. The boy couldn't have been more than fourteen. Had he really killed a soldier? And then it struck Mykola. If anyone saw his uniform, all bundled up, would they think he had killed a soldier for the uniform? This added another layer of complexity to his situation.

Mykola said his prayers and asked God to help him make the right decision. Then he tried to get comfortable in a small space between two buildings near the river. As he was drifting off to sleep he heard in the distance the voices of some tramps, who were warming themselves by a fire and drinking. He thought he smelled hot food as well just before he drifted off.

Just after midnight Mykola was abruptly awoken. Three thugs were rifling through his belongings.

"What do you want?" Mykola asked.

"Everything you've got," the leader sneered at him.

"I have nothing," Mykola said but the thugs had already found his few coins.

"Well we'll take this 'nothing,'" one said.

One of them had undone the bundle containing the army uniform. "What about this?" he asked his companions.

"That's worse than garbage," the leader responded and kicked the clothing away into the night.

"It might be worth something," the second man said almost under his breath.

"I don't want anything to do with that!" the leader replied.

Then finding nothing else of value among Mykola's meager belongings the three decided to give him a beating.

He didn't know why they beat him, they had taken all he had and he hadn't tried to stop them. Maybe it was because he hadn't had much of value. Maybe it was because they were drunk. Maybe it was just something to do – some men are just like that.

Mykola lost consciousness.

When he awoke the sun was well up. Mykola was bloody and bruised. His stomach ached where he vaguely remembered being kicked several times. His right eye was swollen shut and there was dried blood in his hair and on his hands and arms. He tried to get up and realized he could barely move. He rolled onto his side and again tried to raise himself, but fell back down.

"They got you, did they?" a voice fairly near by asked.

"Yes," Mykola groaned.

He looked up and saw a wizened, old man leaning heavily on a walking stick. He then used the stick to point to the uniform strewn around where Mykola lay.

"They didn't take your trophies," the old man commented.

"They are not trophies," Mykola responded slowly with a cut lip. Then he added, "I am a soldier trying to find my way back to the army."

"Are you indeed." the old man stated rather than asked. Then after surveying Mykola and his scattered possessions he added, "Well, we'd best get you cleaned up."

So the old man helped Mykola to re-bundle the uniform and anything else the thugs had not taken and together they walked slowly down to the river. There the old man helped Mykola wash away the blood and bathe his wounds.

"You know sleeping near the train station is very dangerous," the old man commented.

"I was planning to take the eight o'clock to Budapest," Mykola replied.

"Well, let's see what we can do to help you on your way tomorrow instead," the old man replied.

So after Mykola was cleaned up the two men wandered toward the market. There the old man carefully selected a spot near the intersection of two streets. He pulled out Mykola's army cap and gave it to Mykola to hold. Then in a strong voice he began telling a story of his own service in the Emperor's army. As he spoke, some passers-by ignored him completely, as if they really didn't want to see or hear him. Some scoffed, laughed, or taunted him. Occasionally one would even spit at him. To these he would simply say, "Yes, even Jesus was taunted and spit upon." Young boys would throw small stones at them. Rarely, someone would drop a small coin in Mykola's hat. They sat there all morning and into the afternoon. Mykola was surprised that the police had not made them move on but the old man told him this was his spot and he often spent the day there.

"The police know me," he said, "they know I will do no harm."

So by late afternoon Mykola was feeling a bit recovered from the beating, but getting very hungry. The old man must have been hungry as well, for he suddenly said, "It's time to eat."

They walked to a small tavern near by. Mykola had avoided taverns during his journey, buying food in the markets where the prices were better. The old man and Mykola settled themselves in the tavern near the fire. Then the old man ordered a large bowl of goulash to share and two glasses of

Tokaji wine. It was a feast. Mykola had not eaten this well for a long time.

As they ate, the old man asked Mykola many questions and by the end of the meal he knew the whole story and the decision facing the younger man.

After they had eaten and paid, the old man divided the few remaining coins, half for Mykola and half for himself. Mykola protested that the meal had been a generous enough gift but the old man insisted.

"It may be enough to get you to Budapest .... or on your way back home," he said. "Have you decided what you will do?"

"No," said Mykola. "I will decide in the morning."

So the old man took Mykola to a place where he often slept. It was a secluded shelter away from the river and train station. He insisted it was a much safer place to spend the night.

Mykola was exhausted. It had been a very long day. He wrapped himself in the uniform jacket and fell asleep immediately.

When Mykola awoke the next morning the old man was gone. At first he thought perhaps it had all been a dream. But when he began to move, the stiffness and soreness from the beating he had experienced told him it had all been real. Then he reached into his pocket and found the coins the old man had given him. That, too, had been real.

So what would he do? He gathered his belongings, re-tied the bundle of his uniform, and headed for the train station.

Mykola had decided not to go to Budapest after all, but rather to travel east toward Subotica and then northeast toward Debrecen. At that point, if he changed his mind and decided to go to Budapest, he could do so from there. Otherwise, if he decided to head for home, he would have to determine how best to cross the Carpathian Mountains.

Since Mykola was not travelling as a soldier, he used all the coins he had to buy a train ticket to Subotica. From there he would see whether he could earn more money to continue his journey or if he would have to continue on foot.

In Subotica, Mykola tried to beg as he had with the old man in Kaposvar but the local police made him move on. So Mykola set off on foot. Along the way, Mykola looked for people who he could help; sometimes they offered him food or money for his help and sometimes they did not. After several attempts to beg, he became more successful even though he did not like to do this and it was always his last resort when he was very hungry and in desperate need of food. And so Mykola walked on, following the train tracks towards Debrecen.

As he walked, Mykola found his thoughts were constantly consumed with wonder and worry about where he would get his next meal. His mind often wandered back to the feast he had shared with the old man. During this time he continued to puzzle over whether he should head for home or to Budapest and the army.

Eventually Mykola made his way to Debrecen. Finally he had made his decision. He had come such a long way – he was going to head for home.

From Debrecen he continued to travel north and east. The last town of any size in Hungary was Mateszalka, which was in the foothills of the Carpathian Mountains, separating Hungary from Romania and Galicia.

As Mykola drew nearer to the mountains he began to worry about how he would ever cross them. He formulated a simple plan. He would follow the river valley, which surely would flow through a mountain pass.

As Mykola travelled ever higher and further north and east, it became winter in earnest. The temperatures dropped, especially at night. While walking during the day, Mykola could keep warm, but the nights were very cold – too cold to continue sleeping outdoors. Mykola wore all the clothing he had, including his uniform jacket over the peasant shirt for extra warmth. At night he huddled in the shelter of small caves, cliff over-hangs, or in hollows he had made in the earth, lined with pine needles and branches. He did everything he could think of to keep warm.

He found every day he travelled less and less. Some days he barely travelled a few miles. Then one morning he awoke to find that the world had been clothed in white. The collar of his jacket was stiff with frost where his breath had moistened it. This was going to make travelling much harder.

And indeed travelling became even more difficult and much slower as Mykola's feet slipped on the snow-covered rocks and grass. His hands and feet were cold all day as he walked. By early afternoon he had not travelled far but he was cold and weary. Disheartened, Mykola looked for shelter. His meager food supply had been used and he was cold and wet.

"Dear God" he prayed, "don't let me die here alone. Please help me to get back home."

And then he slept.

When Mykola awoke he knew he was in trouble. His fingers were swollen and white. Frost bite. His head ached and his chest felt heavy. He was sick.

"Now I will surely die here," he thought. But he was too sick to think much more than that. He knew he should get up and move around to get his circulation flowing, if nothing else. He had not travelled very far at all the day before but he was just too sick to even move. He tried to pray but even that was too much of an effort. He drifted into a fitful sleep.

Mykola did not know how long he had been there or how long he had been asleep. When he awoke he was even more miserable than when he had fallen asleep. He thought he heard a sound but could not imagine what it might be. He tried to focus in the direction of the sound, but could only make out a small, round figure, not far off. It might have been a person or a wild beast. Mykola could not tell and in his state of mind did not really care.

Baba Komar had been out gathering firewood. She lived alone in a small hut in the mountains. Her husband, a woodcutter, had died the year before but she had nowhere else to go. Besides she loved the little cottage, which they had built together after they were married. It was and always would be her home.

Baba Komar was a healer but during the long winter months, isolated as her hut was, it was very rare that anyone sought her help. So she was quite surprised to see a young man, half frozen like a kitten in the snow, not far from her home. From the look of him, he had been there awhile and was in a pretty bad state. Frost bite for sure, she could see the telltale signs, and fever no doubt. She didn't know if he could be saved but she would have to try. She talked to him. She must get him to respond or there would be nothing she could do for him.

She finally managed to make Mykola open his eyes and focus on her. She told him how serious his condition was and that she would help him but he must help too. She encouraged him to try standing up. If he couldn't walk, she was afraid she could not get him to her hut. With constant talking, poking, prodding, and urging, Mykola finally began to respond. And as he became aware of the old woman he became aware of his dangerous condition as well. He struggled to stay awake and do what she was asking him to do. It wasn't that she was asking much, just to stand, lean on her, and walk. He should be able to do that he thought. But it took much more effort than he expected. The first time he tried to stand up it seemed that his legs were no longer his own. They felt foreign, wooden, and non-responsive. He tried again with a little more success. The old woman, who was stout and sturdily built, supported the young man. Together they slowly, falteringly made their way to her hut. Mykola tried to concentrate on each step. He couldn't believe how hard it was simply to walk.

When they got within sight of the hut, Mykola almost cried for joy. The little old woman was breathing heavily from the effort, but determined to get the young man inside. It had been a real effort for both of them.

Inside, Mykola did not notice how neat and clean the little house was. All he noticed was that it was warm. He couldn't remember ever feeling warm. The sensation washed over him and he almost collapsed with joy at the sensation.

The little, old baba sat him on a bench next to the peitch and then wrapped him in a pyrena (feather quilt) from her bed. She set water in a pot on the firebox to warm. Then she carefully removed his boots and socks. The feet were bad too. The frost bitten areas had to be warmed gradually by bathing in lukewarm water. Later she would make a balm with chamomile and poplar buds, collected last spring, to help the healing process. If he were lucky the damage might not be too bad.

When she had done all she could for the young man's present comfort she made some chai (tea) and helped him to sip it slowly. It felt so good and helped Mykola to warm up from the inside. Then she put some soup into a pot to warm on the firebox. The soup smelled marvelous to Mykola but he wasn't sure he could stay awake long enough to eat it. He was warming up and had an incredible urge to sleep again.

Baba Komar let the young man doze by the fire. When he awoke she helped him to eat some soup. Not much at first - who knew when he had last eaten. She noted that he was thin and under fed. And so, with a bit of soup in him and in a warm, safe environment, Mykola lay down on the bench. The old woman covered him with the pyrena and he slept.

When Mykola awoke he was startled by his surroundings and for an instant could not place where he was. Then slowly the events of his rescue began to come back to him. Could it be that this little baba had actually been able to get him out of the cold and into her hut? How far from the hut had he been when she had found him? He remembered struggling to walk and leaning very heavily on the old woman.

"She must be very strong," he thought.

When she saw he was awake she asked him how he felt.

"Warm," was the first thing he said. Then he realized she was inquiring about his health. "My fingers and toes hurt and my chest and my head," he told her taking stock of his various complaints. She said he had suffered frostbite and she had already made a remedy, which would help. She was concerned about his chest and put her ear to it to listen to him breathing. She had heard him coughing as he slept and that, too, was a concern. She made him a poultice for his chest and a cup of strong tea with rose hips, willow bark, and honey. Later she would make a tincture of herbs, which might relieve his cough. He sipped the tea and was surprised that he wasn't very hungry. His head was pounding and all he really wanted was to go back to sleep.

"Finish your chai then you can sleep," she told him.

The next time he awoke it was nighttime. The little hut was dark and he could hear the old woman snoring softly in her bed along the far wall. He was wringing wet, yet when he removed the pyrena, he began to shake with chills. His head continued to pound and his chest was very sore. He was aware that he had been coughing and now his chest hurt more and more with every cough. He lay there in the dark for a few moments and suddenly he realized that the little old woman had saved his life. He hoped he would get better so he could repay her kindness. And with that thought he drifted into sleep again.

When he woke up once more it was daytime. The little old woman was busy doing something at the table. He coughed and she turned around to see that he was awake.

"And how do you feel now?" she asked.

"A little better I think," he said, more for her benefit than because it was true. He asked where the toilet was and she directed him to a lean-to on the back of the house. When he returned, she made him wash up in a basin of warm water which she had prepared. The simple effort of getting up to the toilet and washing had worn him out. He had to sit down again. He was shivering so he wrapped himself in the pyrena once more.

"You need to eat something," she said matter-of-factly, as she handed him a steaming bowl of rich broth with vegetables.

It tasted so good! Mykola thought it must have been the second best meal he had ever eaten – the only meal that might have been better was the one he had shared with the old man in Hungary.

As he was eating the old woman asked him his name and then told him he should call her 'Baba Komar'. He smiled for she bore no resemblance whatsoever to a mosquito!

"So how does a soldier of his Imperial Highness the Emperor come to be freezing in the woods near my home?" she asked.

"It is a very long story," Mykola started.

At this Baba Komar laughed and said, "I expected it would be but we have all the time in the world here."

And so as Mykola ate the soup, he told his tale. As he spoke Baba Komar nodded, smiled, or frowned, as appropriate for the contents of the story. It was clear she was enjoying having company and was prepared to make the most of it.

Mykola ended his story by saying he had hoped to reach his home by Christmas, in order to celebrate with his family.

"Oh my dear," the old woman said, "Christmas has come and gone. It is now near the end of February. You have been travelling a long time."

The end of February! Could it be that it had been three months since he and his companion had been sent to Sarajevo? Mykola thought hard about his trials and travels. He had completely lost track of time.

"And where is it that your family live?" Baba Komar asked.

Mykola named the village but she had never heard of it, so then he named the town situated where the tributary joined the Dniester River; again, she had not heard of it. Stanyslaviv, then, surely she had heard of the city. No, still no recognition. This old baba must have never travelled far nor heard tales from travellers!

So then Baba Komar named the towns and villages nearest to her home. Mykola's heart fell. He had not heard of any of these places! Where on God's great earth was he?

"In spring, when you are well again, we will travel to the village on the pass. I make the trip every spring."

"And when will spring come?" Mykola asked.

"Later in the mountains than everywhere else but you will need the time to get well," she responded.

Mykola was grateful for Baba Komar's care and hospitality. He knew she was right because, even having this conversation had made him weary and ready for sleep again.

Baba Komar replaced the poultice on his chest, gave him more tea with honey, and helped him get comfortable. Before long he was sleeping again.

"Sleep may help," she thought, "I've done all I can." And she prayed.

As time passed Mykola got a little stronger and stayed awake a little longer. He learned Baba Komar had been married to a woodsman. They had not had children. He had died the year before. Baba Komar enjoyed her life in the little cottage. She had learned about herbs and remedies from her mother and had offered her services as a healer to the local folk. The nearest town was several miles away but when the weather allowed, people would seek her out to help them with all manner of illnesses. So between her little garden, the fruits of the forest, and what she might be given for her services as a healer, she was able to maintain a comfortable living.

The more Mykola learned about the old woman the more he admired her.

Mykola noticed an array of beautifully carved, wooden figurines of animals. Baba Komar told him it was her husband who had carved them, during their long winter months in the hut. She missed him dearly. The lovely carvings reminded Mykola of his Uncle Vasyl and a wave of homesickness washed over him.

As the weeks melted away Mykola began to heal. There would be some damage, perhaps some lingering pain and the loss of some sensation, especially in his toes but the frostbitten areas had not become infected. It might be that the young man would not be able to walk as far or as fast as he once had but he would not lose any toes. The infection in his chest finally succumbed to Baba Komar's remedies and all that remained was a nagging, dry cough.

As Mykola began to feel better, he offered to help Baba Komar in her daily chores. When the weather did not make it too difficult, he helped her to gather fuel for the peitch. Together they ate and entertained each other with stories of their lives and things they had seen and done. Surprisingly the time went very quickly.

Then as suddenly as when the first snow comes, the cold, winter wind turned warmer and the smell of spring was in the air. It would still be some time before it would be safe to travel down into the town at the foot of the pass but now Mykola was getting anxious to be on his way once more.

Finally the day arrived when Baba Komar announced they should head into town. When they entered a local store the proprietor greeted her warmly, although his wife was a bit taken aback by her companion. Her natural curiosity about who he might be eventually overcame her initial reaction.

Baba Komar was aware of the younger woman's reaction, but chose to ignore it. Her business was with the woman's husband. He was a fair and generous man; one who would afford a traveller the help custom demanded.

"This poor young man has been very helpful to me this long winter," she began. "He has become lost while serving the Emperor by keeping the peace far to the south," she continued. "He is still a very long way from home and needs our help to get him back to where he belongs."

The proprietor knew Baba Komar would not ask for help for anyone who was not worthy and so he immediately agreed to do what he could to help the young man.

They began by trying to determine exactly where Mykola's home might be. This was difficult as neither had heard of the towns and villages near his home. Finally the proprietor decided his brother, who lived in a larger town with a train station might be able to help. Surely someone there could be found who would know how to get this lost soul back to his home.

And so it was decided that Mykola would stay with the proprietor and his wife for a week until his planned trip to the larger town to buy stock for the store. There he would introduce the young man to his brother and together they would form a plan to get him home.

Mykola bid Baba Komar a fond farewell, thanking her for her care and help.

And so it was that Mykola slept in the barn in the yard behind the store. He did what he could to help the proprietor, in order to earn his keep. The proprietor noted the young man was always willing to lend a hand and genuinely appreciated his help.

Because the trip to the larger town had several purposes - to buy stock for the store, to visit his brother, and to celebrate Easter, which was quite late that year - the proprietor's entire family would be making the trip. The trip required extensive preparations. A wagon was loaded with the family's essentials for the visit and the celebration. The proprietor, his wife, and two small children would make the journey, riding in the wagon. Mykola was asked to ride the spare horse alongside. On the return trip, the wagon would be filled with supplies for the store, so the extra horse would be needed to pull it.

The trip to town took two days. The travellers started very early one morning, spent the night with friends in a village which was about half way, and arrived at their destination the following afternoon. It was Holy Thursday.

That evening, both families along with Mykola attended the huge, beautiful church in the town. Mykola, who had never attended a liturgy other than in the church in his village or in the chapel of an army detachment, was awestruck by the size and magnificence of the building.

"This is truly a house of God!" he thought.

So he was quite surprised to learn that, though the church and liturgy were very familiar, this was actually an Orthodox church. He would have been even more surprised to know that Easter on the Orthodox calendar that year was a full week later than on the Greek Catholic calendar. As a result, his family had celebrated Easter the prior week and had already begun their journey to Canada.

The four days of Easter celebrations - Holy Thursday, Good Friday, Holy Saturday, and the culmination on Easter Sunday - were like a miracle to Mykola. He thoroughly enjoyed celebrating Easter with the proprietor and his family. He had not had such a joyous celebration for several years. It was almost enough to ease his desire to be on his way toward home.

On Bright Monday the proprietor and his brother took Mykola to the train station to inquire about passage to Mykola's home. The ticket master was surprised to see a soldier from the Austrian Common Army so far from home but he showed them a map. Mykola would have to take a train north and east to Kolamyia, then to the town on the Dniester. From there Mykola could walk to his village.

"But first," Mykola thought, "I will report to the recruiting office and submit my commander's letter."

Because he was a soldier, the ticket master waived the fare. Mykola was very grateful, as he had no money. The train was to leave that evening. The proprietor and his brother took Mykola back to collect his belongings and have the women prepare food for his journey. When Mykola was finally on the train and heading for home he felt relieved and very tired. He fell asleep almost as soon as the train left the station. He was going home – at last!

Pavlo, 1905

Father Mykhaylo arranged for Pavlo to take passage on a ship leaving from Hamburg for Montreal, Canada in the fall of 1905. It was a grand adventure, to be sure, but Pavlo was apprehensive. He had spent some time with Baba Pelik and his brothers and cousins and had said his good-byes to the villagers and, of course, to Father Mykhaylo. He had been very sad to leave the only world he had ever known. Unlike so many who had made this journey, Pavlo did not have big expectations for his life and he would have been more than content to remain in the village and work for Father Mykhaylo for the remainder of it. But the good Father wanted him to go to Canada and make something of himself, so Pavlo would do it. He would make the good Father proud.

Pavlo travelled alone from the village. Many others had left in the spring and summer but now, in autumn, the villagers were preparing for winter rather than a trip across the ocean.

Once on his way, it wasn't long before Pavlo met other young men, who were either travelling alone, with their families, or with families who had taken them on as protégés. These new acquaintances helped ease the pain of separation and homesickness, which would otherwise have overwhelmed the young traveller. And although he didn't know it just then, these new friends would prove to be very useful allies when he reached the new country.

3 NEW BEGINNINGS

Taras, 1902-3

The Bodnars were lucky to be joining an established family farming operation. The arrival of Mr. Bodnar, an adult male, entitled him to the allotment of fifty hectares of land. As his arrival had been anticipated, the parcel of land roughly adjacent to the existing family enterprise had been claimed in advance for the new arrivals. The land itself was not exceptional other than in its size. Mr. Bodnar's first thoughts were that this land would not be suitable for growing grain, as was the custom in the old country. He soon learned the crops of choice in this region were not grain, but sugar cane and tobacco. He would have a lot to learn but fortunately there were many willing to help him and he was eager to start a new life and a new kind of farming.

For many who had immigrated to the Misiones region it had been difficult to adapt to the sub-tropical climate, which was much warmer and wetter than they had been accustomed to. Initially, learning what crops to grow and how to grow them on the new farms had been an exercise in trial and error. Despite advice from those who had settled before them, many of the new arrivals failed to make a success of their farms and often returned to the urban areas for employment or back to their homelands. So having an established family unit into which they would integrate was a huge advantage for the Bodnars.

Taras was eager to learn what he could of this type of farming in the new country. His hosts found him a willing and able worker and were happy to have his help. The hours of work were long and doubly exhausting, due to the unfamiliar heat and humidity but Taras was determined to learn how to be an Argentine farmer – his dream depended on it.

Taras sent brief letters to his father. He described the farm, the crops, and the climate but he didn't know whether he should encourage his family to follow him just yet. He needed to know more about farming prospects first. He thought there would be time as he was sure his father would not want to leave until after Mykola returned from military service. It would be a big decision for his father and Taras wanted to be sure any input he provided would help make the decision a good one.

Toward the end of the year of labour Taras had promised to Mr. Bodnar, and as he was contemplating his future, two separate and unrelated events occurred, which hugely impacted his plans. First, he had heard from Ivan Boyko, the young man who had befriended him on the ship. Ivan had married his sweetheart, Esperanza, and they were planning, with the help of her father, to start a yerba mate (tea) plantation further north in Misiones. Ivan's father-in-law had worked for a man named Volodymyr Hnatiuk, who had been the first person in recent years to grow the local tea. Ivan wondered whether Taras had claimed his fifty hectares of land yet or if he might be interested in joining them in this new venture.

The second event was far more personal. Mr. Bodnar approached Taras to inquire whether he might be interested in joining the family by way of marriage to Maria, his eldest daughter. Taras had long been aware of Maria's intentions to marry him but he was not inclined to comply. He did not want to offend Mr. Bodnar, who had been so good to him, so he asked for some time to think about the offer. Mr. Bodnar was far from being offended but he did wonder why this hard-working and obviously ambitious young man was not jumping at the chance to become a partner in the thriving, extended-family farm. He suspected Taras just needed a bit of time to understand what a tremendous opportunity was being offered.

Taras replied to Ivan's letter the next day. He would join in this new venture. He would leave, as soon as possible, and claim his land along with Ivan to establish their plantation.

When Mr. Bodnar was told of Taras' decision he was very surprised. He also felt badly for Maria, who knew about her father's offer to Taras. She would be humiliated at being rejected and heartbroken at losing the man she had so long dreamed of marrying. Mr. Bodnar decided it would be best for all concerned if Taras left as soon as possible to prevent awkwardness and prolonged pain. As a result, Taras was offered a cash bonus for his work and was released from his obligation a few months before the promised year of labour was completed. Taras was a free man with cash in his pocket and the promise of a new adventure. He was very happy, indeed.

Mykola, 1905

Mykola had arrived by train at the town where the tributary met the Dniester River. He disembarked and went straight to the army recruiting office. There he presented the letter his unit leader had given him so long ago. The clerk in the office looked at the letter and found Mykola's name in the register. Then he wrote in the final column next to the name 'Discharged'. Mykola was free to go. "You may be called up again if you are needed," clerk called after him as he left the office.

Mykola hadn't felt so free, so grateful, and so joyous in a long time. He was almost home. Soon he would see his family. He had learned to walk more slowly and more deliberately, but with a bit of a limp because of the pain he still had due the frostbite he had suffered. Soon he was at the edge of his village. He was home.

Mykola walked up to his father's house. It looked different somehow. And there was no one around – very unusual. Where were Anna and Dariya? With Tato and the boys in the fields? True it was spring and time for planting but, just the same, the house looked strangely changed and empty. Mykola walked around to the shed at the back. Just then someone called to him from Uncle Vasyl's house next door. Had Uncle Vasyl finally married? No it was a neighbor woman he had known all those years ago before he entered the army.

"Who are you?" the woman asked shapely.

"It's me, Mykola … Martiniuk," Mykola answered. "Mrs. Slewka?"

"Yes …" she said hesitantly, "Is it really you? We thought we would never see you again."

"There was a time when I didn't know whether I would ever see home again!" Mykola responded.

"Well your uncle is in the fields - he'll be home soon to eat. Come over and have chai with me and I'll tell you what has happened while you were away."

Mykola had many questions and his neighbor answered as many as she could. She explained how the family had waited and waited for his return and for word from Taras in Argentina. Finally they had sold the family home and farm to Uncle Vasyl, who sold his own little hut to her husband. Then Mykola's father and the rest of the family had left for Canada just after Easter.

"Then I have just missed them!" Mykola exclaimed.

"Oh no, Easter was weeks ago," the neighbor responded.

"How could that be?" Mykola wondered. It wasn't until a few days later when Father Mykhaylo explained to him the different dates for Easter that year on the Orthodox and Greek Catholic calendars that, Mykola understood.

And so it was that when Uncle Vasyl returned from the fields, Mykola was reunited with what was left of his family in the village – all, of course, except for his brother, Mykhaylo, who had married so well.

After the shock, surprise, and joy of the return of his favorite nephew, Uncle Vasyl and Mykola spent long hours talking about what to do next. Mykola was devastated that he had missed the departure of his family. He had dreamed of being reunited with them and at times during his long journey home, it was this dream that had been the only thing keeping him going. But now that he was back in the village with Uncle Vasyl he wasn't sure he wanted to embark on new journey. Furthermore, he realized rather quickly that Uncle Vasyl, though willing to help him follow either Taras or

Tato, could really use help on the farm. Soon it became obvious that Mykola's place was in the village on the family farm with Uncle Vasyl.

The spring that year was especially sweet and gentle in the little village. Mykola worked side-by-side with his uncle, seeding the crops and planting the garden. He was so happy to be back home.

It may have been the lovely spring weather, or perhaps it was the pure joy of living that overwhelmed Mykola, or perhaps it was simply fate, but for whatever reason Mykola's return did not go unnoticed by many of the village girls. Mykola had always been considered a handsome young man but his shy ways had often resulted in him being overshadowed by his more gregarious brother, Taras. Now during this exceptional spring, Mykola appeared to a number of young girls of marriageable age as the ideal mate. Mykola was too filled with joy at being home to really notice this change in the young women of the village he had know all his life.

One fine Sunday morning during Divine Liturgy, Uncle Vasyl, who noticed everything, recognized the stir Mykola was causing among the young women. That afternoon as the two men walked through the small field behind the house, Uncle Vasyl gently suggested perhaps it was time for Mykola to consider marriage.

"Perhaps it is," Mykola responded, "but where would I find someone who would want to marry an old, lame soldier such as myself."

"Where indeed!" Uncle Vasyl exclaimed and then proceeded to describe the young girls who had been mooning over him in church.

Mykola was amazed. He had not noticed any of this. Uncle Vasyl was amazed that Mykola had been so blind!

At any rate on the next few Sundays, with Uncle Vasyl's help, Mykola began to see signs of interest from various village girls. There was one girl who surprised him, as she had always seemed to be attracted to Taras. Mykola thought she was very pretty and didn't expect that she had even noticed him in the past.

"Perhaps it is just because I am Taras' brother," he thought. "She wouldn't settle for me instead of someone like him."

But he was wrong. Nadya had always enjoyed Taras' lively scheming but for a husband she wanted someone stable and sensible. In short she wanted Mykola. Soon the two were seeing a lot of each other and it became clear that soon there would be a wedding to celebrate.

Uncle Vasyl offered to build himself a small hut at the back of the yard next to the shed but Mykola would not hear of it. After they married, Mykola and Nadya wanted Uncle Vasyl to continue living in the family home with them. Uncle Vasyl was overjoyed. It would be just like in the early days of Yuriy and Kateryna's marriage. He would be part of a larger family once more.

Yuriy, Late Spring, 1905

It was past the middle of May and the pioneer family, who had extended their hospitality to the Martiniuks, were busily seeding their fields and planting their garden. Yuriy was anxious to investigate available land for a homestead but he felt he should help his host at this busy time of year.

Many of the men who had arrived with them were planning to select a homestead as quickly as possible. Often the order of business after selecting a homestead followed a pattern. First a shelter had to be constructed. Then any children who were old enough to work for others would be placed in positions of employment. Then the head of the household would walk to Moose Jaw, some one hundred and eighty miles to the south, in search of employment in the town or on the railroad. The woman of the household and any small children were left on the new homestead with the backbreaking and lonely task of beginning to prepare the land and plant and tend a garden, in order to grow essential food for the coming winter.

Yuriy hoped the money he had brought would be enough to sustain his family through the first winter, without having to 'farm out' the boys or leave his family behind to seek employment far away. If he selected a homestead carefully and if he and his two sons worked diligently, they might be able to build a rudimentary dwelling and start breaking the land before fall. It might even be possible to plant a small, late garden.

Both Yuriy and Andriy were eligible for a homestead and later in the year, when Petro turned eighteen, he too would be eligible for a homestead. However, Yuriy had been warned against taking on more than one quarter section of land at a time, since it would be hard to meet the three-year requirements necessary to keep the land.

For the administration fee of ten dollars the Dominion Lands Act provided for any male, eighteen years of age or older, to obtain one hundred and sixty acres of land under an 'Intent to Settle'. In order to keep the land, at the end of the initial three-year period the development and value of the land was assessed and if it met the requirements of the Act, the homesteader would be issued 'Letters Patent', indicating his ownership. The requirements of the Act were that during the first three years, the homesteader must reside on the land for at least six months each year, build a permanent dwelling on the land, and cultivate a total of at least thirty acres at a reasonable rate per year. The Act also provided the option of buying an additional quarter section of land adjacent to the original homestead, provided the requirements were met. Yuriy felt cultivating thirty acres of land was the biggest challenge, since he had never farmed more than seven and a half acres of land in his life! It seemed daunting but his neighbours assured him it could be done. And he was lucky because he had two strong, young sons, who would be a tremendous help in the enterprise.

Yuriy was sure if he and the two boys worked together they could meet the requirements for the Letters Patent on an initial homestead in his name. Andriy and Petro could then each file their own Intent to Settle, hopefully on a quarter section of land adjacent to or very near the 'home place'. At any rate Yuriy hoped each of his sons might have his own homestead before long and by working together they could meet all the requirements necessary to obtain Letters Patent on two, if not three, quarter sections of land in the not too distant future.

Yuriy discussed this plan with Andriy and Petro and both agreed that this was the best way to proceed. Therefore, Yuriy went in search of a homestead with adjoining options for his sons' homesteads, while his sons helped their host with spring seeding.

Yuriy knew exactly what he was looking for in the land he would homestead. First of all, the soil must be a rich, dark chenozem. Second, he hoped to find a homestead with water and some woodland. He had heard it was very difficult to break the land if it was completely covered in bush, but some woodland was essential both for building materials and fuel. Many of the farmers from Galicia were obsessed with woodlands because in the old country, overlords who owned the rights to such land had often restricted access. And so Yuriy was looking for a compromise, some woodland, but some open meadow as well. He did not know whether he would find such a place but he set off with the local agent from the Land Registry Office in search of it.

First the agent took Yuriy north where indeed there were still many homesteads available, providing a good chance that two or three adjacent quarter sections could be had over the next several years. But the soil was not as rich as Yuriy had wanted and there were a lot of trees, including even some evergreens. Then the agent took Yuriy east. Here the land looked a bit better but it was very hilly and still covered in too much bush for Yuriy's liking.

The agent said to Yuriy, "I thought your people wanted trees. That's what everyone asks me for – 'find me land with lots of trees.' "

Yuriy replied, "Yes sir, I do want some woodland but also some meadow; water if possible, but not alkali; good dark soil; and the possibility for my sons to homestead near by."

"You aren't asking for much!" the agent responded. "We'll try again to see what we can find."

But that evening when Yuriy told his host where the agent had taken him and what he had seen the farmer was thoughtful.

The next morning the farmer said: "Yuriy, if you will wait until I finish getting my crop in, which should be soon with the help of your boys, I will take you to see some land which I, myself, have been thinking about buying."

And so it was that several days later the farmer took Yuriy, Andriy, and Petro to see some land not far to the west of the farmer's homestead. The soil was good. There was water but the land was not alkali. There were gently rolling hills covered in bush but there also were some meadowlands among the hills. Yuriy tried to calculate how much of the land could be readily broken initially, without having to clear a lot of bush. It might just work. Then the farmer explained that the best part about this particular quarter section was that there was more land available near by. The land was a bit further from the settlement and the railroad and, of course, there was no road so it hadn't appealed to many settlers yet. Yuriy thought they could make it work.

So the next day Yuriy met the local land agent and showed him the quarter section he wished to homestead. The agent seemed a bit reluctant but finally agreed and the paperwork was filed.

Because Andriy and Petro had been such a help to the farmer he agreed to help Yuriy and the boys find a spot to begin building a dwelling.

"When we came," the farmer said, "for the first year we lived in a dugout in the ground, covered with branches and sod. Later we built a shack over the dugout. The house we have now was just built last year. I had to work on the railroad for two winters in order to earn enough money to build that house."

Yuriy was very much aware of Anna's reluctance to come to Canada. Further, she had suffered illness and lost a lot of weight on the journey and he was worried about her. Yuriy felt he had to try to make all this up to her. With the available trees and three grown men, Yuriy planned to build a modest hut before winter set in. He wanted to give Anna a home that was a bit better than a hole in the ground.

So after the Intent to Settle was filed, Yuriy, the boys, and their host selected a spot, sheltered by a bush-covered hill to the north and with a sprawling meadow to the south. The proximity to the bush would mean that once the trees were felled and dressed they would not have to be moved far to the building site. Using the tools they had brought with them and others borrowed from their neighbor, the three men went to work preparing to build a modest, two-roomed hut.

Yuriy and his sons slept on the homestead in a tent they had borrowed so they could work all the long, summer days on the new dwelling. Anna and Dariya continued to sleep with the neighbour's family but walked the two miles every day to the new homestead. They would bring food and ate with the men, picnic style.

While the men built the hut, Anna and Dariya worked to establish a small garden plot near by. Their neighbor brought his oxen and plough to turn the sod for their initial garden. Then Anna broke up the sod with a shovel, while Dariya raked the grass and weeds and picked up the debris. After several days of backbreaking labour they were ready to plant. The farmer's wife had suggested they plant potatoes, onions, carrots, turnips, and beets for this first garden as it was well into June and, although the days of summer were long, the growing season was short. For the rest of the summer Dariya's job was to carry water from a slough not too far from the garden plot, to water the growing plants, and to pluck the grass and weeds, which threatened to engulf them. Once the garden was in, Anna helped the men drag trees from the bush to the building site. Dariya collected tall grass, which would be chopped up and mixed with the clay plaster. Once plastering began, both she and Anna helped as well.

The hut had some similarities to the home they had left behind although it was considerably smaller. It was made of tree trunks, plastered between and over with a clay mixture. They did not have slaked lime or cow manure so the clay was mixed with dry grass from the meadows. This may not have made a very durable plaster but it would be good enough for the first winter and made for a home that was better than a hole in the ground. The roof was covered with tree branches, then sod, and finally 'thatched' with dry grass. The hut had one, south-facing door and one 'window'. They could not afford glass for the window so it was covered with a semi-translucent hide. Its purpose was more to let in light than to see through. The floor was packed earth, which Anna coated with slurry of mud. When the mud slurry dried hard it could be swept clean of crumbs and debris and recoated as needed. There was a peitch in the corner for warmth and cooking.

Once the house was built, Anna went about the business of turning the hut into a home. She did what she could to arrange their meager possessions in a way to make the hut comfortable and useable. As yet there was no furniture to speak of, save the chests and boxes in which they had transported their belongings from the old country.

"There will be time to build beds and chairs in winter," Yuriy had told her.

As they were preparing to move into the hut Yuriy went with their neighbour to the nearest town, a place called 'Alvena', to buy supplies to add to the few chickens he had purchased earlier from the farmer. They would not go hungry this winter. It took the two men the better part of a day to get to town and buy what they needed and another full day to return with the heavily-laden ox wagon. Yuriy was grateful for his neighbour's wagon and team of oxen, for without them, walking to town and then carrying the supplies home on his back, even with the help of his sons, would have made for an arduous journey.

With her 'kitchen' supplied with flour, lard, sugar, and tea, Anna worked hard to re-establish a home for her family. It was very difficult for her not to compare their new situation with the home they had left behind. But every time she allowed herself to think of their home in the old country she felt her eyes sting and she had an uncontrollable urge to cry. She was not happy. She might never be happy again but she would not cry. What would be the point? She was here now, so she would just have to make the best of it – if she could.

Meanwhile, Yuriy and the boys borrowed the neighbour's team of oxen and plough and began breaking the meadowland nearest the hut. August was approaching; it was much too late to plant a crop this year but they wanted to have enough land broken to be able to plant in spring. As the autumn wore on it was time for the neighbor to begin his harvest, so Yuriy, Andriy, and Petro went to lend a hand. This served as a repayment for the kindness their neighbor had extended to them upon their arrival, as well as a learning experience.

"Next year, God willing, we will be harvesting our own crop," Yuriy said. In the meantime, Anna and Dariya were busy harvesting what they could from their little garden and processing and storing the produce for the winter.

Because they would need money for grain seed in spring, Andriy decided to walk to the town of Saskatoon, on the west bank of the South Saskatchewan River, to try to get a job for the winter. Yuriy was sorry to see him go but he knew that if the boy could earn enough to keep himself fed and for the seed in spring it would be a huge help. Another neighbor asked Petro whether he would be willing to work for him during the winter, taking care of livestock. Petro agreed this would be a good place for him to pass the winter and in this way, he too could add to the family's funds. So after harvest, with both Andriy and Petro gone, Yuriy, Anna, and Dariya settled into the little hut to face their first Canadian winter.

"Our first winter in Canada. Will it be as cold as they say? I don't really like to be cold but Tato and the boys cut and split a lot of wood, so surely we can heat our little house. How wonderful it is to be in our own home again. Living with others was all right at first but as time went on, I was getting anxious to be out of their house and into our own. Mama was too. I think she is much happier now that she has her own little hut to keep. We have been so busy this summer but we have so much already. Tato really can make everything work. Even Mama must see that now. We will be snug and warm this winter. We will be busy making clothing and furniture and planning for spring. I am looking forward to our new life."

Winter, 1905-6

Andriy

Andriy and a young farmer from the neighbourhood set off together on foot for Saskatoon on a bright, clear, sunny autumn day during the gentle reprieve in the late fall, commonly referred to as an 'Indian Summer'. Andriy was glad of the company and very much enjoyed hearing of the young farmer's experiences.

Andriy's companion had arrived in Canada nearly three years prior, as a single man sponsored by an extended family - a husband and wife, two married sons and their wives, and two young children. He had lived and worked with the family during his first summer in Canada and then had headed west to Calgary to work on that growing community's sewer system during the winter. He had liked the foothills and mountains and had spent the next year working on the railroad west of Banff. Now, almost three years since his arrival in Canada, the young man had saved nearly enough money to establish himself on a homestead. He had returned to the neighbourhood in the spring to be near the folk he had immigrated with from his village in the old country. Once again he had lived and worked with the family who had sponsored his trip to the new land. This winter he hoped to finally earn enough for his homestead in the following spring.

Andriy had no idea what kind of job he might be able to get in town or where he would live but his companion promised to help him when they arrived. It took a few days for the pair to walk to Saskatoon, first across country to Alvena, then along the train tracks in a southwesterly direction to another small settlement where the tracks turned directly west and then south into town. The weather was fair and they had brought enough food with them for the journey. Andriy fell in love with the countryside, the rolling hills, the river where the train tracks crossed it, the small farms with their little huts spaced so far apart. But most of all, Andriy loved the wide, blue sky. The expansive horizons made him feel at once small and insignificant, but also privileged to be a part of God's great earth. As Andriy walked and listened to his companion, he began composing a poem - a hymn almost - of praise and thanksgiving for the wonderful new land of which he was becoming a part.

There were actually three communities on the South Saskatchewan River where the train tracks they had been following culminated in a round house and pumping station. On the east bank, across the river, was the village of Nutana. To the south, along the west bank of the river, was the village of Riverdale (later to be called Riversdale). But as his companion explained, the growing town of Saskatoon between the other two villages, afforded the best opportunity for employment. The population had been growing rapidly in recent years. The Grand Trunk Pacific Railway had built its roundhouse and pumping station and there was talk that the Canadian Northern and Canadian Pacific Railways would also run through the town. Furthermore, there had been talk of amalgamating the villages of Nutana and Riverdale with the town of Saskatoon to form a city. If that were to happen there would be a tremendous demand for labour to work on the construction of sewers, water treatment facilities, and electrical facilities.

The first thing the young men did was to find lodging in a boarding house. Many of the townsfolk took in lodgers in order to help maintain and pay for their modest homes. Because many young men came to town from farms to work for the winter the practice of boarding seasonal labourers was commonplace.

The pair found a room to share in a rather small house owned by a woman who had been widowed in the spring. She had three small children to support and was counting on lodgers to help her keep her home and support her family. Andriy had always been fond of and good with children and it was probably these qualities that made the widow comfortable with renting to the two young homesteaders. She had been nervous about the prospect of having strange men in her home but these two seemed to be the type who would suit her needs and family well.

The room they would share was small. It was in the attic of the one-and-a–half story home and sparsely furnished with only a bed and a washstand. The price was two dollars per month for each of them. This included two meals a day, breakfast and supper. Even though Yuriy had given his son a small amount of cash to help him secure a place to stay and hold him over until he could begin earning his own way, Andriy was concerned. His companion assured him they would have jobs very soon and all would be well.

And so it was that on the first morning Andriy ate a hearty breakfast of porridge with milk, toast, and coffee and was off with his friend to find employment. The first stop for the pair was at a hardware store. The owner needed no help. Then a dry goods store and then the flourmill - all with no luck. Andriy was disheartened but his companion was not. The next morning they set off in search of employment once more. By mid-day Andriy was really getting worried about finding a job. His companion decided to head west to the village of Riverdale, while Andriy checked first at the railyard and then at the blacksmith across from the roundhouse. Still no luck. Then he wandered toward a small shop on the ground floor of a building across from the roundhouse.

It became apparent that the shop, which had attracted his attention, was a small café. Later Andriy had thought he might have been led to the café because he had been particularly hungry that day. The café was full of men, who had come in for lunch. A small, black-haired man was bustling around from table to table, at once taking orders and delivering plates of food. The man wore his black hair in a long, thin braid down the middle of his back. He was dressed in light-coloured trousers and a loose-fitting tunic. His skin had a luminous yellowish tinge and his black eyes were narrow and upturned at the outer edges. Andriy had never seen anything like him. He stood at the door staring at the sight before him.

"You want eat?" the black-haired man asked him from across the room.

"No, I want work," Andriy replied.

"No work," the man replied with a wave of his hand, indicating Andriy was being dismissed from the premises.

Just then there was a huge crash, followed by the sound of clattering pots and pans coming from the kitchen at the far back of the small café. A verbal barrage in a language Andriy had never heard before and could not understand followed the initial racket. The general meaning, however, was not hard to comprehend. Something catastrophic had happened in the kitchen. The patrons of the café looked up from their meals and momentarily stopped talking and eating. Just as quickly, they returned to their prior preoccupations. The small black-haired man rushed to the kitchen. Andriy wasn't sure whether he should leave, sit down at a table, or follow the black-haired man into the kitchen. He did none of these, but simply stood and stared at the door, which had swung swiftly closed behind the black-haired man. No one in the café seemed to notice that Andriy was still standing there.

Andriy didn't know how long he had been standing at the entrance to the café. His reverie was interrupted when he noticed that the small, black-haired man had reappeared from behind the swinging kitchen door and seemed to be motioning for Andriy to approach him. Andriy looked around and it was clear there was no one else who might have been the object of the little man's gesture, so Andriy walked toward him.

"Come - you help," the man demanded and held the swinging door open for Andriy to enter the kitchen.

The sight which met Andriy's gaze was even more extraordinary than what had held him spellbound just moments before. There was another small, black-haired man, who was dressed exactly like the first and looked so much like the first that they could have been twins. He was standing on a small stool over a hot stove covered with large, bowl-like pots, round wicker steamers, and long-handled utensils. On the floor around the stool were upturned pots amid the shards of broken dishes and spilled food.

Andriy was astonished by the scene and the man who was summoning him.

"You help," the little man demanded again handing him a mop.

So, Andriy took the mop and began clearing the mess on the floor surrounding the second little man, who continued his ministrations over the stove without giving notice. The first man disappeared through the swinging door into the front of the café. And there he was cleaning up in the kitchen of Chang's Chinese Restaurant. Andriy would not know for some time just how lucky he had been to walk through the door of the café at exactly that moment. God had truly smiled upon him that day.

And so it was that Andriy started working with 'Sam' and 'Tom' Chang in the little café on Avenue A, next to the blacksmith and across from the roundhouse. His job consisted of carrying in wood for the big stove and keeping it stoked, washing dishes, clearing dishes off the tables, and washing the floors. In addition to these routine tasks he would occasionally be asked to run errands for his employers. As the Chang brothers got to know Andriy they trusted him with more duties. Because Andriy was able to communicate, at least a little, in several languages including a little English, which he had learned during the train journey across Canada, he was invaluable to the Chinese brothers, both with suppliers of the goods for their café and with their customers.

In time Andriy learned that 'Sam' Chang, the elder brother, had learned broken English while working with a railroad construction crew. His younger brother 'Tom' had just recently arrived in Canada and had not yet learned any English. 'Sam' and 'Tom' were not their real names but these were as close as most of their customers could come to pronouncing their Chinese names.

Andriy grew to admire and respect the Chang brothers. They worked hard and expected no less of him. They were fair and paid him a decent wage for the work he did. In addition to his pay Andriy could eat three meals a day in the café. This meant he only had to pay for room, rather than room and board at the widow's house. This would help him to save more money for the farm.

It was the brothers' routine that 'Tom' would arrive at the café very early in the morning to get the fire in the stove started and begin preparing for the breakfast customers. 'Sam' would pick up the necessary fresh supplies on his way to the café. The brothers shared a small room in a house a few blocks from the café. It was their dream to one day own a café rather than rent the space for one. But that day was still far off.

As the winter progressed, Andriy was sometimes asked to go early to the café to get the fire in the stove started and to bring in a supply of wood so 'Tom' could focus on preparing for the breakfast rush. Occasionally, 'Sam' would ask Andriy to come early with him to procure fresh supplies for the meals to be cooked that day. Regardless of these early starts, Andriy was always expected to stay until after the last customer had left the café, in order to wash the final dishes and clean the kitchen. As a result, Andriy's days were very long. He rose at four in the morning and met one of the brothers by five. The breakfast customers began arriving at the café before six, since they had to eat before reporting to their various jobs by seven or so. The café was busy most of the day but there was often a lull in customers during the mid-afternoon. This was when Andriy would catch up with dish washing, clean up, and removal of garbage. By the time the last supper customers left the café at about seven in the evening, all three were exhausted. Andriy had little time to see or talk to the young farmer, who he had walked with to Saskatoon.

'Sam' knew what it meant to save every penny he earned – he had been doing so for years. Indeed this was how he had saved enough to bring his brother to Canada and pay the required fifty-dollar head tax levied on Asian immigrants. So after about a month 'Sam' asked Andriy if he wanted to sleep in the café. At first Andriy thought this wasn't such a good idea but as the winter grew colder and the length of his workday increased, he changed his mind. He found sleeping on the floor near the cook stove, which remained warm well into the night, was almost as comfortable as sleeping in the lodging room. So after a few nights of sleeping in the café Andriy went to the widow's house to collect his things and settle his account. The widow was sorry to see him leave but she was confident her other lodger would find a new roommate. Sleeping and eating at the café meant Andriy could save most of his earnings.

One evening 'Sam' asked Andriy if he would like to learn more English. "Yes, of course," the perpetual student answered. "Then you come," and the two left the café and headed out into the dark, cold, winter night.

Andriy had no idea where 'Sam' was taking him so he was surprised when they walked such a distance from the café. They walked almost fifteen blocks to a small, neat house in Riverdale. 'Sam' took off his hat, bowed his head, and knocked at the door. Soon the door was opened and a tall, slender young man stood in a pool of soft, yellow light filtering onto the doorstep from within the house.

"Please come in my friend," the stranger said. "And who is this young man?"

Andriy smiled a shy smile and answered haltingly, "My name, Andriy Martiniuk."

"Well Andriy, welcome to my home," the stranger said and led the two visitors into the small, well-lit, front room.

Since their arrival 'Sam' had not said a word. Now he pointed at Andriy and said: "You teach English him too. I pay."

It was a great gift 'Sam' was offering and Andriy knew it. He had been picking up English from what he heard but he knew he made many mistakes and was speaking broken English, at best. He hadn't known 'Sam' had been studying English. He wondered why 'Sam' had not brought 'Tom' to learn English. It wasn't until much later that Andriy learned 'Tom' had no intention of learning English; he had not warmed to this new country and dreamed only of returning to China.

The stranger told Andriy to call him 'Bill'. 'Sam' interrupted by pointing at the stranger and saying: 'Professor Bill'. Andriy's confusion was obvious.

"I used to teach at a university back east," Bill said. "No need to call me 'Professor', just 'Bill' is fine. I taught English Literature, now I teach English to my friends in the evenings." Then he turned to 'Sam' and said, "No need to pay, I told you, I do this because I want to."

'Sam' just hung his head a bit and said quietly, "I pay," then handed Bill a small envelope.

Bill seemed a bit embarrassed to receive the envelope but he took it and placed on the mantel of the fireplace warming the room.

"Well, now," Bill said as he turned and smiled at his two pupils, "let's get started, shall we?"

Andriy came to love these special evenings. He learned quickly and soon began to teach 'Sam' as they worked. Eventually 'Sam' decided Andriy was as good a teacher as Bill and, while he insisted Andriy continue to study with Bill, 'Sam' was happy learning what English he needed from his employee.

When 'Sam' stopped attending the lessons at Bill's home Andriy offered to continue paying for his own lessons but Bill would not hear of it. By this time Bill had seen the brilliance in his new student and his ability with words.

Bill was the younger son of an English gentleman. As such, he had been well educated but there was little opportunity for him in his homeland. His sense of adventure had led him to Canada and his education had landed him a teaching job at the University of Toronto. He might still have been there if it hadn't been for Ada. Bill had met and fallen deeply in love with a young woman he had met at the home of a mutual friend. Ada was the only child of a wealthy Toronto businessman. Bill did not measure up to Ada's father's idea for her husband. One day Bill had received a brief note from Ada indicating that her father was taking her west where he was planning to invest in new opportunities. Bill had been heart broken. After two years of pining for his lost love, Bill decided to head west as well. Perhaps their paths might cross again, although he suspected by now Ada was likely married to someone, who had earned her father's approval.

Just how Bill ended up in the town of Saskatoon was a mystery, even to him. He had been travelling, teaching English, and writing a book of poetry when he arrived in the small settlement on the west side of the South Saskatchewan River. It just felt like home so he decided to stay. And now there was talk of a university in the new province of Saskatchewan and it might well be situated in Saskatoon, so Bill decided this was as good a place as any.

One day Bill asked Andriy, "Do you read poetry?" This was a simple enough question. Andriy's eyes lit up and he answered, "I love poetry! I have even written some of my own." The words were out of his mouth before he realized it. He had not intended to admit to anyone how he loved to use words to capture the visions and actions his imagination constantly created.

So there it was. Now Bill knew Andriy's secret. It was the secret Andriy had not even told his father or Uncle Vasyl. He felt exposed and vulnerable.

But Bill did not laugh or criticize. He looked thoughtfully at Andriy and then said, "I would like to hear your poetry."

"But it is in Ukrainian," Andriy answered.

"I know a little Ukrainian," Bill responded.

And so Andriy recited one of his short poems. He spoke slowly and deliberately. He watched carefully for signs that Bill had not understood certain words or phrases. He stopped and explained these before continuing. When he had completed the poem he repeated it again, slowly and deliberately. Bill seemed to be truly appreciative.

"You would make a fine teacher," Bill said, "but you are a truly gifted poet!"

Andriy could not believe his ears. Could it be that this learned man actually believed him to be a poet?

From that day on through the long, dark, cold winter, Andriy's thoughts, as he conducted his daily tasks, were of writing poetry in both his beloved

Ukrainian and, with Bill's encouragement, in his new second language, English. Bill was very encouraging because he recognized a real talent in the young Ukrainian homesteader. "Brilliance can be found in the most extraordinary places," he mused to himself. "If it hadn't been for my work with immigrants, 'Sam' Chang in particular, I would have never met this promising young poet." Bill decided Andriy must become a poet and everything possible must be done to ensure that he reached his potential.

When Christmas came, Andriy's thoughts turned to his family – he was very homesick as he had never been away from family at this holy time of year. Christmas was, of course, not of any importance to the Chang brothers, so the little café was open for business. There were fewer customers but still there were the labourers who were far from home and had nowhere else to find a meal and companionship.

January was cold but by February the temperatures had warmed and the small amount of snow, which had fallen in the town that winter, was gone. The temperatures rose further and small hints of spring began to appear - a few green weeds or blades of grass and the swelling buds on the trees. "Well," thought Andriy, "winter wasn't that bad after all." He had heard horrific stories about how cruel the Canadian winters could be. Andriy began to wonder whether it was time to return to the farm to help with clearing the land and seeding. Then March 'came in like a lion', with a huge blizzard, sub-zero temperatures, and terrible wind chills. No, it wasn't quite spring yet!

As April approached the weather began to warm again, the snow from the March blizzard turned to slush in the streets and the west wind held the tantalizing promise of warmer temperatures. Andriy was ready to head back to the farm and his family, so he counted his precious savings - almost ten dollars! He was very proud of himself and grateful to the Chang brothers, without whom he would never have been able to save so much. But Andriy had an even better reason to feel proud for he had written his first poem in English. This last accomplishment was largely due to the teaching and encouragement of his new friend, Bill.

So when it was time to return to his family, Andriy's first stop was the widow's house. His travel companion from the previous fall had moved on – the widow didn't know whether he had returned to the farm or simply moved to other lodgings. Andriy prepared to leave town. He was able to buy grain seed as his father had instructed before he had left the farm. In addition he bought a small amount of salt and tea for his stepmother and a red ribbon for little Dariya. These he carried on his back to the homestead. It took many days to return to his family but the glorious spring weather, the returning ducks and geese, and the lovely green, rolling hills made the onerous journey more bearable.

Petro

Petro's winter was not as successful as Andriy's. Perhaps it was because he never expected or intended to do more than just get by. Perhaps it was because he didn't have the luck of meeting individuals who were willing to give him a hand to succeed. Perhaps he just didn't recognize the opportunities, which may have presented themselves to him. For whatever reason Petro spent that long, dark, cold winter working and sleeping with the animals in the neighbor's barn. The farmer treated him fairly and his wife fed him well. The work Petro did was appreciated but he never went beyond what was asked of him. He did an adequate job, but no more. The farmer paid him accordingly and by the end of the winter Petro had a small amount of cash to take home to his father. Petro was neither pleased nor disappointed with his earnings and his father thought, "Every little bit helps, at least we didn't have to feed the boy through the winter."

Pavlo

Pavlo arrived in Montreal in the late autumn of 1905. His first priority was to get a job. It just so happened that one of the young men who had befriended him on the ship had an idea of how to find employment. He had heard that crews of men were recruited to go into the forests to cut down trees for shipment to lumber-processing yards. It would be hard work but it would mean a place to live, food, and the possibility of saving some money. Pavlo was anxious to get a job so, although he had declared himself to be a farmer on his entrance application, he joined his new friend in a search of work in the bush camps north of Montreal.

Pavlo enjoyed his time in the bush. True it was hard work and the temperatures were colder than he had imagined. There was a lot more snow than he had ever seen in his lifetime. But the food was hearty. The men were a diverse group, mostly immigrants like him, who spoke many languages and had many different ways. On Sundays there was a 'service' in the bunkhouse and then the men could rest for the day. Pavlo took to wandering the countryside on these days. He was in awe of the landscape – so different from his homeland - and eager to learn all he could about this new land. The winter went by very quickly and, although Pavlo had not been able to save much money, he was pleased with the new skills he had acquired and the work he had done.

Toward spring, one warmish Sunday afternoon, Pavlo was out walking in the woods. He stopped near a creek to rest on a fallen log. As he sat in the sunshine he felt a little drowsy. So for that reason he wasn't quite sure he was seeing what he thought he was seeing. Not far off was a black, mother cat and her litter of about six kittens. Pavlo had always been fond of cats and wondered if he could catch one for a pet. These Canadian cats were fluffier than the ones back home but he suspected they needed the extra fur to stay warm in the Canadian winters. The mother cat was hurrying along and the kittens were following behind her as best they could, the littlest one bringing up the rear of their parade. It was clear that neither the mother nor the kittens had seen Pavlo. So he just sat very still and waited until they passed right near the log he was sitting on. Quickly, Pavlo sprang forward and grabbed the littlest kitten. Much to his surprise the kitten did not meow or scratch but suddenly Pavlo was overwhelmed by the most disgusting odor. The mother 'cat' had sprayed him – she was not a cat, but a skunk!

Pavlo reeked. He couldn't stand the smell of himself. His eyes stung. He found a drift of the last of the winter snow on the north side of a tree and rolled in it. Then he decided he had to wash himself in the frigid creek. Even that didn't help. Finally, drenched and cold, he knew he had to go back to camp. The men in camp were not amused. They didn't want Pavlo anywhere near them and made him sleep in the shed with the horses. Even the horses didn't want Pavlo near them. He was desolate!

The next morning, the camp boss came up to, but not into, the shed. He called out, "Hey Paul-o! The men won't work with you today. Instead, they scraped together enough cash to ship you out west. I'll leave it for you under this rock by the door. If you walk swiftly you can catch the freight train in town. Buy a ticket to Winnipeg on the freight – they won't let you ride with passengers!" As he walked quickly away he laughed. How humiliating.

Pavlo couldn't believe it. He was being sent away just because of the way he smelled. He picked up the cash, it was just a little more than he was owed for his work but it was something. He began walking toward town. As he walked, he tried to think of ways to get rid of the smell. Nothing he tried helped and the smell didn't seem to be lessening at all. In town he approached a rail worker and told him of his plight.

The man just laughed and said, "keep your money – you can ride in here." And he opened the door of a cattle car. It smelled almost as bad as Pavlo did! He climbed inside. The cows were not very happy to have him as company but at least it was warm in the cattle car. The rail worker said, as he closed the door, "I'll let know when we get to Winnipeg – you might smell better by then."

Pavlo was hungry and tired but all he wanted to do was sleep and so he made a nest for himself in the straw, as far away from the cattle as he could get, and he slept.

4 TUT Y TAM (HERE AND THERE)

Argentina, 1903

Taras had not sent word for his family to follow him to Argentina. He had seen how much of an advantage it had been for the Bodnars to join an established agricultural colony. It would be very hard, indeed, for a small family unit to come to Argentina and begin to farm alone, from scratch. Even with three sons, Taras' aging father would have to work very hard to become established. Developing a large-scale farm in Argentina was worlds away from his father's experience working the tiny family holding in the old country. No, if his family were to follow him, he would first have to build at least the start of a plantation they could then help him to expand. For this reason Taras delayed in encouraging his father to come to Argentina and at the same time readily agreed to join Ivan in the plan to start a yerba mate plantation in the north.

Ivan was thrilled that Taras would be joining their venture. His father-in-law, who was part Guaraní (an aboriginal people of Northern Argentina), had a wealth of knowledge and was a very hard worker for a man of his age. However, Ivan knew he needed the help of at least one other young, able-bodied man to build his dream. He had liked Taras from the moment they met on board the ship from Europe, but even more importantly, he had seen in Taras a quality he admired – ambition. He had also noted Taras' quick mind and way of finding creative solutions to problems. Yes, his new friend would be a huge asset to their venture.

The Bodnars had insisted on giving Taras a ride to the nearest town, Apostoles, where he met Ivan's family. Ivan had purchased a carro polaco and a horse to convey them, along with their belongings northward forty miles to the settlement of Posadas on the northern border of Argentina. It was the vast, wild region northeast of Posadas in which they intended to claim two adjacent, fifty-hectare parcels of land, one for Ivan and one for Taras. This would be the basis of their partnership and the foundation of their plantation.

On the long trip north, Taras learned a great deal about this new crop he had never heard of before. He had put his faith in his new friends, who believed it would be a profitable venture. Yerba mate, he learned, is an evergreen bush – its use had a long history stretching back to the beginnings of time. It was such an integral part of the culture of this part of the world that it would one day be referred to as 'el product madre de Misiones' (the mother product of Misiones). Its leaves and sometimes even its twigs were brewed as a tea. But this was not an ordinary tea like the chai Taras was used to.

The tea made from the yerba leaves and twigs had been used for generations by people living in South-central Brazil, Paraguay, Uruguay, and Northern Argentina. The indigenous Guaraní people had harvested the leaves of the native yerba bush only every three years to allow the bush to regenerate. The tea, called mate for the traditional gourd from which it was drunk, had become an important aspect of social traditions. Typically, it was made by filling a gourd (guampa) three quarters full of dried leaves and pouring hot, but not boiling (to prevent a bitter taste), water over the organic matter. After it had infused, the tea was drunk through a straw (bombilla). Traditionally, the brewer of the tea passed the gourd to the first individual sitting in a circle. After a few mouthfuls, the gourd was passed back to the brewer who refilled the water and then passed the gourd to the next person in the circle in a clockwise fashion. This tea ritual was, in some ways, similar to the use of a tobacco pipe in other aboriginal societies.

After the Spanish colonization, the use of yerba mate became widespread and by the sixteenth century became Paraguay's main commodity, even outstripping tobacco. In the middle of the next century, the Jesuits domesticated the yerba plant and developed plantations using native labour, in the missions they established in the Misiones region. These domesticated plants rivaled the wild varieties grown in Paraguay. Then in the 1770's when the Jesuits were expelled, their plantations fell into disuse and their knowledge of domesticating the yerba plant was lost. After the War of the Triple Alliance, Paraguay was devastated and some of its yerba growing areas became part of modern Argentina. Brazil then became the major producer of mate. By the end of the nineteenth century the production of yerba mate was struggling in Argentina, due to several factors, not the least of which were the quickly disappearing natural groves. It was just in the last few years that efforts to re-domesticate the yerba plant had been successful. Now it was beginning to become a viable commercial product of Northern Argentina - the same region where the Jesuits had successfully developed plantations over two hundred years before.

The government assisted in making yerba mate a successful product in the region by imposing protectionist tariffs, improving the infrastructure to facilitate the transportation of the product, and implementing a policy to require all settlers to grow the crop on a portion of their new land holdings. As a result, both large plantation owners and small farmers contributed to the production of this important crop. Yerba mate grew to become an integral component of the identity of the peoples living in the region, not just a source of livelihood but a part of their developing culture.

Ivan had procured some ripe, purple yerba seeds, which would be soaked and planted in small pots when they reached their destination. The first small plants would be ready to go into the ground of the fledgling plantation before September. It would be three years before the plants could begin to be harvested, so maize, beans, and tobacco would be planted as well, both for food and as cash crops until the yerbe bushes were mature. Each year another planting of the yerbe would extend the three-year cycle so that, eventually, it could be harvested annually on the plantation. The harvesting of the yerba was very labour intensive and typically large plantations exploited native labour for this purpose. Ivan and Taras did not want to profit unjustly from the labour of those who would work on their plantation. They planned to set up a cooperative, whereby all who worked with them would earn a share of the profits according to what they had contributed.

Canada, 1906

The winter had been good for Anna. She had managed to prepare and store sufficient foodstuffs to keep her abbreviated family in good health throughout the cold months. The dreaded winter had not been as bad as she had anticipated. She had had time to make the little hut into a home and to rest and regain her strength after the horrendous journey to this place. She had even learned a bit about local flora and fauna and especially native healing herbs to add to the knowledge she had gained from the old village healer before marrying Yuriy. She had also made up her mind to make the best of her situation although, in her heart, she would never forget nor stop longing for her homeland.

Dariya was in her element. She loved the crisp, bright winter days and always volunteered to fetch wood or water for her mother – anything to get out of the little hut. She loved the freedom and open spaces. The only thing she missed were her brothers and the fact that there were no other children her age for miles around. But she enjoyed spending the long winter evenings with her parents and was learning, every day, the household tasks she would some day need for her own home. She kept busy and was never bored. She did still have trouble falling asleep at night. Long after hearing her father's soft snoring in the night, she would be thinking – her mind racing with ideas and stories. This was how she had always amused herself and it seemed that at night her mind was more active than ever.

Yuriy was glad when his sons returned from their winter employment, for he had started to turn the land by hand on the small plot they had cleared the autumn before and he wanted to get seed in the soil before turning to the task of clearing more land for planting.

Petro was the first to return home. He brought his earnings, which his father immediately set aside along with what was left from their journey. He was saving to buy oxen to help clear the land. Until he could buy his own oxen he would have to rely on borrowing his neighbour's team, whenever these were not being employed on that farm.

It was still a bit early to plant the fields, so Yuriy and Petro went to town for replenishing supplies. They walked as far as their neighbour's farm and then rode with him to town. They would be gone for a couple of days.

Anna had saved a few potatoes from the late garden of the prior season to be used as seed and she still had most of the seeds she had brought from the old country. Yuriy had been so intent on his fields that he hadn't had time to pay attention to her garden, so she was determined to spade and extend the little garden plot herself while he was gone. So while Yuriy and Petro were away, Anna and Dariya worked to turn the soil to increase the size of their garden. After a spring rain Anna decided to take Dariya into the woods to look for mushrooms. They found a few, which she planned to prepare as a treat for Yuriy and Petro when they returned.

On the day she had expected their return, Anna was surprised to find instead two aboriginal men at her door. Although she was frightened she tried very hard not to show it. They did not speak Ukrainian and she did not understand their language but they made it clear they were hungry. So Anna found some left over soup and some kasha (corn meal) for them. They ate it on the spot then turned silently and disappeared into the bush.

It had been a relatively mild winter, so much so that established farmers were in their fields preparing the soil and seeding by early April. Andriy returned a week or so after Petro with the bag of grain seed. Yuriy wanted to get seed into the ground as soon as possible. Anna was happy to have Andriy back, but was even happier to have real chai – a luxury she cherished. Dariya loved the red ribbon and insisted on wearing it in her hair daily, despite Anna's sharp words about saving it to wear to church.

Toward the end of the previous century there had been a few Ukrainian Catholic priests from the United States, who had visited the various Ukrainian settlements in the Canadian West but these visits had been few and far between. Then in 1902, Metropolitan Andrey Sheptytsky of Lviv, who at that time was not allowed to travel abroad, sent Rev. Basil Zholdak to Canada. He brought with him three Basilian Fathers and four Sister Servants of Mary Immaculate (SSMI). These few Ukrainian Catholic Religious were soon joined by Belgian-born, Roman Rite, Redemptorist Fathers, headed by Rev. Achille Delaere and a few French-Canadian priests. These priests learned the Ukrainian language and customs and were permitted to celebrate the Divine Liturgy in the Eastern Byzantine Rite, as well as to baptize, marry, and bury members of their Ukrainian Catholic flock. The non-Ukrainian clergy sacrificed much to gain the trust and respect of their new parishioners. While very much needed, this small contingent was still insufficient to serve the needs of the growing Ukrainian Catholic communities spreading far and wide across the Canadian West.

A number of Ukrainian Greek Catholic Churches had been established in the area east and south of Rosthern since 1902 but only one of these was a reasonable distance from Yuriy's homestead. The family would leave on Saturday evening, walking to their nearest neighbour's homestead, spend the night there and then travel together very early in the morning to the church. The Divine Liturgy, if a priest were present, would last all morning. Then the families would gather in front of the church and share a picnic lunch. If the weather was inclement, the people would even eat in the church itself. It was harder, sometimes impossible, to get to the church during the winter months. Even in summer, there was not always a priest available every Sunday to conduct the Divine Liturgy in the little church. If there was no priest, the small group of worshippers would sing the parts of the Liturgy, which were usually sung by the diak or cantor. The people came as often as they could, with or without a priest, to pray together as a community. For the most part, the faithful had to be content to pray on their own or in groups and only occasionally with the luxury of the services of a priest.

The Ukrainian Greek Catholics, who at this time were still underserved by their own priests, at times relied on French, Roman Catholic priests, who served their own near-by parishes. Despite an inherent distrust of the Roman Rite, born of centuries of attempted conversion by Polish overlords in the old country, out of necessity and genuine Christian love there grew a bond between some French priests and Ukrainian Catholic settlers. Some of the frontier French priests had learned the Ukrainian language and the customs of the Eastern Catholic Rite. And so it was that in the absence of Ukrainian Catholic Priests many settlers sought French Priests to administer to their religious needs.

There were more new settlers arriving in the region at an increasing pace. The little settlement nearest Anna and Yuriy's homestead was growing and many more homesteads were being established around the settlement. When the Martiniuk family went to the little church they often met new arrivals. Anna always wanted to know where the newcomers had lived in the old country and was thrilled when she heard they had come from or near her own village. When that happened she entreated the new arrivals to tell her everything they could about the home they had recently left.

One such family was the Ciones. They had arrived the previous fall and had lived in the settlement with another family during the winter. Ivan and Maria Cione had four fine sons, who would no doubt be a big help in establishing a homestead. Maria was pregnant and was hoping for a daughter. Anna told her that when the time came, she would be happy to help with the birth. Anna had been called upon to help a few women give birth in the year since she had arrived in Canada and was gaining a reputation in the surrounding community for her skills and healing knowledge.

Both Anna and Yuriy, on learning of the Cione family, could not help but miss the sons who had not accompanied them to Canada - Mykola and Mykhaylo who had stayed in the old country and Taras who had gone to Argentina. Yuriy in particular felt the loss of the sons from whom he had been separated.

Other families had arrived from villages and towns a little further away from their home village but Anna still wanted to know everything they could tell her about the land of her birth. She had met a woman from one of those neighbouring, old-country towns one day when she had accompanied Yuriy to town. It seemed the family had no intention of homesteading. It may have been because they had only three daughters or perhaps the husband planned to start a business in town. Even after a lengthy conversation, Anna came away without a clear idea of the family's plans.

"Oh well," she thought to herself, "not everyone wants to share family information. I never used to be so nosey; I guess a year in this new country has changed me! Here it seems everyone knows everything about everyone else. I guess it's because we all rely on each other so much."

But there was something slightly unsettling about this new family. Anna couldn't quite put her finger on just why she had not felt particularly comfortable after her first interaction with Mrs. Bastiuk.

On the homestead, Anna and Dariya planted the hardier vegetables in early May and the seeds for more delicate plants a week or so later. Then they carried water from the slough to water the garden plot. Soon small plants began to poke through the earth. Anna had always loved gardening and Dariya was beginning to see it as more than just a chore.

Once the initial 'field' had been planted, Yuriy and the boys set to clearing bush and breaking more land – these occupations would consume their time and energy for the better part of the summer until it was time to harvest their first, small crop. The only two other accomplishments of that summer were the construction of a small lean-to against the original hut for Anna's chickens, as well as a small cow shed a few hundred feet away from the hut for the newly acquired cow.

As the spring turned to summer, Anna took Dariya into the bush, which virtually surrounded their little 'yard'. She had noted the trees and bushes, which had bloomed in early spring and now went in search of their bounty. Early in the summer, the tiny wild strawberries began to appear, then in early July she found Saskatoon berries and a bit later pin cherries. As autumn approached Anna and Dariya picked mushrooms, hazel nuts, and chokecherries. Anna was always on the look out for healing plants and was beginning to build a store of dried herbs, which she kept in a cupboard built by Yuriy specifically for that purpose. She found native willow bark and chamomile, of course, which grew in abundance but she also found Seneca root. This was a valuable commodity. The roots were dug, washed, and dried in the sun, then sent with Yuriy to town where they could be sold for cash. Anna was very proud of her contribution to the family's funds.

Dariya was always recruited to accompany her mother into the bush and the prairie meadows in search of nuts, berries, bark, roots, and herbs. At first, she saw these forays as a lark and only half-heartedly looked for the things her mother directed her to find. But as the summer wore on, Dariya began to develop an interest in the plants her mother was gathering.

"And what is this one for, Mama?" she would ask.

Anna was always glad to share her knowledge with her young daughter. She knew that healing knowledge was a great asset at the best of times but in this wilderness it was a necessity.

The early warm spring weather had continued with only a few mild frosts and good rainfall throughout May. The unusually warm summer temperatures and breezy conditions were perfect for the field and garden, alike. By late August, the grain in the field was ready to harvest and the garden harvesting and processing was beginning to slow down. There had been some issues with gophers and cutworms in both the field and garden but the mosquitoes hadn't been too bad and, thankfully, there had not been many grasshoppers either, so the crops were good. The fields planted early that year had had the prefect growing conditions, so they ripened early and produced good yields.

The good crops meant there was a need for extra labourers to help bring in the harvest – young men and boys arrived from the east by train to help the established local farmers. Yuriy and his boys took advantage of this need for harvest labour and worked for several farmers in the region, earning some much-needed cash. If the boys could earn as much during the following winter as they had the previous winter, Yuriy hoped by spring he would have enough saved to buy a team of oxen.

This first gentle winter and summer had been a relatively easy transition for the family and they were all growing to appreciate their new home. Even Anna thought less of the home she had left behind.

Then earlier than expected the bitter, cold, biting winds and heavy snowfalls of the winter of 1906-7 set in. This would prove to be one of the most severe winters on the Canadian prairies. It was a winter that would live on in memory and myth for generations.

"How could this winter be so different from last? I don't remember ever being this cold before. Everything is so cold that it creaks – including me! I must be cheerful, because Mama is not. She has been whispering under her breath about how much she misses our old home. Tato just ignores her but I know he is worried. Sometimes, I think he believes he made a mistake to bring us here. I know it will be all right. Tato always makes things work out. But it is so cold!"

Ukraine, 1907

After his return from the army, Mykola had worked with Uncle Vasyl through the summer of 1905 and had married Nadya in the spring of the following year.

In the early spring of 1907 the rhythm of life in the little hut and in the village on the tributary of the Dniester continued as it had for millennia. Nadya had given birth to a son, who was named Anton for her father. Uncle Vasyl was almost as delighted with the baby as were Mykola and Nadya.

Late in the prior year another birth had taken place in the family. Mykhaylo and Larysa had had a son as well. His name was Volodymyr, after his maternal grandfather. Mykhaylo had not turned out to be the husband Larysa had expected. He had worked half-heartedly with her father, who had tried very hard to train his son-in-law to one day take over the large land holding. Unfortunately, Mykhaylo was more interested in being the heir to the holding than in learning how to operate it successfully. As the years since their marriage worn on, Mykhaylo had spent less and less time with Larysa's father during the day and after the first year of their marriage, less and less time with Larysa as well. It seemed Mykhaylo had developed a weakness for drink. This was a serious disappointment to the father and a source of frustration and embarrassment to the daughter. So it was, as if by divine intervention, that Larysa had conceived and bore a son. The son was destined to be the one and only, truly wonderful result of the marriage.

During the winter of 1906-7 word had finally come from Taras in Argentina. Mykola was overjoyed to hear from his brother. He was enthralled by the description his brother gave about his plan to create a tea plantation out of the rain forest! That really did sound like one of Taras' schemes. Mykola was glad Taras had found a business partner in Ivan and the letter contained another, most amazing surprise! Mykola quickly wrote a letter to Tato and sent the two letters together to Yuriy in Canada.

The next fall, Uncle Vasyl had a serious discussion with Mykola. Perhaps he was feeling guilty about his promise to Mykhaylo regarding inheritance of one fifth of the original family farm. Perhaps he realized that as Mykola's family grew, the farm would not be large enough to sustain them. Perhaps he knew the money he had so carefully saved might be put to better use than simply being hidden away. At any rate he had no intention of spending it all. It was important to always have a bit put away for difficult times. But Uncle Vasyl believed a portion of his savings would be best spent on a bit more land. And so it was that Uncle Vasyl and Mykola discussed the possibility of buying a small, thin plot, almost adjacent to their existing land. The owner was leaving for Canada and was anxious to sell. Mykola wasn't sure they should be spending Uncle Vasyl's savings to increase their small holding but if that was what his uncle wanted, Mykola was willing to help him farm it. And so the little farm grew to be just over eight morgs in size, about twelve and a half acres. It would mean more work, but also the possibility of more surpluses, which could be sold to buy other necessities. Mykola was grateful his uncle was such a prudent and careful businessman.

5 LIFE GOES ON

Ukraine

One warm evening in early spring after Nadya had taken little Anton to bed, Mykola and Uncle Vasyl were sitting on a bench in front of the house enjoying the sunset. Uncle Vasyl turned to Mykola and said, "Are you sure you don't want to follow your brother to Argentina or the rest of the family to Canada?"

"I am sure," Mykola replied, "everything I need to be happy is right here in this house, in this village. God has truly blessed me."

"Well," said Uncle Vasyl, "if you ever change your mind, I want you to know that even after buying the new field, I still have a little money saved and it is yours to do with as you will. Between that and the price you could get for the land and house, it would be enough to take your family to the new world."

Mykola was grateful for Uncle Vasyl's generosity, but had made a commitment to stay and farm with his uncle.

"Dyakuyu, (Thank you). If I ever need your money," Mykola replied, "I will not hesitate to ask for it. But for now let's just enjoy what we have."

Mykola's long journey to return home after his military service had made him eager to be settled and he was very happy to be settled on the land of his forefathers, living a life that had changed very little for generations.

In a little while, just after the sun had set, Nadya came out to join the two men. Uncle Vasyl stayed for a few minutes and then discretely left the young couple to enjoy the gentle spring evening alone together.

The garden would be coming up soon. Uncle Vasyl and Mykola had almost finished planting the grain in the fields. Little Anton was learning to walk and getting into everything. He was a real little boy and Mykola was so proud of him.

They had seen Mykhaylo and Larysa with little Volodymyr in church on Sundays but had not had much interaction with them beyond that. Mykola hoped that now their sons were getting a little older, the two toddlers could get to know each other and grow up as brothers.

Mykola missed his brothers, especially Taras. They had always been so close. Now the void in his life, resulting from the absence of his beloved brother, was filled by Nadya and little Anton. But he still missed Taras – especially all his imaginative schemes and plans!

Before long it would be time to cut hay for the cow and then to pick the cherries to dry for the winter. Nadya would be kept busy weeding the garden and all too soon, harvesting the produce to prepare and store for the winter. Mykola loved spring when everything was growing and full of promise.

Spring turned to summer and then an early fall came upon the village. The seasons were shifting once more. Mykola noticed Uncle Vasyl was slowing down. He wondered how his father was doing with the heavy farm labour that the new land demanded.

One season followed the next. Nadya gave birth to a daughter, Dora, in the spring of 1908 and another son, Taras, in the fall of 1910. The little hut was full of noise and commotion but both Mykola and Uncle Vasyl loved every shriek, every giggle, and every wail.

The fall harvest of 1911 was hard on Uncle Vasyl. He was only fifty-four years old but he had been bothered by arthritis of late. His hands were gnarled and painful to the point that he had stopped carving. Nadya had treated his hands with herbs and wrapped them in soft warm cloths but the relief was only temporary. That winter, arthritis had settled into his hips and back. He stayed in bed on the worst days and sat in the sun on the bench in front of the house on the better days. He always brightened whenever one or more of the children came running over to him.

Then in the heart of that winter Uncle Vasyl fell ill. At first it seemed to be just a cold. But then the symptoms intensified and soon it was clear he was very sick indeed. One night Uncle Vasyl called Mykola to his bedside.

"Remember I told you I have some savings?" Uncle Vasyl asked.

Mykola nodded solemnly.

"In the attic, in a box, under the extra bedding," was all Uncle Vasyl could say before a fit of coughing made it impossible for him to go on.

That night as Mykola sat by Uncle Vasyl's side, holding his hand and praying with his beloved Uncle, the man who had been a second father to him quietly breathed his last.

Mykola mourned his Uncle's death. He called Father Mykhaylo to arrange for the prayers and funeral. He wrote letters to his father and his brother, Taras, to tell them about Uncle Vasyl's death. He was surprised by Mykhaylo's reaction to the news. It seemed that when their father was leaving for Canada, Uncle Vasyl had bought Tato's part of the family farm and the house. Mykhaylo had been upset at the prospect of losing his inheritance - a fifth of his father's property. To satisfy Mykhaylo, Uncle Vasyl had promised him one of the five morgs of the total, original family farm instead of a fifth of his father's half share, which would have been the inheritance from their father. Not satisfied with what he had been promised, Mykhaylo now wanted to claim one fifth of the newly expanded farm, including the strip of land Uncle Vasyl had bought in 1907.

Mykola had not known of the prior arrangement but he took the news in stride. He agreed to cede one morg of the original farmland, but was adamant that the new field was not a part of the prior agreement. This became a permanent wedge between the brothers. What had especially bothered Mykola was that Mykhaylo had been more interested in his inheritance than in his uncle's passing. He wondered why with so much land he would inherit from his father-in-law, Mykhaylo was at all interested in inheriting the tiny portion of Uncle Vasyl's land.

When Mykola finally remembered Uncle Vasyl's savings and searched for it he was surprised at how much money there was, even after the purchase to increase the size of the farm. He was tempted to approach Mykhaylo to buy back the morg of Uncle Vasyl's land. However, when he discussed this idea with Nadya, she cautioned against the plan.

"If Mykhaylo learns Uncle Vasyl left you some money as well as the new field, he will want part of it as well. Better to save it. We might need it some day. In the meantime we can manage."

After Uncle Vasyl died the tiny house seemed a little less cheerful. Mykola missed his uncle. So did Nadya and the children. It was over a year before the pain of their loss began to fade a little. In the summer of 1912 Nadya again gave birth, this time to a fine, healthy boy. Mykola and Nadya looked at their new son and without any discussion both agreed he should be called Vasyl. And so it was that with the birth of this new son, slowly the rhythms of daily life returned. The children were growing up. Anton was five; little Dora, the apple of her father's eye, was three; Taras was one; and then there was baby Vasyli. It was a busy, joyful home and Mykola never let a day go by without thanking God for all he had been given.

Argentina

Taras and Ivan were able to obtain two adjacent plots of land on a tributary, actually an arroyo or stream, of the great Parana River, over one hundred and fifty miles northeast of the frontier post of Posadas. It took two days by river steamer to reach their land from the post. The little party had to take everything they would need with them, since it would be a long time before they would be back to Posadas for supplies.

Their land was part of the Interior Atlantic Forest, which is the natural habitat of the wild yerba plant. The Guaranis had picked the leaves of the wild plants to make their daily brew for centuries. The Spanish had found the production of yerba to be a source of wealth in this region and its production had been regulated by seasonal royal grants. Eventually the Jesuit missionaries of colonial times had domesticated the plant and developed huge plantations to allow for export of the material throughout the region, as well as to the old world. With the expulsion of the Jesuits in the 1770's, the secret of domestication of the plant was all but lost, although a few, small farmers continued to harvest and process the wild plants for local use and for export.

After the War of the Triple Alliance in 1870, most of the yerba mate-producing regions were in Brazil and Paraguay. The only Argentine areas suitable for this crop were in the provinces of Misiones and Corrientes. Because Argentina did not wish to depend on importing yerba from Brazil and Paraguay, its production became not only an important commodity but also an issue of national economic security. As the Argentine demand grew, over harvesting of the wild groves led to degradation of the natural plants. New germination techniques were developed to secure the production of the important crop. This was the birth of the modern yerba plantations.

At the end of the nineteenth and beginning of the twentieth centuries the Argentine government provided subsidies for the development of large yerba plantations, imposed tariffs on imported material to protect the local growers, and encouraged colonization of government lands by immigrant 'colonos', who were to plant yerba on at least a portion of the land they farmed.

The land in this region was covered with sub-tropical trees and shrubs. Some of the larger trees, notably of the laurel family, could be used for lumber for building and as an initial cash crop. Other indigenous plants included those of the legume family, important for nutritious seeds and nitrogen production in the soil; latex bearing plants, which could be exploited for their sap; and citrus plants, which could provide valuable, edible fruits. In order to prepare the land for planting yerba, it was first cleared of the forest growth then the unusable remnants were burned and finally the rich, reddish-brown soil was tilled in preparation for planting. Along with yerba, sugar cane and tobacco were planted, as more immediate crops, since it would be several years before the yerba could be harvested.

The yerbateros (cultivators) harvested the berries of the yerba plant, the Ilex paraguariensis, from January till April when these matured to a deep purple colour. The berries were then soaked for several hours and the pulp removed from the seeds. The seeds were planted in germination boxes. After seventy to one hundred and twenty days, the seeds germinated and after a year the seedlings were transplanted into the field, approximately three meters apart, with a shade over the seedlings to prevent them from drying out. It was important to keep the seedlings watered and weeded to allow them to grow, consequently the growing of yerba was very labour-intensive.

After three to four years the leaves were ready to harvest. The shrubs reached maturity after about five years. Most shrubs lived for decades, but produced fewer and fewer leaves after reaching maturity. The plants were either male or female. The female plants produced a milder flavor and less caffeine than the male plants, but were less prevalent. The branches and leaves were harvested and dried in a secadero (dryer) with hot air produced by a wood fire and then milled to produce the vegetable matter (yerba canchado). This was then aged for six to twelve months before it was re-milled for brewing into a 'tea' for consumption.

Ivan and Taras built a single, modest building on stilts, which served as their first communal home. It had two adjoining rooms. Ivan and Esperanza slept in one room and the second room served as both the gathering room and a makeshift bedroom for Taras and Esperanza's father. The cooking was done outdoors where Ivan and Taras had constructed a traditional peitch in the style they were used to from their homeland.

For this venture to succeed everyone had to work very hard. Esperanza cooked the meals, cared for their house and clothing, planted and tended a small vegetable garden, collected food from the abundant forest, and helped clear the land and plant crops in the field. Taras and Ivan worked their combined plots of land together as the start of a single plantation. They worked hard from sun up to sun down to make the rich, red soil bear fruit.

This was an economic boom time for Argentina. The country had natural resources and agricultural products for a ready global market. The natural transportation system of inland waterways combined with the rapidly expanding rail system facilitated the transport of goods to the large Argentine ports and thence to the world. The rapidly growing population, thanks to immigration from Europe, provided a ready work force. Foreign investment, largely from Great Britain, encouraged the development of industry and railways. The advent of refrigeration allowed for Argentine beef to become a major export, along with grain from the vast Pampas.

This was indeed a golden age for Argentina. It was a good time for two ambitious, hard-working, young men to establish themselves.

As the land of their plantation was gradually cleared and more and more crops were planted, it became important to attract additional labourers. Here Esperanza's father was invaluable. He recruited descendants of the indigenous peoples, who lived in the region, to work on the plantation. He also contacted workers he had known during his days as a peon on the estancia of the English Patron in the south. Many of them were willing to throw in their lot with the two, young yerbateros, who were developing a large yerba plantation.

When Taras first arrived at the arroyo flowing past their land, he had been overwhelmed by homesickness – the location reminded him of his home in the old country. Not that there was anything in this new land - its soil, vegetation, or climate – which was at all like the village he had left behind. It was simply the fact that his new home would be located on a tributary of a mighty river. During the exhausting days of the first years of establishing the plantation, time slipped away. Taras wrote once to his father, detailing the nature and location of their land and their plans. The letter sat on a shelf above his bed awaiting the opportunity to be sent first to Posadas and then onward. It wasn't until some time after it had been written that Taras realized he had neglected to send his letter.

The occasion, which brought the letter once more to mind, was a life-changing event. Along with several peons, who had migrated north from the southern estancia, came a few women. One of these was a young girl, the daughter of one of the labourers. Her name was Carmen Garcia. She was a shy girl with huge brown eyes and beautiful, long, dark hair. The first time Taras saw her with her mother and father as they were disembarking from the riverboat, he couldn't get her out of his mind. She had captivated him body and soul before he had even spoken to her.

Taras could not contain himself. He spoke to Ivan about his overwhelming attraction to Carmen. Ivan was cautious and implored his friend to be cautious as well. Carmen was only fourteen years old. Ivan was concerned her father would not want her to marry at so young an age. Furthermore, Ivan did not want her father to think he had to agree to a marriage because Taras was one of the landowners.

Taras listened to Ivan's counsel but he was adamant that he would marry Carmen – sooner or later.

Taras spoke as often as he could with Carmen's parents. He was friendly to Carmen but he took his time. He wanted her to get to know him. He wanted her to like him. After an infrequent trip to Posadas to refurbish supplies – a trip that saw Taras much too preoccupied to remember to take the long-forgotten letter to his father – he returned with small presents for the women of the plantation. He believed the women were key to the success of their enterprise, as they were the heart of each small family unit of workers.

The present Taras brought for Carmen was a length of beautiful, brightly-coloured cloth, imported from a foreign land. It was a substantial gift. This gift drew the attention of Carmen's father. He approached Taras and asked why such an extravagant gift had been given to his daughter. Taras had to admit he had fallen in love with Carmen and hoped to marry her one day. The father did not respond. He bowed deferentially to the landowner and returned, in silence, to his hut.

Taras was in agony. He was sure he had damaged his chances of obtaining the father's blessing to marry young Carmen.

So it was a huge surprise and relief when Taras found Carmen and her family at his door the next morning. It seemed Carmen had grown fond of Taras as well and when her father told her of the landowner's desire, she had surprised him by telling him just how much she had hoped this might be. The father was willing to oblige his daughter. And so it was that Taras was betrothed to Carmen. It was this event that made Taras remember the long-forgotten letter to his father. It had been over two years since the letter had been originally written. Now Taras added several paragraphs, first describing the growing plantation and finally announcing his betrothal to Carmen. He ended the letter by begging his father's blessing on his upcoming marriage and forgiveness for the long-overdue letter. And then, in his exhilarated mood, Taras decided to travel once more to Posadas in order to mail the letter to his old home, the little village where the two streams joined to form a tributary of the mighty Dniester River.

By 1902 the Ukrainian Greek Catholic settlers in Misiones had joined with the Polish Roman Catholics to build a shared church in Azara. The Immaculate Conception Greek Catholic Church was not built until 1911, so in the spring of 1906 it was to the 'shared' church that Taras took his intended to be married. Taras was twenty-five and Carmen was fifteen.

Taras built a fine home for his new wife, just across the compound from the original two-roomed hut, which he had shared with Ivan and Esperanza when they first arrived. Ivan also had built a new home for his growing family. In addition to his father-in-law, Esperanza had given birth to a fine son a year after they had arrived at the settlement and was now pregnant again. Taras had continued to live alone in the original hut until just before his marriage.

Business was good. The little plantation was growing both in size and in population. Ivan and Taras bought more land adjacent to their original plots whenever they had available cash from the profits of the farm. As the plantation grew, the need for more labourers increased and more were recruited to join the enterprise. Unlike many plantation patrons, Ivan and Taras treated their labourers fairly, paid them in cash, and even shared the profits of the plantation with them, according to their contributions. This was highly unusual, as at the time, the norm was for patrons to hire itinerant, indigenous Guarani labourers, called Mensu, not for cash but for private bonds, which could only be used to purchase necessities at over-priced plantation stores. This was a system of labour bondage and was brutally enforced by armed guards, who prevented escape and, by the law, returned escaped labourers to their patron. Because Taras and Ivan were more humane in their dealings with labourers on their plantation they were able to establish a loyal and dedicated work force, which contributed to the success of the plantation.

Another key to their early success was that Ivan and Taras decided to ensure their plantation would not only grow and harvest the yerba but also dry, mill, and age it. Their aim was to have a self-sufficient operation, which would control their crop from planting to distribution. This would avoid the large operations springing up to service small farmers, paying lower prices for the unprocessed raw yerbe (hoja verde) and reaping huge benefits on the backs of the small producers.

The optimism and joy of the growing plantation was reflected in the happy family life Taras and Carmen had established in the little hut. There was much rejoicing when, in the fall of 1907, Carmen gave birth to their first son. Taras had wanted to name the boy after his beloved father, Yuriy, but Carmen had a hard time pronouncing the foreign-sounding name. After much discussion, the young parents agreed to call the boy Jorge, which is the Spanish equivalent. Taras was happy that they had come to this compromise but he sometimes caught himself referring to the baby as Yuriy – much to the amusement of Carmen who enjoyed teasing him about such slips.

"The poor boy will not know what his name is if you insist on calling him that," for she still had difficulty pronouncing the name in Ukrainian. And then the two young parents would laugh as Taras made a great show of practicing to call the baby 'Jorge'. As the child grew into a toddler Taras was still having trouble remembering to call the boy by the Spanish name and over time began using the nickname 'Yory'. The nickname stuck and soon everyone called him Yory.

Two years after the arrival of their first son, a second son arrived, who they named Nicolao after the favourite brother, Mykola, who Taras had been inseparable from as a boy. In the growing family tradition of giving their sons nicknames, this son would be referred to as 'Myko'.

And now a couple of years later Carmen was pregnant again. Taras smiled to himself as he thought of his own boyhood, growing up in a large family of brothers. Would this next child also be a boy? If so he wanted to call him Guillermo, in honor of his beloved Uncle Vasyl. But of course a daughter would be very welcome, as well. Taras had missed his mother greatly and was determined that if his family were graced with a girl, she would be called Kateryna.

In 1911, the Greek Catholic Church, Iglesia la Immaculada Concepcion, was built in Azara and this became the church Ivan and Taras took their families to, whenever it was possible. It was in this church, as well, that their children were baptized, confirmed, and received their first holy communion, as well as where the families celebrated the holy feasts of Christmas and Easter.

Argentina, as a nation, continued to prosper and began moving toward a democratic society. All Argentine men - that is all Argentine-born, working, and middle-class men - were granted suffrage by the Saenz Pena laws of 1912, which made voting compulsory and secret. Aspiring foreigners were not yet granted such rights. But none-the-less, it was easy to be optimistic and happy in these boom years, especially for two young people such as Taras and Carmen, who were so much in love and working together to make their dreams come true.

Canada

Winter came early in 1906 and it lasted a long, long time. It was a bitterly cold winter. Yuriy had wanted the boys to go to Prince Albert to find work in a bush camp. Petro didn't want to go back to working for their neighbour as he had in the previous winter and Andriy really wanted to return to Saskatoon. In the end, Yuriy agreed they might have a better chance of finding work in the city – Saskatoon had been incorporated as a city earlier that year and there was a lot of work needed to develop the electrical and sewage systems and the water works. Hence there would be plenty of jobs. Now that the full force of winter was upon them, Yuriy was glad his sons were not in a bush camp in the north.

Andriy and Petro had walked along the railroad track to Saskatoon, as soon as the early harvests were completed and before the cold, early winter had set in. This was a stroke of double luck for them. First, it made their journey more bearable and second, they arrived in the new city before many of the other men from the farms. As a result, they had no trouble finding employment. The two brothers got jobs working on the water works. This meant digging deep ditches into which the lead pipes were laid. It was hard work. Moreover, it was outdoor work in that bitterly cold winter. They lived in a bunkhouse near the river, where the water treatment plant would eventually stand. Every morning they were fed a hot breakfast and taken by horse-drawn wagon to where they would work for the day. At mid-day, they were brought food, often sandwiches and hot soup. At the end of the day they were taken back to the bunkhouse for supper. Some of the men spent their evenings playing cards, singing, playing instruments, and telling stories. Some spent their earnings on cigarettes and liquor, although they were not supposed to have liquor in the bunkhouses. Andriy spent his evenings writing poetry. He had wanted to visit the Chang brothers and his old friend, Bill, but the workdays were long and exhausting. The thought of venturing out at night filled him with dread, especially in the cold, blustery weather.

The men did not work on Sundays. Many spent the day sleeping or in their customary evening pursuits. Andriy and Petro were used to going to church whenever possible on Sundays and Holy Days. In the city, the brothers would hear from others of their faith if and when there would be a priest in the community to conduct the Divine Liturgy. This would often take place in someone's home, where the visiting priest was staying. It would be another six years before the first organizing meeting for the formation of the Greek Catholic Parish of St. George would be held and not until 1917 before the first church would be bought for the fledgling parish.

The long cold winter wore on and the brothers worked through it with determination, sustained by the belief that all of this would someday be worth the effort.

Back on the homestead it was very cold in the little hut. Even with the peitch burning day and night, the door and window covered in heavy blankets, and the inhabitants dressed in as many layers of clothing as they could find, it was never truly warm that winter. When the early killing frosts and snow falls started, Anna was worried she had not completed her winter food preparations for her family. Some of the root crops had not even been harvested. On the first day that it was possible to get back into the garden, she brushed away the snow and dug. The potatoes and carrots might still be all right but they would have to be eaten soon – they would not last the winter. The garlic and beets, if properly dried might be all right as well. The onions however were lost. All Anna had of them were the ones she had pulled to thin the plants, having dried them earlier in the fall. Thankfully she had made the cabbage into sauerkraut just before the freeze. It was possible that Yuriy would not be able to make a fall trip to town for winter supplies. She took stock of her pantry. There was still some flour and some grain, which she could grind into flour if need be. She had corn meal; lard rendered from a pig they had butchered with their neighbours just the prior week and salt pork from the same pig. And then there was the cow – how grateful she was that they had her – with luck, they would have milk, cream, butter, and cheese all winter. And the chickens too – they should continue to lay all winter, provided they could be kept warm and fed. Of other supplies - salt, sugar, and tea - there was little. They would have to make do. With this in mind Anna began to ration the foodstuffs they had on hand. The meals she prepared were adequate, but just, and nothing was wasted. She had known lean years in the old country and she was determined her family would not starve in this new country.

Just after Christmas Yuriy fell ill. It was just a cold but he was miserable. Anna did what she could to ease his discomfort. She knew the best thing for him was rest so she insisted he remain in bed. Therefore, Anna had the full responsibility for the house, as well as the cow and chickens. This was not new to her but she hated going out in the blustery winter to feed and milk the cow. Thank God the chickens were closer in the little lean-to against the hut. Yuriy had relieved her of these duties when the weather had turned cold but now he must rest and she must do what was necessary.

One very cold day, a huge blizzard developed. Anna insisted both Yuriy and Dariya stay in bed while she stoked the fire in the peitch and prepared hot food and drink. Then she prepared to go out into the blizzard to tend to her cow. She could not see the cow shed – just a few hundred feet from the hut. She was afraid she might not be able to get to the shed and if she did, she might not be able to find her way back to the hut. She decided to tie a rope to the door of the hut. Then she bundled up in Yuriy's big buffalo robe and took the other end of the rope. She headed in the direction of the cow shed, but after battling the wind and stinging snow for what seemed like a very long time, she had not yet reached it.

"I must have wandered in the wrong direction," she thought.

So she began walking in another direction and then another, changing her course each time by just a few degrees. She was sure she was far enough from the house so she would have to find the shed sooner or later. She was getting very cold. Her hands were beginning to slip on the rope. She knew she could not loose a grip of the rope or she would be lost. She could see absolutely nothing but the blinding white of swirling snow. Anna was not one to give up but that day she had to admit she could not find the cowshed in the storm. Grateful for the rope, she struggled back to the hut.

Inside she found Dariya anxiously waiting for her. Anna removed the great buffalo robe and her half frozen shoes and babushka (scarf). The rest of her clothing would become wet as soon as it warmed in the hut, so that too would have to be removed. She asked Dariya to fill the kettle with water from the snow barrel. The barrel was placed by the peitch and filled with snow to melt for their water supply in winter. Anna then stripped off her clothing and wrapped herself in a pyryna. She had Dariya pour the warmed water into a tub to soak her feet.

"That was very dangerous," Anna thought to herself. "But as soon as the blizzard lets up I must try again to get to the cow shed." The very thought of going outside again made her shiver.

"Are you all right Mama," Dariya anxiously asked. She had been very worried about her mother, who had been gone a long time in the whiteness that engulfed their little hut.

"I'll be all right," Anna responded but she wasn't so sure herself.

Yuriy had slept through the entire ordeal and Anna decided it would be best not to tell him every detail.

The blizzard blew all day and all night and all the next day. She was worried about the cow in the shed – no food or water and in desperate need of being milked. Finally, on the third day the storm let up. By this time, Yuriy was feeling a bit better. He dressed and went out to see the cow. She would survive but there would be no more milk this winter.

Anna felt guilty that she had not been able to get to the cow during the storm but Yuriy did not place any blame on her. He knew Anna had done all that she could. Even if he had been well, he could not have done better. When he finally heard the story of Anna struggling against the storm with a rope tied to the door of the hut, he was so proud of how ingenious she had been. He would not have thought of or bothered with a rope and he might not have survived.

Through the rest of the long, dark, cold winter, Anna kept her thoughts to herself. Her experience in the blizzard had re-enforced her homesickness and her longing for her old home but she no longer vocalized these thoughts. Since they had arrived in this new land she had been quick to comment on whatever was not as good here as it had been at 'home'. In spring she lamented that she could not run barefoot under the cherry trees and watch the petals of their blossoms floating on the air. In summer she pined for the rich dark soil of the garden she had left behind. It would be years before her garden patch here was as fertile, despite the manure and rotted leaves she continued to work into it. In autumn she missed the shimmering reflection of the yellow leaves along the banks of the two streams flowing through the village. In winter … in winter she longed to be warm, the way she had been in their little house in the old country. Such thoughts still filled her mind and deepened her sense of loss for her homeland but she no longer spoke these longings aloud.

Yuriy noted the change in his wife and was worried. He knew she had not wished to travel to this new land and did not like being here. He himself had often wondered if he had made the right decision. His sons, Mykola and Taras, who had been inseparable most of their lives - not only would he never see them again but they would not likely ever see each other. Perhaps it was all because he had wanted to leave. But no, Taras would likely have gone regardless. Mykola and Mykhaylo - surely it was all his fault then that these two sons were to be forever separated from the rest of the family. So much sorrow he had caused. Would it ever be worth it?

Finally. Finally spring came. It was a painfully slow spring and after the long, bitterly cold winter, it was much anticipated. The boys returned from the city. Their earnings were even better than Yuriy had hoped for. They could buy the oxen this spring. As soon as it was possible, the three men set off for the settlement, which had grown tremendously. They came home with all the necessary supplies in a cart drawn by a team of oxen, along with a used plough and a rifle. Yuriy had never felt so rich in all his life.

That spring, planting the fields they had broken in the past, was delayed by inclement weather. The late start to the spring would result in a poor crop that year. However, with the oxen it was now possible to clear and work much more land far more easily. It was still hard work but at least it felt as though they were truly making progress. Next year, Yuriy would have to report on the progress they had made in the first three years on the homestead. He was now confident they would meet the conditions necessary to retain ownership of the land.

During the summer of 1907 each of Yuriy's boys claimed a homestead of a quarter section of land adjacent to the original homestead. Petro, who was twenty years old, decided he would continue to live in the little hut with his family until some of his land had been cleared but Andriy, at the age of twenty-two, built himself a dug-out hut, covered with logs and sod. There he lived throughout the rest of the summer and fall, while working with his father and brother on all three homesteads.

Petro had become quite a good shot with the rifle. He had taught himself the skill by shooting gophers and rabbits, which had threatened the crops and garden. And so it fell to him to hunt ducks, geese, and even the occasional deer, to supplement the family larder.

The following winter, Petro decided to continue to stay with the family, as he could make a much-needed contribution to their food supply by hunting. Andriy went back to the city to spend another winter working. This time he was able to get a job as a clerk in a store. The city was growing and there were people moving in every day. As a result, there was a need for many more shops to supply the new settlers. Andriy, who was becoming fluent in several languages, was a real asset to the storekeeper who hired him. And for his part Andriy was grateful not to have to work outside that winter.

That winter was not nearly as severe as the previous one had been. Andriy had more time to himself because of the shorter workday in the store. As a result, he was finally able to reconnect with his old friends from two winters previous.

Andriy first went to see 'Sam' Chang at the little restaurant across from the roundhouse. The restaurant hadn't changed much except that 'Tom' was no longer there – he had finally saved enough money to return to his beloved China. 'Sam' was happy to see Andriy and the two men drank chai and told each other all about what had happened since they had last seen one another. Andriy enjoyed talking with 'Sam' so much that he often went to the restaurant that winter, sometimes for a meal, but often just for a visit.

Andriy, the consummate student, loved to hear about 'Sam's' homeland, his experiences travelling and living in Canada and all the adventures, which filled his days as he worked the little restaurant. 'Sam', for his part, appreciated Andriy's intelligence and gentle nature. He had met many people throughout his lifetime but Andriy was one of a kind, a valued friend.

Andriy also called on his old friend, Bill. 'Sam' had told Andriy that Bill was still living in the same house so one Sunday afternoon, Andriy set off to pay him a visit. Bill was delighted to see Andriy.

"So how is the aspiring poet?" Bill asked when he met him at the door.

"I am well," Andriy responded "and I have some new poems ... in English."

"Wonderful!" Bill exclaimed, "Let's have a cup of tea and hear them."

So the two men drank tea and talked about what had happened to them since they had last met. Bill told Andriy the much-needed university had finally been established in the city the prior spring. He had taken a position at the newly created University of Saskatchewan, teaching English Literature and Poetry. After getting caught up, Bill asked Andriy to share his poems.

Bill was as astounded as he had been when he had first learned of the young man's talent for poetry. The crisp neatness and use of language characterizing Andriy's creations were remarkable. Once more, Bill tried to persuade Andriy to become a scholar rather than a farmer.

"Cannot I be both?" Andriy asked. And then he told Bill about the homestead he had taken adjacent to his father and brother's land. Bill understood Andriy's family commitments but he wanted to do whatever he could to encourage the young man to continue to develop his poetic talent.

Andriy's winter in the city was one of the most pleasant he had spent, due in large part to his two, old friends.

In the spring of 1908 Yuriy was required to appear before a Commissioner of Oaths in Prince Albert, to provide a sworn statement of his application for a homestead patent. This legal process was a bit daunting for him as it was for many of the immigrant farmers. On the advice of his neighbor, Yuriy hired a local lawyer to help him with the process. It was advisable since Yuriy did not speak English and it was likely the Commissioner would not speak Ukrainian. Because it was a busy time on the farm, neither Andriy nor Petro could be spared to make the trip and the lawyer, who spoke several languages, would be there to help Yuriy as he had assisted many of the farmers in the region with homestead patents and other legal issues.

The oxen could not be spared for the journey so Yuriy borrowed a neighbour's horse and buggy. The lawyer met Yuriy on his arrival and took him aside to prepare for his appointment before the Commissioner.

"Now there is nothing to worry about," the lawyer told him, "just tell me about your farm and I'll make a few notes."

So Yuriy told the lawyer the legal description of his homestead, the fact that he had built a home on the land and had resided in that home with his wife, daughter, and sons since the fall of 1905. He detailed the number of acres he had cleared and planted each year and the livestock he owned.

It was evident Yuriy was nervous.

"OK," said the lawyer once he had all the necessary information. "When we go before the Commissioner, I will be acting as your interpreter. Whenever the Commissioner asks you a question just begin to talk very loud and very fast. It doesn't matter what you say; he won't understand you. You can talk about anything you want – even swear if you want to – it doesn't matter. I have all the information and I will tell the Commissioner. It is important that you appear passionate about your farm."

Yuriy was a bit puzzled but he trusted the lawyer, who had been successful for so many of his neighbours.

When the two men were called to face the Commissioner, Yuriy was very nervous. He knew if this interview did not go well he could lose his homestead. He looked at the lawyer, who was shuffling the papers on which he had written his notes. Yuriy took off his cap and bowed his head in a deferential manner. He held his cap with both hands before him. It was all he could do to keep from turning the cap round and round in a gesture, which would have shown how very nervous he was.

Then the Commissioner looked up and asked him a question. It was an easy question. He was being asked his name. This much Yuriy understood of English. He pulled himself up to his full height and proudly stated his name. The clerk wrote something down in a large ledger book. Yuriy looked at the lawyer, who appeared calm and in control.

Next the Commissioner asked a rather long question. Yuriy looked at the lawyer again and saw him nod as if to tell Yuriy to start his answer. Yuriy started speaking quite loudly. He almost forgot how nervous he was as he talked about how much he wanted to keep the land he had worked so long and hard for. After a moment or two, the Lawyer touched Yuriy's arm and then said a few words to the Commissioner. The Commissioner nodded and the clerk wrote down more words in his ledger.

Then the Commissioner asked another long question. Yuriy didn't know what to say this time so he began waving his arms around and then he began cursing. Yuriy didn't curse often but he did know a few choice words. He noticed the slightest hint of a smile on the lawyer's face but this time, the lawyer let Yuriy continue for a bit longer. Then the lawyer nodded to him and Yuriy was silent. The questioning went on like this for about thirty minutes. Yuriy was actually beginning to enjoy himself and it was clear the lawyer was, as well.

Finally the questioning was over. The Commissioner asked the clerk to read back what he had written. The Commissioner looked thoughtful. Yuriy held his breath. Then the Commissioner said one word, 'Approved'. Yuriy was instructed to make his mark next to the place where the clerk had written his name and it was all over. Yuriy now owned his land!

It wasn't until some time later that Yuriy began to feel foolish about his performance. It came on gradually but eventually Yuriy began to feel embarrassed that due to his lack of understanding and speaking the language of his new country, he had performed for the Commissioner like a trained animal. He didn't blame the lawyer – it had just been his way of doing business and, of course, it had all turned out for the best. But Yuriy felt foolish. He determined there and then to learn to speak English.

Andriy and Petro, of course, had been learning English a bit at a time since they had arrived in Canada. Andriy, thanks to his natural talent for languages and his friend Bill in the city, had become proficient. But up until now Yuriy had thought it wasn't necessary for him to learn a new language. Now he felt differently. He had his sons begin to teach him. At first it was hard to get the words and the pronunciation right. And of course, he felt self-conscious trying to express himself in this new language. But little by little Yuriy began speaking English, first with his sons, then with neighbours, and eventually with anyone he met. It wasn't long before Yuriy could make himself understood in the new language. Anna, on the other hand, thought it was totally unnecessary to learn English and stubbornly never tried to learn even a few words.

Immediately after receiving the patent for his homestead, Yuriy, with the help of the lawyer, applied for his certificate of naturalization. It was a proud day for him when he became a naturalized British Subject in Canada. From that day forward, Yuriy was a very proud Canadian and took his responsibilities and rights as a Canadian Citizen very seriously.

When the time came for Andriy and Petro to appear before the Commissioner for their own applications of homestead patents they did not need the services of the multi-lingual lawyer and spoke for themselves. They too became proud naturalized British Subjects and Canadian Citizens.

Yuriy and his sons worked well together and their labours were rewarded.

Petro married a neighbor girl, Svetlana Moroz, in the fall of 1908. His brother and father had helped him to build a new, wood-framed home on his homestead. It was well known throughout the community that Petro's new wife was very pleased with her new home, for she never lost an opportunity to brag, to anyone who would listen, about it as well as about her husband. This, of course, pleased Petro very much. The boy who had never applied himself over-much, except in hunting, had found his perfect match and had matured into a man, who was proud to be a good farmer and provider for his family.

Andriy had built himself a modest home on his own land, as was required to retain his homestead. His requirements for a home, as it was just for himself, were not great. All he needed was a peaceful place to write his poetry when the daily work of farming was complete. Andriy was perfectly content in his simple abode and his simple, solitary life.

And so once more, Yuriy's little family consisted of just himself, Anna, and Dariya. They too had built a bigger, new home. The new house was built of lumber. It had a lean-to porch and one large room on the ground floor. The room had two glass windows with screens for summer and storm windows for winter. At one end of the room was a wood/coal stove with an oven and reservoir for heating water. At the other end was a table with six chairs. Upstairs were two small bedrooms each with a tiny window. Dariya had never had a room of her own and she was delighted with it!

In the summer of 1909, an amazing story circulated throughout the community. It seemed that three young children, a brother and sister and their cousin, had been tending cows in a pasture on a hill near a small village to the southeast. All three of them had seen a beautiful lady, dressed in blue and white flowing robes just like in the holy pictures. She had smiled at the children, but had not stopped or spoken. She simply walked toward the bushes and disappeared into them.

At first the children were afraid to tell anyone what they had seen. Eventually they could keep the secret no longer and told their parents. The parents were astounded. They didn't know whether or not to believe the children. They questioned the children separately and in detail and then compared the stories. The whole thing may well have been a product of their imaginations. It may have been the result of boredom with herding the cattle or even an attempt to get out of the chore. It might have been a story they had concocted and agreed to tell in order to get attention. But there was something very moving in the sincerity with which the children described the lovely lady. Finally the children were taken to a priest to tell their story. He was skeptical at first but he too was taken with the children's sincerity.

Soon the story was circulating throughout the region. People from the area began to gather in the pasture on the hill to pray. The children still spent much of their time there, tending cows.

The people would ask the children, "What exactly did you see? Where did it happen? What did the Lady look like? Where did she go?" The children always patiently answered all their questions.

Then one day in early autumn, while the children's families were with them in the pasture, the youngest boy suddenly said, "I see a golden cross on a chain on the ground."

"Well, then, pick it up," said his father, who saw nothing on the ground. The young boy stooped and appeared to be picking something up. He held it to his chest and whispered "Dyakuyu, Thank you."

The father was concerned his son was losing his mind.

That night the young boy developed a fever. He was taken ill very suddenly. By morning he was dead.

Whether or not this untimely death was in anyway related to the prior sighting, it served to draw more and more people to the pasture. Soon families were travelling from far and wide to meet on the hill to pray.

At the end of June in the following year, after the crops had been planted, many of the homesteaders took their families to pray on the hill. Eventually a priest from the village near the hill would plan an entire weekend of prayer and the site became important for pilgrimage in the region in years to come.

In 1910, news spread among the homesteaders about a very important visitor who was coming to the region. It was the Servant of God, Metropolitan Andrey Sheptytsky. He would be visiting the Church of the Assumption of the Blessed Virgin Mary four miles northwest of the town of Alvena. The small log church, which had been constructed in 1905, might have been selected for the visit because it was situated nearly in the middle of the Ukrainian bloc settlement of the region. The trip from

Yuriy's homestead would be about nine miles, a whole day of travel by Oxen and cart. But the excitement growing in the community was destined to overwhelm the obstacle of distance. By this time Yuriy had obtained his own team and wagon and so there was no excuse. The family would make the trek. They would attend the Divine Liturgy performed by the great man from their homeland. They would hear all he had to tell them about the old country they had left behind and what he had seen on his long journey across their new country.

Soon after the trip to see the Metropolitan, Yuriy decided it was time to replace the oxen with horses. Oxen were best for the business of hauling heavy loads of wood for building and for breaking brush and removing tree stumps but they were slower than horses. With a team and wagon, the family could travel further in a shorter time. So with the new team, one spring after the seeding was completed, he decided to take his family to the pilgrimage hill to the southeast. This would become a tradition in his family for many years to come.

Yuriy was beginning to feel his age. It was in the summer of 1912 that Andriy had read him Mykola's letter about Uncle Vasyl's death. When they had parted, Yuriy knew he would not likely see his brother again, but death made that a certainty. The brothers would not be together again in this life and it filled Yuriy's heart with sorrow.

Yuriy was filled with the knowledge that his days, too, were numbered. He knew his sons, here in Canada, would be fine. They could continue to work all three homesteads without his help. But he was worried about Dariya. True, she was young but soon she would have to marry. He hated the idea of losing her but he knew she would have to find her own life, sooner or later, and he hoped she would marry before he died. His younger brother's death had created a sense of urgency to have Dariya settled.

Lesya

Lesya Bastiuk was the middle of three daughters. Her father had been disappointed when the eldest daughter had been born. He had hoped a son would eventually become indispensible to his father-in-law on the farm and in due course the farm would then pass into his own hands. When the second daughter had been born, the father gave up on this plan for his future fortunes and lost all interest in the family. Any future children, if they were to come, could not re-kindle his interest. Lesya's mother had recognized the change in her husband at the birth of their second daughter and had, in the depths of her heart, blamed the child for the change. A third and final daughter had been born almost completely unnoticed by the distant father.

Lesya's older sister, Petrusia, ruled the roost and her younger sister, Marusia, followed wherever Petrusia led.

Lesya had always felt she was different and that she existed on the distant edge of her family circle. For a long time she had tried to fit in, tried to be like her mother and sisters, but no matter how hard she tried the fact remained - she was different. She was different in ways she could not help or change.

Although the differentness went much deeper than physical appearance, even physically there was no question Lesya was, indeed, different. Where her sisters were big girls, tall, large-boned, with large, round faces, Lesya was short, slight, and small boned. These physical differences were reinforced by the dispositions of the three girls. Where her sisters were loud, self-assured, and self-centered, Lesya was quiet and introverted. From her earliest days, she had felt not only different, but also unwanted and insecure. Her early attempts to be more like her sisters had not helped and in some cases had even made matters worse. Petrusia especially recognized the insincerity of the behavior and rather than being flattered that her sister was trying to emulate her, took Lesya's attempts to be more self-assured as a form of parody or insult. Petrusia's cruel response to Lesya's attempts to fit in made her feel even more isolated and insecure.

Lesya's sisters instinctively hated her for being different and teased her ruthlessly.

"You were left on the door step by Gypsies," they taunted her. She knew this was not true but it hurt none-the-less.

Lesya's mother was very much like her sisters. She was self-centered and not particularly 'motherly'. When Lesya had been quite young she had recognized these qualities in her mother and, in an attempt to shield little Marusia, had tried to be a substitute mother to her. But as time went on it became clear that her efforts were neither effective nor appreciated. Petrusia, jealous of what she perceived to be Lesya's attempt to monopolize the baby of the family, formed an alliance with Marusia. And so it was that the eldest and youngest sisters alternately ignored or tormented the middle one.

Lesya's father was almost a non-entity in the family. He worked only when necessary and then only at part-time jobs for other people. He had acquired the little house in which they lived, across the tracks from the main part of the town, shortly after arriving in Canada and had done absolutely nothing to it ever since. As the years wore on the little house became shabbier and shabbier. Mama showed no more interest in the house than did Tato.

The little house sat on a small lot with a shed at the far end. In between was a large garden. If it had not been for the garden the family might well have starved. While Mama planted the garden each spring it was left to the children to tend it all summer long. Often, Petrusia and Marusia would disappear when their help was needed most. So it usually fell to Lesya to keep the garden free of weeds. Mama did little to process or prepare the garden produce for the winter months, so from an early age Lesya learned from her baba what needed to be done and how to do it.

Baba Ditka lived alone on a farm not far from town. Diedo had died a few years ago but Baba insisted on staying on the farm. Tato had hoped Baba would move into their little house in town and he would take over the farm but Baba would not hear of it. She knew she was much better off hiring help for the farm than turning it over to her son-in-law. He was no farmer. He could no sooner take care of the farm than he could the little house in town, let alone his family.

Baba Ditka, mama's mother, was Lesya's saving grace. She and Diedo had come to Canada before Mama and Tato and had been in Canada for many years.

Lesya looked a lot like Baba Ditka. Baba was a small, wiry woman. Lesya was a lot like Baba in many other ways - they both were willing to do whatever had to be done. When things at home got to be too much for Lesya she would escape to Baba's home. Baba never asked what was troubling the young girl, she would just fix a cup of tea and the two of them would sit quietly and drink it together. Lesya cherished her time with Baba.

Once when Lesya needed new shoes, it was Baba who had given her a pair of her own shoes. Because they both had small feet Baba's shoes almost fit Lesya and were much better than any other shoes she had ever had. Lesya cherished the shoes, not only because they were so fine, but also because they had been a thoughtful gift from her beloved baba.

It was not long after having received the gift of the shoes that Petrusia and Marusia began making fun of the fact that Lesya was wearing Baba's 'old shoes'. They teased Lesya about it but when she didn't react as they had hoped, with shame and anger, they began telling the other children in town about the shoes and where they had come from. Even though most children would have seen a good pair of shoes as a blessing, no matter where they had come from, children can be cruel. As a result it was not long before many of the children of the town took up the taunting and teasing Petrusia and Marusia had instigated. They even began calling Lesya 'Baba Shoes'. Lesya's feelings of isolation and pain increased.

"Is this how it will always be?" she wondered. "Am I really so terrible that I only draw cruel attention?"

She loved her baba and the present of those shoes but she hated being singled out and teased so ruthlessly. One day she decided not to wear the shoes to school. That was a mistake. For when she returned home from school the shoes were gone. Lesya searched everywhere but the shoes were not to be found. Feeling ashamed that she had not worn the shoes and then lost them, she felt very, very low. There was nothing to do but to tell Baba what had happened.

Baba Ditka was a wise woman. She knew all about the teasing that Lesya had endured because of the shoes. She also knew the source of the teasing – Petrusia's jealousy. Baba was not at all surprised that the shoes had disappeared at the first opportunity. It was not Lesya's fault. And so Baba comforted her favorite granddaughter when Lesya came to confess the loss of the shoes. Baba was determined that some day she would give Lesya something, which could not be taken away from her by her overbearing sisters.

Lesya prayed daily that she could be a good person and some day, someone might appreciate who she was and what she had to offer.

When Lesya was twelve years old she was staying for a few days with Baba to help her in the garden. The eldest Cione boy, Stephan, was working as a hired farm hand for Baba at the time. His responsibilities were to feed and water the farm animals and keep Baba's little farmhouse in good repair. He was very good with animals and tools. Baba always said Stephan could fix anything. It was clear Baba liked Stephan.

Stephan was the eldest of the four Cione boys. He had worked hard with his father and brothers to clear the land on their homestead. But he hadn't been very strong as a child and as he grew older, it became clear that his body could not cope with the rigors of farming on the Saskatchewan prairie. From the time he had been a youngster he had been troubled by episodes of aching long bones and painful joints. His mother had tried every thing she could think of and had consulted anyone who had healing knowledge, but nothing seemed to help. As Stephan approached puberty, the pain and swelling of his joints bothered him more and more frequently. And so it was that his younger brothers became the farmers, while Stephan did what he did best. When his health allowed Stephan was responsible for the animals on the family farm and, if anything needed repair, it was Stephan who would do the job.

Because Baba Ditka lived alone on the homestead she and her late husband had established, she had to rely on hired neighbours to help her with the actual farming. During the summer Stephan turned sixteen, Baba had asked him whether he would be willing to work for her, taking care of her cows, horses, chickens, and pigs. Stephan had talked it over with his father and they decided the cash he could earn from Baba Ditka would be a valuable contribution to the family's income. Tato had told Stephan that if he found the job too difficult, he must tell Baba Ditka he had to quit and return to his family's farm. Stephan was determined he would keep the job with Baba Ditka.

And so it was that, while Lesya was working with Baba in the garden, she often saw Stephan as he went about his chores. She knew Stephan, of course, from church and school. But he was four years older and she had never paid much attention to him.

Stephan knew the Bastiuk girls from school. He didn't much care for the eldest and youngest but the middle girl was different. He knew she worked hard and her home life was not pleasant. Stephan did not like to see anyone or anything suffer. His own pain had taught him to be compassionate and empathetic.

As Stephan worked, he had the habit of stopping occasionally to consider what he had done and how best to proceed. He was a careful worker. At these times he would take a small, round, white peppermint candy out of his pocket and pop it into his mouth as he considered his work. Lesya had seen him do this many times. She had only ever had one candy in her entire life and she was fascinated by the fact that this boy had a pocket full of them.

Stephan noticed Lesya watching him one day as he was repairing the back door from Baba's kitchen to her garden. He asked Lesya what she thought of his work. She replied that it looked as though he might be finished soon.

"Not too soon," he said, "I still have a pocket full of peppermints so the work can't be finished before they are gone."

Lesya thought this a funny response. She wondered if he was teasing her but if he was, she didn't quite understand whether or not she was being laughed at or what the comment really meant. She wanted a peppermint but she was not about to ask him for one.

A few days later, after having helped Baba with the work she had been asked to do, Lesya returned to her family in town.

Lesya didn't think about Stephan Cione for a long time afterwards.

Stephan had all but forgotten the shy, little girl, who had watched him working and eating peppermints at Baba Ditka's. Lesya too had had little time to think of the young man, who had worked for Baba because his health did not allow him to be a farmer like his brothers.

It had happened as a result of meeting at a dance in the town hall. Stephan noticed Lesya sitting with other girls her age, on a bench along the long wall of the hall. She was very petite and looked younger than her age. She wasn't a striking beauty but there was something about her. She listened to her companions, nodding and encouraging them to continue talking. She was not distracted by the boys and men standing at the back of the hall. She was not trying to get the attention of someone who might ask her to dance. There was a 'solidness' about her - a sense of caring for others - that attracted him. At first he hadn't recognized her, so he had asked one of the other fellows who she was.

"Why that's the Bastiuk girl – you know, the nice one!" his companion responded. Stephan immediately remembered spending a few summer days in her company at Baba Ditka's.

And so Stephan bolstered his courage and walked over to Lesya and asked her to dance. She didn't hesitate or act surprised or gush and make a scene, but simply smiled and rose to her feet. This girl didn't play the flirting games most girls did. An offer to dance was just that and she was happy to oblige. Stephan liked that.

They danced an old-time waltz and seemed to move quite well together. Stephan had always liked music – he had a wonderful, deep singing voice - so when his body allowed it he was a natural on the dance floor. After the first dance in the traditional set of three, Stephan took Lesya's hand and they walked slowly around the hall, as did the other dance couples. Stephan struggled to find something to say to Lesya but it was she who spoke first.

"Are you farming with your brothers?" she asked.

"No," Stephan replied, "I have a job at the hardware store here in town."

"Do you like the work?" Lesya asked.

She was so easy to talk to! Soon the band started to play again and the two began a lively foxtrot.

As time passed after the dance, Stephan made it his business to meet Lesya on the street or in a shop. He wanted to spend time with her. One day she smiled as she saw him coming toward her.

"Isn't life funny," she said. "When I was twelve I would have followed you around for a peppermint candy and now you seem to want to follow me."

They both laughed. And as time passed they found they had much in common. Both had felt like outsiders, she because of the way her sisters excluded and tormented her and he because of the episodes of ill health, which had prevented him from full-time farming with his father and brothers.

It was by no means a surprise to many of the town's people that Stephan Cione and Lesya Bastiuk should marry. However, Lesya's father was less than impressed with her choice. Surprisingly he had something to say on the matter.

"How will he keep you? He can't even work full time. And besides he will never inherit his father's land – that will go to his brothers. Couldn't you marry one of them?"

Lesya's mother had never spent much time thinking of her middle daughter but when she heard of the planned marriage to the 'invalid', her response was typical.

"You can't get married before your older sister. She will look like an old maid. You must wait."

Of course Lesya had no intention of marrying someone else or waiting to marry Stephan. She was in love and she knew that, despite the difficulties they would no doubt encounter, she could be happy with him as with no other. At last she would have a chance at happiness.

Baba Ditka had always favoured Lesya, much to the chagrin of her daughter and other two granddaughters. She also had been fond of Stephan. She thought it was a good match and she supported it. Luckily, neither Tato nor Mama cared enough to actually try to prevent Lesya from marrying Stephan.

Stephan's parents had always worried about what would become of him and how he might support himself. They were concerned it would be difficult for him to support a wife and family. But they had always loved him and had supported him through his bouts of illness as well as periods of relative health. They were happy that he had found someone to love and she, indeed, loved him. They decided they would have to do what they could to help the young couple.

And so it was on a bright, sunny day in early May of 1913, that Stephan and Lesya were married after the Divine Liturgy. Stephan was twenty-two and Lesya was eighteen. At the end of the Divine Liturgy, Father led the congregation in singing the time-honoured song, 'Mnohaya Lita' (Many Years) to bless and wish good fortune for the young couple. No one sang with more gusto than Baba Ditka and Mrs. Cione.

The Ciones had invited the town's people to their farm for a celebration. Of course everyone who could attended. There was food and drink and a wooden platform had been built to serve as a dance floor. Some of the guests noted that it was usually the bride's family who hosted the wedding celebration. But then again no one was surprised that the Bastiuk's had not even offered to help. The Bastiuk's, of course, took great pride in being the bride's family and full advantage of the Cione's hospitality. Mr. Bastiuk, it was said, had enjoyed the refreshments so much that early in the evening he had disappeared – no doubt to sleep it off.

The day had been perfect as far as Lesya was concerned. The only shadow, which had briefly crossed her sunny day had been the ugly comments of her older sister. Petrusia had not been pleased that Lesya had married before her. She had made her feelings about the inadequate match known throughout the community. She was jealous and vindictive. But for her the final straw had been Baba giving Lesya her strand of coral beads – the ones she had worn when she had married Diedo in the old country. Petrusia, as the eldest granddaughter, of course, considered these should have been saved for her on her own wedding day. She considered this no less than a betrayal by her baba and the probable reason for Lesya rushing to marrying before her – and to an invalid, no less.

Pavlo

Pavlo had worked for one winter in Winnipeg but he didn't like the city. He had heard some people from his home village in the old country had travelled through Winnipeg on their way to Saskatchewan and had settled north of Saskatoon. So he decided he would go there too. He had been homesick and thought if he lived among people from his home village it might help.

Pavlo had learned, the hard way, about 'riding the rails' so it had been easy for him to get from Winnipeg to Saskatoon and then to the northerly communities. He found employment with one of the farmers, who had come from his home village, and settled into life on a homestead. He lived, worked, ate, and went to church with this family for several years.

Pavlo began to dream of a homestead of his own. Although he had listed 'farmer' as his occupation when he landed in Canada, his only farm experience in the old country had been tending geese and taking care of Father Mykhaylo's horse. Over the past few years with the settler family, he had learned a great deal more about farming and decided he enjoyed the work and lifestyle.

One day in church Pavlo noticed a young girl. She wasn't like the other girls who giggled behind their hands and shot him admiring glances. No this girl was prim and proper. Her father, Pavlo noted, was quite a bit older than her mother. It appeared the young girl lived alone with her parents. She was reserved, perhaps a bit shy, and very pretty. Pavlo especially noted her grey eyes and slim figure.

After returning to the farm that day, Pavlo asked his employer who the young girl was. "You mean old Yuriy Martiniuk's girl?" the farmer replied. "Her name is Dariya and she is but thirteen or fourteen years old. She is much too young for you to be thinking about. Besides, I thought you wanted your own farm. You will need a strong, sturdy girl for a wife to help you on a farm."

Pavlo was not deterred. He resolved to marry Dariya.

Pavlo began by looking for a homestead. The farm he had been working on was some seven miles from the church but in the opposite direction of old Yuriy Martiniuk's homestead. It would be a bit far from her family but perhaps she wouldn't mind too much, he thought. But when he began to inquire about available homesteads in the area, he was very disappointed.

Many, many people had moved into the region in the last several years and the only available homesteads were quite distant from the church, the Martiniuk's farm, and the farm he was working on. The closest available homestead was over fifteen miles to the southeast. Pavlo looked at the land. It was hilly and had a lot of bush. The soil was not bad but there were a lot of rocks. He knew enough about farming by now to know it would be a challenge to make a go of it on this homestead. Worst of all, he didn't know anyone in the small farming community near the homestead. He wasn't sure what Dariya would make of all this but he decided he had to make a start.

So Pavlo left his former employer's farm very early in spring and claimed his own homestead. He began to clear the land where he planned to build a house. He helped seed a neighbor's crop and, in return, after seeding was complete the neighbor helped him clear more land.

Then Pavlo prepared to build a small rectangular house. He had felled some black poplar and white aspen trees of moderate size when he was clearing the land. He had put these aside to season. By fall he was ready to dress the logs and use them to build his house.

And then the most amazing thing happened. The fall had been long and gentle so most farmers in the area had completed their harvest. As a result, when they heard that the quiet, young man who was homesteading about two miles from the hamlet was preparing to build a house, all the neighbours gathered to help him!

Within a few days, the walls were up and plastered and the roof thatched. Pavlo couldn't believe his luck. He was eternally grateful to his new neighbours.

At that time there wasn't yet a church in the vicinity, so the farmers had come together to talk about constructing one. Pavlo attended the meeting. It seemed the biggest obstacle was a plot of land to build on. After a moment's thought Pavlo suggested the corner of his new homestead on the road and closest to the hamlet. His neighbours were astounded at his generosity but in Pavlo's mind, it was only right, since they had all helped him.

And so it was that the neighbours got together once more to build a church. Someone donated lumber, someone else donated whitewash, and others donated money to buy a bell, etc. Before long, the community had a modest, wood-framed church. The next thing was to find a priest who would serve their church.

Pavlo again volunteered to see if he could do anything to help. There was a rail line running through the hamlet and on to a larger community to the north. Pavlo took the train to visit the priest who served that church and several surrounding churches. Unfortunately, when Pavlo arrived he learned he had just missed the priest, who was heading for another church that Sunday. When Pavlo heard where the priest was headed he thought it must be fate. The church to which the priest had gone was none other than the church attended by the Martiniuk family.

Pavlo managed to get to the church in time for the Divine Liturgy. It was good to be back among the people he had lived with for several years. Afterwards he approached the priest with his request. At first the priest was dismissive.

"Where would you have me conduct the Divine Liturgy, in a barn?" the priest demanded.

"No, no, your reverence," Pavlo said with humility – he had long known how to address a reverend priest! "We have built a small church. It sits on my own homestead not two miles from the hamlet. A train comes through the hamlet on Friday and again on Monday. I, myself, would pick you up on Friday of the weeks when you could conduct services in our church. You could stay in my humble home or of one of my neighbours'. I would then return you to the train station to take you back home on Monday."

"You have thought this through," was all the priest said. "Let me think about it."

The priest admired the young farmer but there was more to having a church than simply having a building. So the priest wrote to Bishop Nykyta Budka in Winnipeg to seek his council.

When, as a result of Metropolitan Andrey Sheptytsky's visit to Canada, Bishop Budka was appointed as the first Canadian Ukrainian Catholic

Bishop in 1912, the clergy of the Ukrainian Catholic Church consisted of five Basilian priests, seven diocesan, four Belgian-born Redemptorists, and five bi-ritual French Canadian priests, as well as four tiny communities of Sister Servants of Mary Immaculate. This handful of religious had been looking after the spiritual needs of the Ukrainian homesteaders, who were scattered over thousands of square miles, from Winnipeg to Edmonton and beyond. In 1913, when the new bishop received his Dominion Diocesan Charter, he took responsibility for over eighty parishes in Western Canada.

So it was within this context that the new bishop greeted the request of Pavlo's community. He insisted the priest who had made the request add the new parish to the list of parishes he was already serving. The bishop himself would visit the church to consecrate it and give it a name. And thus the church of Saint Nicholas was founded.

The next spring Pavlo worked diligently to plant his first crop. It wasn't large because he had only cleared a small field. Because of his faith and the role he had played in building a church and getting a priest to come at least once a month in summer and at least once during the winter, his neighbours were happy to help him again after their own fields were planted. Pavlo was becoming a member of the community and he was very proud.

So it was with renewed confidence that Pavlo once more made the train journey to attend the church where the Martiniuk's worshiped. He then asked his former employer to accompany him to the Martiniuk farm after the Divine Liturgy.

Yuriy was surprised to see this young man coming to visit him. He had known of Pavlo from his time working in the area but had not known him personally. However Yuriy did know the farmer who had employed Pavlo and now accompanied him.

The farmer spoke to Yuriy telling him about how Pavlo had obtained his own homestead, built a modest house, cleared some land, and had planted his first crop. Then he told of Pavlo's role in building a church on land he had donated and getting a priest to serve the church. By now Yuriy was very much impressed. Finally the farmer vouched for Pavlo's work ethic and character. And then Pavlo, himself, asked Yuriy for the hand of his only daughter. Anna had been listening to all this and couldn't help but gasp at the thought of losing her daughter. One look from Yuriy and she made not another sound.

"I must think about this," was all Yuriy said. "Please come back again after the next Divine Liturgy in our church and we will talk further."

Dariya had been out of doors that afternoon so she had not seen the visitors nor suspected anything about their visit. When she returned home the visitors were gone. Yuriy took her aside and told her what had transpired. At the age of fifteen, Dariya was still very much a girl and had not thought much of marriage. She knew her father worried about what would happed to her after he died but she had always assumed Andriy would move in to take care of her and Mama when the time came. Petro had married a neighbor girl five years before and had a growing family of his own but Andriy, it seemed, might remain a bachelor farmer.

Dariya was filled with mixed emotions. She was flattered that someone wanted to marry her, to be sure, but she was not prepared to leave her home and family.

"I will not force this marriage upon you," Yuriy said gently, "but you must consider it - seriously - the young man deserves that consideration."

"But Tato, I don't even know who he is!" Dariya exclaimed.

"Of course," Yuriy consoled her. And then he told her of the young man's work on the neighbour's farm, of how he had seen her in church over a year ago, how he had taken a homestead, built a house, donated land for a church, helped obtain the services of a priest for the church, and planted his first crop. All of these things were in his favour. But for the first time in her life, Dariya was actually frightened.

That night Dariya hardly slept. She turned over in her mind all that her father had told her. She knew Pavlo would be coming back in a few weeks and she wanted desperately to have a decision made by then … but she couldn't imagine making a decision before even seeing him!

She knew her mother was desperate to talk to her about the offer of marriage but Dariya also knew that her mother would be opposed to it, simply because she did not want to lose her daughter. Anna had grown to depend on her daughter's help in the garden, around the house, and on their foraging excursions for herbs, nuts, and berries. Speaking to her mother about this decision would not provide anything new to think about. Besides, she had to make this decision on her own.

Anna was hurt that Dariya avoided talking with her about the marriage proposal. She felt if her daughter left her it would be a very personal slight.

Dariya spent many nights thinking more and sleeping less. Finally, the Sunday of the priest's next visit to their church arrived. Dariya dressed with special care. She still didn't know what she wanted to do but she did want to look her best to meet this young man who might become her husband.

When Dariya saw Pavlo she remembered him from prior Sundays. He was not exceptional in looks, rather short and perhaps a bit stout. But he had a nice smile and his eyes lit up when he smiled at her. Perhaps…

Once again, Pavlo came with his former employer to the Martiniuk home. This time neither father nor daughter was not caught off guard. Pavlo spoke gently and reassuringly to both Yuriy and Dariya. He told her of his good neighbours and how everyone in that community worked together – while this was not unusual in and of itself, the way Pavlo told of it showed how much he appreciated and valued such neighbours.

Pavlo returned several more times that winter to visit the Martiniuks. Perhaps it was his persistence, or perhaps his gentle way, or perhaps Dariya saw in him some of the caring Pavlo had always shown to those he loved. At any rate by spring she had decided.

And so one day in spring, Pavlo brought a thin, gold ring to Dariya. She was to keep it safe until they could have banns read in the church and then be married. It was such a lovely thing. Dariya had not seen anything as beautiful and it would be hers to wear for the rest of her life! One day, she decided to wear the ring, just to see what it would be like. She put it on and admired it. Then some chore took her mind away and before she knew it, the band was gone!

Dariya was frantic. She searched the house and then the yard. She retraced her steps. She prayed to St. Anthony to help her find the lost ring. She dared not tell her mother or father. She was terrified Pavlo would no longer want to marry such a careless girl! And he was coming later that week. What would she do? What could she do?

When Pavlo arrived Dariya asked if they could walk together out toward the field as she had something she had to tell him. Anna and Yuriy looked at one another questioningly. Both had noticed how distracted Dariya had been of late and they wondered what had been bothering their daughter. Secretly, Anna hoped Dariya had changed her mind and was telling Pavlo she couldn't leave her family to marry him. The same thought had crossed Yuriy's mind and he hoped his daughter would not go back on her word after all that had passed between her and the young man over the winter.

As soon as they were out of earshot of her parents, Dariya confessed her grave sin to Pavlo. He was silent. She had seen the disappointment in his eyes – that look of disappointment would haunt her for the rest of her life. Then he took her hand. He knew she was still very much a girl, despite being almost sixteen years of age. He could see she had suffered enormously over the loss of the ring. He didn't want her to suffer any more. So he simply said "Don't worry, it will be all right."

"I don't need a ring," she responded. "We can get married without a ring."

"No," Pavlo said softly, "you must have a ring to marry me."

For a split second Dariya expected the worst. She had lost his ring and now he no longer wished to marry her. Pavlo saw it all in her eyes and quickly reassured her, "I will get you another ring you don't even have to tell anyone about the first one. It will be our secret."

Whatever Dariya had felt for Pavlo before that moment - fondness, admiration, respect - now she knew she loved him and always would.

Early in the spring of 1914, Dariya and Pavlo were married in the church where he had first seen her. She was almost sixteen and he was twenty-six.

Dariya had proudly worn the coral necklace her father had given her on the morning of her wedding day. The necklace had belonged to Yuriy's beloved first wife, Kateryna, and he was glad he had brought it to Canada so Dariya could now wear it. Anna had been surprised by the gift. She had not known Yuriy had the necklace all this time. She was hurt he had saved it for Dariya rather than giving it to her. Anna had never owned a coral necklace of her own since her father had been very poor. Her first husband might have bought her coral beads but he had died young. It seemed to Anna that after all she had done for Yuriy, not the least of which had been coming to this God-forsaken land, he should have given her the necklace. It added to Anna's despair over losing her daughter and made it a very difficult day for her.

After the wedding party at the Martiniuk's homestead, Pavlo took his new bride back to his own homestead. Dariya had never seen it before. Her first impression was how very far away from her parents it was, for she knew she would miss them dearly. But Pavlo was with her and he would make everything right just as Tato had always done.

That first evening in the little house on the homestead, just after they had turned down the coal oil lamp and gotten into bed, there was an amazing racket outside their door. It was the sound of banging on pots and pans, whistles blowing, stomping, and yelling. Dariya was frightened out of her wits!

Pavlo went to the door and there, in the moonlight, were his neighbours! They had come to 'shiveree' the young couple. Of course the neighbours had to be invited in to meet his bride. Dariya was overwhelmed by the welcome but wished it had been at a more appropriate time of day.

Dariya had grown up in a quiet home. Her aging father was quiet. Her mother was increasingly quiet since that terrible winter of 1906. Her brothers were living in their own homes on their farms. It had been a very quiet household. Now Dariya was faced with rowdy neighbours and a husband who seemed to welcome all their noise. She wasn't sure she could get used to this.

"A wife. I am a wife!" It was hard to believe. She now had a husband and her own home. "What a strange and wonderful life this is." She thought of her childhood in the far away village. She thought of the years since they had arrived in Canada – all the hard work and how much they had accomplished. "And now it is my turn – no, our turn - my husband and I will now have to make a life for ourselves." It was exciting and daunting all at once.

6 THE GREAT WAR

Ukraine

Change was coming and it wasn't going to be good. There had been political tensions in the region for generations, notably but not exclusively, between the Austro-Hungarian Empire and the Empire of the Russian Tsar. It came to a head on the 28th of June 1914 in Sarajevo, with the assassination of the Austrian Archduke, Franz Ferdinand. Austria-Hungary declared war on Serbia; Germany fell in line as an ally of the Austrian Emperor. Russia came to the defense of Serbia. In order to pre-empt France joining forces with Russia, Germany attacked Belgium and France. The violation of Belgium's neutrality brought Great Britain into the conflict.

Since the Third Partition of Poland (1795), Ukrainian people had lived in one of two autocratic empires, the Austro-Hungarian in the west and the Russian in the east. In the late summer of 1914 the Western Austrian province of Galicia was on the front line of a war between these two empires.

It was a hot summer day and Mykhaylo was resting in the shade under a tree behind the big house. He had spent the entire morning surveying the crops with his father-in-law and wanted nothing more than a few moments of peace. He never enjoyed these mandatory trips into the fields with Larysa's father but today had been worse than usual. Larysa had been unhappy of late and her father blamed Mykhaylo. He was very harsh and it was clear he expected to see changes in Mykhaylo's behavior.

Mykhaylo sat at the base of a large oak tree; his back slumped against it and his head in his hands. He had a headache. It was as much from the heat of the morning sun as from his father-in-law's words and, of course, it was compounded by a hangover. Mykhaylo had spent the evening before, as he spent most evenings, in the company of friends, drinking until very late. The morning's outing had not been appreciated.

He heard the dog bark and was about to yell at it to be quiet but when he looked up there were two men standing in front of him. They were soldiers. The older of the two was obviously in charge.

"Are you Mykhaylo Martiniuk?" the soldier asked.

"I am," Mykhaylo responded as he slowly got to his feet.

"You will come with us," was the reply.

"But why?" Mykhaylo questioned.

"Your country needs you," was the curt reply.

"You make a mistake," Mykhaylo said. "My father-in-law needs my help. We have just returned from surveying the fields."

"Your father-in-law will have to do without you."

"But I can't be conscripted," Mykhaylo continued, "I have a wife and a son to care for."

"They will have to do without you, as well."

"This isn't right," Mykhaylo continued, "You must be looking for my brother, Mykola. He served in the army. You must want him not me."

The soldier in charge paused for just a second. He turned to his assistant.

"Is there a Mykola Martiniuk on the list?"

"No Sir."

"Find out why."

"Yes, Sir"

"Now come along," he said to Mykhaylo and there was nothing more to be done.

Mykhaylo was taken from his home. He saw Larysa and her father standing just outside the house. He wanted to call out to them to put a stop to this. But they did not come forward to plead his case. Perhaps it was even because of them that he was being taken.

Of course it was not because of Larysa or her father. They had been as surprised by the arrival of the soldiers as Mykhaylo had been. The reason for the conscription was the coming war. Men were being rounded up in the whole village, throughout the countryside, and in all the towns and villages of the empire.

When Mykola heard that his brother had been conscripted he was sure the soldiers would be coming for him next. He tried to prepare Nadya but she was horrified by the prospect of being left alone with the children in a war zone.

In the following days the news of events in the wider world filtered into the village. The empire was on the brink of war. All men were being conscripted into service, young and old, those who had served previously and those who had not. Everyone would be needed.

And yet no one came for Mykola. He wondered why but thanked God daily that he had not been called.

Mykola would have been surprised to learn the reason. When he had finally made his way back home after his required military service, he had stopped at the recruiting office in the town where the tributary met the mighty Dniester. He had given the clerk the letter from his commanding officer recommending discharge. The officer had duly made the entry 'Discharged' next to his name on the roll. Then some time later, word had come to the recruiting office that rebels had destroyed Mykola's unit. Another clerk went through the list of the unit members, marking each as 'Died in the Line of Duty'. It had caused only a passing moment of curiosity that one of the unit members had been marked as 'Discharged' on a date after the demise of the unit but mistakes could happen. And so it was that when the officer's query regarding a 'Mykola Martiniuk' had come, the clerk in the recruiting office sent off a reply that the soldier had died in service. Therefore Mykola no longer existed as far as the Austro-Hungarian military was concerned.

The soldiers came to the village a few more times, looking for additional conscripts. Once they inquired of a neighbor: "Who is the man working the field over there?" referring to Mykola.

"Oh," the neighbor responded, "that's the cripple, Martiniuk" somewhat exaggerating Mykola's condition. For although it was true Mykola had suffered frostbitten toes and fingers on his long trek home after he had completed his required military service, over the years he had learned to cope with the lingering effects of this trauma. He walked with a slight limp and suffered pain and stiffness in his hands and feet but these maladies merely slowed rather than prevented him from doing his daily chores.

The neighbor continued, "He farms his uncle's small plot of land. The uncle died a few years ago. It's a wonder he can manage since he can hardly walk. His feet were damaged when he served in the Emperor's Army."

Mykola was one of the few men remaining in the village after the conscriptions. Because of Nadya's fear that he would be taken, Mykola had agreed not to do anything to draw attention to himself. Everyone in the village knew, of course, that Mykola was still there but they also knew he was slow moving and suffered pain from his previously frostbitten feet. So the villagers were not surprised that Mykola was not conscripted, after all, he had done his military duty. Mykola thanked God every day that he was allowed to remain with his family.

Events moved quickly. By the first of August war had been declared between Austria and Russia. By September the Russian army had swept across much of Galicia. Many prominent Ukrainians, including the Metropolitan Andrey Sheptytsky, were arrested and deported. Retreating Austrian soldiers were ordered to shoot anyone suspected of being pro-Russian. Thousands, many of whom were innocent of the suspected collaboration, were executed or deported.

For a brief period the Tsar's Imperial Army had control of the region and went to work attempting to eradicate the Ukrainian language and the Greek Catholic Religion. Fortunately there had not been enough time to inflict these policies on the insignificant little village before the Austrian army re-captured the area in the following spring.

The little village had long lost any prior prominence it might once have had. In the distant past its advantageous location, where two tributaries joined forces to rush toward the Dniester, had made the village a notable centre of trade. But now that transportation links crisscrossed the landscape and the village had been by-passed by major roads and railroads alike, it was the town on the Dniester that was prominent in the region.

This being said, there was no doubt the entire area was in a war zone. Villages, no matter how out of the way or insignificant, were plundered and burned, their residents displaced, raped, and murdered. Food was in short supply and disease was rampant. Many, many civilians and soldiers alike died.

Mykola's family prayed and put their faith in God to preserve them and, somehow, they survived. Because the weather had been favourable, they had produced a good crop and garden during the summer of 1915 but then almost all of it had been lost to army scouts and scavengers, who had moved through the region. One army or another had consumed everything edible in its path that autumn.

Larysa's father had thought about taking his wife, daughter, and grandson to the city of Stanyslaviv. He wrote to a relative there, but the reply came: "Stay where you are. Travel by train, wagon, or even on foot is very dangerous. There are soldiers everywhere and they don't care who they shoot. There is no food here. No safety. Nothing. Stay put."

And so the family stayed in the little village. The servants and farm labourers drifted away. It didn't matter. There was nothing to tend in the house or the fields. There was nothing to pay them with or to feed them. There was little or nothing for the family to eat either.

Larysa's father, once a proud landowner, thought wryly to himself, "What good is land if you are starving?"

At the first indication of trouble he had bought all the food and supplies he could get his hands on. He had hidden some in the forest on the edge of one of his fields. He had taken anything of value, small enough to hide, and buried it in what he hoped would be a safe spot in the yard under the large oak tree. He had moved his family out of the big house and into one of the labourer's huts. The soldiers came and took everything from the big house that wasn't nailed down. In the next wave of scouts and soldiers, anything edible disappeared. The family huddled together in terror in the hut. When the few foodstuffs Larysa's father had managed to hide and the animals were gone, he went into the forest only to find the stash of food and supplies had been found and taken. There was nothing left to do but scavenge for nuts and roots like everyone else. Soon there was nothing left to scavenge. Larysa's father feared they would all die of starvation.

His wife had given up. She lay motionless day and night on a small cot. One morning she simply didn't wake up. They buried her in the churchyard but there was no way to mark the grave except with a simple wooden cross. If things ever improved he would erect a proper marker over her grave. He wasn't sure it would ever happen.

But as bad as things were, Larysa's father tried to go on for the sake of his daughter and her son.

The winter of 1915-16 had been filled with hunger, fear, and turmoil. 1916 had not been an improvement on the prior year but Mykola's little family was still there, just barely surviving. All around them people were starving, as food supplies dwindled to famine levels. There were political forces from every direction pushing and pulling on the people and everywhere there was conflict. Would there ever be peaceful times again?

One day a stranger appeared in the yard behind the hut, surprising Nadya. He had a gun and was demanding food. She calmly told the children to go inside and then said to the stranger, "We don't have much but what we have we will share. Stay here and I will bring you something."

The man was suspicious but he knew she couldn't get away and he could take her or her children if she didn't do as she had said.

Shortly, Nadya returned with a cup of tea, made from herbs, which grew wild in the ditches; a piece of hard, dry bannock, made from ground weed seeds and a little water; and a bit of wild honey, which almost made the bannock palatable. The man consumed these meager offerings as if he had never seen food before. Nadya apologized for the poor fare but indicated it was all she had. The man nodded as he finished the last lick of honey. Then he rose and nodded to her as if he had been an invited guest. He turned and strode off down the road. Nadya almost collapsed with fear.

Nadya hadn't wanted to tell Mykola about the 'visitor' but, of course, the children were very excited to tell him all about it when he returned. Mykola had gone to the tributary as he had done every day. He had been trying to catch a fish for their supper. It seemed the once plentiful fish had disappeared along with all other sources of food. But today he had been lucky. He had caught one. Not a very large fish but it would provide a bit of protein for the nearly starving family. Mykola watched as the children smacked their lips and wished for more. He had not touched a morsel, although he had insisted Nadya share the delicacy with the children. 'What would become of them?' he wondered.

Early in 1917 the Russian Revolution erupted, adding to the chaos and turmoil. Lenin had been allowed to return, from exile in Switzerland, to Russia via Germany. In return his Bolshevik government pulled out of the war against Germany and gave up much territory along its western borders.

While many in the world thought of the end of the Great War as the signing of the Armistice Agreement on November 11, 1918, conflict in the area surrounding the little village persisted. In October of 1918 there was an attempt to establish an independent Western Ukrainian Republic, including the region. This lead to conflict with the Poles, who also claimed the area. The issue would not be resolved for several more years when Poland and Russia agreed that the region be annexed by Poland, while the eastern part of Ukraine became a Soviet State.

And so after several years of war, its misery, starvation and hardships, the little village was back, politically, where it had been prior to and sometimes during the Austro-Hungarian Empire, with Polish overlords.

Canada

Dariya and Pavlo were married early in the spring of 1914. They worked very hard from sun up to sun down to establish their farm. They spent the spring preparing the fields, which Pavlo had previously cleared, and planting a crop. Then they spent the rest of the summer clearing more land. It was backbreaking work.

Dariya didn't mind the work and she enjoyed married life but she missed her parents, especially her father. One day, an overwhelming sense of homesickness swept over her while she toiled in the field along side Pavlo.

"I'll be right back," she told him as she shuffled off into the bushes. Pavlo assumed she had gone to relieve herself. Dariya sat down on a fallen tree, put her head in her hands, and wept silently. She stayed there for just a few minutes, weeping. Then she thought to herself, "What a foolish woman you are! Yes, you are a woman – a married woman. Now get back there and help your husband!" And so after she had given herself a stern talking to, she got up, wiped her eyes with a corner of her apron, and marched back out into the field.

"Are you alright?" Pavlo asked.

"Dobra, I'm fine," she responded with a forced smile and continued with her labours.

In early summer they heard about the war in Europe. Dariya was worried about her brothers – the ones in Canada and the ones back in the old country. Likewise, Pavlo was worried about his own brothers back in the old country. Since coming to Canada he had not heard much from or about them.

"What would a war in the old country mean – for them and for us here in Canada?" he wondered.

The farmers in town said there was nothing to worry about. "The war effort needs grain," they said, "so the farmers won't have to fight."

Dariya was grateful. She couldn't bear the thought of Pavlo leaving her alone on the farm.

And besides, she thought she might be pregnant. So as news of the war filtered into their little community, Pavlo and Dariya prepared to welcome their first child. Within a year of her marriage Dariya gave birth to a son, Ivan. Both young parents were overjoyed!

On August 4, 1914, when Britain entered the Great War, Canada as a British Dominion was at war as well. The Canadian forces were to be comprised of volunteers. The Militia Act of 1904 limited enlistees to those male inhabitants, who were British Subjects between the ages of eighteen and forty-five and were not exempted or disqualified by law. At that time a large proportion of the Saskatchewan population were 'foreign born' and, on those grounds, may have been exempted. Furthermore the demand for agricultural production, particularly for the war effort, and the urgent need to maintain a work force in that sector resulted in many exemptions for farmers. As the war progressed and the Allied Forces faced devastating losses, the Canadian Military Service Act of 1918 allowed for conscription and the farm labourer exemptions were eliminated.

Among the farmers of the west, who were struggling to establish their farms and a new life, the war might have seemed very far away. The immediate pressures on the pioneer farmers were great just prior to the war. The west was in an economic slump created by low grain prices, difficulties regarding the transportation of grain, and three prior years of drought and crop failures.

Although Yuriy was a very spiritual man and he lived his religion faithfully, he was conflicted by Bishop Budka's pastoral letter, urging Ukrainians in Canada to return to Austria to serve that country in the Great War. The political complexities, which had resulted in the Bishop's urging, were beyond the understanding of many of the immigrant farmers of the time. It might well have surprised them to learn that the Bishop was doing what he believed was necessary to protect the beloved Greek Catholic Church from proselytism by the Russian Orthodox Church.

In Yuriy's case, he thought about his eldest son, who had done his required military duty for the Emperor and, as a result, had missed emigrating with the family. His second son, Taras, had immigrated to Argentina, partly to avoid the required military service. Yuriy himself had emigrated with his remaining sons partially for the same reason. He still had two sons in the old country, who would likely have to fight in this war. That was enough of a contribution from his family. He prayed for their safety every day.

Yuriy held the bishop and all clergy in high regard with respect to issues of the church but he really wondered whether they should become so involved in a worldly issue such as this war. While some of his neighbours agreed with the Bishop, deep in his heart, Yuriy simply could not. He had worked very hard to become a naturalized British Subject and he really did feel he was Canadian. Although he had been born in the old country, he had never felt a strong allegiance to the Austrian Emperor or his empire. If Canada needed his sons to fight in this war, that was one thing, but to return to the old country to fight against his adopted country – that was something else.

Perhaps it was because Yuriy was in his sixties and his sons were required to farm their combined family farm of three-quarter sections of land, or perhaps it was just luck, neither of Yuriy's sons were conscripted. Nor were any of them sent to internment camps during the war. Actually, in their neighbourhood, inhabited almost solely by Ukrainian and French settlers, no one had even heard of such arrests. It was only after the war, when stories of the internment of Ukrainian Canadians reached their community. It was a dark episode in Canada for Ukrainians and non-Ukrainians alike.

"We are Canadians now," Yuriy had said, "we left the old country behind us thanks be to God."

The war years were actually a boon for the farmers of Western Canada. The harvest of 1915 was the best that had ever been recorded in Saskatchewan. There was a huge demand for grain and the ever-increasing farm capacity and production was well timed to meet those needs.

The amazing crop of 1915 was a real boost to Pavlo's little family. Not only did it mean Pavlo, as a farmer, would not likely have to go to war but also the increased yield and price of grain would make life on the farm a little better.

As the years passed and the war continued, some of the young men in town volunteered and later some were conscripted. Their families heard more about the war after that from letters sent by their boys from overseas. It made the whole war seem more real when a neighbor told of his son in the trenches in France. And then there was the news of the young Warona boy who had been killed. Suddenly, the war was very real to everyone in town.

On the farm Pavlo's little family flourished. Baby Ivan grew into a toddler and in 1916, Dariya was again pregnant. The growing family, of course, did not decrease her workload. In addition to the responsibilities of childcare, she continued to toil side-by-side with her husband in the fields. Most days, Dariya was exhausted by the time she could crawl into bed after the supper cleanup, putting the baby to bed, and helping with the evening chores.

But with all the hard work the little farm was flourishing. In 1917, in the face of a potential shortage of grain to meet the needs of the war effort, the price of grain was three times the pre-war level.

Shortly after their second child, Maria, was born, an itinerant worker had arrived at their door. Pavlo was glad to have help with the farm, as Dariya had her hands full with the two children. And so it was that this man came to live with them – sleeping in the barn and working along side Pavlo with the animals and in the fields.

One day Dariya was washing clothes in a tub in the yard. Baby Maria was lying on a blanket near by. Little Ivan was running around the yard playing. At one point he came over to her to have her open a small tin box he had found. She recognized the box – it belonged to the hired hand.

"No," she said, "this is not yours. You cannot have it." And she put the box in the pocket of her apron. The child was not happy to have lost his new toy, but was soon distracted and ran off to play again. After washing the clothing and hanging the laundry on the clothesline to dry, Dariya took the baby into the house to prepare lunch. She hung her apron in the porch and got busy in the kitchen. After awhile, she heard her son come into the porch, but thought nothing of it. When it was time for lunch she called out to her son to come and eat. There was no reply. Curious - she went into the porch. There lay her son, still and lifeless, with the small tin opened in his pudgy little hand. He had opened the tin box and eaten the contents, presumably thinking the little pills were candy. Dariya snatched up the toddler and ran to find Pavlo. It was too late. There was nothing that could be done.

Pavlo was devastated but Dariya was beyond devastation. She blamed herself for not taking better care of her son. She cried day and night for many weeks. She could not take care of her daughter or do any of her usual work. Pavlo asked a neighbor lady to come and help with the baby and the household chores but things did not improve. Eventually, Dariya stopped crying but it was as if she had become a ghost of her former herself. She walked through her life in a daze for weeks on end. Pavlo was very worried about her. He tried to talk to her. He had the priest talk to her. Nothing helped. Nothing changed. Pavlo was worried he had lost her, as well as his son.

Dariya had retreated into herself. She had always had a good imagination and had used it all her life to amuse herself and to help pass the time as she worked. As the days and weeks since the loss of her son drifted by, Dariya began to think of him – what he might have been, what he might have done. In her mind, she created a running story about this lost son, one that she would hold secretly in her heart and mind for the rest of her life. It was perhaps the best therapy for her. It may have been the only way she could learn to cope with the loss. The loss of this first son was very painful and it took a very long time for Dariya to come to terms with it.

One day in the spring, after that long, dark winter and Dariya's long, dark period of mourning, she awoke to a bright sunny day. She hadn't even noticed the weather for months. But on this day she arose, dressed, and announced to Pavlo that she must visit their son's grave. Pavlo did not know what to think of this sudden change in her. He was afraid she had finally lost her mind. He decided it would be best to take Dariya to the grave, so he hitched the horses to the wagon, dropped their little girl off with neighbours, and drove to the graveyard.

The graveyard was on the outskirts of town, some two miles from their farmyard. It was on a small plot of land designated by the municipality to be used by both of the town's churches, the Ukrainian Catholic Church and the French Roman Catholic Church. Dariya had not been to the little grave since the day of the funeral. Pavlo had been there often to pray for the little fellow. As they approached the grave Dariya fell to her knees. She shuffled across the young spring grass on her knees until she reached the grave itself. There she hung her head and prayed. She remained like that for some time. Pavlo was beginning to wonder how he would get her to leave the grave and return home. But then Dariya looked up at him.

"He's with God now," she said.

"Yes," was all Pavlo could manage as he choked back his own tears of grief.

"The sun is so hot on his little grave," Dariya continued. "He needs some shade to protect him."

This statement again sent Pavlo into near panic as he worried over his wife's mental state.

Then Pavlo decided to say a prayer out loud. Dariya joined in. When it was finished Pavlo said, "Time to go home."

And so they returned to the farm. Things began to get a little better after that. Dariya began to take an interest in her daughter. Pavlo was greatly relieved.

A short time later Dariya told Pavlo she wanted to plant some lilac bushes around the little boy's grave. Lilacs had come to be Dariya's favorite flower. She had planted a row of the leafy bushes in front of their home and she relished their sweet perfume, which always seemed to coincide with her birthday in June. Pavlo promised to help her. And so the two young parents took lilac shoots from the bushes, which grew in front of their home, and planted them around the grave to shelter the lost little one. Dariya walked to the graveyard every week to carry pails of water from a nearby slough to encourage the lilac bushes to grow around the little grave. By the next summer it was clear the lilac bushes would form a protective little alcove. Dariya smiled when she thought of it.

In the fall of 1918 the joyous news came that the war was over! The world was filled with great hope for a brighter future … and Dariya was pregnant again. During that winter the child came too soon. It was a boy and it was stillborn. Pavlo was very concerned this set back would put Dariya into depression once again. But she was much stronger this time. She knew that if the babe had not waited to be born at the right time he would not likely have survived. It was hard but not as hard as losing a toddler, who had been healthy and active. She asked the priest if the baby could be buried next to his brother. The priest had been very close to the couple, as he stayed with them every month when he came to the little church on their farm. He knew how hard it had been for them to lose their first son. It wasn't the way of the church to bury an unbaptized baby inside the graveyard but he agreed to bury the little lost soul next to his brother, within the growing alcove of lilac bushes.

Maria, their daughter, was a joy. She had a sunny disposition and reminded her mother so much of herself when she had been a child. Maria loved to help her mother and Dariya loved to have Maria's help. She was actually getting big enough to be of some real help in the garden and in the kitchen. Dariya thanked God daily for her daughter.

While Dariya was grateful for Maria, Pavlo adored her. He loved to take her into the fields and explain to her what he was doing on the farm. And, to his delight, she seemed to enjoy spending time in the fields and the barn as much as she enjoyed helping her mother.

"What a strange world we live in. Lives started and lives lost. Some far away, across the sea, and some right here on our little farm. It really doesn't matter how, whether by accident or in a war, the loss of a child is so very hard. My heart goes out to those mothers, those many, many mothers, who lost sons in the war. Please God, don't let such a terrible thing happen again. Grant those who have died eternal memory, Vichnya Pamyat, grant them eternal memory."

Stephan and Lesya

After their marriage in 1913, Stephan and Lesya had moved into a little house in town not far from Lesya's parents. It hadn't been her choice location but the house was available at a rent they could afford. Stephan had been working in the hardware store for several years now. It was a good fit because he knew everything there was to know about tools and how to use them. Everyone always said that if something could be fixed, Stephan Cione would be the man to do it. Prior to being married, Stephan had lived in a rented room but with a new wife, he had found the little house and arranged to rent it from the day they were married.

Despite the proximity to her parents and sisters, who seemed suddenly to be very interested in her new life, Lesya was very happy in her new home. When they first moved in she spent long hours cleaning the little house from top to bottom. Stephan fixed the broken windows and loose hinges and before long the little house was a cozy home.

Lesya was well aware of the concerns of her parents-in-law, regarding how the young couple would live on Stephan's meager salary. She was determined that together, she and her husband would make their own way in the world. And so she decided to take in laundry and do sewing and mending to contribute to the family income.

Of course, Stephan's parents often brought gifts from the farm. One Sunday they brought a couple of chickens, which delighted the young couple. Stephan immediately built a small coop in the backyard. Another time, Stephan's father stopped by with some meat from a recently butchered cow. These gifts were very much appreciated as the young couple struggled to get on their feet.

The financial struggle increased somewhat when Lesya became pregnant within two years of their marriage. But despite their limited funds the growing little family was very happy. The first child, born in 1915, was a girl, Olena, whom the family always called Lena. She was bright and intelligent and very playful. The young parents doted on her. Within two years their second child, a son, Pylyp, was born. What a delight. Lesya and Stephan could not have been happier.

Lesya and Stephan were members of the local Ukrainian Catholic Parish. There was a fine church in the town with a priest who lived in a small house next to the church. Lesya volunteered to launder and mend the church linens and vestments. It was not a big job but there was no pay and it did take away from other, paying opportunities. Despite this, she was very proud to be able to make a small contribution to the parish. Stephan had a fine, deep singing voice and was one of the members of the church choir. And so the young couple found community in the parish.

As the little family grew, Lesya worked harder and harder to supplement her husband's income. He had shorter periods of good health as the years went by and longer periods of inability to work. The owner of the hardware store knew the family well and always made allowances for Stephan's illness but he could not pay Stephan when he could not work.

Argentina (1914-1918)

There was a war going on but it was far, far away and would have little impact on many of the citizens of Argentina. Falling in line with the stance of most of the Americas (Canada, as a British Dominion, was the exception), Argentina declared itself neutral in the conflict. Even after the United States entered the war, Argentina maintained its neutrality.

The Great War had proved to be a double-edged sword for the Argentine economy. On one hand, since its trading partners were at war, they had a drastically reduced demand for some Argentine imports, while at the same time, those nations decreased production of their exports in favour of manufacturing for the war effort. As a consequence, industries sprang up in Argentina to produce the goods that had traditionally been imported.

Taras first heard about the war during an infrequent trip to Posadas for supplies. He had heard some men talking about the 'world going crazy'. Interested in what had prompted this comment, he bought a newspaper to find out what it was all about. He was amazed to learn that, while he had been completely oblivious to the situation, the German and Austro-Hungarian Empires had declared war on Russia, France, and Britain. And now, it seemed that nearly the entire world was at war, on one side or the other of this conflict.

Taras' first thoughts were of his brother, Mykola, and his family, who still lived in part of the Austro-Hungarian Empire. Had Mykola been conscripted and sent to fight? What about his other brother, Mykhaylo? Was he fighting as well? Then he realized if Canada were in the war, his brothers, Andriy and Petro, could be fighting too. It would be cruel if two of his brothers were fighting for the Central powers and the other two for the Allies. The very thought of it sent a shiver down his spine.

"Dear God," he prayed, "don't let it be so." And that was all he could think to say in his spontaneous and desperate prayer.

In a frantic effort to discover how his family in the old country was faring, Taras delayed his return to the plantation. Instead he wrote a quick, brief letter to Mykola. He wanted to know if they were all right and if there was anything that could be done for them. Taras hoped that if all were well, perhaps now his brother would bring his family to Argentina. Taras had hoped and prayed for that to happen for some time but every time he wrote to his brother to encourage him, the response had been the same, "We are fine where we are." Now Taras just hoped they were still alive and safe.

Taras also sent a brief letter to his father in Canada.

"Are Andriy and Petro still on the farm? Or have they been sent to war? I pray that they are safe and everyone there is well. Please let me know as soon as you can."

After posting the letters Taras asked the postmaster to send word to him on the plantation as soon as a reply appeared. For a small fee the postmaster agreed to send any responses immediately to the plantation.

And then there being nothing more he could do, Taras returned to the safety and serenity of the plantation, the daily cares of his life as a yerbatero, and the joy of his loving wife and growing family.

The initial cash crop of hardwoods, which had been a by-product of clearing the land for the yerba trees, had helped establish the plantation. The ongoing citrus crops supplemented the main yerba production. The market had never been better for the products of the plantation. And how the plantation had grown. There were now over fifty people living and working with Taras and his partner, Ivan.

Taras and Ivan had worked very hard to establish their yerba plantation. As their sons outgrew the limitations of schooling at home, their fathers decided these boys should be sent away to complete their education. It was Ivan who sent first his eldest son and then his second son to live with a family in Posadas, in order to attend school. In 1917, at the age of ten, Yory, too was dispatched.

Yory missed his parents and his home tremendously during the first school term he was away. But he had literally grown up with Ivan's sons, who had been attending the school in Posadas for over a year before Yory's arrival.

The three boys worked diligently at their lessons. With their host families they attended Divine Liturgy at the new Greek Catholic Church, San Vladimiro de Posadas, which had been built in 1916, and soon learned to appreciate town life.

Taras thanked God that he had been guided to this wonderful land of plenty. True, there had been some dissention down in the capital, Buenos Aries. It seemed there were labourers who were fighting for more rights and some of the demonstrations had gotten out of hand. The reports had even called these events 'riots'. But in the peaceful world of the plantation life was good. Taras just wished that he had been more successful in guiding the rest of his family to join him. Every time he thought of them he felt a little guilty that he had not been quick enough to encourage his father to come to Argentina, rather than Canada.

Argentina remained neutral throughout the Great War and had benefited from being able to supply Great Britain and its allies with large volumes of grain and beef. There had been internal pressures for the country to enter the war, both from ethnic groups within the country and from the countries engaged in the war. These pressures increased when the United States entered the war. But Argentina remained neutral.

On one hand this neutrality resulted in profits for the wealthy landowners from exported Argentinian beef and grain. On the other hand, foreign-owned companies re-directed their efforts to operations in their homelands and reduced activities in Argentina. This resulted in Argentinian workers being laid off. Unemployment, a general decline in wages, and a rising cost of living for the Argentinian working class, resulted in a growing demand for labour unions to protect workers' rights. By the last two years of the Great War labour strikes were common in Argentina.

After his initial shock at hearing of the Great War and his immediate concerns for his family, those still in the old country and those in Canada, Taras was very uneasy until, finally, he heard from his father. Andriy had written on behalf of Tato to assure Taras that they were all well and safe. Neither he nor Petro would be conscripted. They were working extra hard on the farm to produce grain for the war effort. The only note of concern in the letter was that they had not heard from Mykola in the old country.

Taras wrote again to his favorite brother, begging him to respond if he was at all able to do so. Then Taras polled all the families he knew, who had immigrated from the same part of the world, in the hopes of gaining any information about how the people there were faring. There was very little to learn. Taras prayed devoutly that his two brothers in the old country were safe. He had a very uneasy feeling every time he thought about them. He knew his father was suffering the same concerns.

It wasn't until early in 1919 that word from Mykola finally came. The war had been horrific. Many, many people from their region had died, if not as a direct result of the fighting then due to starvation. There had been so little to eat that Mykola had thought often about how his family would survive. But survive they did. Taras was overjoyed and relieved to hear all this.

Mykola had no information about their other brother, Mykhaylo. He had been conscripted soon after war had broken out. Neither Mykola nor Mykhaylo's wife, Larysa, had heard a word from him from that day to this. He was most likely dead.

Despite the fact that Taras had never been close to Mykhaylo, he grieved for the loss of a brother and said many prayers for his soul, if indeed he had been lost.

"Now maybe Mykola will come to his senses and join us here in Argentina," Taras hoped.

7 AFTER THE GREAT WAR

Canada

Andriy

The year 1918 saw the end of the Great War and tremendous rejoicing but there were other events that year, which were not as joyful. Fairly early in the growing season on the Saskatchewan prairie, farmers first began to notice rust developing on the wheat in their fields. Some farmers who had seen the devastation of rust in the past, set to cutting their crops down to be made into hay for their animals. Yuriy had never seen rust before. Together with his sons they inspected their crops. There was some evidence of rust but the wheat was growing thick and tall. They just couldn't imagine cutting it down for hay. And so they waited and watched. The rust progressed. Soon it became evident - there would be no crop that year. Sadly they headed into the fields to cut down their crop. The damaged wheat was bundled for feed for the cows. Unfortunately, they had waited too long. The rust-ridden wheat stalks were unpalatable to the cows and they would not eat it. This was a huge economic blow to the family.

Yuriy was very concerned when Petro took a loan from a businessman in town, in order to keep his family through the winter until the next growing season. Yuriy felt he and Anna would be able to manage on the savings he had always kept for such hard times. Andriy decided to return to Saskatoon to work for the winter.

It had been almost ten years since Andriy had last been to the city. He was amazed by the changes he saw on his journey, this time riding the train. Where once there had been a few scattered farm communities and even fewer farm homes among the small, cultivated fields, now there was a small hamlet or town every seven or nine miles along the railway line. The number of farmyards and the number and size of the fields surrounding them had virtually exploded!

And in the city itself – what progress had been made! What had once been the loosely knit amalgamation of three villages now had become a real city, with a teeming down town, full of shops, cafes, multi-story office buildings, and hotels. There were sidewalks, streetlights, and streetcars!

One of the first stops Andriy made was to see his old friend, Bill. They enjoyed an afternoon discussing the city, the University, and Andriy's poetry. Bill told Andriy that their mutual friend, 'Sam' Chang, had finally saved enough to fulfill his lifetime dream of owning a restaurant. Unfortunately the price of properties in the city had risen to such an extent that 'Sam' had had to move to a smaller, nearby town, in order to make his purchase. Andriy was determined he would make the journey to see 'Sam's' restaurant and visit with his old friend.

Bill, as always, was very enthusiastic about Andriy's poetic talents. During the following winter he helped Andriy to submit several of his poems to a regional newspaper for publication. After the first few had been published, Andriy, with Bill's continued help, submitted a proposal for a book of poetry to a publishing company. After submitting samples of his work and waiting impatiently for weeks to hear whether the proposal would be accepted, Andriy was ecstatic to learn that it was! With Bill's help and advice, Andriy worked tirelessly to refine several of his existing poems and write new ones for the book. By the end of the winter the manuscript of poems was ready for submission.

Andriy had earned some money that winter in the city but more importantly, he had submitted his first book of poetry for publication. If published there might be a small stream of money but the most important thing was the joy of sharing his poems with a wider audience.

It was only toward the end of the winter, when Andriy was preparing to return to the farm, that Bill encouraged him to seriously reconsider enrolling at the University to study poetry. Andriy said he would think about it. But he knew his father was aging and it would take both his brother and himself to continue working the family farm, at least until Petro's sons were a bit older.

"And how would I pay the tuition?" Andriy had asked Bill.

"Why with the money from your book," Bill had responded. "and, of course, you can count on me for a loan if you need one."

This was a generous offer, indeed, but Andriy did not think he could accept it. And so the poet-farmer returned to the land, which had so inspired him.

For several years after the lost crop of 1918, life on the farm was rewarding. Crops were good as were prices. Demand for grain was high as international trade grew after the war. Farming communities were prosperous and reveled in the celebration of the fruits of their labours.

Yuriy

In the fall of 1920, Yuriy would be sixty-five years old. He had lived longer than he had ever imagined he would. He had out-lived his younger brother and two of his grandsons. When he thought of Dariya's two, lost boys, it broke his heart.

He was much slower these days. He couldn't help as much in the fields. His sons, Andriy and Petro, had taken over the responsibilities of seeding and harvesting. He still helped with the livestock when he could. But recently he began to feel very tired. More than once Anna had found him napping in the sunshine on the bench, just outside their lean-to porch. She didn't say anything but he knew she was worried about him.

The past winter had been especially hard on him. He had caught a cold early in the fall and had never really gotten over it. It had settled in his chest. He had coughed violently for weeks on end. Anna had nursed him and used every remedy she could think of, willow bark and rose hip tea and even onion juice with honey, but Yuriy's condition had continued to worsen. Over the winter he had lost weight, had had difficulty breathing, and seemed to be perpetually tired. He had not thought he would see another spring. Yet here he was, enjoying the spring sunshine and listening to the returning songbirds.

Yuriy had grown to love the sights and sounds of his adopted land. He gazed out across the farmyard toward the closest field. He remembered the days of hard toil to clear that patch of land and the first crop they had coaxed from it. He watched the large, white, puffy clouds, which always looked like sheep to him, sail through the unbelievably big, brilliant, blue sky. He gazed at the fresh, spring-blue slough, not far from the house, and allowed himself to be mesmerized by the sparkling glint of sunshine on the water. He felt the gentle breeze ruffle his thinning hair. God had been very good to him. He had had a good life.

An hour passed. And then another. Yuriy's mind drifted back to the early days in the old country, with his mother and father and brother. How he missed them. He smiled when he thought of the little wooden creatures, Vasyl used to carve. His heart warmed when he thought of his first wife, Kateryna. They had been so young and so in love. And then the boys had come, one by one. His five sons. And then he thought of Dariya – the joy of his life.

"The business of life is the making memories and in the end, that's all there is," he thought.

A little while later Anna called him for lunch. When he didn't come she assumed he was sleeping again. She walked outside and saw him slumped on the bench. She gently nudged his shoulder but he didn't respond. And then she knew. He was gone. Her life would never be the same again. She was forty-four years old but she felt like she was one hundred and four.

Anna

Andriy and Petro were in the fields seeding. Petro's wife would be taking them lunch now. There was nothing she could do but sit beside Yuriy and pray for his soul. She hated having to leave him slumped over on the bench in the sun but until she could get help, that's the way it would have to be.

Anna's thoughts wandered. Now that Yuriy was gone she could go home. How often she had thought of returning to the land of her birth. She could live with Mykola's family in the little hut, she thought. Oh, but the journey! She was much older than she had been when they had come as a family …. and she dreaded the long ocean crossing …. and she would have to go alone, for there was no one who would travel with her.

She knew it was impossible. Just a cruel trick her mind was playing on her. As much as she hated it, she was in Canada to stay.

Dariya

As soon a word reached them of Yuriy's death, Pavlo insisted Dariya take the wagon to the train station in town, despite the fact that it was seeding time. Dariya hitched the team to the wagon, readied little Maria, and headed off. Dariya was expecting a child later that year, so it was a long, hot, dusty, uncomfortable trip, the fifteen miles or so by train to the town closest to her father's farm. She was grateful to see Andriy at the station to meet her and take her home.

When she arrived, her father's house was full of people. The ceremony of prayers for the dead (parastas) would be held that evening and Tato would be buried the next day. She was so glad she had been able to get there in time.

Dariya had been filled with grief over the loss of her father. Little Maria, who was only four years old, did not seem to know what to make of all the people in Baba and Diedo's house. And she too missed Diedo, who had been a warm and loving presence in her short lifetime.

It was after they had laid Yuriy to rest that Anna announced she would be going back with Dariya. Dariya was astounded. She had assumed her mother would continue to live on the farm in her own home.

But Anna had made up her mind. During Yuriy's decline there had been numerous occasions when they had needed help around the house. Andriy always came willingly, as soon as he could, but Petro had, often as not, tried to get out of giving aid. Anna blamed his wife.

In truth Petro's wife had never grown accustomed to Anna's sharp tongue and demanding ways. And since Petro had never really been close to Anna, except during the very early days after she had entered his life, he preferred to keep his own wife happy, rather than cater to Anna.

And so it was that, when Dariya and Maria returned home after the funeral, Anna accompanied them. Anna brought all of her clothing, kitchen utensils, healing herbs - in short - all of her earthly possessions. Her one, prized possession was the holy icon her husband had brought with them from the old country. It had been given to his parents when they had married and had been a part of his home ever since. It was her one concrete link to her former life in the old country. The icon had hung on the wall of the room in which she slept from the day she had married Yuriy and would continue to do so for the rest of her life.

Later that summer Dariya had another son. She called him Yuriy, in honor of her late father. She prayed to God she would be allowed to keep this son. He was healthy and strong and Dariya made a promise to God that she would do everything she could to keep him safe.

After the child had been baptized, the priest and neighbours gathered at the parent's home for a celebration. Some of the neighbours were saying how unfortunate it was that these parents had had such bad luck with boys. At that one of the neighbor men tossed Pavlo a 'two-bit' coin, took the baby out of Dariya's arms, and walked toward the door. As he stepped outside the house he called over his shoulder: "I've bought your son, it is a sure-fire way to ensure you'll have better luck with him!" Dariya was appalled. Over the years she had gotten used to the raucous and sometimes strange ways of her neighbours. She had grown to enjoy their antics, for the most part, but this - this was outrageous! Pavlo saw the look of horror on Dariya's face and smiled secretly to himself. It wasn't long before the neighbor returned to the house and 'gifted' the baby back to Dariya and Pavlo.

Dariya wasn't sure what to think of all this but she was glad to have her baby son back in her arms.

"What a strange, strange life this is! My poor Tato, gone now. How I wish I had seen him just one more time before he died. How I miss him. He was truly a good man. And now, Mama has come to live with us. My poor husband, this will be hard for him. Mama can be so difficult. And it's not even as if we invited her – she invited herself! I will have to do whatever I can to make it easy for both of them. How I wish she had stayed on the farm, where the boys could take care of her, as Tato wished. But it is just like Mama to do exactly what she wants, no matter what the consequences are for those around her. God give me the strength to keep peace between my husband and Mama. And into this turmoil, I have brought my new son. God, please, let me keep this precious one. I couldn't bear to lose another son. Maybe he will be the balm to soothe the aggravation, which is inevitable between Pavlo and Mama. So much to hope for. So much to expect from such a small bundle. I pray that it will be so."

Andriy

After his father's death and Anna's departure to live with Dariya and Pavlo, everything on the farm seemed different for Andriy. He loved the land and the feeling of being a part of it as he worked alongside his brother, Petro. But something was missing for him.

Andriy saw how marriage and family had transformed his brother and sister. For the first time in his life, poetry wasn't quite enough to fill his entire being. Poetry was still a critical, integral part of who he was. He could never imagine his life without continuing to write poetry. By this time he was actively engrossed in writing another volume of poetry for publication, but still a haunting, hollowness lurked in his soul.

Andriy prayed for guidance. What was missing? What must he do to fulfill his destiny?

Perhaps it had more to do with his brother, Petro, than anything else. His brother had three sons, the eldest, Ivan, was now eleven. Andriy remembered growing up in the old country, knowing that his father's small land holding would not be adequate to support all five sons. Tato had made a brave choice to come to Canada so his sons could prosper. Andriy wondered if Petro was worried about having enough land for his own sons.

Andriy knew Petro had borrowed money after the rust-infested crop failure of 1918. Also, he knew that Petro had had difficulty paying back the loan, despite the better crops that followed. Tato had worried about Petro's loan but Petro had been too proud to ask for help. He was embarrassed that Tato had been right about the dangers of borrowing money. Andriy was concerned Petro might need to borrow again, in order to buy more land, as his own quarter section and the joint quarter-section left to the two brothers would not be adequate to support Petro's growing family.

Before his death, Tato had told the brothers he expected them to take care of Anna after he was gone, so Andriy had been diligent in sending money from grain cheques to Anna after each harvest. He knew Petro had not. Andriy did not judge his brother. He knew Petro's family, his wife in particular, demanded whatever his part of the farm could provide.

And so it was with all these things in mind that, to his own astonishment, Andriy discovered at the age of nearly forty, he might like to have a wife.

Andriy had always enjoyed the time he had spent in the city but he didn't think he would want to actually live there. He liked living on the farm but he was not as dedicated a farmer as his father or brother. Perhaps there was something in between city life and farm life that would suit him.

There was a funeral in the community. Mr. Slewka, the owner of the dry goods store, had died after a prolonged illness. His wife had died a few years earlier. He left behind his only daughter, Elena. Andriy knew Elena had been devoted to her father. She had nursed him through the long years of his illness and had taken care of his business at the same time.

It was clear Elena was an astute businesswoman. She had focused the store's inventory in order not to compete, but rather supplement, the offerings of the other stores in town. Andriy knew Elena was a self-sufficient woman and he liked that about her.

Andriy began to formulate a plan. If he could somehow convince Elena to marry him, perhaps he could live with her in town and rent his land to

Petro. The income from his land would be his contribution to the union and some day, when Petro could afford it, perhaps he would buy Andriy's portion of land to increase the size of his farm. It seemed like a good plan but how to bring it about?

So as Andriy contemplated his plan, he began to think about his old friend, 'Sam' Chang. Andriy had always meant to visit 'Sam', in order to see his new restaurant but somehow a visit just never seemed convenient. But now as he recalled 'Sam's' dedication and determination to achieve his own dreams of success, it seemed that a visit with his old friend was just what was needed. So bright and early one morning, Andriy borrowed a neighbour's truck to drive to the small town near the city.

Andriy angle-parked the truck on the main street, right in front of 'Chang's Café'. It seemed to be the only restaurant in town. It was a typical building with a narrow front, facing the street. There was a tall window on either side of a door. The door had a tall oval window. A sign in one of the side windows proudly proclaimed 'Canadian and Chinese Food'.

Andriy walked into the café at about ten in the morning. It was almost completely empty. There were two old men drinking coffee at a corner table. There seemed to be some activity in the back but no one to greet him as he entered. Andriy walked toward the back of the long, narrow room.

"I help you?" came a familiar voice from the kitchen. And then 'Sam' saw Andriy and a huge smile lit up his broad face. "Andriy!" he exclaimed, "You come for lunch?"

Andriy didn't want to distract 'Sam' from preparing for the lunch rush but 'Sam' assured him today would be quiet. It was a busy time on the surrounding farms. There would be a few town's folk - from the bank and stores who might stop in for lunch but the bulk of his business today would be from the teenagers after school and then a few farmers and their families this evening. And besides, as always, 'Sam' was prepared to handle any amount of business that might come his way.

"How are you, old friend?" Andriy asked.

'Sam' kept smiling and nodding, "I am doing very well," he responded.

Andriy immediately noticed 'Sam's' English had suddenly improved dramatically!

"Your English has improved," he responded.

"I have learned English very well," 'Sam' replied. "It is necessary for business. But here my customers expect to hear me speak the way I did when I first came to this country – it is a small thing."

Andriy was astounded. At once he felt sorry for 'Sam' and proud of how astute he was.

'Sam' brought two cups and a pot of coffee and the old friends settled in for a long visit. They were interrupted a few times and on one occasion, 'Sam' returned from the kitchen with two bowls of steaming soup and egg rolls to share.

Andriy learned that 'Sam' was able to make a comfortable living and, for the most part, he enjoyed the community he served. He had comfortable living quarters above the restaurant and a large garden behind it, where he grew vegetables for the cafe. He bought milk and eggs and some meat from the local farmers. Every two weeks he drove his panel van into the city to buy additional supplies.

Most of the people appreciated having the café in their town but 'Sam' had never really felt an integral part of the community. Some people still referred to him as 'the Chinaman' rather than by name. Some of the older children and teenagers still made fun of him. But he was always kind to them and was slowly winning them over.

'Sam' had added a display of candy for sale next to the till. The children always wanted their parents to buy them a treat. Sometimes 'Sam' would reward a child, who had been well behaved in the café, with a free sample. The teenagers were always looking for a place to congregate and the only other option in town was the drug store. The druggist had made it clear they were not welcome to read the comic books unless they intended to buy them. And so 'Sam' had installed a new invention, which he had seen in a city restaurant, a Whirlitzer. It had a constant, colour-changing, light display and played records for a nickel a play. The young people loved it. So after school they would throng to the café for Cokes and French Fries, which they called 'chips', and to listen to records. They even danced among the tables. 'Sam's' ingenuity had made him a success, despite the odds.

Andriy told 'Sam' all about his life on the farm, his most recent time in the city, and his poetry. Eventually Andriy got around to telling 'Sam' about Elena.

"Have you ever thought about getting married?" Andriy asked.

"I have," said 'Sam', "but … here ... My brother returned to China to get married; I don't want to go back. I want to stay in Canada. There are few Chinese ladies here! And who else would have me?" he added laughing.

"Don't you get lonely?" Andriy asked.

"Of course. And don't get me wrong, I would marry if I could but it is just not in the cards, as they say."

After a long visit the two old friends said good-bye. 'Sam' wished Andriy well with his plan to win Elena and Andriy promised to bring her to the café to meet 'Sam'.

As Andriy drove home he realized just how blest he was and he resolved to follow his plan.

Stephan and Lesya

In 1920 Stephan and Lesya welcomed into their happy home their third child, another son. They named him Miroslav. Miroslav was the most delightful baby and grew into an amazingly brilliant toddler. He loved to sing and dance and often entertained his parents and older siblings with his impromptu kitchen performances.

When Miroslav was three years old he went with his parents to the Christmas concert at the town school, which his brother had just started attending and where his sister was in grade three. He was in his glory. He watched every recitation, every song, every dance, and every play with incredible attention. Lesya had never seen her youngest son so enthralled. "Perhaps he will be a singer, like his father," she thought.

The next morning, as the family was getting ready for the new day, Miroslav pulled a chair into the middle of the kitchen floor and climbed up onto it. "I am on a stage," he announced. And then he began to imitate what he had seen the night before. His recitation was not word for word what he had heard but much of the meaning was there. Lesya and Stephan were astounded! Then he sang a song, granted it was a Christmas Carol, which no doubt he had heard several times before but he had the perfect tune and words. Amazing! And then he tried to do a little dance but of course the chair was not a stage and so, he got down onto the floor and while humming the tune, proceeded to imitate the intricate steps of the Ukrainian dancers he had so enjoyed. The family clapped for Miroslav's performance and he was very pleased with himself.

For several days after the concert, Lesya would hear little Miroslav practicing songs he had heard that night. In her heart, she loved all three of her children but this little performer was very special indeed.

It seems that great happiness is often followed by great tragedy. In the fall of 1924, first Lena came home from school with a sore throat and fever. Within two days Pylyp was also sick in bed with the same symptoms. On that day the town's people heard there was a case of diphtheria in town. Any family afflicted was quarantined. Stephan heard the news while he was at work. He knew two of his children were sick and he feared they might have the dreaded disease. He asked to leave the hardware store and rushed home – the quarantine sign was already posted on his front door. Stephan could not believe it. He called out to Lesya, who was in shock and shaken with worry.

"You cannot come in," she told Stephan through the door, "you must go to a rooming house until this is over. I only wish I could send little Miroslav with you. So far he is well but I worry we will all be sick before long."

Stephan stayed near his front door for some time comforting his wife. Finally he returned to the store. He would work very hard and take food to his family every day until this horrific epidemic was over. Many people in town knew that Stephan Cione's house was quarantined but then several other houses were as well. Everyone tried to keep his or her distance from anyone who might have been exposed. Stephan worried his boss would tell him not to come to work but that dreaded news did not come.

Every day after work Stephan took fresh water in a bucket to put outside his front door, along with milk, bread, and eggs. Sometimes he could bring a little meat or a few root vegetables from their backyard garden. His family in the house was not even allowed to journey into the backyard.

Inside the little house Lesya nursed her two sick children and tried to keep little Miroslav away from his brother and sister. Lena, who had fallen ill first, began to recover slowly. The fever broke. Her sore throat eased and she was able to eat a little bread soaked in milk without too much pain. The coughing continued but seemed to be lessening. Pylyp, on the other hand was very sick for many days. He tossed and turned in his sweat-wrenched bed, coughing and crying from his extremely sore throat. The mucous from his nose was foul smelling and blood stained. His neck had swollen and he had a persistent 'barking' cough. Lesya was sure that, despite all her efforts, her eldest son would soon die. She was heart-broken. And what was worse, her beloved Stephan could not be with them. Although she thanked God for the health of the rest of the family, she was devastated by the prospect of losing her first-born son.

Lesya slept little. She ate little. She bathed her son with rags soaked in water and tried to get him to eat or drink – "just a little". In the end there was little she could do to comfort him but sit by his side and hold his hand and pray.

Meanwhile, eight-year-old Lena was recovering and taking on the responsibilities of the house, little Miroslav, and her mother.

The worst was yet to come. Little Miroslav began complaining of a sore throat. "Oh God, NO!" Lesya prayed. "Please no more illness. Please not little Miroslav!"

But sometimes prayers are not answered in the way we want them to be. God has His ways.

As little Miroslav began getting sicker Pylyp slowly began to recover. This gave Lesya hope. If her two older children recovered perhaps Miroslav would as well.

It was not to be. The little boy's throat swelled. His breathing became rapid and laboured. He couldn't eat, talk, or even swallow without extreme pain. When he was awake he was in agony. When he slept his limp little body looked pitiful. But she stayed at his side for hours, days … doing what she could for him as he struggled to fight off the infection.

Poor little Miroslav. He did not have the strength to win the battle. Just a few days after falling ill he was dead. Lesya was distraught. Lena, who had completely recovered, told her father the sad news through the door when he came to the house that evening. Stephan knew he could not enter the house until the quarantine had been lifted, so he ran to the doctor's home.

"Please, sir," he said with his hat in his hand, "my daughter and older son are well again. My wife was never sick but our little boy is dead. Can the quarantine be lifted?"

The doctor looked at Stephan with pity. It was not the first time he had had to make a hard decision about lifting a quarantine.

"Tomorrow," he said gently. "I cannot lift the quarantine until tomorrow. I will go to your house first thing in the morning and examine your wife and children and, if they are well, the quarantine sign will come down and you can bury your son."

Stephan went back to his home. He told Lena through the door what the doctor had said. He wanted to come into the house but Lesya made him wait until morning, until after the quarantine had been lifted.

Lena made pancakes for her brother for supper that evening. Stephan stayed outside the front door whispering to Lesya and trying to comfort her. Lesya sat near the front door, holding the body of her dead, beloved child. She listened to Stephan but said little. Something inside her had broken.

In the morning the doctor arrived. He insisted Stephan stay outside while he entered the little house. First Lena then Pylyp were checked and declared recovered. Then Lesya was questioned. No she had not had any of the symptoms. The doctor examined her and found her to be weak but not ill. Caring for sick children can take its toll.

The doctor offered to remove Miroslav's body but Lesya would not allow it. At that moment Stephan entered the house.

"Thank you sir," he said to the doctor. "We will take care of this now."

The doctor removed the quarantine sign as he left the little house. He went straight to the priest's home beside the church and told him the sad news. Shortly Father Alexi arrived to comfort Stephan and his family. This would be a very difficult loss for them all. Such a lively, talented little soul, to be taken so young. Father Alexi prayed with them and for them. It would not be easy, he knew.

And so after Miroslav was buried, slowly life in the little house returned to the previous routine. Lena and Pylyp went to school and played in the schoolyard with the neighbor children. Stephan went to work. Lesya did laundry and mending. She spent time every day in the church and at the grave of her beloved son. She had become even more quiet than usual. She took care of her family and did everything she had to do but it was as if she were walking through a dream rather than living her life. It was not unusual for Stephan to return from work to find Lesya crying. She didn't cry in front of the children but the tears often overcame her during the day, when the rest of her family was away.

It was fall, then it was winter, and then the spring returned. Had she even noticed the seasons that year? No, she hadn't noticed much.

One spring day Lesya was standing at the washtub in the kitchen, doing laundry. Pylyp had fallen during a rough game of shiny and twisted his ankle, so he sat on his bed with a cold, wet rag wrapped around his elevated injured joint. He was reading. Then he heard the sound of soft weeping coming from his mother. Pylyp knew his mother had not gotten over the loss of little Miroslav but he had not seen her cry since the funeral. Lesya cried almost silently – no gasps or gulps or wails, just a soft intake of breath and the hot tears rolling down her checks. Pylyp was so sad to see his distressed mother and wanted to do something to ease her pain but he could not think of anything to say or do for her. And so as he had been taught, "when you don't know what to do, say a prayer and leave it in God's hands". So Pylyp prayed. He prayed his little brother was safe with God and that his mother would know and be comforted by the thought.

Just then a small, bright, yellow bird sat on the limb of the tree just outside the kitchen window. It began to sing. For such a small bird it had an amazing voice – clear, bright, and quite loud. Lesya looked up at the little bird and thought of Miroslav. He had been just a little boy but with such a beautiful voice. Surely God had sent this little bird to remind her of him. So Lesya watched and listened to the little bird. It sang for a long time. Pylyp watched as his mother's tears dried and for the first time in a very long while, a faint smile crossed her lips.

"Thank you, God, for sending the little bird with the big voice!" he prayed.

It took a long time. Stephan was caring and gentle with Lesya and eventually she began to come back to him. In his heart he knew something had changed in her, which might never be the same again but he was glad to have his wife back – in whatever form that would now be. Then an amazing thing happened. Lesya was once again pregnant. She wasn't sure how she felt about having another child but Stephan was overjoyed. This was an answer to his prayers.

"She will be better now," he thought.

And so in 1927, three long years after little Miroslav was lost, Lyudmyla was born.

Dariya and Pavlo

It had been an adjustment to say the least, having Anna living with Dariya and Pavlo. Anna could be difficult and, although he generally kept his feelings largely to himself, it was clear that Pavlo neither welcomed her uninvited invasion of his home nor particularly cared for Anna and her sharp ways.

Dariya had been grateful enough to have her mother there to help with little Maria during the remainder of her pregnancy in 1920. It also had been a comfort to her to have her mother present for the birth to her son, Yuriy, later that same year.

Anna was a good cook and often took over the kitchen, which allowed Dariya to tend to her two, small children, the household chores, and to help Pavlo in the fields during the busiest farming times. However, it also meant

Dariya had to play the role of peacemaker between her mother and her husband. It was, at the best of times, an uneasy peace.

As the years rolled by the little family grew. Dariya had another daughter, Iryna, born in 1923 and in 1925 a son, Mykola, named for her beloved half-brother in the old country. As the family grew, so did the farm. Pavlo knew that, although a huge plot of land by the standards of the old country, the homestead quarter section of land would not be a big enough farm to sustain his family in this new world. And so as others around him were doing, he saved in the good years and invested in more land. He now owned two full sections of farmland, although not contiguous – all the land was still close enough to conveniently farm.

And now it was time for Pavlo to repay the great debt he owed to Father Mykhaylo in the old country. For, if it had not been for the good Father all those long years ago, Pavlo would not be here in Canada. He would not have met and married Dariya. They would not have had this wonderful family. It was time to repay his debt.

Difficult though it was to live with the tensions of strong personalities under the same roof, having Anna living with the growing family had had an unexpected benefit. It meant Dariya and Pavlo could more easily visit friends and neighbours without taking along their brood. Their neighbours made a very social and fun-loving community. There was always a reason to get together and celebrate – the end of seeding, the end of haying, the end of harvest, birthdays, anniversaries, and during the long, dark winter, just the opportunity to get out and see someone! And so it often happened that Dariya, who had grown to love these visits with neighbours, and Pavlo often went visiting and left Anna in charge of their children.

Dariya, like many of the women of the area, was often called upon to help prepare for weddings, funerals, and church functions. These events meant she had to be gone from home for a couple of days to help with the cooking and preparations. The women peeled potatoes; cooked rice; killed, cleaned and cooked chickens; made soups and pies; etc. They baked bread and made holubtsi (cabbage rolls) and pyrohy (perogies) – all labour intensive activities, especially when cooking for an entire neighbourhood. The women worked and talked and laughed all day long and late into the night. One would always have to stay awake to keep the stove fire burning, while the others threw coats on the floor and slept for a few hours. These events were a very important part of the social fabric of early life on the prairies and Dariya was always very involved in such community events.

Anna resented being used as a 'babysitter'. In her own house she had maintained a neat, clean home and had had absolute control over her environment. In Dariya's home this was less possible. The children were rowdy - running, jumping, yelling, and fighting. This was completely at odds with the quiet, orderly home she had maintained with Yuriy.

And so Anna was not the most patient of grandmothers. She often scolded the children for their hi-jinx and when they became just too much for her, she would turn them out into the yard to continue their ruckus. She was fond of warning them to be good or "the Tartars will get you." None of the children had any idea what a 'Tartar' was and it wasn't long before they came to the conclusion that, whoever they were they were either too far away or too busy to actually be troubled with poorly behaved children in the middle of the Saskatchewan prairie.

When Anna was feeling sorry for herself she thought about moving back to the farm. Andriy had been good enough to honor Yuriy's wishes and had always sent her a share of the grain cheques. Petro, on the other hand, had totally disregarded his father's wishes.

"It is all the fault of that wife of his," Anna thought bitterly. "She has high expectations of what Petro can provide so he has nothing left for me."

It was at times like these that Anna knew she could no more easily go back to living on the homestead than she could go back to the old country. She didn't like the situation in which she found herself but there was really nothing she could do about it.

And so it was that Anna became more and more bitter and sharp-tongued. This of course increased the tensions in Dariya's home. Dariya longed for the happy home she had dreamed of creating with her husband.

Dariya loved spring on the prairies. When the last vestiges of snow finally disappeared and the ice on the sloughs melted, the water was such an incredible blue! And then the geese and ducks and song birds returned to fill the air with their mating songs.

At this time of year if you knew how to gauge the weather and temperature and knew just where to look, you could find wonderful smorzhi (morel) mushrooms. Dariya loved this delicacy and she looked forward to picking the mushrooms with great anticipation. Although spring was an incredibly busy time on the farm, she would always manage to wander off into the bush behind the pigpen to spend an hour searching. It was strange how at first you could look and look and see nothing but then suddenly you would see one gorgeous mushroom and then another and another and soon your eyes would be trained and you could pick a whole apron full. On those occasions Dariya would walk back to the house carefully with her apron cradling the precious horde. She would clean and slice the delicacy and then sauté them with sweet cream and dill. How the family loved this special treat. The fact that the morels had a very specific and short season made the treat even more special.

And then as the days grew warmer and longer still and the lilacs brought forth their annual blessing of cone-shaped clusters of tiny, fragrant purple blossoms, Dariya knew that another year had passed and she was a year older. It was always a bittersweet realization. She didn't mind growing older; she loved her family and her life on the farm but she saw how her mother was aging and growing more and more miserable with the years. "Is that what is in store for me?" she would wonder. And then her thoughts would shift to her father who had left this world in the springtime. It was far too busy on the farm to make the trek to visit Tato's grave just then but she usually found a way to get there sometime during the summer. When she visited the old, original farmstead, she often spent time with Andriy and sometimes with Petro's family. Andriy usually accompanied her to their father's grave where they prayed for his soul. It wasn't until many years later on one of those occasions, Andriy confessed to Dariya that he always said a silent "thank you" to his father for having brought the family to Canada. After that, Dariya continued the tradition of thanking her father for bringing her to Canada, as well. Many years later, this would become a family tradition, upheld by Dariya's son George and in turn by his son, Paul.

Life on the farm followed a typical routine. Everyone was up early to do the morning chores before breakfast. Everyone had a job to do. Pavlo rose first and started the fire in the kitchen stove, which heated the whole house. Then he headed out to the barn to feed the animals and milk the cows. Maria, as soon as she was old enough, accompanied her father. This was her favorite time of the day because she loved the farm chores and this was the only time she could have her father entirely to herself. Even after young Yuriy was old enough to accompany his father during the morning chores, Maria insisted it was her job and Yuriy could bring in wood or water or some other chore. Anna and Dariya started the day by getting the younger children up and cooking breakfast so it would be ready when the morning chores were done.

Breakfast usually consisted of hot, cooked cereal - oatmeal, cornmeal (kasha) or cream of wheat - with fresh milk, home-baked bread, homemade jams and jellies, and coffee or tea. Only on Sundays, after Divine Liturgy, or on Holy Days were eggs cooked for breakfast, as these were otherwise used only in baking or sold for cash.

After breakfast the children were dispatched – the older ones to school or chores, depending on the day of the week and time of year. In addition to the standard school year, school-aged children walked to the hamlet school during two weeks each summer to learn catechism from two nuns of the order of Sister Servants of Mary Immaculate. After breakfast, the pre-school children were sent off into the yard to amuse themselves and each other. Pavlo went to the fields, the barn, or the workshop, while Anna and Dariya mended and washed clothing, tended the garden, baked bread, and prepared foodstuffs and meals. Everyone had a job to do and everyone knew what was each one's responsibilities and contributions to the family welfare.

The daily routine on Saturdays was different. On Saturday, Dariya, Anna, Maria, and later Iryna, cleaned the whole house from top to bottom. Soon after Anna had come to live with them, Pavlo had decided that their little hut, while perfectly comfortable for Dariya, Maria, little Yuriy, and himself, was just too small to accommodate Anna as well. The very next year, with the help of his neighbours, he constructed a larger, timber-framed home.

This house was in the typical style of farmhouses in the area. It had a dugout, dirt basement, primarily for storing root vegetables. The rectangular shaped home consisted of a large kitchen, which served as the main living area, with three small bedrooms, all in a row, opening onto the kitchen. There was a small pantry behind the kitchen and a lean-to porch, which served as the entrance to the kitchen.

Initially, Pavlo and Dariya shared one of the bedrooms with baby Yuriy, Maria slept in another small bedroom and Anna in the third. As the family grew Anna had to share the bedroom she had occupied since her arrival and had come to think of as her own with Maria and Iryna, while Yuriy and Mykola shared the middle bedroom. Anna often thought all four children should have the middle bedroom so that she could have 'her' room to herself but she knew Pavlo would not approve of such a plan.

At any rate, Saturdays were different from every other day of the week. It was the day on which the family prepared for Sunday, God's Day. So the women and girls cleaned the whole house and laundered the bedding, while Pavlo and his sons did the daily chores, as well as tidied the workshop and yard. By the end of the day everyone was exhausted. After supper, Dariya heated water on the kitchen stove for weekly baths. A large, square, aluminum tub was placed in the middle of the kitchen in front of the stove and filled with heated water. Then one by one, from the youngest to the oldest, family members took their turn in the tub of warm water. By the time it was Dariya's turn, the water was neither as warm nor as clean as she would have liked but it was necessary to wash away the grime of the week's labours. In spring, summer, and fall, Anna preferred to wash herself outdoors with water directly from the well, as did Pavlo.

By the time the children were put to bed on Saturday night, Dariya was exhausted. She would slip into the bed she shared with Pavlo and luxuriate in the cleanliness of her body and the freshly laundered sheets and pillowcases. It was something she looked forward to all week. It was the one luxury in her life and she cherished it. Unfortunately she was usually so tired that she had little time to enjoy the luxury before drifting off to sleep.

Sunday was also different. Everyone got up early and did the morning chores as usual but then it was time to get dressed in 'church' clothing. If the priest was coming and there was Divine Liturgy in the little church on the corner of their land, there was no breakfast that morning. The days of a priest arriving by train on Friday and staying with the family until Monday's train had long passed. Now the priest who served their little church, along with several others in the region, had an automobile. He came, along with the diak (cantor) for the scheduled Divine Liturgy, then usually stayed for lunch with one of the parish families before returning home.

Pavlo was always the first to enter the church on Sundays. In summer he opened the windows to air out the building. In winter he started a fire in the small, pot-bellied stove to warm the building. Then he set about preparing the candles and sacristy for the priest. Pavlo served in the church as stárshyi brat (church elder and priest's assistant). He took these responsibilities very seriously.

Dariya, Anna, and the children followed on foot to the little church, as soon as everyone was ready. Anna, Dariya and the girls sat on the left side of the church in one of the wooden pews, about halfway between the door and the altar. The boys, when they were old enough, sat on the opposite, right-hand, side of the church with the men. When they were a little older still and had had their first communion, the boys were altar servers. Soon the church filled with neighbours from the parish. The little yard in front of the church was full of horse-drawn buggies and a few trucks or automobiles.

By the time the service was completed several hours later, everyone was famished. Often Father, the diak, and a selection of neighbours would accompany Pavlo and his family on foot, from the little church back to the farmhouse. Lunch was actually a feast. It consisted of soup; usually borscht or chicken broth with homemade egg noodles (sometimes referred to as 'wedding soup'); roasted chicken (put in the oven before leaving for church); an array of vegetables (fresh from the garden in summer or home-canned in the winter); fresh bread and butter; and Dariya's specialty, pie. From her first taste of the delight on the ocean crossing many years earlier, she had promised herself this dessert would be her specialty. As a result, she spent long hours learning how to make the flakiest pastry crust and the most delicious fruit fillings from the wild berries she collected. It was said in the community that a piece of Dariya's pie was worth walking many miles for.

Life on the farm was good. It was hard work, surely, but the rewards were great, indeed.

Ukraine

While the rest of the world celebrated the end of Great War, hostilities continued in the region of the village on the Dniester tributary. At the end of the war, the Austro-Hungarian Empire was no more. Poland was re-established as a nation, the Second Polish Republic, and was anxious to regain Galicia, which it had lost to Austria in 1772.

In November 1918 the short-lived Western Ukrainian National Republic, encompassing Galicia, Bukovyna, and Ukrainian Transcarpathia, was declared. In January 1919 unification with the Ukrainian National Republic (eastern Ukrainian territories formerly under Russian control) was ratified.

Because Poland particularly opposed the loss of Galicia, the Ukrainian-Polish War in Galicia (1918-1919) ensued. Fears in the wider world of westward advancement of Bolshevikism resulted in Poland being allowed, by the Paris Peace Conference in June of 1919, to occupy all of eastern Galicia.

Meanwhile, the Ukrainian National Republic (the area formerly under control of Russia) was fighting the Ukrainian-Soviet War (1917-21) to gain independence from the Soviets.

The Polish-Soviet War (1919-1921) concluded with the Peace Treaty of Riga in March 1921, whereby Poland and Russia agreed to a division of territories. Galicia (briefly part of the Western Ukrainian National Republic) became part of Poland, while Russia agreed the border between Poland and the Soviet Ukraine (formerly the Ukrainian National Republic) would be the Zbruch River. In March 1923, the Conference of Ambassadors recognized Ukrainian Galicia as part of Poland, provided the region would retain a degree of autonomy.

The inter-war years under Polish governance saw increased efforts to Polonize and minimize the Ukrainian population by restricting their religion, language, education, and rights and by colonizing the area with Polish immigrants. In 1923, in order to gain international recognition of Poland's new borders, promises were made to protect the rights of minorities. Though laws were passed these were never ratified by the Polish government.

Because of his efforts to support the Western Ukrainian National Republic, Metropolitan Andrey Sheptytsky was placed under virtual house arrest and was not allowed to leave Lviv for over a year. When he was finally allowed to travel, he did so extensively within Europe and North and South America, visiting Ukrainian immigrant parishes and promoting the Ukrainian nationalist cause. Because of this he was accused of anti-Polish activities and for a time refused entrance back into the country.

Education was centralized and the only way to maintain schooling in the Ukrainian language was in privately operated schools. Ukrainians were ineligible for government jobs and the Ukrainian language was no longer used in business or government. Electoral boundaries were re-drawn and regional differences among Ukrainian peoples exploited in an attempt to divide them. Ukrainian political representation was limited so Ukrainian efforts to participate in the Polish government had little impact on preserving the rights of the Ukrainian people. As a consequence, several anti-Polish, political movements and parties attempted to work directly against the Polish government. In 1921, there was a boycott of the census and in 1922, a boycott of the national elections. In addition, an underground movement, the Ukrainska Viiskova Orhanizatsiia (UVO), comprised largely of former Ukrainian militiamen, conducted a guerilla war against the Polish government.

Mykola and Nadya

After Uncle Vasyl died, Mykola had continued to farm the land his father and uncle had farmed, as well as the new field Uncle Vasyl had bought in 1907. His brother, Mykhaylo, owned one morg of the original farm but since he had had no interest in farming it himself, he had demanded rent from his brother. After Mykhaylo was conscripted and war devastated the region, there was nothing with which to pay rent. Mykola continued to try to coax a living out of the small land holding. When there was finally a crop, Mykola had to pay taxes to the new Polish Government, so even if he had wanted to pay rent to Mykhaylo's wife, Larysa, it was not possible. Larysa was embarrassed that Mykola had even thought to try to pay her rent. She had been disgusted by Mykhaylo's insistence on taking possession of the tiny strip of land in the first place and as far as she was concerned, the land rightfully belonged to Mykola and his family.

It was a small concession but it meant a great deal to Mykola's family. If he could continue to grow a small crop on the land, he might be able to pay the require taxes and eventually replace the livestock, which had been lost or eaten to stay alive during the war. Perhaps life could be, once again, what it had been. Mykola prayed this would be so.

Mykola and his family struggled to get back on their feet. They had survived the war, but not unscathed. Little Taras had died at the age of eight of influenza in the spring of 1919. Nadya was heart-broken. Mykola couldn't believe that both his brother and his young son, who shared the same name, were lost to him. But perhaps God had something better in store for his family in the future. So many of his neighbours had succumbed to hunger or disease or had been the victims of the violence of war. "God grant them eternal memory", he thought, "Vichnya Pamyat."

It was very difficult to re-establish any semblance of normal life after the war. Many villages were devastated and in the villages that had survived, one invading army or another had destroyed many homes. Many buildings had been completely obliterated by bombs, artillery, or fire. Displaced people who had survived the attacks might have initially hidden in the forests but as the hostilities subsided they wandered into the towns and villages that were still standing.

It was equally difficult to re-establish farming life after the war. Mykola relied heavily on the help of his son, Anton, who at the age of eleven had to work very hard along side his father to get the small holding to produce enough grain to pay the taxes and meet the family's needs. Mykola's wife, Nadya, along with nine-year-old Dora and little Vasyli, who was five, tended the chickens and garden. Everyone worked very hard. And because of their faith, determination, and hard work, life was slowly improving. While the threats of disease and starvation were still very real, at least it seemed there was hope. Hope that, with patience, hard work, and the grace of God, they would survive. Armed conflict continued but largely to the north and east of the little village. And so with optimism and faith in God, the little family struggled on.

It was during this struggle that co-operatives played a key role in helping small Ukrainian farmers by promoting modern farming methods and providing financing and marketing opportunities. They also fostered Ukrainian-language publications, which played a role in deepening the feelings of Ukrainian nationalism. These co-operatives were based on the belief that military and political action against the ruling Poles could not be effective and only a growing and strengthened Ukrainian farm community could alleviate the harshness of Polish rule.

Larysa

Mykhaylo did not return from the war. He was presumed dead. Larysa and her father devoted themselves to caring for little Volodymyr, who they planned would one day take over the family farm.

Larysa's father had worked with Polish overlords in the past. At first he thought living under Polish rule once more would be as it had been in the old Austro-Hungarian Empire but this was not to be. Despite passing laws to provide for autonomous Galician rule, prevent Polish colonization, and support a Ukrainian University, none of these laws were enforced. Ukrainian language, religion, and culture were severely restricted. Polish colonization was accomplished through land reforms in 1925, which broke up large estates and sold the land to Polish veterans. Large, local landowners were 'advised' to sell off most of their property and if they resisted, the Polish Government would enforce the redistribution of land from former large holdings.

It soon became clear that the only large landholders in the area would be Polish. Not wanting to be reduced to a marginal farmer, when once he had been a significant landowner, Larysa's father began to make a plan for the future of his daughter and grandson.

When it had become evident that he would not be able to retain his land, Larysa's father retrieved the few treasured items he had buried when the Great War had begun. These items could not have helped them in those dark days, as they could not have been sold even if there had been a buyer, and any resulting funds could not have been used to buy the required food, as virtually no food existed. The more likely scenario would have been that these items would have been stolen, but now … now, along with the meager funds from the sale of his land, it just might be enough to buy a new life.

Unknown to Larysa and Volodymyr, who was now an adolescent, the former landowner was planning their escape. One day he told his daughter he had some business to conduct in the town on the Dniester. She, of course, assumed the 'business' had something to do with his attempts to retain his land – a problem, which had consumed him since the end of the war. In reality the former landowner was meeting with a man, who he had heard had helped others in a similar situation.

A few days later Mykola was astounded to find his brother's father-in-law coming to the door of his little hut. Mykola invited the great man in, anticipating there had been word of Mykhaylo – perhaps he was not dead after all, perhaps he had returned.

But what the landowner had to say surprised Mykola even more than would have the news of his brother's return.

"No, I am sorry to say there is no news of Mykhaylo," the landowner replied to Mykola's inquiry.

But the landowner did have an important mission. He wanted Mykola to keep a few of his late wife's belongings. The small, soft, leather pouch contained a few of her favorite personal items, the landowner explained.

"Please keep these few mementos safely and … secretly," the landowner begged. "It isn't much but some day Mykhaylo may return and if he does, there will be nothing for him. This is all that I can spare but perhaps it will help him. If he doesn't return, use them for your own family's benefit. You are a good man and I know you will handle this matter fairly."

Mykola was astonished. The landowner had said nothing about leaving but Mykola knew there could be no other explanation for his words and actions. He also knew that it would be best to keep his conclusions, as well as the existence of the small pouch, to himself.

And so a few weeks later the former landowner, his daughter, and grandson departed the village without any great show or farewell. The former landowner had discretely sold his land, all be it at a value far less than it was really worth. He had obtained Polish passports for himself, his daughter, and grandson. He had arranged travel, which took the abbreviated family first by train and then by ship. They were going to America.

Larysa, when she realized they were leaving and would never return, had a sense of sorrow as she thought of her husband and the father of their son, who was most assuredly dead. It was suddenly certain she would never see him again and the thought filled her with grief. Larysa had not liked what Mykhaylo had become but she still had feelings for him and the probability of never seeing him again in this lifetime had a profound effect on her.

News of the departure of Larysa, her son, and her father spread through the village. Mykola acted as surprised as everyone else. Some people asked him whether he had known that they were leaving and, in all honesty, Mykola could say he did not. People wondered what it meant if someone like the former landowner had fled. Surely this was not a good omen for things to come.

Anton

In 1924, Mykola and Nadya noticed a change in their eldest son. It was almost imperceptible but his loving parents noted it. Anton, at seventeen, continued to be devoted to his family but something was different.

"Do you think it is a girl?" Mykola asked his wife, almost hoping the change they had noticed in their son could be something so natural.

"I don't think so," replied Nadya. "I think it is something darker. I can't explain it but I worry that Anton is some how 'leaving' us."

"I know what you mean," Mykola said. "He does everything he should, as he always has, but I feel there is something between us, something that wasn't there before. I am worried about him."

"So am I," Nadya answered.

Based on their conversation Mykola felt he had to speak to his son about their concerns. But when he did, Anton denied that anything had changed.

"Perhaps it is the influence of friends…" Nadya speculated after Mykola described his unsuccessful conversation with Anton.

"He does go out some evenings. Not like Mykhaylo used to, to drink and gamble. He never comes home drunk. But perhaps this is the clue to the change in him."

And so Mykola tried to speak with his eldest son again. This time, he asked about his friends and what they did when they went out in the evenings.

"Nothing much," Anton replied. Then he added, "Didn't you go out with friends when you were my age?"

"I was very lucky to have a close brother when I was your age. We did everything together. We did go out sometimes, it's true. But we never did anything we wouldn't tell our father about."

Anton just looked at his father. Mykola was sorry the minute the words had left his lips. He had not wanted to be critical and yet what he had said had hit the boy hard. He immediately apologized.

"I am so sorry. Of course you have a right to do as you please in your free time. Please forgive my intrusion. But please know that your mother and I love you and we would do anything for you, should you ever need help."

This last statement was intended to assure Anton that, no matter what he did, his parents would support him. Unfortunately, the effect of the statement was to emphasize for the young man just how very different he felt himself to be from his parents.

Anton had lived through very difficult times in his young life. He had seen the effects of war and hunger on his own family and their neighbours. What impacted him the most was the cruelty and brutality, which some men displayed toward others. His sense of righteousness had been developed and strengthened through the war years.

During the latter years of the Austro-Hungarian Empire, the Ukrainian people in Galicia had gained equality with their Polish neighbours. Then after the war, with the fall of the old empire, they had fought for and briefly achieved an independent nation. So now it was unthinkable for them to accept the status of being a downtrodden 'minority group' in the newly reconstituted Polish Republic. As the injustices of Polish rule toward the Ukrainian people continued after the war and ensuing conflicts, Anton's sense of righteous indignation deepened. He felt duty bound to do something about it.

Anton saw his parents as good people but people who seemed to have no further ambition than to return to the life they had known before the war. In fact, the life generations of his forbearers had lived. Anton believed there could be something better and he had dedicated himself to bring about his dreamed of better life.

It was this mindset, which left Anton and many of his friends ripe for recruitment into the UVO, a military organization intent on sabotaging the Polish Government. Anton believed whole-heartedly that the only way to achieve a better future was by working for an independent Ukrainian Nation. Only then could Ukrainian people be free to speak their language, attend their churches and schools, and govern themselves. The UVO was very much aware that it was not just the present Polish Government, but also the threat of Russian dominance (which might some day replace it) to be opposed. No, the only way was to establish an independent nation. And that was what they intended to do, by whatever means it would take.

Anton's friends were not just young men of his own age. They included older men as well, men who had been soldiers in the war. They were united by their beliefs, rather than by their age. They met in small groups to plan covert activities. Not everyone knew exactly how many men were involved and not everyone knew exactly what each person's role was. Anton had been involved on the periphery of the group. Perhaps it was because he was young. Perhaps it was because he had not been a soldier. But at any rate, he knew only a handful of those in what he believed to be a much larger group of like-minded people.

Anton was intelligent. He, along with his brothers, had learned from his father to read and write. He had a natural talent for expressing his feelings through writing. It was this talent, which he had been told, would be his best contribution to the cause. And so it was that Anton wrote heart-felt, pithy, and provocative text for pamphlets to support the movement. At first, one of the older men would talk to Anton and tell him the direction the texts should take, the major points to be addressed, and the call to action to be made. But as time went on it became obvious that Anton knew what had to be said and how best to say it for maximum effect. So Anton would write the text for pamphlets and deliver it to another member of the group, who would print the pamphlets and pass them on to someone else who had them distributed. Anton wanted to do more. He wanted to be more actively involved in the movement. But every time he mentioned these desires, he was told that what he was doing was of the utmost importance and no one else could do what he did. And so Anton had to be content with his small role in the bigger movement.

One day, Anton's colleague asked him to attend a meeting of a larger group. Anton was proud and excited to have been invited to such a meeting. But on that evening, as Anton was hurrying to where the meeting was to take place, he had run into Father Mykhaylo. The good Father had also noticed a change in this young parishioner. Father Mykhaylo knew Anton's family well, as he knew all his flock. There was something in the deep intention of the young man as he hurried on his way, that made Father Mykhaylo want to know more.

"And where are you going in such a hurry this fine evening?" he asked.

"Just to meet with some friends," Anton replied.

"Oh, I see and who are you meeting?" the priest continued.

"Just a few of the fellows … I have been working with, writing some …" Anton was flustered by the direct questioning of the good Father. He had prepared responses for his own father, but to lie to a priest – he just couldn't do it.

And at that moment, Father Mykhaylo knew. He knew Anton was involved with a group he was well aware operated in the area. He fully understood the boy's feelings of frustration and need to do something to improve his people's lot. But Father Mykhaylo believed there was a better way. So he detained him by speaking with him about their common beliefs and goals and the different paths, which might be taken to achieve them.

At first, Anton was simply anxious to be on his way. He knew what had to be done and he wanted to be a part of it. Father might be a learned man but he just didn't understand how urgent it was to fight for what you believed in. After all, he was a man of the church … a man of peace.

And then, suddenly, Anton was nervous. Father Mykhaylo had guessed. He knew what Anton was doing and where he was going. Would he try to stop him? Would he tell his father?

But Father Mykhaylo was an intelligent man. He knew the best way to reach the young man was through his sense of righteousness.

"Anton," he said evenly, "before you give your time and talents to a goal, be sure you know how it is to be achieved. I know, as well as you do, that our Ukrainian people are suffering injustices but does that give us the right to perpetrate injustices on those who impose them upon us? There is a way to fight for what we believe in without hurting others the way they hurt us. It is not easy to walk the path of righteousness, rather than revenge."

"But Father," Anton responded, "all I do is write pamphlets."

"And what do the others in your group do?"

"I don't really know…"

"Well, perhaps you should know before you continue your involvement. Please think about this."

Anton did not want to believe what he was doing was not the right way to achieve an independent Ukraine but he knew Father Mykhaylo was wise and cared about what was happening to his people. So rather than hurrying on his way, he thought perhaps he should find out more.

And then Father Mykhaylo really surprised him.

"Come with me to the church, Anton. I want to show you something."

Anton didn't want to go to the church. He didn't want to go home. He wasn't sure he wanted to go to the meeting either. He needed to think.

"Please, it won't take long," the priest said gently.

And so Anton and the good Father walked to the church. First, Father knelt briefly to pray and then motioned for Anton to follow him. At the far end of the church was a small office. The priest pulled a small box out of the desk drawer and extracted several papers.

"These are reports of some of the activities some people think are justified in their attempts to free our people from oppression. What do you think of these?"

Anton read several reports of destruction of government facilities. These were unfortunate but sometimes it was necessary to do such things to highlight injustice and take a stance against the perpetrators. But then there were reports of violence against people who were not part of the oppressive government. And finally, the report of the assassination of a government official.

"The question you must ask yourself, Anton, is just how far you are prepared to go? What are you willing to do? Can injustice ever bring about justice?"

Father had a point. Anton would not destroy anyone's property and he would not hurt anyone. He had seen enough of that during the war. Could there really be another way?

And so Father Mykhaylo sent Anton home.

"If you would like to take another path for the same cause," the good Father said, "please come to my house next Monday evening. I think it might help."

On that Monday evening when Anton arrived, Father Mykhaylo greeted him warmly. Anton recognized a few, but not all of the men gathered there. When everyone had assembled, the good Father led them in a prayer. It was a petition to the Mother of God for Her protection of the group as it went about its work. Then they spoke of ways to work with the people to strengthen their sense of identity through language, religion, and customs. This was the approach Metropolitan Sheptytsky had taken. It was slower and less revolutionary but it did get attention from outside the country. Because Poland really only existed as an independent country, as a result of an international agreement, perhaps there was something to this approach. Anton could appreciate that there might be a right and just way to work toward Ukrainian independence.

Anton soon learned that one of the ways this group worked to achieve its aims was to publish a Ukrainian language newspaper. Writing pamphlets for the UVO was one thing but writing about the Ukrainian identity, culture, and religion served two purposes. It strengthened the resolve of the people and it provided critical information for those outside Poland, who might support the cause. Anton was to become part of a team, regularly writing for both the Ukrainian people and a broader audience. Anton was thrilled with this project and vowed to do his utmost.

It may have been a coincidence. A few days after Anton's first meeting at Father Mykhaylo's home, Mykola Martiniuk appeared at the good Father's door. He asked whether he might have a word with the good Father. Father Mykhaylo wondered exactly what Anton's father knew about his son's recent activities.

Father Mykhaylo invited Mykola into his kitchen. His wife was doing the marketing and so the two men had the house to themselves.

"Please sit and I will make us some chai," Father said.

Mykola sat at the kitchen table. He liked Father Mykhaylo, who was only a few years his senior. He began to tell the good Father why he had come.

"Father, we are very worried about our oldest son, Anton. He seems changed … distant. He meets with friends we do not know. He spends hours writing and yet we never hear about what he has written. What can this mean?"

Father Mykhaylo knew why Anton was behaving as he was. He also knew his father might not approve of his activities. But the young man was old enough to decide what he believed in and what he must do about it. Mykola might understand but he might not. And so the good Father listened to Mykola's worries. He comforted him and they prayed together for guidance. When Mykola left he felt better, although he still had no idea what was happening with his son.

Father Mykhaylo

"Perhaps I have done a little to help this young man," Father Mykhaylo thought. And as he mused about his role in Anton's 'conversion' the thought of another young man drifted into his consciousness. It had been over twenty years since he had sent young Pavlo Dannyk off to Canada to find a better life. He had often wondered if he had done the right thing. Pavlo's baba had died. His brothers and cousins had struggled at menial jobs to keep body and soul together. One brother had been killed in the Great War. Surely Canada would have afforded young Pavlo better than that.

And then, just a few days later, as if God had sent it as an answer to the good Father's musings, a letter arrived from Canada. It was from Pavlo. He described his farm, his family, and his life. It all sounded so wonderful. But best of all he had sent money – the sum which the good Father had given him to travel to the New World and more. This would be very useful to support the work the good Father was undertaking in these difficult political times. Father Mykhaylo thanked God and prayed for his young protégé, Pavlo. "I wish you all the best, you deserve it!" he thought.

Argentina

The Great War had had a huge impact on the attitudes of nations and the people who populated them. The world beyond Argentina seemed to have changed dramatically. The British were looking to trade more within their Empire and with the United States, which had been its ally in the war. Foreign investments in Argentina, which had been largely, though not exclusively from Britain, began to shift to new investors. In addition, social attitudes changed after the war, notably the efforts of workers' unions to protect the rights of their members.

Before the Great War, Argentina had been a wealthy nation, relying on agriculture, free trade, and British investment. After the war, Argentina was anxious to resume its pre-war export economy, along with renewed foreign investments, immigration, and an expanded domestic market. In the decade following the Great War, Argentinian agriculture benefited from the development of an agricultural machinery sector, improved animal breeding for exportation via the improving frigoríficos (refrigeration transportation), and an expanding meat packing business. Along with agricultural machinery, a new automobile industry developed. During the war, traditional trading partners had put all their manufacturing efforts into meeting the demands of the war and, as a consequence, Argentinians had had to begin to produce what had previously been imported. Light industries in textiles and leather, as well as luxury goods, began to develop.

Trade increased tremendously immediately after the war. In 1918, the Allies, who were short of food supplies bought large quantities of grain and beef from Argentina. Argentina loaned large sums of money to the Allied nations. While foreign investment from Great Britain declined in the post-war years, the rising new power of the United States became a major investor in Argentina.

When Hipólito Yrigoyen of the Radical Party had been elected in 1916 as president for a six-year term, there had been great hopes for democratic changes in the country. However, the reality was that there was little change for the working classes. The affluence of the upper class increased as the poverty of the workers increased. Efforts to improve working conditions were often suppressed and a growing unrest was developing. In 1919, the Argentine army violently attacked striking metalworkers in an event, which was referred to as 'La Semana Trágica' (The Tragic Week).

The aftermath of the war had wrought many changes in the world, in the country, and on the prosperous yerba plantation on the arroyo of the Parana River northeast of Posadas. The market for their main product, yerba mate, was largely South American and demand was increasing.

There was something, seemingly insignificant at the time, that would prove to have major consequences in the future. In 1920, Taras had been living in

Argentina for eighteen years. Since his arrival, he had grown accustomed to the local traditions and rituals of consuming mate – after all, his livelihood was built upon the foundation of this lucrative local crop. But Taras had grown up drinking a different kind of chai, black tea, which had been available in the old country for centuries. Occasionally he had craved a cup of chai, possibly because it brought back memories of his youth and home. Such tea was available, of course, but it was imported and quite expensive so it was considered a luxury item.

In 1920, Taras had heard about some farmers who were trying to grow black tea from seeds, which had been brought to Argentina from Russia. A few years later, in 1924, he was fascinated to learn that the government had obtained tea seeds from China and was encouraging farmers to grow it. Taras, always the innovator, was among the first to obtain seeds and begin to experiment with growing this non-native tea on the plantation. Ivan was supportive, if mildly skeptical, of Taras' venture but, like Taras, he had missed the chai he had grown up with and thought at least they would have a less expensive source for their own use.

It had taken some doing to get the Chinese seeds to grow and prosper in the hot, humid climate and rich, red soil of Misiones but Taras had persisted and was rewarded for his efforts. The price for such tea on the world market was quite low in those years. In addition, this tea grown in Argentina was considered inferior to that grown elsewhere. As a result, many farmers who had experimented with growing it soon gave up in favour of more lucrative crops. But because both Taras and Ivan enjoyed drinking this chai and because Taras had perfected growing it on their plantation, they had continued to grow the new crop on a modest scale.

Taras and Carmen had a fine family of three sons and one daughter. Yory, had been sent, along with Ivan's two sons, to Posadas at the age of ten in 1917, to attend school. Meanwhile, the younger boys, Myko and Guillermo, learned to help weed and tend the young yerba plants, as well as to help in the garden and with other tasks on the plantation. Taras and Ivan schooled the younger children in the evenings, as they had their older sons.

Little Katya (Kateryna), at the age of five, was the pride and joy of both her parents. She had the sweetest personality. From her earliest days she was referred to in the family as 'little Katya' for she was petite, not unlike her mother. But that was where the physical resemblance to her mother ended. While Carmen had huge, brown eyes and thick, dark hair, little Katya had fine, sandy-coloured hair and beautiful, soft grey eyes. Every time Taras looked at his beautiful little daughter it took his breath away, for she resembled his favorite brother, Mykola, so much that it was astounding. Taras still missed the brother he hadn't seen in almost twenty years. He had heard so little from him since the Great War. Taras thought often about this brother and prayed that some day they would be reunited. But until that day came, he would cherish his little daughter who looked so much like Mykola.

Only one shadow fell across little Katya's young life. She was often the object of Myko's resentment. In actual fact, Myko resented everyone and everything but, like most bullies, he had singled out Katya as an especially vulnerable target. He plagued her with criticism and made fun of her constantly. As a very small girl she once asked her mother, "Why does Myko hate me so much?"

Carmen was well aware of Myko's treatment, not only of Katya but all the other children and it distressed her deeply.

"He doesn't hate you," the mother tried to reassure her daughter, "it's just the way he is. He doesn't mean what he says and does. He doesn't even know how much he hurts others."

Myko

Despite what Carmen told her other children about Myko's behaviour toward them, she knew very well that Myko had a deep-seated need to make others feel small so he could feel big and important. She talked to Taras about this disturbing nature of their second son but neither parent knew exactly what to do about it. Taras tried talking to Myko but met with the same sort of behaviour that Myko displayed toward everyone else.

"He thinks he is better than everyone," he reported to Carmen after having tried many times to talk to his son about the way he treated others, "even me, his own father!"

"Actually he reminds me a lot of my brother Mykhaylo," he thought to himself. "Maybe some people were just like that and there was nothing anyone, even a parent, could do about it."

Taras tried to remember what his father had done to handle his difficult brother but nothing helpful came to mind.

So Taras and Carmen tried to bolster Myko's own feelings of worth, hoping he would have less need to belittle others. But this only served to emphasize Myko's deeply engrained belief that he was better than everyone around him. Then they tried to show him the value of the contributions of the other children and how, what he did, complimented the communal effort but this had little effect. In the end, they decided to try to be patient with him and pray he would out-grow his disturbing behaviours.

Myko often felt Yory's ideas, though seen by others as brilliant, lacked practicality. In his heart, he believed that his own suggestions were at least as relevant as those of his older brother. Myko was so consumed with his feelings of being overshadowed by his older brother that he did not recognize Yory as his strongest supporter. As a result the natural distance, based on their diverse characters, which had existed between the two brothers since birth widened as the years went by.

Meanwhile, Myko continued to act as if he were much better than everyone else. He had little regard for, and perhaps was actually even unaware of, the negative impact his actions and words had on those around him.

The years after the Great War were marked by increased immigration to Argentina in general and of Ukrainian immigrants to Misiones, in particular. After the initial arrival of Father K. Bzhukhovsky in Misiones from Brazil in 1908, several more priests from Ukraine had followed. Then in 1922, an amazing event took place. Taras and Ivan took their families to the Ukrainian Catholic Parish of San Vladimiro in Posadas, where, whenever it was possible, they attended Divine Liturgy. The reason for this family expedition was to see the Metropolitan from Lviv, Andrey Sheptytsky. The great man had come to consecrate the churches and chapels built by the Ukrainian immigrants since their arrival. He spoke passionately about the importance of maintaining a cultural identity, as this was, even at that very moment, under attack in the homeland. This event had a tremendous significance for the parishes in the far-flung hinterland of Northern Argentina.

Yory

It was during the family visit to Posadas in 1922 that Yory, who had been living in town during school terms since 1917, had a serious conversation about his future with his father. Of the original three boys who had been sent from the plantation to school in Posadas, only Yory remained in town. Ivan's eldest son had completed his schooling and returned to the plantation. His younger brother had decided to return as well, even though he had not yet completed his studies.

Yory's younger brother, Myko, had shown no interest in joining his brother in Posadas and had convinced his father he had no need to attend the school in town. Taras' youngest son, Guillermo, had just started his schooling in Posadas. Yory, at the age of fifteen, wanted very much to complete his schooling, which would take another two years. He expected his father would be willing to allow this. However, what Yory really wanted, more than anything else, was to continue his studies by undertaking advanced and specialized training at the Posadas Practical School of Subtropical Agriculture. This, he was concerned, would be more than his father would be willing to support.

Taras and Carmen spoke often over the next two years about Yory's dream of advanced education. There was no doubt that, with Ivan's sons and Myko, the plantation could do without Yory, should he continue to study. And it was likely that Yory might learn better and more modern farming methods, which could be useful to the plantation as a whole. But Taras had another concern. He worried that if Yory were absent from the plantation for too long, he might not retain his position as Taras' eldest son in the hierarchy of the next generation. Myko had already begun to act as if he were Taras' representative in discussions among the young men regarding the directions the plantation should take. It was clear his two sons were very different from one another but Taras had a strong instinct that there might be a threat to the future harmony of the plantation if Yory did not return after standard schooling.

Thus it was that Taras asked Yory to return to the plantation for a year after completing his basic education in Posadas. A compromise had been reached whereby, if Yory spent a year working with his brother and Ivan's sons, in the following year he could return to Posadas to undertake advanced training. So, in 1924, Yory returned home. He was happy to be living at home once more and enjoyed working on the plantation. He had subscribed to an agricultural publication and eagerly shared any new ideas he thought might be applicable. Taras watched these interactions very carefully for any signs of divisiveness. It soon became clear that Yory was seen as well informed and the source of potentially valuable new ideas to improve the plantation. Ivan's sons knew first hand from their shared time in Posadas of Yory's academic abilities and were more than happy to defer to him when he proposed a new idea. Myko would always have questions about how such new plans might actually be implemented but he seemed willing to listen to his older brother, even if he saw no value in such new ideas.

So after a year of watching the four eldest sons work together to improve the plantation's production and sales, Taras agreed to send Yory back to Posadas. Yory was thrilled to be heading back to town. While he loved the plantation and living and working with his extended family, he had grown fond of life in town and he burned with the desire to learn all he could about agriculture in this very unique part of the world.

This time when Yory returned to Posadas, Taras rented a house in which Guillermo and Yory would live. So as Yory attended the agricultural school, Guillermo attended the town school.

In 1927, a new Patron established a five-hundred-acre yerba plantation a bit further up the Parana, five miles from the German settlement of Montecarlo. Ernesto Guevara Lynch and his wife Celia called their plantation 'Puerto Caraguatai'. The young couple, obviously from a moneyed family, earned the respect of Ivan and Taras, because they paid their labourers in cash and treated them well.

The young couple had departed for a few months in June of 1928 in order that their first son, Ernesto (Ernestito) Guevara de la Serna be born in more civilized environs. The young family grew and prospered and truly enjoyed life on their plantation on the Parana River. A Galician-born woman was hired to help with the children and remained a close family friend, even after she left them to get married. In 1929, the family was called south to deal with other family business, leaving a relative in charge of Puerto Caraguatai. The family did not return.

Taras

Yory loved his time studying at the Posadas Practical School of Subtropical Agriculture. One of his teachers had recognized the quick mind of this young man from the backwaters and had encouraged his natural ability for creative thinking. Toward the end of Yory's studies, the teacher had built on one of Yory's exciting ideas for an innovation and the two had published a paper based on the concept. Yory was ecstatic about the work he had done with his professor and when their paper was selected for presentation at an agricultural meeting in Buenos Aries, he could not contain himself. He wrote immediately to his father. Taras was proud of his son but concerned Yory was drifting away from the family and its business.

Taras and Carmen spoke often about Yory. Carmen seemed much less concerned than Taras was. She tried to tell her husband how much Yory was like his father, always coming up with new ideas, always convincing others to try them. Taras wanted his son back on the plantation but feared that the attractions of the greater world were pulling him away.

Taras' father, Yuriy, had died in Canada seven years before. When he had heard of his father's passing, Taras had been grief stricken. He hadn't seen his father since he had left the old country almost twenty years before and now would never see him again. Taras wished he could talk to his father about his concerns for his two eldest sons – the brilliant scholar who was being drawn away from the family plantation and the second son, who believed himself to be better than everyone else. How Taras wished he could talk to his beloved brother, Mykola, to seek his advice. In the absence of advice from his father and brother, Taras prayed for guidance.

In 1928, Yory and Guillermo returned to the plantation. Taras felt his prayers had been answered. Yory seemed to fit back into the routine of family and plantation life effortlessly and Taras gave thanks to God for having all his sons around him once more.

It is a cruel trick of human nature that sometimes parents cannot see themselves in their children. Taras had left his family to travel half way around the world to follow his dreams and schemes, yet could not help worrying over Yory leaving the family plantation to do the same. Likewise, Taras dreaded the coming of age of his lovely daughter, despite the fact that he had married her mother, Carmen, when she had been the same age as Katya was now.

Little Katya was turning fifteen and Carmen insisted that the event be marked in her traditional manner with a quinceanera celebration. The thought of his beloved daughter coming of age was something that bothered Taras almost as much as his concern for his eldest two sons.

So while Taras fretted over his eldest and youngest children, Carmen focused her attention on their middle son. She recognized Guillermo as an altogether different character from his siblings. She knew he was keenly aware of the distance, which had been growing between his older brothers. He was astute enough to know that, what on the surface might appear to be a constant competition between the two, was in fact a competition solely in Myko's own perception. Both Carmen and Guillermo understood fully that Yory was completely unaware of Myko's need to compete with and better his elder brother. For his part, Guillermo had no desire to be involved in the dynamic between his brothers, nor did he wish to take or be seen to take sides. Guillermo loved both of his brothers and his greatest wish was for peace and harmony in their family. And it was for this reason Carmen loved this third son so much and yet worried about him, as well.

Guillermo loved life to the fullest. He always saw the positive side of every situation, even when others could not. He always did whatever was expected of him and could be counted upon, no matter the situation. For this reason, many members of the younger generation went to Guillermo with their problems. Carmen saw that, although he didn't have the spark of innovation which was so much a part of her husband and her eldest son, nor the ambition of her second son, he was by far the most sensitive and caring of her four children. And it was exactly this aspect of his nature that caused her some concern, for she knew just how much of a burden it could be to be the person everyone turned to for advice, comfort, and solace.

After a brief hiatus, Yrigoyen was re-elected as president of Argentina in 1928 but politically, nothing much changed in the country. In that same year, the Argentine government purchased a large tract of land in the region of the Iguazu, in the far northwest of Misiones province, eventually to become a national park.

Life went on. The plantation prospered. A dirt road, running parallel to the Parana River along with the slow introduction of automobiles made travel to Posadas from the plantation faster than it had been by steamboat. It became much more convenient to travel to the town of Posadas and the plantation began to feel less isolated.

Ivan's sons met and married the daughters of Ukrainian immigrants from Posadas and brought them to live on the plantation. With the birth of their children the next generation was forming.

In 1929, Yory, who had maintained close contact with his former teacher, learned that the paper they had written together and presented two years earlier, had drawn the notice of someone in the department of agriculture. The two were being asked to travel to Buenos Aries to discuss it with officials. Yory was elated and left the plantation as if walking on a cloud. While Taras was proud of his son, his old concerns about losing him resurfaced.

Myko had been unusually pleased about his brother's triumph and decided to travel with him as far as Posadas, ostensibly in order to collect supplies for the plantation.

The Letter

In 1929, Mykola received a letter from his beloved brother in Argentina. It was so good to hear from him. Taras described the successful plantation and as always, implored Mykola to join him in Argentina. After Larysa and her father had left, it was very tempting to do the same. Now that Galicia was part of Poland, Uncle Vasyl's savings, in the currency of the old Empire, were worthless. Even if he sold the land, together with the proceeds form the belongings entrusted to him on behalf of his lost brother, Mykhaylo, it would not have been enough to take his whole family across the sea.

Taras had a special reason for writing. It seemed his eldest son had completed advanced schooling and was being enticed to share his ideas about new farming methods beyond the family plantation. Taras was afraid of losing his son.

"Oh Taras!" Mykola mused. "And how do you think our father felt when you left for Argentina! And can you really be so concerned about a son who is so much like you that he can invent new and better ways of doing things?"

And so Mykola wrote to his brother to congratulate him on having a son so much like his father.

"Rejoice," he wrote, "for there is another in this world as creative and intelligent as you! How I wish I could know him. And how much I wish our sons could know each other. Have faith, my dear brother, enjoy your family, for they mean more than even the prosperity of your plantation."

And so, Mykola, in writing to his brother, suddenly realized he must follow his own advice and rejoice in his own son – an apple is never far from the apple tree.

8 THE GREAT DEPRESSION

Canada

It all started in 1929. First a drought hit the prairies. It had been a hot, dry summer and the lack of rain had dried and withered the crops in the fields. Then in the fall there was news of a 'market crash'. It had happened in far away New York City, so it might have been inconsequential to the farmers of Saskatchewan. This, of course, was not to be the case. The crash of the markets would affect everything and everyone. Trade and demand for farm products declined, prices dropped, unemployment rose, and an international economic depression set in. The young country of Canada, where a third of its gross national income came from exports, was hit very hard. The farmers of Western Canada, who relied almost exclusively on exports of their farm products, were hit hardest of all.

One year of crop failure could be survived but ongoing drought conditions alternating with hailstorms and hordes of grasshoppers were devastating. And this is what Saskatchewan farmers faced.

1929 … drought. 1930 … drought. 1931 … drought. Could these weather conditions possibly continue? Could the people continue? Three successive years of crop failure were devastating, not just economically, but in terms of morale, as well. Pavlo heard of farmers just walking away from their farms – some had moved into the city to find work, some had moved to other areas where they hoped better weather conditions would prevail in order to start again. He had even heard of a man who had returned to the old country believing the dream of prosperity in the new world was just that – a dream.

1932 was no better than the prior three years had been. It was getting more and more desperate. Then finally … finally in an answer to the collective prayers of the prairie farmers … finally in the spring of 1933 - it rained! The crops looked beautiful. Hope swelled. Everyone was overjoyed. And then …

And then in late June they heard the devastating sound - the sound of hungry hordes of grasshoppers. They were everywhere. The years of drought had resulted in their numbers swelling well beyond normal. And they devastated the crops.

In the spring of 1934 the farmers headed out to the fields again. Maybe this year …

It was a hot year. Farmers prayed the crops would have enough moisture to grow and mature before the tender young plants burned in the heat. And then, as can happen on the prairies with high summer temperatures, the clouds rolled in from the west. The farmers looked to the clouds and thanked God for the coming rain – just in time to save their crops. But in the cruelest twist of fate, the clouds brought not only rain but also hail. It pounded the young crops into the ground and there was little left after the storm clouds departed.

Toward the end of summer, the repeatedly parched fertile prairie soil was subjected to high winds. It was as if the very soil itself had decided to abandon the countryside; it lifted up into the wind and blew away. The swirling black clouds of prairie soil were what gave this dark period in Saskatchewan farming history the ominous name, the 'dirty thirties'.

Once again in the spring of 1935 it rained. Maybe this year. The crops began to poke through the ground and were looking like they might have a chance … this year. But the winds blew and blew and the soil flew and flew and the crops could not withstand the onslaught.

The winter of 1935-36 was unbelievably cold - one of the worst in recent memory. And then, as if the fates were playing an even crueler trick, the summer of 1936 was incredibly hot! From one extreme to the other.

Saskatchewan farmers knew what it meant when their home was referred to as the 'land of extremes'.

People perished in the heat of the summer and, especially in the south of the province, the winds continued to blow the treasured Saskatchewan soil away. The crop was lost once more.

The year of 1937 started out well. Maybe this year. In early June the crops were coming up green and lush but by the end of the month the heat and blowing dust had once more devastated them.

Throughout these years of paralyzing weather, the gardens had fared little better than the crops in the fields. Many people suffered greatly from heat exhaustion and lack of food. Would there ever be an end to this tragedy? The news reports said the economic depression in the wider world was coming to an end but to the farmers of Saskatchewan, this sounded like a fairy tale with no bearing whatsoever on their own lives.

During the fall of 1937 the rains came again. It rained in the spring of 1938 as well. Maybe this year. But this year there were grasshoppers again … and rust. Some small portions of the crops could be harvested and some of the gardens could be salvaged. Maybe next year.

Lyudmyla

Lyudmyla was a quiet child. She had been quite small when she was born, early in 1927, and she had been ill many times during the first years of her life. Lesya had worried constantly about this child, who might be taken from her as little Miroslav had been. Between her mother's worry and the constant shadow of the lost child who had preceded her, Lyudmyla had developed into a quiet, thoughtful toddler, who seemed much older than her years.

One day Baba Ditka had come to help with the house and children, while Lesya was occupied taking care of her ailing husband. Stephan's health was failing rapidly.

Baba Ditka made supper for her grandchildren and prepared them for bed. She had noticed little Lyudmyla had several warts on her hands and was quite self-conscious about them. She had a habit of hiding her hands, almost as if to avoid giving offence to anyone who might happen to see them. Baba Ditka knew her youngest granddaughter needed to develop self-confidence. So very early the next morning she woke little Lyudmyla and took her out to the yard behind the house.

"Come and wash your hands in the grass," Baba said to the sleepy toddler.

Lyudmyla was mystified but much of what adults did mystified her, so she did as she was told. She bent down and ran her fingers through the short, dew-covered vegetation, which passed for grass in their backyard. Her hands became surprisingly wet from the dew, so she began to rub them together as if washing them in a basin of water.

"That's right," said Baba, "let's get our hands clean." Then Baba Ditka took the little girl's hands in her own and said a prayer to banish the warts.

"Now go back to bed," she told the girl, "it is much too early to be up yet."

And so little Lyudmyla went back into the house and crawled into the bed she shared with her big sister, Lena. It was warm and comfortable and before long the child was asleep once more.

In the morning, Baba Ditka was making breakfast when the two sisters came into the kitchen. As usual two-year-old Lyudmyla quietly took her place at the table and sat with her hands on her lap. Fourteen-year-old Lena came to help Baba with breakfast preparations. Soon twelve-year-old Pylyp arrived in the kitchen as well. As the four of them prepared to eat, Pylyp noticed something different.

"Lyudmyla," he said, "what happened to your warts?"

Lyudmyla looked at her hands and was surprised. There was no sign of the warts.

"The grass must have washed them away," she replied.

Pylyp had no idea what his little sister could possibly mean but he decided it didn't matter. He was happy the warts had disappeared. And Baba Ditka smiled to herself.

The Hermit

The years of drought and depression were hard on everyone. Farmers lost crops and sometimes their farms. Business people lost customers, sales, and sometimes their businesses. No one was left unscathed. Different people had different ways of coping with the hard times.

One spring morning, Baba Ditka was walking over the hills behind her farmhouse looking to see where the Saskatoon berry bushes were blooming the best that year. She would make note of it for later in the summer, in case it was not too dry or hot and there were some berries to pick. To her surprise she saw a small man carrying something, hustling over the crest of a nearby hill. Her curiosity got the better of her, so she followed him. When she got to the top of the hill there was no sign of the man. Where had he gone?

Baba Ditka mentioned this strange occurrence to her farmhand. He liked Baba Ditka very much but he thought perhaps she had just imagined the little man. She was, after all, getting older and old people sometimes saw and heard things that just weren't there.

So it was with great surprise a few days later that the farmhand met, face to face, a little man just as he approached the rise of the hill behind Baba Ditka's house.

"Who are you?" the farmhand asked, "and what are you doing here?"

The little man gave an unfamiliar name. When he saw the quizzical look on the farmhand's face he said: "I am from a little place just east of here. I lost my farm. I have no family. I mean no harm. I just need a place to live." And with that he walked away over the hill and was gone.

The farmhand followed but when he crested the hill there was no sight of the little man.

"Where did he go?"

It wasn't until some time later that Baba Ditka and the farmhand learned the little man had built himself a small dug-out in a hillside in her pasture. The entrance was well concealed. Inside, he had a little bit of this and a little bit of that but it was all he needed. He never took anything from anyone unless it was offered. He lived on what he could gather from nature. Occasionally someone would offer him a bit of food or some clothing but he never begged. Once in a while someone would offer him a temporary job but he always declined. It seemed this little man had decided his needs were very few and he preferred to live alone in his little dirt cave. Before long, everyone in the neighbourhood knew of him. He became accepted as part of the neighbourhood and, what had originally seemed very strange, with time became just an ordinary aspect of life in those parts.

Baba Ditka

The first years of drought had been a hardship. Eventually Baba Ditka could no longer employ a farmhand. There really wasn't too much to be done on the farm anyway. A neighbour might help her plant a field next spring. Baba Ditka didn't have much for savings and what she did have would be exhausted soon. The animals were sold one by one since there was nothing to feed them. When she, like so many others, could not pay the taxes on the farm she tried to sell the land but there were no buyers. So she talked to the banker in town and put a mortgage on the farm. But that was not a solution. Without a crop she could not make the payments on the mortgage.

All this was very difficult. Baba Ditka had worked hard all her life. She and her husband had homesteaded this land and after he had died, she had stubbornly continued to live on the farm and work the land. With the help of hired hands she had managed to maintain the farm. But now it seemed there was no way to continue.

Baba Ditka had always been a very practical person but this dilemma was proving to be her undoing. One night after her meager supper she walked around the farmyard. It was so sad and barren - it almost broke her heart to look at it. Dust was piling up against the unused barn and empty granary doors. The fields were a wasteland where even weeds could not grow. There were no sounds of cows or chickens in the farmyard. The desolate garden patch brought her to tears. She sat down on the bench by her front door and brought her apron up to her eyes and cried. That night she went to bed and didn't wake up the next morning.

Lesya was devastated. Baba Ditka had been her supporter - her strength. And now she was gone. It was almost as hard as it had been to lose little Miroslav.

The Bastiuks

Lesya's Mama and Tato were at first excited when they heard of Baba Ditka's passing, as they had hoped for years to inherit her farm. But when they learned that the bank owned the farm, it was the end of their long-cherished dream. Bitterness set in. Since Tato had never worked much and owned no land of his own he and his wife were among the poorest people in the town. They relied on whatever charity they could come by and made a point of getting what they could from Stephan and Lesya. However, since Stephan's condition had worsened his family had very little to share and, as a result, there were always hard feelings between the two homes.

One day Lesya sent Pylyp to take some flour to her mother. There was no one in the house so Pylyp went into the backyard. Still no one. He called out but there was no reply. Finally Pylyp approached the shed at the back of the yard. As he opened the door there was a great deal of commotion. Diedo and Baba had been doing something they obviously didn't want anyone to discover. Pylyp was mildly curious but he really didn't like visiting Baba and Diedo, so he just said, "Mama sent me to bring this flour to you," and handed over the small sack. Baba took it and hustled him out of the shed. She didn't even say "thank you" but sent the boy on his way. Pylyp didn't think much of this as he had always found these grandparents rather odd.

Several weeks later Lesya heard the news - her father had been caught making horiwka in the shed behind their house. She had long suspected he did this. She even suspected he sold his home brew, for if he did not, she had no idea how her parents survived. Although she and Stephan had always shared whatever they had with her parents, lately there had not been much to share.

And so Tato had to pay a fine. Lesya didn't know whether he had managed to pay it and if he had, where he had found the cash to do so. She never brought the subject up and neither did her parents. But from then on she felt an even greater distance between her parents and herself and really didn't know why.

Petrusia and Marusia had married and moved out of the neighbourhood with their husbands. Though their husbands had been relatively prosperous farmers before the depression, these two daughters had done nothing to help their parents. When the depression hit, although her sisters were still better off than Stephan and Lesya or Baba Ditka, they were even less inclined to do anything for their parents.

If Petrusia visited her mother and father she would bring her two young sons and expect to be fed by Lesya, since there was virtually nothing to eat in their parents' home. While visiting she would scold Lesya for doing so little for Mama and Tato.

"After all they have done for you," she was fond of saying, "you could at least share what you have. No doubt Stephan's parents bring food from the farm. Mama tells me you never give her meat. It is disgraceful. How ungrateful you are. And how could you turn in your own father! You know making home brew is the only way he can make any money. How could you be so jealous of what little he has as to turn him in to the Mounties?"

Lesya was astounded. She knew there was a reward of fifty dollars to turn in people who made moonshine but she would never have dreamed of doing such a thing. She had no idea her father had thought she had turned him in. She protested her innocence to her sister but, of course, like everything Lesya said to her sisters, it fell on deaf ears. Like Mama and Tato, Petrusia would believe what she wanted to believe and, unfortunately, that was always to Lesya's detriment.

And so Lesya had to live with this false accusation on top of all the other criticisms her sisters continually leveled upon her. She knew she had done what she could for her parents, although she would have been the first to admit it had not been much. And she knew she had never done or said anything to harm them. But as Stephan assured her, when things go wrong, people always want to have someone to blame.

So Petrusia rattled on, "And how disgraceful it was that Baba Ditka mortgaged the farm and did not tell anyone. Why could she not have left the farm to Mama?" for as the eldest daughter, Petrusia had expected Baba's farm would one day be her own.

Stephan

Stephan had been ailing for many years. The crippling disease he had suffered most of his life had progressed. As a young man he had suffered joint pain but had been able to work during periods of relative health. As time went by the crippling effects worsened. First he had to walk with the aid of a cane. Then he needed two canes. Eventually he could not propel himself at all. He had suffered incredible pain. He had become a bedridden cripple.

The loss of the breadwinner's earnings was devastating for his family. Lesya did whatever odd jobs she could find to earn a little cash. In spring if she could afford it, she bought a piglet to fatten on table scraps during the summer. In fall it would be butchered and, if she were very careful, the meat would last most of the winter. Then of course there were the chickens. Each spring she tried to buy a few chicks. She kept them in the kitchen near the stove until they were big enough and it was warm enough for them to be put into the coop in the backyard. The chickens provided eggs and ultimately a roasted chicken and soup. And most important of all was the garden. Lesya loved gardening and in good years, when there was rain, she could coax enough produce from her little garden patch to feed her children with fresh vegetables in summer and canned and pickled ones throughout the winter.

During the winter of 1929-30 Stephan would, with Lesya's help, move from the bed to a chair to sit while the bed linens were changed. During these times he often called little Lyudmyla to come and sit on his knees. He loved holding this youngest daughter of his. It gave him comfort to have this gentle little girl sit quietly on his lap as he told her stories.

Lyudmyla had a hard time enjoying these brief visits with her ailing father. She knew how he suffered and she was always concerned about hurting him more. Consequently she sat very still and tried very hard not to do anything to cause her father pain.

As Stephan's health declined, he was not able to get out of bed at all so Lesya and the children took turns sitting by his side, holding his hand, and talking or praying with him.

On Palm Sunday of 1930, Stephan knew he would not live to see the Great Day, Easter Sunday. Baba Cione came into town to help Lesya and to be with her dying son. At one point when the two of them were alone Stephan told his mother he had such a long, long journey ahead of him. She cried and pleaded for him to take her with him.

"Yes, Mama, come with me," he said. Then he was silent for several minutes. A shadow fell over his brow.

"What is it?" she asked.

"I just turned around to see where you were. You are so far behind me now. Stuck in the snow. I'm sorry, Mama, I can't wait for you."

Baba Cione cried and cried. She held her son's hand and prayed. He drifted off to sleep and she thought he would not awake.

But as the week wore on Stephan was awake some of the time. He told stories about what he had seen and done during his lifetime to whoever was sitting with him. Someone was always with him day and night. Sometimes it seemed he was talking to someone who was not there. He seemed to be having a conversation but the person watching with him heard only his side.

He was in pain. Lesya and Baba Cione did what they could for him. The doctor had been to see Stephan and had given him something for pain but it only lasted a few hours and the next time the doctor came, Stephan told him he didn't need any more medication. He continued to suffer, mostly in silence as he had much of his life.

Good Friday on the Julian calendar that year was on April fifth. That was the solemn day on which Stephan Cione breathed his last. Baba Cione stayed with her son while Lesya took the children to church for the plashchanýtsa service. When they returned, Stephan was drawn, pale, and weak. There was no cooking to be done, as everyone was fasting. Lena took her little sister out into the yard so Mama could care for Tato. He lingered through the rest of the day. Uncle Myron, Tato's brother, came from the farm and began reading the Psalms. He did so all afternoon and late into the night. Lena put little Lyudmyla to bed and reluctantly, she and Pylyp also slipped into bed. During the night Lena awoke and found her mother silently weeping. Tato was gone. He had been only thirty-nine years old.

The neighbours started coming early the next morning to help wash and prepare the body. Six large candles were set up around the body and would burn continuously until it was time to take him for burial. Stephan's brothers, Myron and Bohdan, arranged for the digging of his grave and then went to their farm to build the coffin.

Poor little Lyudmyla. She was only three years old and didn't really understand what was happening. The little house was so full of people. Mama, Lena, and Baba Cione were crying. Pylyp was off somewhere - she didn't know where. There was so much activity in the little house. She didn't know what to do, so she crawled under the kitchen table as if to hide.

Stephan was buried in the graveyard next to the church on Easter Sunday after the Celebration of the Great Day. The priest and congregation came from the church to the little house. They prayed, sang, and then picked up the coffin and carried it toward the graveyard. Because Stephan had been a noted member of the church choir, they sang and sang as they processed. Three times Father Alexi stopped to read a gospel before the procession continued. Finally they reached the graveyard. Father led the final prayers and committed Stephan's soul into God's hands. It was over.

The little house was quiet and full of sorrow. Baba Cione came from the farm to stay with the family for a few days. Her husband had died a few years before. She was a kind-hearted woman who had lost the husband she had loved and now her first-born son. She grieved with his widow and children. Lesya was glad to have Stephan's mother with them. She had lost her own dear Baba Ditka and, because of the nature of her relationship with her own parents and siblings, Stephan's mother seemed like the only family she had left.

Lesya

Times were hard. Due to the diligence of a kindly town administrator, who knew Lesya would need financial help, she began receiving a small Mother's Allowance of sixteen dollars a month. It was a big help but the amount barely covered rent and wood for heating the little house. She continued to do whatever she could to feed her family. Her husband's family provided what they could spare from the farm. And life went on.

Stephan's brother, Bohdan, usually came to town once a week. On most of these visits he would bring milk, flour, or even a bit of meat, depending on what was available. Each fall he would bring a load of wood for winter fuel. If it had been more than a week since they had seen Uncle Bohdan, Lesya would have little Lyudmyla stand on a chair to watch out the window for him. Sometimes he did not come. Lesya knew that times were hard on the farm and Bohdan would bring what he could for his dead brother's family but the times he did not arrive with the life-sustaining contributions were a dreadful blow. Lesya often went without food, sustaining herself with tea made of wild herbs and weeds, so her children might have what little there was to eat.

Then just two years after Stephan died Lesya became ill. She had had a difficult life. From the start she had felt unwanted and unaccepted within her family. Growing up the only love she had ever received had been from Baba Ditka. She had been fortunate to love and marry a wonderful man but his ill health had placed a tremendous burden on her. She had always done whatever she could to contribute to the family income, whether taking in laundry and mending or helping neighbours with their gardens - anything to bring in a bit of cash to supplement and later replace Stephan's income. She had nursed her three children through a course of diphtheria and had lost one of them to that dreaded disease. She had lost her beloved baba and her husband. She had gone without food on numerous occasions so her children might not starve. She had been through a lot in her short lifetime.

The illness at first did not seem very serious but Pylyp walked the three miles to his uncles' farm to ask Baba Cione to come and help. When she arrived Baba was quite worried about Lesya and sent for the doctor. The doctor noted that Lesya was malnourished and knew that if she didn't get some proper food, her body would not be able to fight the infection that had taken over. So he told Baba Cione to make some meat broth and feed Lesya as much of it as she would take.

As one day dragged into the next, Lesya slept more and more. She tried to eat the broth her mother-in-law had prepared and diligently coaxed her to take. She asked for her children to sit by her side and pray with her. One evening when Pylyp had gone to the schoolyard to talk with his friends and Baba Cione was getting little Lyudmyla ready for bed, Lena was sitting alone with her mother.

Lesya seemed unusually pale. As Lesya held Lena's hand she said to her eldest daughter:

"When I am gone, Lena, you must promise me you will take care of your brother and sister. You must keep the family together. Please promise me this."

"Nothing will happen to you Mama!" Lena responded, "You will get well. You must!"

But Lesya repeated her request. "Promise me, please."

"I promise," Lena vowed.

That night while the children slept and Baba Cione dozed at the bedside of her late son's wife, Lesya slipped away. She died as she had done everything in life, quietly and with dignity. She was only thirty-seven years old. Lena was seventeen, Pylyp was almost fifteen, and Lyudmyla was five.

Orphans

As soon as the news reached Lesya's parents, they descended on the little house. They took anything they thought was of value - a holy picture hung above the kitchen table and Baba Ditka's coral beads, which Lesya had been given to wear when she married Stephan. Baba Cione had been gone to fetch Father Alexi and the grief-stricken orphans were in too much shock to do anything to prevent this ultimate cruelty.

Baba Cione was outraged by the behaviour of Lesya's parents. This episode, along with the fact that she knew there had been times when her own son, Bohdan, had not taken food to Lesya and the children, made her realize what she must do. She decided then and there that her grandchildren needed an adult living with them. Her sons thought it would be better for the children to move to the farm but Baba Cione had made up her mind. And so she moved into the little house on the far side of the tracks.

After Lesya was buried in the graveyard next to her beloved Stephan, Lena and her siblings went daily to pray at their graves. Lena knelt in the middle, with Pylyp on one side and Lyudmyla on the other. They prayed together out loud. Often Lena would cry as they prayed. Lyudmyla suspected Pylyp was crying too but she couldn't see him.

"Don't cry," she would whisper to Lena, "when you cry it makes me cry."

Lena tried very hard not to cry.

Lena had just finished grade twelve and had earned a scholarship to attend Normal School in Saskatoon, in order to become a teacher. When Mama died, leaving her brother and sister seemed impossible. She had promised Mama she would take care of them. But Baba Cione insisted Lena go to the city to study.

"Go! Study hard. Become a teacher. Get a job. Then you can take care of Pylyp and Lyudmyla. I will stay here with them until then."

And so in the fall of 1932, Lena took the only two dresses she owned and a small amount of cash, which Baba Cione had given her, and went to the city to attend Normal School. She stayed with the Sister Servants of Mary

Immaculate in their house on Avenue E. The fathers of most of the girls who were boarding with the Sisters would bring potatoes, cabbages, and sometimes farm-grown beef or even wild game to barter for their daughters' keep. But Lena was an orphan who had little more than the scholarship she had earned, so the good Sisters accepted her without payment. Resourceful, as always, Lena was able to survive on very little while completing her studies. After one year she had earned a first class teaching certificate and could look for a job as a teacher.

Pylyp

Pylyp had wanted to quit school to find a job in order to support his siblings. But jobs were few and far between. Baba Cione insisted Pylyp continue going to school. So that autumn he joined his uncles' threshing crew. Uncle Bohdan had made the investment in a threshing machine in better times and it had added greatly to the income for the farm. And so it was that Uncle Myron worked with the threshing crew but left the details of running the side business to his younger brother, Bohdan. There was less and less to thresh every year but his uncles had the machinery and were willing to travel to thresh whatever crops there were. Pylyp hoped he could earn at least enough to buy his schoolbooks and clothing for the winter.

Pylyp worked hard with the threshing crew, which this year consisted only of his uncles and cousins. When the work was done, Uncle Bohdan paid everyone except Pylyp. He then paid all the bills associated with the threshing business and bought winter supplies for his family. When Pylyp asked for his wages, what was left was only a small portion of what he had hoped to earn. Uncle Bohdan's response was "You are just a boy, you can't expect to earn what the men earn."

Perhaps Uncle Bohdan felt he had contributed enough to his dead brother's family and Pylyp's work was some small repayment. Perhaps it was because he did not pay his own sons and felt there was no need to pay Pylyp. Regardless of his reasons, Pylyp felt he had been treated poorly and this added to his growing frustration.

Pylyp was frustrated by the fact that he had not even earned enough to return to school. Now he must find a job. But where?

A friend told Pylyp he was going to catch a freight train heading north to Melfort. Harvest was a bit later up there so there might still be work.

"You might be able to earn enough money to at least be able to go back to school," his friend said.

It sounded like a good plan so Pylyp decided to join him. Pylyp and his friend waited until dark, then headed for the train station in town. Each had brought the only clothing they owned, wrapped in a bundle, and a bit of bread and cheese. Between the two of them they had a very small amount of cash Pylyp had a dollar and seventy-five cents and his friend had about four dollars.

The two boys had never caught a free ride on a freight train before but they had heard about how others had done it. So they hid in some tall grass along the tracks and waited for the train to back up before pulling out. It would be going slowly, so the plan was to run up to a freight car and climb onto the axles underneath before the train started to pull out of the station. Unfortunately, the hiding spot they had selected was too far from where the freight cars were, so when they started running there was no way they could reach a freight car and get positioned on an axle. The engineer and conductor both saw the boys running and when the train stopped backing up before beginning to move forward, they called out to the boys and asked what they were doing.

"We wanted to catch the train," Pylyp's friend answered.

"Well you almost missed it," the conductor replied. "Do you have the fare?"

The boys looked at each other. They hadn't planned on paying for their train ride but now it seemed to be the only way to get to Melfort, so they showed the conductor the little money they had.

The conductor suspected the boys had intended to ride under the freight car for free. He knew how desperate they must be for work and heading north meant they hoped to get jobs helping with the harvest. He took pity on them and just took twenty cents from each boy before letting them board the train.

Less than a quarter of an hour after the train pulled out of the station it suddenly screeched to a halt. Then the train backed up slowly. It had hit something on the tracks. The boys looked at each other in amazement. If they had been riding on the train axles, they surely would have been killed. It had been a close call.

When the train arrived in Melfort, the boys found the streets filled with hundreds of men. These men, like the boys, were carrying bundles containing their meager worldly possessions. On the sole of one shoe each had written the wage they were willing to work for, '$3.00/day', '$2.00/day', etc.

Pylyp looked at his friend and simultaneously they realized the chance of getting a job here, where there were so many, full-grown men looking for work, was very low.

What could they do?

They still had the bread and cheese from home and by now they were hungry, so they found a quiet place to sit and eat their meager supper. As they ate, they listened to the men talking. Some were talking about jobs in Winnipeg.

"I have a cousin in Winnipeg!" Pylyp's friend exclaimed. "We could go there. When we get jobs you could send money home to your sisters. It would be *better* than going back to school. Even if you finished school in another two years, then what would you do? There are no jobs here. Would you work on the farm with your cousins? You know what that would be like – you would never earn what your labour is worth. Would you go to Normal School to become a teacher like your sister? If you didn't get a scholarship, how would you pay for that?"

His friend was right. There was no point going home. Pylyp needed to find a way to earn money. That was the only way he could help take care of his sisters. Pylyp was sad to leave Lyudmyla and Lena but what could he do? He couldn't afford to go to school and he couldn't get a job here. He would go to Winnipeg with his friend.

When he had left home, Pylyp had not told Baba Cione, as he was sure she would not approve. And, after all, he had only intended to go to Melfort to get a harvest job. Now that things had changed he decided he must write a letter to Lena, explaining his plan. By the time Lena, now studying in Saskatoon, got the letter, Pylyp was long gone.

Lyudmyla

Meanwhile little Lyudmyla became quieter than she had ever been. She helped her baba around the house. She missed her father and her mother. There were days when she sat by herself just trying to remember how her father had actually looked. She had been only three when he had died. She tried desperately to conjure her mother's face so that it, too, would not vanish from her memory. She missed Lena and Pylyp desperately. The little house was so empty. Some days she would drag a kitchen chair to the window and climb up on it to stare out the window.

"What are you looking at?" Baba Cione would ask.

"Nothing," little Lyudmyla would reply.

She was looking for Lena or Pylyp to return. She ached to see them. She hoped and dreamed that one day she would see them walking toward the little house. She didn't want to tell Baba Cione how lonely she was and how much she missed her sister and brother, mother and father. After all, the only good thing in her young life now was Baba Cione and Lyudmyla didn't want her to think she was ungrateful.

Baba Cione

Baba Cione had been beside herself. She had not anticipated Pylyp's departure. She knew he was frustrated by not being able to support his sisters or even earn enough to return to school. She was annoyed by her son's behaviour toward the boy and knew it may well have been the last straw for Pylyp. She had hoped he would finish school but she knew there really wasn't the money for him to do so. She was fully aware there might not be a job for him after completing school but perhaps he might have worked on the farm with his uncles and cousins. But it was not to be.

And so Baba Cione prayed that Pylyp would be safe, would get to a place where there would be a job, and when things got better he would return to them.

Despite all the recent tragedies in her life, Baba Cione's love of life could not be dampened. She was always singing and laughing, especially at herself. She soon learned she loved to live in town! She visited with neighbours, she went to church, she went to the shops, and she took care of little Lyudmyla. She made a cozy little home for the poor, sad orphan. Life would be hard for this child but Baba Cione was determined she would do everything she could to make this granddaughter's life as pleasant as possible.

The young girl had had great difficulty falling asleep each night. It was to be expected given all she had been through in her short lifetime. So Baba Cione would take Lyudmyla into bed with her. They would nestle under the great pyrena and Baba would tell her stories. At first these stories were about far-off Ukraine and the long journey to Canada. Then the stories were about all the hard work of homesteading. Eventually Baba began telling stories about the husband and son she had lost. Lyudmyla especially liked to hear stories about her father, as she really had so few of her own memories of him.

Pylyp

He would go east, get a job, and send his pay home to his sisters. Some day when things were better, he would return.

And so Pylyp and his friend caught a freight train from Melfort to Winnipeg. They were inexperienced but soon learned the necessary skills and conventions of 'riding the rods'. When they got onto the freight train they now knew the best place to ride was on top of a boxcar as far back from the engine as possible, to avoid the blowing smoke and cinders. The weather was fair and bright and the trip was uneventful. When the train approached Winnipeg and began slowing down the boys jumped off in order to avoid the railway police, referred to a 'bulls'.

They made their way to the Salvation Army where there were a few free beds (always taken), but additional beds for the price of fifty cents a night. The beds were in a clean dormitory with clean sheets, pillows in pillowcases, and blankets. There were also washrooms, where the grime of rough travel could be washed away. These were luxurious accommodations and the boys were grateful for a clean, safe place to spend the night.

Early the next morning the boys set out in search of the cousin who lived in the city. They hoped they would be able to stay with her while they looked for work. It so happened that the cousin's son was away, so the two boys were welcomed to stay in his room for a few nights. They were fed a good meal and told that the best places to look for work were at one of the two, large packing plants, Swifts or Canada Packers. Before seven the next morning the boys were at Swifts along with about fifty other men. As the regular workers arrived and entered the building everyone waited expectantly outside. Soon the security guard came out and said, "Nothing today boys," and the crowd of dejected men dispersed. The next day they would try Canada Packers, but in the meantime, they bought a newspaper in order to look through the want ads. The only jobs being advertised were for skilled labourers. Day after day the boys lined up with the scores of other men who were looking for jobs and day after day they came away without any luck. It was very discouraging.

More discouraging was the fact that their host was becoming anxious for them to move on. They had been staying with her for almost two weeks; perhaps this was too much to ask, even of a cousin. So the boys decided Winnipeg was not the place for them. They had heard there were jobs in Kirkland Lake, Ontario, in the gold mines. So the boys thanked their host and prepared to leave. It was clear they had outstayed their welcome but the lady of the house prepared a fine farewell breakfast and sent the boys off with some bread and butter sandwiches.

So they were on the road again. Pylyp was still hoping to get to Kirkland Lake, get a job, work for a bit, and then return home.

In order to continue their journey they had to walk twelve miles to the Transcona Rail Yards. When they got there, they cut across the rail lines and hid in the tall grass along the sidings. There they ate their bread and butter sandwiches. As it happened, a rail worker came by, checking a switch. He spotted them in their grassy refuge.

"What are you two doing here?" he asked, even though he knew exactly what the boys were up to.

There was no point trying to lie so they told him they hoped to catch a freight train east, heading to Kirkland Lake to get jobs in the gold mines.

The rail worker had seen many fellows in similar circumstances. He was impressed that these boys had a plan and were earnest about finding jobs, as some of the men who rode the rods were much less intent on actually working. So taking pity on the young fellows, he gave them some pointers and told them that the freight train they wanted to catch would be leaving at eleven at night.

"And don't forget," he reiterated, "never break the seal on a boxcar – it is a criminal offense and will land you in jail for at least six months."

The boys were grateful for his information and advice.

So they had some time to kill. They walked a short distance from the rail yard and came upon a large garden next to the tracks and a good quarter of a mile from the house it seemed to belong to. It was late fall and there wasn't much left in the garden but there were a few cucumbers, carrots, and potatoes. The boys picked and ate some vegetables. Just then they saw a Model T truck trundle up the lane heading for the house. It came to a halt. A man got out and lifted the hood. There appeared to be a problem with the engine. Then a woman and small child got out of the vehicle and walked toward the house.

Pylyp thought they should try to help since he, like his father, could fix almost anything. So the two boys approached the man and his stalled vehicle. The three looked over the situation and decided to push the vehicle the short distance to the house to work on it there.

After pushing the truck to the house and working on it for about an hour, they got it working again. So the man invited the boys in to clean up and have supper with his family.

Supper seemed like a feast to the boys. They hadn't eaten since their bread and butter sandwiches and were famished. They noticed a smaller garden nearer the house and asked why there was such a large garden so far away. The man explained that they planted the garden for the men who rode the rails. These were very generous and kind-hearted people, indeed.

By the time the boys had to leave to catch the freight train, it was dark and drizzling rain. They found the track the rail worker had indicated earlier and made sure they were watching the east-bound train, as sometimes a train appeared to be heading in one direction but would actually end up moving off in the opposite direction. They hid once more in the tall grass in easy reach of their target boxcar. They were gaining experience and this time it was easy to catch the train and climb up onto the top of the boxcar they had selected. It was dark, cool, and wet and the boys were exhausted after a very long day. They soon fell asleep as the train rolled along the tracks in the darkness.

Pylyp woke with a start! His feet were dangling over the edge of the boxcar and someone was fiercely gripping both of his arms. The stranger pulled him back up onto the top of the boxcar. By now Pylyp's friend was awake as well. They were both shaken by the close call.

The stranger wore a plaid shirt and a mismatched suit jacket and pants. He introduced himself.

"They call me 'Frenchie'," he said. "You boys need to use a rope or belt to tie yourselves to the walking rail in case you fall asleep up here – otherwise you'll fall right off and that'll be the end of you."

He didn't have to tell them twice. This was the most important piece of advice they had heard.

Then 'Frenchie' produced a loaf of bread and a can of beans. He opened the beans and poured them onto a piece of newspaper and told the boys to 'dig in'. 'Frenchie' ate little while the boys devoured the shared meal. Then 'Frenchie' stuffed the dirty newspaper into the bean can, put it into his suit jacket pocket, and walked off along the top of the boxcars into the darkness.

The boys had been aware there were many men, maybe as many as seventy-five, riding the same train they were on but none of the other riders had paid much attention or even spoken to them. They were very grateful for having met the generous 'Frenchie'.

The boys tied themselves to the walking rail but Pylyp wasn't about to sleep again that night. In the morning they talked about the experience of the night before. If each hadn't remembered the events in the same way they would have thought it had been a dream.

They rode the same boxcar all day and night and all of the next day. Soon they would have to change trains to continue heading east toward Kenora, Ontario. So when the train slowed down they jumped off and went in search of their next freight.

Not too far from the tracks they saw a number of men, with bundles like their own, gathered around a fire over which hung a cooking pot. The boys approached the 'jungle' and were challenged.

"Got anything for the pot?" one of the men called out to the boys.

They had nothing to contribute so they knew could not even warm themselves near the fire. The two boys wandered off a short distance and hid in the grass to wait for their next train. By now they were hungry again but they had nothing to eat and there was nowhere to get any food.

The next morning the boys followed some of the men from the jungle, who they had heard talking about Kenora. They watched the men and caught the same freight train and were on their way again.

By that evening the boys were very, very hungry – they hadn't eaten anything since the bread and beans, compliments of 'Frenchie', on the first night out of Winnipeg. The boys tried not to think about how hungry they were and then, as if in answer to a prayer, 'Frenchie' appeared again walking toward them along the top of the boxcars.

"Hungry boys?" he called out to them. It was obvious they were very hungry so 'Frenchie', once more, produced a loaf of bread and can of beans. Once again he ate little, while the boys consumed the impromptu feast.

This time 'Frenchie' lingered and talked with the boys. He gave them more tips about riding the rods. Then he told them he was a 'steeple jack' – he made a living by painting flagpoles and smoke stacks. Neither boy had ever heard of anyone doing that for a living. 'Frenchie' was an enigma. All too soon he got up and walked off into the darkness along the tops of the boxcars, just as he had the last time.

The train rolled along and eventually arrived in Fort William. The boys had to walk to the twin town of Port Arthur, where they would catch their next freight train heading east. Most of the men who had been on their train were heading east so the boys continued to follow them.

When they got to Port Arthur, the boys washed off the grime of rail travel in the cold water of Lake Superior and then sat on the shore to watch the huge ships and the dock activity. The Canadian Pacific Railway (CPR) freight train, which they wanted to catch, was to leave at eight that evening. So the boys took stock of their situation. They had no money left. Pylyp's friend had found a small, gold tiepin among his possessions, which he had forgotten all about. They walked into town and, after considerable negotiation, were able to pawn the tiepin for ninety-five cents. So they bought a loaf of bread and a can of pork 'n beans for their supper. Then it was back to the port to catch their next freight train.

As the train approached Nipigon, Ontario, the boys had heard they would have to get off the train as soon as possible. The 'bulls' in Nipigon were notorious and the boys didn't want to risk getting caught.

Unfortunately, the 'bulls' were also very experienced and managed to catch a number of the men who had been riding that freight train. The two prairie boys were among those apprehended. The motley crew was hauled to the station and their bundles thoroughly inspected. Then they were given a stern lecture and told to head out of town on the highway or risk being jailed as vagrants.

The experienced travellers were grumbling about trying their luck with the Canadian National Railway (CNR) but the boys, who tried to follow them, were not fast enough and lost their trail.

By now the weather had turned cold and the boys' clothing was not adequate to keep them warm. They were lost in a foreign town, cold and hungry once more. Just as despair was setting in their old friend 'Frenchie' appeared once more.

"I saw you guys get picked up by the 'bulls'," he said. "I figured you might need help getting on your way again." So once more 'Frenchie' shared bread and beans with the boys. He told them where to go to catch the CNR freight train heading east. This time he also gave them another pearl of wisdom, which would prove to be very useful. Because it was getting too cold to continue riding on the top of boxcars, 'Frenchie' told them how to find an empty box car and jam the doors to prevent them from slamming shut and locking.

The boys were once more satiated and knew where they were going and how to get there. They arrived at the CNR yards and found several of the men who had been caught by the 'bulls' earlier that evening. The boys climbed aboard an empty boxcar with six men. These were 'professionals' and had all the equipment necessary to make rail travel as comfortable as possible. The men immediately jammed the doors of the boxcar and the boys watched carefully so they would know how to do it themselves.

As soon as the train pulled out, the boys understood why the doors had to be jammed. The train had one engine pulling and another pushing, so the ride was jerky and the boxcar doors would have been opening and closing with every jerk. Eventually, if the doors hadn't been jammed, they would have slammed shut and locked.

The train made frequent stops at pulp and paper mills, mines, and sidings to let other trains pass. At some stops the train picked up full cars and left behind empty ones. The boys slept as much as they could. At noon on the second day the train stopped at a large bush camp. Some of the men from the boxcar jumped off and ran for the camp kitchen. They returned with bread and pies, which they had bought. The men knew the boys had no food but they did not offer to share their bounty. So the boys continued to go hungry.

As time passed more and more men joined them in the empty boxcar. Soon there were so many that the boys had to ride on top again. Around the middle of the afternoon one day the train was approaching Capreol. Once again the boys had heard that the 'bulls' in this town were very mean, even to the point of having shot a 'rider'. So they jumped off early and walked through the town to the tracks beyond the settlement. At Capreol the train was broken into two; one would travel east and the other would head south. Once again the boys followed the experienced riders who were heading east, in order to be sure to get on the right train. This time they rode on a flat car.

Once more 'Frenchie' appeared with food to share. This time he told them they wouldn't see him again as he was heading south from North Bay.

Early the next morning the boys were preparing to board a Northland freight. Some friendly men told them there was a house near the tracks where a 'rider' could get a free breakfast. The boys were reluctant to knock on a door for a 'lump' but they were hungry, so they followed the directions the men had given and were rewarded by a fine breakfast.

Their freight train was leaving at eleven that morning. This time, Pylyp had another close call when attempting to catch his ride. As they were running to climb on board, they realized the train was travelling faster than they had thought. Pylyp's friend caught the ladder of a boxcar, jumped, and pulled his feet up onto the lowest rung, then climbed up. But when Pylyp caught the ladder and jumped his feet missed the lowest ladder rung. He was being dragged along with the car. Instinctively he began moving his feet and running, then with a burst of energy, he jumped once more and his feet landed on the rung. He climbed up onto the boxcar where his friend had been watching in horror.

"I was sure you were a goner," was all his white-faced friend could say.

Once on the train the boys found a flat car loaded with huge pipes. It was raining again so each of them backed into a pipe for shelter. At Englegart, the train would once again be divided into two. Since it would not be continuing until the next morning, the boys got off and walked along the tracks. They found an unlocked shack next to the tracks, where they took refuge from the rain for the night.

In the morning, the boys started walking along the tracks until there was only one set and found a place to hide in the bushes to wait for their train. It was cold and wet. Despite their dry night in the shack, the boys were now soaked through and there was a hole in one of Pylyp's shoes, so his sock and foot were drenched as well. As they watched the train approach from the station, it switched to another track several hundred yards from where they had been waiting. In no time the train was gone and they had missed it.

There they were thirty-two miles from their destination, Kirkland Lake. They walked to the road, which ran through the town, and began trudging along the shoulder. There was very little traffic on the road that cold, wet morning and what traffic there was seemed unmoved by the plight of the bedraggled, drenched youths.

After about two hours of slogging along, the boys happened upon the yard of a small, dilapidated house. There were some children playing in the yard so they approached and asked whether they could have some water from the well. The children stopped their game and stared at the strangers. Then one spoke to the others and the smaller children ran into the house. Pylyp had recognized that the older child had spoken in French. So in his very best, high school French, he asked for water from the well. The older child helped the boys get a drink. Then Pylyp's friend attempted to ask for bread. The child ran into the house and came back with two small pieces of bread. The boys were sure this was all the youngsters had to share and were grateful for it.

The boys walked on. Eventually they caught a ride with a farmer for a few miles and then later in the day, another ride took them all the way into Kirkland Lake. They had arrived.

They walked around the settlement looking for a place to settle for the night. They were wet, cold, exhausted, and hungry. It had been a very long day and a very long trip from Winnipeg. Pylyp was ready to curl up somewhere out of the rain and sleep but his friend said he smelled something good coming from a two-and-a-half story house near by.

"Let's get a 'lump'," he said to Pylyp in Ukrainian. At that moment a large woman came out of the house and overheard what he had said.

"Shcho te hochesh? (What do you want?)" she asked the boys in Ukrainian.

So the boys explained that they had come all the way from Saskatchewan to find work in the mines.

The woman owned the large house and rented rooms to mine workers. It didn't take long for her to assess the boys' miserable condition. Being a kind-hearted woman, she decided these young fellows needed help to get established in the rough and tumble mining town.

"Dobra," she responded, "come in and we'll see what we can make of you."

So the boys followed the large lady into the kitchen on the main floor of the house. She gave them a basin and towels and sent them to the backyard pump to wash as much of the grime off their bodies as they could. Then she called them back into the house. She had prepared a meal consisting of bread, fried potatoes, and sausage. It was the best meal the boys had had in weeks.

As the three ate together the landlady asked questions to learn as much as she could about her supper guests. Although she had a kind heart, she had learned to disguise it with a brisk mannerism so she wouldn't be imposed upon. She listened carefully to the young Saskatchewan farm boys and wondered if they could make a go of it in this rough mining town.

"But they did manage to make it all the way here by riding the rails," she thought. "They are determined or desperate or both."

When she heard of the sad circumstances, which led Pylyp to leave the only family he had, her heart was touched. But to hide her tender feelings for the orphan she simply commanded:

"You must write to your sister and baba immediately. You must tell them where you are and that you are well. You will write tonight."

Pylyp had often wanted to let Lena know that he was still ok but during their travels there just hadn't been an opportunity. Now, though his friend bristled at the demanding landlady's order for them to write to their families, Pylyp was grateful to her for helping them to do so.

After eating their fill, the boys asked how they could repay the landlady's generosity. So as she cleared the supper dishes, the boys headed out to the backyard to chop wood.

The landlady had a tiny room in the attic, which was not currently being rented, and that is where she installed the boys.

"When you get jobs you will pay rent. Until then you are my guests but you will work for your keep."

This was a generous offer, indeed, and the boys were very grateful to her.

So that night the youngsters slept on two narrow cots in an attic room, which was not much bigger than the two cots put together. The beds had worn, but clean, sheets, pillowcases, and blankets, but the room itself was cold and windowless. Compared to the places they had been sleeping while travelling it was safe, dry, and indoors, which was a vast improvement.

The next morning the boys found the landlady's dining room crammed with husky miners, some were renters and others had come just for breakfast. They were directed to sit at the table and ate with the miners, who all but ignored them. The conversation was minimal but the youths did learn a few things about where they might go to apply for mining jobs and a little about what those jobs might be like.

After breakfast Pylyp helped the landlady clear and wash the breakfast dishes, while his friend brought in water from the well and chopped more wood. They had written letters home the evening before, so the landlady gave them some small change to mail them at the post office. Then they headed to the four mine offices along the main drag to apply for jobs. Neither boy was immediately offered a job, so they wandered around the town to get their bearings and see if there might be other work opportunities.

Pylyp spotted a 'Help Wanted' sign in the window of a café and was quickly offered a job as a dishwasher, starting that very moment. His friend continued walking around town and eventually found a job in another restaurant but his job would not start until the next morning. The two friends were reunited late that evening at the landlady's house. The miners who rented rooms had eaten their supper and were nowhere to be seen, so the landlady presented the boys with bread and sardines for their supper.

Pylyp's job was hard work, over long hours but he could eat all his meals at the cafe. The owners and most of the people working at the restaurant were Ukrainian so he fit in. The café was a cold, twenty-five minute walk from the landlady's house. The only clothing he had was threadbare and hole-ridden and his shoes were barely holding together. He was earning thirty dollars a month but now he was paying rent. He had to work five shifts before he had any cash to buy a pair of shoes, his first priority. Every time he saved a few dollars he would buy a piece of clothing, mostly something to help keep him warm. Although he ate his meals at the café, besides rent and the much-needed shoes and coat, he had other expenses. He had to buy soap; pay to have his clothing, such as it was, laundered; and buy stamps, so that he could keep in touch with his family back in Saskatchewan. It would be a long time before he could afford a whole suit of new clothing and longer still before he could save any money to send home.

The landlady never failed to demand of him, "Have you written to your sister?" And so in his next letter Pylyp mentioned that he needed warm clothing. It was with tremendous gratitude that, a few weeks later, Pylyp received a package from Saskatchewan. Lena and Baba Cione had sent him some of his father's clothing as well as hand-knitted socks, mittens, and a scarf. When Pylyp wore these precious items he always felt he was wrapped in the loving arms of his family, who he missed desperately.

1933 - 34

In fall, Lyudmyla was ready to start school. Baba Cione had a great idea. She told her sons on the farm to bring two of their daughters to live in the little house during the school week. This way the girls wouldn't have to walk from the farm to the school in town and Lyudmyla would have her cousins' company. This arrangement worked wonders for the little orphan.

That same fall Lena was getting ready to take her first teaching position. The school she had been assigned was situated about ten miles to the west of the town in which she had been raised. When the school had been built, early in the new century, it had been named for a large village in the old country.

The school itself sat alone on 'School Land', a two-acre portion of a section of land designated for a school. The better part of the section of land had been sold to a neighbourhood farmer, in order to pay for the construction and upkeep of the school. The two-acre schoolyard sat at one corner of the section of land, nearest the gravel grid road. On the schoolyard was situated the one-roomed schoolhouse of typical design. Stairs led up to the only door of the building. Through the door was a small, porch-like, 'cloakroom', with benches on both sides and hooks on the walls for coats. At the other end of the cloakroom was another door, which lead into the schoolroom itself. It was a single, large, rectangular room, with four tall windows along the western wall and one on the eastern wall. On the north wall was a large blackboard, the teacher's desk, and in the northeast corner, the pot-bellied stove. Along the back wall were bookshelves, a water cooler, and the door to the cloakroom.

Situated a few hundred yards from the schoolhouse were a small, one-roomed 'teacherage'; a barn for the horses children rode to school; a well; and two outdoor toilets, one marked 'boys' and the other 'girls'. A page-wire fence encircled the schoolyard and a hedge of caragana bushes helped shelter the buildings. While there were farmhouses as near as a mile or so from the school itself it seemed very isolated in the vast, open expanse of the Saskatchewan Prairies.

When Lena arrived in fall, the School Board Trustee, a local farmer, took her to the teacherage. He brought several sacks of garden produce, potatoes, carrots, beets, cabbages, etc., and a few small sacks of sugar, flour, salt, tea, etc. Each family in the neighbourhood had contributed what they could for partial payment for the teacher. A small cash salary was to be paid in two portions, the first at Christmas and the second at the end of the school year in June, if it would be possible to do so. Lena knew these folk would pay her what and if they could.

Lena's first year living alone in the teacherage was very busy but lonely. The days were filled with chores as well as teaching. When she awoke she had to start a fire in the wood and coal stove in the teacherage. While that was warming her small dwelling, she headed to the school to start a fire in the pot-bellied stove there, in order to prepare for the arrival of the students. Then back to the teacherage for breakfast and to prepare a lunch to take with her to the schoolroom. Then back to the school to prepare for the day of teaching.

The children mostly arrived for the start of the school day at nine o'clock. They did not enter the school building until the hand bell was rung, unless it was a very cold, winter day, in which case the children could gather inside the school until the bell was rung for classes to begin. There were twenty students, ranging in age from six to sixteen and in grades one to ten. In some grades there were only one or two students and in others, as many as six. It was a juggling act to get everyone working on something while teaching a lesson to a specific grade.

The school day followed a formula set by the provincial education authorities: classes from nine until ten fifteen, a fifteen-minute recess, then classes until noon, a one-hour lunch break, classes again until two, another fifteen-minute recess, and classes again until three-thirty. In winter, the school day began in the dark. Throughout the year the children spent recesses and the better part of the lunch hour outside. Only in the coldest winter weather were children allowed to remain in school. Lena had to be in the school or in the schoolyard whenever there were children present.

After the last student departed, Lena would clean the blackboard and brushes, sweep the floor of the schoolroom with sweeping compound, and take out the trash. Then she would haul wood from the woodpile and water from the well for both the school and the teacherage. Then it was back to the teacherage to prepare supper and spend the evening grading papers and tests and preparing lessons for the next day. Despite the long hours of work Lena was very lonely much of the time. Darkness engulfed the little schoolyard increasing her feelings of isolation. One evening, though she knew it was futile, she climbed up on a kitchen chair to see if she could spy the lights of the nearest farmhouse.

"It is out there," she told herself, "even if I can't see it."

Lena put her heart and soul into preparing the Christmas Concert, in order to show off her students' talents and delight their parents. She taught the youngest children to perform a recitation about the meaning of Christmas.

This was delivered in both English and Ukrainian. Next the entire student body sang two Christmas Carols, one in English and one in Ukrainian. After that the middle classes presented a one-act play in English. Then the older students performed two Ukrainian dances while those who could, played violin, mandolin, accordion, or piano to accompany them. Finally, the entire group of students took the 'stage' to sing 'We Wish You a Merry Christmas'. The concert had been a triumph and all the long hours of preparation and rehearsing had paid off. The parents were very happy with their new, young teacher.

At the end of the concert, one of the fathers brought in a sack, which had been left by Santa on the schoolhouse steps. The sack was filled with brown paper bags, one for each child. Inside each brown paper bag was an orange, some nuts in the shell, and a piece of hard candy. The parents produced loaves of sandwiches, thermoses of coffee and hot cocoa, and cakes and squares. As the adults ate and visited the school children enjoyed their Christmas treats and reveled in the knowledge that they would be free from school for two full weeks.

When Lena returned to her home for the celebration of Christmas that year, she planned to ask Baba if she could take Lyudmyla back to the teacherage with her after the Christmas break. She was worried Baba would be opposed to the idea. Baba had grown fond of living in the little house in town and might feel she had no need to continue to do so if Lyudmyla were gone.

Little did Lena know there was a more serious reason for Baba Cione's resistance to the idea of Lyudmyla leaving with Lena. While Lena had been away, a relatively prosperous but childless couple had approached Baba to inquire whether they might adopt the little girl. Baba Cione feared that if the child were allowed to live with her unmarried sister in the isolated teacherage, the authorities might intervene and require the child be put up for adoption. Baba had been touched by the local couple's sincere wish to give her granddaughter what might have been a better life but she had vowed to raise her son's young daughter. She wanted Lyudmyla to remain a Cione and know her family and where she had come from. She never told Lena about her reason for wanting to keep Lyudmyla with her in the little house.

Lena and Baba cleaned the house and prepared for Christmas. They were going to go to church for the holy celebration of Christ's birth and then back to the farm with the uncles and their families for the traditional Sviata Vechera (Holy Evening Supper).

It was such a joyous celebration! The women had been cooking for several days to prepare the traditional, meatless meal. The house was full of steam and warm as they entered from the brisk cold of the evening. Everyone had been fasting throughout the day, so by the time they returned to the farm from church everyone was famished. The large extended family gathered around the table as Uncle Myron, the eldest male in the family, lit the candle in the Kolach (Christmas bread) and pronounced, "Khrystos Rodyvsya" ("Christ is Born") and they all responded "Slavite Yoho" ("Let us Glorify Him"). Then they said a prayer of thanksgiving.

Even in these lean times it was still possible to have the special Christmas Eve Supper. First came the kutya, cooked wheat, mixed with hot water and honey. Uncle Myron took great delight in flinging a teaspoon of the mixture up to the ceiling to see whether it would stick – the amount that did was an indication of how good the next crop would be. Everyone looked up in anticipation for there had not been a good crop in several years.

After the kutya, the family sang a Christmas Carol. Then, course after course of the twelve special dishes were served, borscht, holupsti, pyrohi - with a variety of fillings - mushroom gravy, fish, peas in sauerkraut, dried fruit, etc. And after each dish they sang another carol. After the supper dishes were cleared away and the women began cleaning up, the men went out to feed the animals. It was especially important to take care of the animals on this holy night, as they represented the sheep and cows present at Christ's birth. The evening continued with more singing and talking. The children dove under the table to search for nuts in the straw, which had been strewn on the floor as a reminder of Christ's birth in a manger.

The next morning Baba was anxious to get back to town. It was so easy to go to church for every service when she lived in the little, town house. Her age was showing and she did not enjoy the long sleigh ride from the farm into town. After attending Divine Liturgy on Christmas Day Lena presented Baba and Lyudmyla with the precious gifts she had worked so hard to be able to buy for them. For Baba it was a beautiful new babushka (scarf), mostly black with large red roses and a black fringe. For Lyudmyla it was a new dress. Both had been ordered from the catalog. She had sent Pylyp a heavy, plaid shirt. For herself she had bought a radio but it had been left in the teacherage. It would be her defense against loneliness in the months to come.

Lena talked to Baba about taking Lyudmyla back to the teacherage with her after Christmas and, as expected, Baba didn't like the idea. She said she didn't think Lyudmyla could walk the ten miles back to the school with Lena. Lena explained that one of the farmers was going to take her back to the teacherage in his caboose, so they wouldn't have to walk.

"Well what about when you have to walk three miles to the nearest town for mail and groceries?" Baba asked. "You can't leave Lyudmyla alone in the teacherage."

This was true thought Lena. Perhaps it would be too hard for Lyudmyla to walk with her when she needed to get to town.

Baba told Lena that she worried about her being alone in the teacherage and she would worry even more if the little one were there as well. This was the final argument. Lena knew she would not win against Baba's logic. Perhaps it had been her desire to keep her promise to her mother or perhaps she had just been selfish to want her little sister with her. So after the feast of Jordon, Lena returned to the teacherage alone.

Lyudmyla

Lyudmyla loved living with Baba Cione. In summer, she played with the neighbour girls who were close to her in age. They played in her backyard or one of their backyards. They made necklaces by putting the pointed end of a hollow stem of grass into the open, opposite end and joining these grass links together. They made grass and mud pies with rock decorations. They played school and took turns being the teacher.

Sometimes, Lyudmyla and Baba would go to the farm to spend a few days - Baba to help with the garden or cooking for the men during busy farming times and Lyudmyla to play with her cousins. During the school year Lyudmyla went to the school in town and in winter, two of her cousins from the farm would spend the week with her and Baba in the little house. They loved to dance and Baba would sing for them and teach them the dance steps. When it was warm enough the girls would find pieces of cardboard to use as sleds and slide down the snow-covered hill in the schoolyard.

For Lyudmyla, having her cousins stay in the little house made the winters more bearable. Not only did she have someone to play with in the evenings but also someone to walk to school with. In winter it was dark in the morning when the girls headed off to school and nearly dark by the time they returned to the little house. Lyudmyla had always hated walking home alone in the darkening evening, especially when she had to cross the train tracks.

It was cold walking to and from school in winter. The girls wore knee-high, felt, lace-up boots and woolen, hand-knitted socks, scarves, and mittens. Even so, on brutally cold days it was not unusual to arrive at school or home with half-frozen fingers and toes. It was also cold in the little house in winter. There was always a thick layer of frost on the inside of the windows. It was especially cold in the little house when the supply of wood for the stove was running low. Baba relied on her sons to bring a load of wood from the farm in the fall but often this would not last the entire winter. Sometimes a second load would be brought to the little house in town, sometimes it wasn't.

Lyudmyla knew that her Uncle Myron always had his rifle at hand when he travelled. He was an excellent hunter and never missed an opportunity to shoot game. So it was not uncommon for him to arrive at the little house with a rabbit, freshly killed and ready to be dressed for a rare meal with meat. The only other source of meat was when a cow or pig was butchered on the farm in fall or on the even more rare occasion when Baba actually killed one of her beloved chickens. Lyudmyla was not fond of the activities of butchering day at the farm but she loved to help Baba clean and draw a freshly killed chicken. Sometimes there would be the surprise of an egg inside!

One year, in early fall before the snow fell, Lyudmyla begged Baba to let her stay at the farm for a few days so she could walk to school with her cousins. On one of these days as the children were walking home from school, it was very hot, dry, and windy. As they left the protection of some bushes and moved into the open, about a mile from the farm, the wind really started to blow violently. There was always dust in the air in those dry, hot days of the thirties but this year had been worse than usual. Soon the children were having difficulty seeing each other let alone where they were going. The oldest cousin said "Everyone hold hands so we don't get lost," and the children trudged along with full confidence in their leader. Sure enough after about an hour of battling the swirling dust and choking on it as it threatened their mouths and noses, the bedraggled, dust-covered little band arrived safely at the farmhouse. That night it rained and the next morning was brilliant and sunny, the perfect day to walk back to town and school.

One autumn day, after a very hot, dry summer, a tragic event took place in town. One of the grain elevators beside the train tracks caught fire. The men of the town came running with buckets of water and sacks and blankets but they could not put out the fire and the elevator burned and burned. The air was filled with smoke and the strong odor of burned grain. After the fire had burned itself out, Baba took Lyudmyla with a feather duster and a pail to collect what unburned wheat they could find. This would be used to help feed the chickens. Baba had always watched for when rail cars were being loaded with wheat and after they had departed would take Lyudmyla to gather what grain she could find for the chickens. After the elevator burned there was much more wheat to be gathered but you had to be careful to select the unburned kernels.

Baba kept a few chickens in the backyard for eggs as the staple of their diet. Baba made egg noodles. Uncle Bohdan brought flour once a year after grain from the farm had been milled. Baba kept the flour in a large covered tub in the cool pantry. So she made noodles all year by keeping the chickens fed so they continued to lay eggs. On rare occasions there would be chicken soup to go with the noodles – that was a feast!

So little Lyudmyla grew and her character was shaped by the circumstances of her life situation. She had always been a thoughtful, introspective child.

She became aware of feeling somehow less worthy than others around her. She often felt insecure. She couldn't remember exactly when she had started to feel this way; it was probably after the death of her mother. Her cousins were all confident and close-knit. Lyudmyla loved spending time with them but sometimes felt a bit like an outsider. They often talked about things that had happened when Lyudmyla had not been with them, contributing to her feelings of being left out. She tried very hard to be as much a part of her cousins' lives as they were of hers. She had no one to talk to about these growing feelings about herself. Lena and Pylyp were away and Lyudmyla did not want to say anything to Baba Cione. She loved her baba and did not want to be needy or ungrateful.

Pavlo and Dariya

Pavlo and Dariya labored on. Each year they struggled to survive and by the grace of God and their own hard work, they did … just barely.

In 1933 Maria married one of the neighbourhood farm boys. Pavlo was grateful his daughter settled relatively close by as she had always been his favorite child. She had enjoyed working with him on the farm and he had considered her to be as valuable to him and the farm as any son ever could have been. She could handle the team of horses to plough, harrow, and seed as well as he could. And she loved working the land. In his heart Pavlo had hoped she would not marry, but rather stay on the family farm. He had even thought the farm should one day be passed to her when he could no longer work it himself.

But it was not to be. Like many young women, Maria had felt the need to start her own family. The young man she had chosen was hard working and would take care of her as best he could in these difficult times. And, of course, it did mean one fewer mouth to feed on the farm.

And so when Maria left the family farm, Pavlo had to rely on young Yuriy to help with the farming. Yuriy, who insisted on being called 'George' from shortly after he had started going to school, seemed much less interested in farming than his older sister had been. He loved school and Dariya often commented that he reminded her of her half-brother Andriy.

George

George was thirteen when his sister left home to start her new life as a wife. He knew his father favoured Maria and, because he knew he could never measure up to her in their father's eyes, he had turned to school instead of farming as his preferred occupation.

George loved learning although going to school itself could be challenging. Maria had not gone to school so George was the first in the family to attend. When George started school at the age of seven it had been at his mother's insistence. His father had not seen the need to send his son to school. But Dariya had insisted and, in this, she had gotten her way. He didn't start going to school in the hamlet, two miles from their farm, until late in September after the harvest was complete. During the busy harvest time neither parents nor horses could be spared to take him to town and, though only seven, he had his share of chores to do.

And so when George finally arrived at the two-roomed school in the hamlet the other students had been attending for almost a month. He was behind. But what was worse, he spoke only Ukrainian. Most of the students in the community spoke either French or Ukrainian at home, depending on where their parents had come from. But the children from the hamlet had at least a rudimentary understanding and ability in English. The teacher was an older man from down east. He was English and did not want to hear anything but English being spoken in his school. As a result, George was severely disadvantaged, not only because of his late start in the school year but also because of the language barrier.

After suffering teasing from the other students, many of whom considered him to be 'slow', and the occasional whack across the knuckles with a ruler from the teacher for speaking Ukrainian instead of English, George realized that going to school would not be quite what he had hoped. Fortunately George found a friend in John. John was actually Ivan Kaminsky. George knew John's family, even though they lived in the hamlet, because they went to St. Nicholas Ukrainian Catholic Church situated on the corner of the Dannyk farm. John was older than George and had been going to school for a whole year. John relived his own humiliating start in school when he saw George struggling and so he decided to help his new friend.

“The first thing you have to do is to start calling yourself ‘George’ rather than Yuriy. The teacher has a hard enough time with our last names so make it easy for him to call on you by your English, first name,” John advised.

“Next you must learn to understand and speak English as quickly as possible - don’t worry, I’ll teach you,” John continued.

And so it was that at every recess and lunch hour, John took on the role of teacher to help his new friend learn English.

Pavlo and Dariya were mystified when their son announced he must now be called ‘George’. Pavlo never could remember to do so but Dariya tried to remember to do as her beloved son requested. She had promised God if He let her keep this son, after having lost her first two, she would do whatever she could to keep him safe and strong. She sensed he needed this new name in order to be successful in school and she recognized in him a love of learning, similar to that in her beloved half-brother, Andriy. So she tried very hard to call him ‘George’. Baba Anna, of course, threw her hands in the air at all of this and shook her head. “He is Yuriy, like my husband – the priest said so when he was baptized – no one just changes their name when they want to!”

It was doubly fortunate that George had a good friend and teacher in John but also that he had a natural ability for language, not unlike his Uncle Andriy. And so in a very short time, George was speaking and learning in English. He also learned some French from other students. It wasn’t long before his fellow students realized that George was by no means ‘slow’. It took the teacher a bit longer to come to this conclusion but he eventually saw just how remarkable George’s progress had been.

George was determined his younger sister, Iryna, and brother, Mykola, would not suffer the humiliation and hardships he had suffered when they eventually went to school. And so he made it his job to teach his siblings English and French and anything else he was studying at school. Both Iryna and Mykola loved to learn as much as George did and George was a very good teacher, so by the time Iryna was six, she was more than ready to go to school. Pavlo could not understand why a girl should go to school. He himself had never attended school, although Father Mykhaylo had insisted on teaching Pavlo rudimentary reading and writing in Ukrainian. Dariya had never had the opportunity to go to school. She could not read or write. The importance of reading was brought home to her when she heard Andriy's poetry. It was so beautiful and she loved to listen to him read it but how much more wonderful it would have been if she could read it for herself, whenever she wanted to. She was determined her children would learn to read and write.

The City

In the deepest, darkest days of the depression, Pavlo began to give up hope for his farm. At first he didn't share his thoughts with Dariya but eventually he knew this subject had to be discussed. It was in the evening after they had been forced to sell yet another of Dariya's beloved cows, 'Albena'. Pavlo knew Dariya had even shed a tear over this most recent sale. But there was nothing he could do about it so he decided the time had come to have a serious discussion about their future. And so that evening, as they lay in bed after the particularly long and discouraging day, he asked her:

"Have you ever been to the city?"

"Only when we came by train when I was seven," she replied. "Andriy marvels at how it has grown and changed since then."

"Would you like to see it?" Pavlo asked.

"Some day perhaps," she responded.

"Well," he hesitated, "I am thinking of going to the city. Would you like to come with me?"

"Why would you do that?" she asked in astonishment.

"Do you remember the farmer I worked for before I took this homestead?"

"Yes," she replied cautiously.

"Well," he continued, "he has given up his farm and moved to the city. He has a job there. He wrote to tell me there is a job where he works, if I want it."

Dariya was stunned. She didn't know what to say. The farm was their life. She knew just how hard it had been with the drought, hail, and grasshoppers and how crushing the loss of crops had been. But they weren't starving. They were no better off than their neighbours but no worse either.

It had been so long since she had spoken that Pavlo thought perhaps Dariya and fallen asleep. Gently he tried again…

"What do you think?" he asked.

"If you must go to see what this may be like," she said slowly, "I will go with you. But it would have to be better in the city than living here on the farm before I would agree to move." This last statement was said with a firmness Pavlo had learned was to be taken seriously. In their marriage there had been very few times when Pavlo's decision was not final but once in a long time Dariya showed her stubborn side. He knew she would go with him and consider what was best for the family but if she found the farm was still the best that would be the end of it.

And so Pavlo took a small amount of cash he had been saving from the sale of cream and eggs and bought two train tickets for a trip to the city. Anna was mystified about the sudden need for her daughter and son-in-law to go to the city but she was much more concerned about being left with all the farm chores and children to contend with on her own.

Pavlo had written to his former employer and it had been arranged that he would meet them at the train station in downtown Saskatoon and take them to his own home. The next day Pavlo and his host would visit the meat packing plant where there might be a job for him. Dariya would spend the day with their hostess to see what living in the city was like.

The house was a small, one-and-a-half story, wood-framed house on Avenue H. It was clear their hosts were very proud of their modest home. There were four children in the family, who all slept in one of the two bedrooms on the upper level. The hosts had insisted that Pavlo and Dariya sleep in their bedroom on the upper level.

The evening passed pleasantly enough. The hostess had prepared a large pot of vegetable broth and Dariya had spent the afternoon helping her to make noodles for the soup and bake bread. This was the adequate supper they shared. After supper Dariya helped with the clean up, while the men talked about work in the city and the children raced around playing noisy games. When Pavlo and Dariya were finally alone in the upper bedroom, Pavlo asked hesitantly, "Well?"

"It is too soon to know," was all she could manage. Dariya had found the house small and too close to the other houses on the street. She could barely breath for the closeness of everything and everyone inside and outside the house. In her heart she knew this wasn't the place for her or her family. But she had given her word. She would wait and see what tomorrow would bring.

In the morning, while the men prepared to go to the meat packing plant, the children gathered around the stove. The hostess had mixed up a thin batter of flour and water and was dropping it by the spoonful directly onto the hot surface of the stove. As quickly as a 'pancake' was cooked a small hand snatched it off the stove and gobbled it down.

"Like chickens feeding," Dariya thought, but said nothing.

The process of 'breakfast' continued until there was no more batter in the bowl. At that the children, with a unified moan, wandered off to get ready for school.

Dariya had never seen anything like this in her life. She couldn't imagine her family in a similar situation. At least on the farm they had milk, cooked cereal, and a few vegetables from the garden – she had noted there was a very small garden plot behind the house, hardly enough to feed the family in summer. "Where would you plant enough potatoes to last through the winter?" And then the most amazing thing happened. A man appeared at the back door of the little house. He was bringing water to fill the tank by the stove. The hostess had to pay him for this water. "Imagine! Paying for water!" Dariya had never heard of such a thing. No, this was no place for her family.

When the men returned later that afternoon Dariya was ready to return to the train station for the trip home.

It was curious. Dariya never did hear anything about the job Pavlo had gone to see. He never asked her what she thought of city life. And in the silence on the subject, both knew their life was on the farm – come what may.

A Winter Visitor

There had not been an extremely cold winter since the record-breaking cold of 1906. Dariya remembered that bone-chilling winter very well. It had been only their second winter in Canada and it had been a real shock. The winter of 1935-36 was to be a winter to rival the one of 1906.

One cold, blustery day, while the family was tucked up safe and warm in their farmhouse, there came a knock at the door. Strange in such weather. Pavlo went to the door and found a cold, snow-covered Mountie (Royal Canadian Mounted Policeman). He pointed out into the yard at his poor, exhausted horse and said in Ukrainian, "Please get him into your barn and give him some food and water for he has saved my life by bringing me to your door."

George was dispatched to care for the horse while Dariya heated water and Iryna fetched a pyrena to wrap around the half-frozen stranger.

"I need something to eat," the policeman said, "I was caught in this blizzard yesterday afternoon and haven't had anything to eat since."

Dariya, with Iryna's help, heated some soup and presented it with a slice of fresh-baked bread and a cup of rose-hip chai.

One look at the tea and the stranger said, "What's this? Do you not see that I need whiskey? Not tea!"

"Whiskey?" Pavlo asked incredulously. "But we don't have any," and he was telling the truth. Pavlo had never had a drink of alcohol in his life. Not that he hadn't had the opportunity but from his earliest days, back in the old country, he had seen the trouble strong drink could cause and as a result, had decided never to drink alcohol.

"What do you mean you don't have any?" the Mountie asked with just as much incredulity. "You homesteaders always have home brew. Can't you see that I need some. Don't worry I won't turn you in," for it was not legal to make home brew at that time.

"No, sir," Pavlo replied. "We really don't have any. I have never touched the stuff all my life."

The Mountie just stared at him. He couldn't believe this shortish, slightly stout, Ukrainian immigrant. How could it be that he had no home brew and he didn't drink? It seemed impossible!

So the Mountie contented himself with the soup, bread, and tea. When he had finished he rolled into the pyrena and lay on the kitchen floor in front of the stove and fell fast asleep. He was obviously exhausted.

In the morning Dariya made sure to provide a good breakfast of hot cooked cereal with cream, more fresh bread, and rose-hip chai.

The Mountie was grateful for their hospitality. He knew times were hard and that what he was being offered was the very best they had to share with him. Overnight the blizzard had increased in intensity, so it was clear he was bound to stay with this family for some time.

So after breakfast the Mountie called Pavlo over to have a frank discussion.

"Look, I know you say you don't drink alcohol. That's fine but you really should have some on hand for emergencies … for health reasons."

Dariya was listening intently. She knew how helpful a drink of home brew could be to ease the pain of an injury that needed to be stitched or even a difficult birth. Dariya had learned much from her mother about healing. She had been called upon many times to help deliver babies or to tend to some farm accident.

Pavlo was resistant and felt there was no place in his home for hard drink.

So it was with some trepidation that Dariya spoke up.

"I understand," she said softly and hesitantly. She did not want to say anything contrary to her husband, especially in front of a stranger. "I have seen the value of alcohol for medicinal purposes but I know it can also be misused. I agree with both my husband and with you, sir."

"Good," the big Mountie said. "Then I will teach you how to make it. You must promise me you will never sell what you make and you will only use it for medicine."

"Yes, sir," Dariya responded, "I promise."

Dariya half expected Pavlo to object but he simply put on his great buffalo coat and went out to the barn, as if to put as much distance between himself and what he knew was going to be happening in his own kitchen.

And so the Mountie showed Dariya what to use - potatoes, water, sugar, and yeast - to prepare the mash. He told her how long to let it work and what had to be done after that, in order to distill the alcohol. He would be long gone before that process began, so she had to listen very carefully to remember his instructions.

In another day the weather finally cleared and the big Mountie departed.

Pavlo never said a thing about the large crock behind the kitchen stove or the strange smell that permeated the room. But on the day Dariya was getting ready to distill her first batch of horiwka, he took her aside and said very quietly and very sternly so she would know he was serious:

"You realize that if you are caught doing this you will go to jail."

And that was all he said. It was all he ever said on the matter.

To the day she died, Dariya defended her right to make and use horiwka for medicinal purposes. Later in life, after Pavlo was gone, she even had a bottle of beer or a glass of wine – and not only for medicinal purposes. She never was caught making home brew nor did she go to jail. The neighbours all said Dariya made the best pies … and the best home brew!

Anna

In 1938 things were finally beginning to get better on the farm but not in the farmhouse. Anna had never been a very happy woman but over the winter and into the spring she had become very difficult, indeed. Pavlo had lost all patience with her. The children avoided her. Only Dariya continued to try to please her mother. Dariya had been around sick people enough to know the change for the worse in her mother was probably due to illness. She had noticed her mother wince occasionally but Anna refused to admit to pain. Over the winter Anna had lost weight, more than was usual. In spring she showed no interest in the garden, which had been her domain since moving in with Dariya and Pavlo so many years ago. Dariya desperately wanted to help her mother but Anna would have none of it.

At last in a desperate attempt to make her mother more comfortable, Dariya moved fifteen-year old Iryna to a makeshift bed in the kitchen so Anna could have the bedroom to herself. Anna began to spend more and more time alone in the bedroom and then, actually in bed. Dariya knew her mother was dying but still Anna refused any help whatsoever.

Finally after months of decline, toward the end of June, Anna breathed her last. It came as a relief to the entire family, who had been walking on eggshells for months. It was very hot, so important to bury Anna as quickly as possible. Unfortunately the priest could not get there for several days, so as often had been necessary, neighbour women came to help Dariya wash the body and prepare it for burial. Dariya dressed her mother in the Sunday dress, which had been her favorite, and did her hair in the fashion she had always preferred in life. Pavlo and George built a coffin and a wooden cross. They put Anna in the coffin and the community descended upon the farmhouse, where they read the gospels, said the prayers for the dead, and sang the mournful Vichnya Pamyat.

Then they hauled the coffin on the horse-drawn wagon to the cemetery on the outskirts of the hamlet. The men had dug a grave and the coffin was lowered into it. The community joined once more in prayers for the deceased, sang the mournful tune, and filled in the grave. After most of the neighbours had drifted away, Dariya and Pavlo went to the lilac-embraced graves of their two, lost sons. George, Iryna, and Mykola (who now called himself Nick) followed at a distance. They knew the sad story of their two 'little brothers' and joined their parents in praying for them.

And then it was time to go home. There were chores to do.

That evening it was still very hot outside and even hotter in the farmhouse. The outside door was left open, with only the screen door closed. Dariya and Pavlo were talking in low tones. Dariya was exhausted – it had been a very long, difficult several months. Soon she was asleep. Pavlo rolled over.

Just then he heard the screen door open and close. "That darn dog," he thought and as he was about to rise to lock the screen door so the dog wouldn't be coming and going all night. He saw sparks fly across the bedroom floor. And then, standing at the foot of the bed was Anna. She was dressed just as she had been in the coffin. She didn't say a word and in an instant was gone.

"Did you see her? Did your see her?" Pavlo asked as he shook Dariya awake.

"Who? Who did I see?" she asked sleepily.

"Anna, you mother – she was just here – at the foot of the bed."

"You were dreaming," Dariya said and rolled over to go back to sleep.

Pavlo slept very little that night.

He and Anna had never gotten along but he had always tried to treat her with respect and fairness. He knew there were things he did, which Anna had not agreed with, but it was, after all his home. Why had she come back? Why was it he who had seen her?

The next morning even before breakfast, Pavlo hitched the team to the wagon and went to the next town to fetch the French priest. He explained the situation to the priest, who was used to helping out the Ukrainian Catholics when their own priest was not available. The priest agreed to follow Pavlo back to the cemetery where he sealed Anna's grave.

Pavlo slept much better the next night and Anna never visited him nor anyone else again.

Iryna

Iryna was fifteen. She had been going to school since she was six. She was very bright and loved school. Her brother, George, had taught her to read when she was only four years old and she had been reading everything she could get her hands on ever since. As she grew older, she grew to appreciate Uncle Andriy's poetry. He had given Mama a copy of each of his books and, because Mama could not read but loved his poetry, Iryna often read the Ukrainian poems to her.

Even as a very small child, Iryna had had a very active imagination and had loved to invent and tell stories. She told stories to herself when she was just a toddler and learning to speak. When she got a little older, she told stories to her little brother, Nick, whenever she was asked to help keep an eye on him. She told stories to her cats, the cows, and the chickens. She told stories as she played and did her chores. She told stories to anyone who would listen to her.

Iryna was a keen observer and always listened carefully, especially when the adults talked in the evenings about the trials and tribulations of early life on the Canadian Prairies. This content often featured in the stories Iryna told, although her imagination embellished upon what she heard, resulting in very entertaining narratives.

As Iryna grew older she began to write down her stories in school scribblers. She had dozens of them tucked away in her bedroom. Sometimes she would look through these stories and think about what she had been doing when she had written them. Sometimes she would re-write the stories to improve the content or to add dramatic effect. Iryna loved writing and storytelling.

But now that she was fifteen, Tato wanted her to quit school and spend more time helping Mama at home. It was time, he thought, she started thinking about getting married and having a family of her own.

Iryna wanted desperately to continue going to school. She was taking grade ten. There was only one more year offered in the school in town. Students who wanted to complete grade twelve had to either go to the city or take the required courses by correspondence in order to complete their studies.

She knew her father would not be supportive of her taking the correspondence courses, let alone going to the city, but she hoped to convince Mama to get Tato to agree to let her finish grade eleven.

At every opportunity, Iryna talked to her mother about completing grade eleven. Dariya was well aware of both her daughter's wishes and her husband's position. She wasn't sure she wanted to get involved in the coming battle of wills. Iryna was very much like her husband.

Pavlo had never been as close to Iryna as he had been to Maria. Iryna was much less enthusiastic about farming than Maria had been. Dariya often commented that Iryna was a lot like him but he didn't see it. To him, she appeared to be a headstrong, stubborn, young girl with a head full of silly stories. He was sure that what she really needed was a husband.

This was going to be a battle indeed. Dariya longed for a quiet, peaceful home, like the one in which she had spent the last years with her mother and father. Her half-brothers had been living in their own homes and it had been just her father, mother and herself. In those years her father was getting on in age. He had long since learned how to accommodate her mother's sharp ways in order to maintain peace and harmony.

The early years of her marriage had been hectic with farm work, child bearing and raising, and then her mother had moved in with them. From that moment on there had been little peace in their home. Now that Anna was gone, Dariya hoped a peaceful home could finally be achieved.

When Baba Anna died, for the first time in her life, Iryna had a bedroom to herself. Dariya remembered what a luxury it had been for her when Tato had built them the new farmhouse and she had had the privacy of her very own room.

Dariya wondered if her daughter might be less interested in school if she began to think about a family of her own. On this topic Dariya was torn. She had been sixteen when she married – just a year older than Iryna was now. She remembered how hard it had been for her to leave her home to make a new life with Pavlo. Although she had no regrets about her own life she did feel her youngest daughter should have the opportunity to enjoy her girlhood, as she herself had not.

And so in her subtle way Dariya made a plan. She wouldn't take sides. Instead, she would do what she could to help Iryna enjoy being young and if, by chance, in that process the young girl happened to find a life mate, perhaps the whole issue of schooling might fade away. It was worth a try.

So Dariya began to save the cream money. This was one of the few ways in which farmers could earn cash throughout the year. The cows were milked twice a day and the cream separated from the milk using a large, hand-operated contraption known as a 'separator'. The cream was collected and stored in metal cream cans. These cream cans were emblazoned with Pavlo's name and the name of the hamlet. The cream cans were stored either in the icehouse or down the well to keep cool until they were full. Then on the days when the train came through the hamlet, Dariya would take a full cream can to the train station and leave it with all the other cream cans from the surrounding farms. She would pick up the empty cream can, which would have been returned from the prior trip. When the train came through town, if there was a demand for the cream, the cream cans would be picked up and taken into the city. Every month a cheque would come by mail for the cream that had been picked up. Occasionally there was too much cream left at the train stations in all the hamlets, towns, and villages, so some cream cans were be left on the station platform. In those cases there was no cream cheque.

Pavlo had decided Dariya should have the cream money to use for household needs. After all, it was she who usually milked the cows, separated the cream, stored it, and took it to the train station. It was only right that she manage the use of the cream money. Dariya knew how to save money and how to use it carefully. So her new plan was to encourage Iryna to go to the dances in the town hall and, for each occasion, she should have a new dress. Sometimes Dariya would sew the new dress but recently there was another option. For a small amount of cash, about two or three dollars, a new dress could be ordered from the Eaton's catalog. The order form and money would be sent by mail on the train and within a week or two the dress would arrive the same way. It was an amazing new way to purchase, not only dresses, but all manner of things for the home and the farm. Of course Dariya had to rely on George to actually place the order but she always picked out the dresses from the pictures in the catalog.

On the day Dariya received the first catalog dress and gave it to Iryna, the girl could hardly wait to try it on. Dariya heard a squeal of delight and then Iryna came bounding out of her bedroom to show off the new dress. She was so excited she threw her arms around Dariya to hug her and then tried to kiss her mother on the cheek. Dariya was taken aback by this unusual show of affection and pulled back from her daughter.

"You look nice," she said, "now take off the dress before you get it dirty."

Iryna had always craved physical closeness but this was something that did not seem to come naturally for either of her parents. She was a bit ashamed of her exuberance for the new dress, which had resulted in her own show of affection. Yet at the same time, she was hurt that her mother had recoiled from her embrace. Iryna decided if she ever had children of her own she would cuddle and hug them the way she had longed for.

And so during the summer and fall of 1938, Iryna went, accompanied by George and always in a new dress, to all the dances held in the hamlet and neighbouring towns and villages. Dariya was a bit concerned about what Pavlo might think of all this but to her surprise he said not a word.

"When Mama died, I thought my home could be quiet and peaceful but now it's Pavlo and Iryna who are constantly in conflict. Will we ever have peace? Those two are just so much alike. Both have strong views and both think they are always right! I know that in his heart, Pavlo wants what's best for our daughter but he just can't see that she needs something different from what we needed to be happy. She is a writer like Andriy. She needs to tell her stories – and they are beautiful stories. I wish he could see that she really does know what she needs and it is not what he thinks she needs. How can I help them both? God give me strength!"

Andriy

Andriy and Elena had been married in 1924. He was almost forty and she was twenty-five. It had come as quite a surprise to his family as well as to the entire town. And yet when they were wed, it did seem to be the perfect solution for everyone concerned. Elena, who had been too busy with her ailing father and his business to have contemplated marriage, had slipped past the prime marrying age and was, in the eyes of the community, doomed to be a spinster. Andriy had been considered a confirmed bachelor.

When Andriy announced that he would move into town so Elena could continue to run the dry goods store, Petro, and more especially his wife, felt soon they would have all three quarter sections of land to farm with their boys. Andriy had even suggested that Petro rent his portion of the holding with the idea of eventually buying it. For nearly five years the arrangement had been working well. In 1929 when drought and depression set in however, it became clear Petro could no longer afford to rent Andriy's portion of the land, let alone buy it. Petro's eldest son was seventeen and he and his brothers were farming fulltime with their father. If times had been better they would have been able to take over the entire holding. Andriy, though he continued living in town, began to farm again with his brother. Seeding time was busy each year, harvest time, unfortunately, was not as busy in those lean years.

Early in the drought-ridden years, Andriy and Elena began to plant a garden in the patch on the home quarter that Anna had so lovingly developed. At first they were able to water their garden from the slough near the original family home. However as the drought progressed the slough all but dried up and the garden produced less and less. Whatever the garden produced, Andriy and Elena shared with families in town, many of whom were in greater need than farm families.

Charity had started at home. Those who could produce more than they needed shared with their neighbours. Churches collected from those who had something to distribute to those who had nothing. As the economic depression continued, local help began to fail. Saskatchewan had been the breadbasket but now it had been hit harder than anywhere else in the young country. Railcar loads of fruit, canned goods, fish, and clothing were sent from the east to the stricken province. Every hamlet, village, and town received the benefits of this generosity. In many cases these gifts meant the difference between survival and not.

Soon after the drought had begun, Petro's wife had suggested that Andriy use the money he earned from his books to help make life on the farm more bearable. Andriy asked Petro if he wanted to borrow money but this seemed not to be what had been in his wife's mind. She had hoped for a gift from Andriy of money or his portion of the land or both. Perhaps Petro had hoped for the same but he never mentioned any such hopes to Andriy, who only knew of them from comments dropped at opportune moments by the wife:

"We have sons who could farm all three quarters, while he will likely not have children at all."

"All we have to scratch out a living is the land, while he has money from his books and his wife's business, surely, he has more than he needs."

"What kind of brother has more than he needs, yet watches as others suffer and want."

It is often difficult to meet the expectations others have for your generosity. It is always easy to accuse others of being selfish when those expectations are not met.

Andriy would have been more than happy to help Petro and his family but he had never particularly liked Petro's wife. While he had offered Petro a loan and was willing to help them in any way he could, he was not about to gift his own, hard-earned savings, nor relinquish his land to his brother's family. The dry goods business suffered as much as the farms during the hard years of the '30's and even if this had not been the case, Andriy would never have considered using any funds from the business for his brother and the farm. And so Petro's wife's constant comments went unheeded and her resentment toward her brother-in-law grew with each passing, difficult year.

Andriy knew hardships affected people and often brought out the worst but sometimes the best in them. He felt it was his duty to help those who he could but in those difficult times he had little patience with those who wanted something for nothing and weren't willing to work for what they wanted or needed. It was a principle he had learned from his father and which had guided him throughout his lifetime. It was what he believed to be 'doing what was right'.

And part of doing the right thing, for Andriy was taking on the role of preserving family continuity. He took the time to write to his brothers, Mykola in the old country and Taras in Argentina. He shared their letters with Petro and Dariya. Petro was not particularly interested in the ups and downs of his far-off brothers' lives. His wife always cautioned him against keeping close contact with those brothers for fear this might invite requests for monetary help or even sponsorship to come to Canada. Many who had come to Canada and left relatives behind in the old country were besieged by requests to sponsor their relatives to travel to the new world. Dariya, on the other hand, had fond memories of her two, eldest half-brothers. They had been kind and generous to her when she was a small girl. She missed them, as she missed her dead father. They were all a part of who she was and she would always love them even if she would never see them again.

And so, Andriy continued to keep alive the connections among the far-flung members of his family by writing letters and keeping everyone informed of what everyone else was doing. The letters he received were read and shared and carefully kept in two separate bundles, marked 'Mykola' and 'Taras', in a shoebox with all his other important papers.

Ukraine

In Ukraine, the predominance of small farm holdings, the lack of modernization in farming methods, and the generally low productivity of farms added to the impact of the economic depression gripping the world. Market size had been affected by the re-drawing of national boundaries after WWI and the resultant reduced market size, along with declining prices for agricultural products, added to the economic difficulties. Additional drivers were protectionism and reduced foreign investment. So there was a sharp economic downturn in the newly re-established country of Poland and one of the government's responses was to increase taxes.

In the area that had been Galicia, as in many places in the world, co-operative movements sprang up to deal with the hardships rendered by the great depression. Small farms did not allow for intensive crop production and prices had dropped so dramatically that farm income was decimated. Farmers relied heavily on their animals and what grain they grew for their own use in order to sustain themselves.

And so the family grew what grain it could, not for sale, but to grind and cook for their own meals. They planted and tended a garden for the only vegetables they would have to eat all year long. They scrimped and saved and eventually were able to replace their lost cow and chickens, which added greatly to their diet, supplying milk and eggs. The fish slowly began to come back into the streams flowing through the village and Mykola and his sons often went fishing to supplement their diet. Of course coffee, chai, and sugar were unheard of. There was no money for such luxuries and even if there had been, such items were scarce and hard to come by. But with hard work, determination, and faith in God, the family struggled on and survived.

In 1929, the Organization of Ukrainian Nationalists (OUN) continued the struggle against Polish rule, including attacks on private and government property such as railroads and telegraph lines. This was a highly disciplined, revolutionary, underground group, whose aim was to destabilize the Polish government in order to establish an independent Ukraine. It had rejected the other two prominent strategies, which had emerged in response to Polish rule. Those strategies were the co-operative movement, which was dedicated to working with the Polish Government in order to establish the best possible conditions for the Ukrainian minority, and legal lobbying through political parties for the cultural, educational, and religious rights of the Ukrainian people.

The actions of the OUN resulted in severe government reprisals, notably the 'Pacification' of 1930, in which many Ukrainians were beaten and imprisoned, regardless of whether or not they had been involved in anti-government activities.

Polish aristocrats led the army and were reluctant to have minorities, such as Jews, Ukrainians, or Belarusians, in the ranks of soldiers. As a consequence there was little threat of conscription of Ukrainian peasants into the Polish Army. Quite the contrary. It was well known that if a man, who was not an ethnic Pole, attempted to enlist, he would more likely than not be classified as category 'D' – physically unfit to serve. So unlike during Mykola's day in the Austro-Hungarian era, his sons did not have to do military service before they could marry. The reasons for marrying later in life in these times had more to do with the decreased number of available partners, as the population had been dramatically reduced due to the direct and indirect effects of the war. In addition, for those remaining and any future generation they might contemplate, the difficulty of making a living had increased dramatically.

Mykola's son, Anton, like many young men had burned with the fire of nationalism and revolution. He had had a brief involvement with the UVO, a revolutionary organization that had preceded the OUN. But thanks to the intervention of Father Mykhaylo, he had re-directed his youthful zeal and considerable literary talent to a more moderate movement. That movement, advocated by Metropolitan Sheptytsky, sought to work through the legal means of lobbying for the rights of the Ukrainian people. Anton had continued to work diligently to help achieve the goals of the moderate movement for many years. When the 'Pacification' of 1930 came, he was grateful he had abandoned his initial association with a group known for tactics, which could only be described as guerilla warfare. Now he was ready to focus on his personal life rather than on the cause, which had consumed him but as yet had shown few signs of being achieved.

Mykola and Nadya continued to watch and worry about their eldest son. From the age of seventeen he had seemed to grow somewhat apart from them and the family. It always seemed he had other concerns to consume his attention. Not that he was inattentive to his family responsibilities – it just seemed there was always something more on his mind.

One night Mykola turned to Nadya in bed and whispered, "Do you think he is being called by God to become a priest? He seems to spend a lot of time with Father Mykhaylo."

"I don't know," answered Nadya. She hadn't thought of that possibility. It was worth considering.

"Perhaps you should talk to the good Father again," she added.

Perhaps he should. He really hadn't gotten any information to help understand his son from the last conversation he had had with the priest but perhaps now there would be more to be learned.

Father Mykhaylo had grown quite fond of Anton Martiniuk. He was a serious and dedicated young man, who had an extraordinary literary talent.

At one time the good Father had thought to encourage the young man to extend his education and perhaps consider the priesthood. But now, after many years of careful observation, it had become clear that Anton had another calling.

Anton had fallen in love. His sister, Dora, had married and already had a fine son, whom she had called Bohdan. But until recently, Anton had not been the slightest bit interested in starting a family of his own. Now all that had changed.

Anton had known Luba all his life. She was a serious, quiet girl. She had suffered many things during her youth, things that had shaped Anton and most of their generation. But perhaps her guarded nature was as much a part of who she was as the nature of the world in which she had grown up.

Luba Olynyk was the only daughter of Father Mykhaylo. Anton had often met her at the good Father's home where he and likeminded men assembled to discuss, plan, and work to support the Ukrainian identity. Luba was sympathetic to the cause but it was difficult to know whether she was as passionate about it as her father and the others were.

Father Mykhaylo, like all Greek Catholic priests, had suffered for his beliefs and his dedication to the Eastern Right and his church. Like many of his fellow priests, he had worked hard to defend the rights of Ukrainian Catholics to continue to practice their religion in its ancient form. But as in the old days of the Austrian Empire, there had been continued and ever-growing pressure from the Polish rulers to convert the Ukrainian people to Roman Catholicism. Some Ukrainian people actually did convert in order to get better jobs and suffer less discrimination but most clung stubbornly to the rights and traditions of their forefathers.

People were intimidated and ridiculed for continuing to attend the beautiful, domed church on the hill where the two streams met in the village. But for priests it was worse. They were harassed by Polish youths, who used the excuse of 'differentness' of the Eastern Rite to 'encourage' priests to stop ministering or to leave villages all together. Father Mykhaylo would do neither so he and his family felt the constant scrutiny and threat of Polish animosity. Fortunately for him, his wife and daughter bore these burdens with as much strength and grace as did the good Father himself.

Despite all this, the Ukrainian Catholics were better off than those of the Ukrainian Orthodox faith. Because the latter did not recognize the Pope and had been associated with Tsarist Russia, those Ukrainian people received even worse treatment at the hands of the Poles. They were a minority within a minority. Many of their churches were closed, destroyed, or confiscated and turned into Roman Catholic Churches.

Anton had seen a steely reserve in Luba and admired it as much as he admired her father. In time, as he saw more and more of her, he felt she was the only person who could share his deep faith and devotion to the Ukrainian cause. She understood who he was - his values, strengths, and weaknesses. He knew he had fallen in love with her and hoped she did, or would soon, feel the same way about him.

Anton, like many young men in the village, had little to offer a prospective bride. But his father owned just over eight morgs of land and the young couple would be expected to continue working and living with his family so that was something. Eventually when his father was gone, he and his younger brother, Vasyli, would have to share the small land holding but that was a long time off. A lot could happen before then.

In 1929, at the age of twenty-two, Anton married Luba. The little two-roomed house was full once more. Mykola and Nadya continued to sleep in the east room while the newly weds, Anton and Luba, slept in the common room and Vasyli slept in the attic.

Nadya was very pleased with her new daughter-in-law. It was so good to have another woman in the house again. She had missed her own daughter, Dora, tremendously since her marriage. Not that Luba was anything like Dora. Dora was bright and lively and was always coming up with new ways to do things in a more efficient and fun way. She sang, talked, and laughed as she toiled alongside her mother and always seemed to make the work more bearable and more pleasant. Luba on the other hand was very quiet and reserved. She seldom spoke unless spoken to. And Nadya could count on one hand the number of times she had heard Luba laugh.

"It's all new to her, she'll get used to us soon," Nadya thought.

But as time went on, Nadya began to realize it was just the way Luba was. She worked hard but she spoke little and laughed even less.

One day, Luba had been in the shed with Vasyli, helping to care for the animals. By now they owned a cow, a pig with piglets, and a few chickens and ducks. As Luba milked the cow, Vasyli was forking hay into the manger. Suddenly he lost his footing on a slippery patch and fell with a thump on his backside. When Luba looked up she was astonished to see her brother-in-law wallowing in a muddy mass of straw and manure. And she laughed out loud. It was a rare, melodic laugh that was infectious and soon Vasyli was laughing too. Nadya heard the commotion and came running from the house to see what had happened. The comical scene and the merry laughter of the participants was a welcome diversion and she, too, began to laugh. It was a small incident but it gave Nadya hope that soon Luba would be feeling more at ease in her new home.

Although Luba still didn't speak or laugh often, when she did it was heartfelt and all the more worth waiting for. And Vasyli, who had broken the ice with his sister-in-law, decided it was his job to be as entertaining as possible in order to encourage Luba's rare bouts of joviality.

A year rolled by and then another and another and still there were no children. Nadya wondered if it was because the couple married later in life. Then she wondered if it was because of the hardships of their childhoods. But other couples were having children. It seemed strange. So Nadya did what she always did when she didn't understand something - she prayed.

Vasyli soon wanted to marry as well. He had long been fond of a neighbour girl and, unlike his older brother, did not need as much time to feel ready to start a family. It would not have been unheard of for the three couples to share the little two-roomed hut but Mykola remembered how when he was a small boy, his Uncle Vasyl had built the little house of his own just next to the main house. That little hut had been sold to a widow who had lived in it until she died several years ago. Someone else now lived in it but Mykola decided there was enough room at the back of his home to build at least another room for Anton and Luba. And so Mykola and his sons built an add-on room to the original two-roomed house. The new room was attached to the back of the house with a doorway into the central hallway.

Luba was thrilled with the new room and the privacy it afforded her and her husband. She took great pride in keeping the little room clean and tidy. It was as if it were her own small home within the larger family home. Anton noticed the change in his wife as did the whole family and Mykola was pleased with himself for having come up with the idea. But of course it had not been all his own doing; it was what Uncle Vasyl had done to give his father's family room to grow. And so Mykola said a special prayer of thanksgiving for having had such a thoughtful and loving uncle.

Finally Luba was pregnant. Anton was ecstatic as were Mykola and Nadya. It was difficult to tell exactly what Luba thought as she continued in her quiet, thoughtful ways. As time passed she did not grow as large as Nadya would have expected. She hoped and prayed there was nothing wrong with the baby. But in due course the child was born. She was small, but perfectly formed and seemed completely healthy. It was in the quiet moments when Nadya observed Luba with her baby that she knew what a very good mother Luba would be.

"Not everyone is the same," Nadya thought. "We talk and sing and laugh, while Luba thinks and observes. She is different but she is good. And she is good for Anton. He needed a quiet, thoughtful wife. Thank God he found her and brought her into our family."

Luba called her baby Maria and everyone in the family doted on her.

And before long Vasyli's wife also had a baby girl, who was named Halia.

The two little girls grew up together as if they were sisters. Nadya loved to spend time with her granddaughters and, as the years went by would often ask their mothers to do certain household chores, not because she needed help but because she wanted an excuse to take care of the little ones.

And before long two more babies were welcomed into the little house. Luba had a son whom they named Ivan. He was a chubby, cheerful little brother for Maria. And a year latter little Halia had a brother as well. Vasyli named his son Taras, not for the far-off uncle in Argentina, whom he had never known, but for his beloved older brother who had died at the tender age of eight. Maria, three, and Halia, two, were as enthralled with the baby boys as if they were living dolls rather than brothers.

Mykola was in his mid fifties and beginning to slow down.

"We are so blessed to have our sons to carry on with the farm and our daughters to take over the house and garden," he would say to Nadya as they sat on the bench in front of the little house each evening.

Events in the world were not as pleasant as in Mykola's home. The worldwide depression was easing but the economy and the political state in Poland were still very uncertain. An aggressive leader in Germany was looking for ways to recapture what he thought of as lands inhabited by German peoples in the north and west. Some Ukrainians looked to the rising power of German Nazism as a way toward freedom from the Polish yoke.

The Soviet government to the east was also looking at territory currently in Polish hands. The Soviets promoted the idea that Ukrainians in Poland had never been treated well as a minority and should be allowed to join with their 'brothers' in the Ukrainian Soviet. There were some Ukrainians who shared this political view and believed communism would finally allow them to get out from under the Polish thumb and be able to set up an independent Ukrainian Nation. But others were skeptical – they had heard the rumors and then the personal stories of the government-orchestrated famine in the Ukrainian Soviet during the early thirties. Times were difficult in Poland but at least the people could work for their food and no one took it away from them, leaving them to starve.

Still others feared they would once again be caught in the midst of strong rival forces with little concern for the Ukrainian people. Being part of Poland was not ideal but there might be far worse fates.

And then in April 1938, ethnic Germans in the northern and western regions of Czechoslovakia, known as the Sudetenland, prompted by the new German leader, demanded autonomy and the freedom to align with Germany. France, the United Kingdom, and Czechoslovakia wanted to avoid another war at all costs. After several months of negotiations, on September 29, the Munich Agreement was signed by Italy, Germany, Britain, and France to require Czechoslovakia to cede the Sudeten territory to Germany. Tensions in the region were high and increasing rapidly. And worse was yet to come.

Argentina

When the worldwide depression produced an economic crisis, crippling the world economy, Argentina found itself in a precarious position. Following the Great War Argentina had resumed its pre-war export economy but then the great depression hit. There was a sudden and sustained decline in demand for Argentinian exports and available foreign investment capital. Foreign-owned companies in Argentina downsized dramatically, resulting in major unemployment in the country. The economic downturn affected everyone in the country from the wealthiest, who struggled to pay their mortgages; to the government, which struggled to pay its employees; to the middle class and poor, who simply struggled to survive.

The export economy, which had made Argentina wealthy in the past had come to a screeching halt and the country's economy went into free fall. In 1930 a military coup overthrew the government. But the new military government lasted only two years, ushering in a decade of political instability. In 1934 a new trade agreement sought to exchange the export of Argentine grain and meat for preferential manufactured goods from Great Britain and concessions to British-owned meatpacking plants and railroads. This agreement helped Argentina weather the depression but slowed domestic industrialization and planted the seeds for nationalist dissatisfaction.

Yory

Times were hard for the yerba mate producers. There had been a boom in production resulting in supply vastly outstripping demand. Prices dropped dramatically causing the government to create the Commission Reguladora de la Yerba Mate (CRYM) in 1935. The CRYM instituted price controls, quotas, subsidies, and technical assistance to increase efficiency and yield. A side effect was the displacement of many peasant labourers from the land where they had previously worked.

The economic challenges seemed to fuel Yory's creativity as he strove to find new ways to increase the efficiency of the family plantation. He introduced modern equipment and methods, as well as additional crops to supplement the staple crops, which had been the focus of the plantation.

It was largely due to Yory's innovations that the plantation continued at all, despite the economic downturn swirling around it. Demand and prices dropped; markets beyond Argentina dried up; and, even within the country, people just didn't have the money to continue to buy the plantation's products.

Fortunately for those who lived and worked on the plantation it was possible to grow more food than was needed for their own use but little of the surplus could be sold and there was little cash coming in. Maintenance of the yerba trees, which had been the mainstay of the plantation, was crucial for the future but for now, what they produced was difficult to sell and when it did sell, it was for a fraction of its prior value.

Yory's efforts did not go unnoticed. His friend from earlier days at the Posadas Practical School of Subtropical Agriculture, with whom he had written a paper on modern methods of farming in Northern Argentina, had kept in close contact. They had shared ideas over the years and his friend had never hesitated to promote Yory as a very capable and knowledgeable source of agricultural innovation. As the depression continued and government bureaucracy grew, in order to create middle-class jobs, Yory's services were called upon for a new government agency in Posadas. The purpose of the agency was to provide innovative methods to support struggling farmers in the state of Misiones and beyond.

While Yory was thrilled with the prospect of this new government position, Taras was loath to see his eldest son leave the plantation once more. But Yory was confident there were ways to improve the lot of farmers, even in these difficult times and he welcomed the challenge to be a part of the effort. And there was another reason Yory particularly wished to return to Posadas. Toward the end of his last sojourn in the capital he had met a fascinating woman. Despite the fact they had only seen each other twice and had spoken but little, Yory just could not get her out of his mind. And now he was heading back to Posadas and perhaps would be able to see her once more.

"She is probably married and has a houseful of children by now," he told himself but he could not help dreaming that it was not so.

Therefore when Yory arrived in Posadas, one of the first things he did was to visit his old friend and former teacher, for it had been at his home where Yory had last seen Oxana. Oxana's father was a bureaucrat in the local government and a friend and colleague of Yory's former teacher.

Yory was welcomed warmly by his friend and they spend a long, lazy afternoon in the sunshine on his patio, sipping yerba mate and talking about old times and new challenges. Eventually Yory bolstered his courage and asked about Oxana's father and, of course, his lovely daughter.

"I was wondering when you would get around to asking about her," his friend laughed. "I am afraid you won't be seeing her here for some time."

So it was as Yory had suspected. She had married and moved to some far off locale. He was surprised at just how affected he was by this thought.

"She has been sent by her mother to stay with her aunt in Buenos Aries," his friend continued.

"Her aunt?" Yory asked incredulously.

"Yes, it seems her mother thinks there is no one suitable for her daughter here in the backwaters of Misiones and so she has been sent to the big city – presumably to find a suitable husband," this last bit of information was delivered with an undisguised air of contempt.

"But," he continued, "I believe the lovely Oxana will be visiting her parents for Navidad."

Yory was elated. Even if Oxana were already married he would at least be able to see her once more. And then perhaps he could put her out of his mind and concentrate on his new job and life in Posadas.

Yory had long been concerned about the way in which the land was being used in the subtropical area along the Parana River. The virgin forests were being cut down to make way for plantations of yerba, citrus, tobacco, and other cash crops. These crops depleted the soil of its nutrients and, in the past, the only way to ensure the continued prosperity of the plantations was to increase the size of the land holdings. Yory believed these methods would eventually eliminate the forests completely and impoverish all the land in the region. His goal was to find ways to protect or re-establish the natural forests and to revitalize the soil in order to ensure continued prosperous farming for future generations.

To this end he proposed re-forestation via the planting of indigenous trees where these had been previously removed. Unfortunately it was necessary to find ways to revitalize the soil, which had been depleted by the production of cash crops, before the young trees could be established. Several potential crops, which might accomplish these goals were being considered including legumes, such as soya beans. However the local plantation owners were resistant to adopt these new crops, which were seen as less profitable than the prior cash crops. While the market for the traditional crops had declined dramatically, at least there was a market – how and where would they even begin to sell the new crops being proposed? In addition, it was much harder to convince the plantation owners that it was necessary to replenish and revitalize their land when there was so much land available. Their response had always been simply to clear more land rather than worry about the depleted areas left behind. Yory and his colleagues had a difficult task ahead of them.

Myko

Myko had been doubly glad in 1929 to travel with Yory to Posadas. This trip meant Yory would be leaving the plantation and finally, he would be the prominent son of one of its two founding owners. Myko had grown up believing himself to be better than his elder brother, better than Ivan's sons, better, in fact, than everyone around him. In his mind he had convinced himself that it had been an accident of birth alone, which placed him in the position of the second rather than first son in his family and he was determined to show the world it was he, and not his brother, who would turn the fortunes of the plantation around.

Myko had always rankled at the fact that Yory was forever coming up with new ideas, which everyone seemed to think were so wonderful. Why was he given so much attention for just thinking up new ways of doing things, while he, Myko, had continued to work tirelessly in the time-honoured ways for the good of the plantation? Why were his efforts always in the shadow of those of his elder brother? Myko put little store in Yory's ideas and could never really understand why others did.

But there was another reason Myko was especially excited about travelling to Posadas. It had been some time since he had taken notice of a girl, who attended San Vladimiro Church in Posadas. She was exceptional in one way and that was the magnificent colour of her hair. Mykhalia Kostiuk was short and plump, with a round face, and indistinct greenish eyes, but her hair – her hair was red. Myko had been captivated by her hair from the very first time he had seen her and that had been almost two years ago.

Myko had made a point of introducing himself to the family. He had made sure the father was aware of what a large plantation his family owned and what a prominent position, he himself, held in the family business. Then he had turned his attentions to the daughter. She was quite flattered to have such an eligible man so obviously interested in her. The father, too, seemed pleased by the possibility of Myko as a future son-in-law. And so it was that Myko had taken every opportunity to travel to Posadas, over the last two years, in order to press his case with the father and daughter. And now that Yory was leaving the plantation, Myko hoped for good, it was time for him to make his move. He would ask her to marry him and he was confident she would agree.

Myko had not mentioned any of this to his parents or anyone else on the plantation. He had long ago learned that whatever he did, no matter how impressive, it would always draw a reaction less than it deserved in his opinion. And so, he kept his plans and dreams to himself. He would do as he pleased without consultation or input and eventually everyone would have to see just how much he could accomplish on his own.

Myko asked the father for the daughter's hand and was approved. He then asked the daughter and was accepted. He would now have someone to honour and respect him and support all he did. Myko was triumphant.

When he returned to the plantation, he told his parents he was to be married. They were surprised, to say the least, as they had no idea of their son's two-year courtship nor whom he had chosen. But they expressed their happiness for him and were eager to meet the girl, who would be their new daughter-in-law and her family.

Yory was as surprised as everyone. He too had noticed the redheaded girl in church, as no doubt did everyone, but he had had no idea of his brother's attraction or intentions. Myko was well aware he had caught his elder brother by surprise and congratulated himself on being the first to marry.

The wedding took place in Posadas early in 1930, with the bride's family hosting a celebration on their nearby farm. Then the young couple travelled with the groom's extended family back to the plantation.

Myko's wife was a bit taken aback when they finally arrived at the plantation, dusty and weary from their long journey. Based on what she had been told she had much higher expectations than the reality afforded. But she comforted herself in the knowledge that her husband was the eldest son, at least in theory, of one of the plantation owners and she would share his prominent position in the enterprise.

It soon became obvious to everyone that this new arrival had high expectations of her position. Taras and Ivan had always promoted the concept of fair treatment and compensation based on contribution to the enterprise. So while Myko's wife was now part of one of the two founding families she was expected to participate in the work of the plantation. She had grown up on an estancia working along side her parents and siblings but somehow had gotten the idea that in her new home, her position would be somewhat more exalted.

Carmen and Taras were dismayed by the fact that their new daughter-in-law seemed uninterested in the family business and less than willing to participate in it.

"She will learn," Taras said. But Carmen was not so sure.

And then just a few months later Myko announced they were to have a child.

"Well, that's something," Carmen said quietly to Taras.

Myko was so excited about becoming a father. He insisted a new house be built for his growing family, as soon as the busy farm season was over. He selected the site himself, a bit further from the other houses and closer to the arroyo. The new dwelling was to be situated just so in order to catch the evening breezes from off the water but far enough to avoid flooding and excess insects.

Taras was impressed that Myko was taking such care in providing for his family and hoped this was an indication that the young man was finally maturing.

Guillermo

Guillermo also came of age during the decade of the Great Depression. He had completed his studies in Posadas but, unlike his elder brother, Yory, had decided he much preferred life on the plantation to life in town. After returning he had married one of Ivan's daughter's, Vasylyna, in 1931. They had grown up together, played together, worked together, and so it had been a very natural match. Everyone, especially the two fathers, were very pleased by this event.

It was only Myko, himself recently married, who seemed to be less than enthusiastic about the marriage of his youngest brother. Carmen suspected it was Myko's jealousy based on his competitive nature, which had thrown a shadow over the happy event for him. Myko was likely concerned that Guillermo and his bride, by joining the two founding families, might have a more prominent place in the family enterprise.

The young couple, however, was oblivious to any under currents, which might have dampened their happiness.

Guillermo's first child was a son. The proud new parents named him Juan, after his mother's father, Ivan, the co-founder of the plantation. As he grew it became evident that Juan was very much like his father. He was kind-hearted and helpful. Those of the younger generation went to him for advice, just as many of the generation before had sought his father's advice.

Katya, too, found happiness and marriage. In 1932 she married a local boy, Dmytro Kulyk, the son of one of the original Ukrainian farmers who had followed her father and Ivan into the wilderness to establish the plantation.

Yory

Oxana Karpenko had returned to Posadas to visit her parents for Navidad. Yory thought her as beautiful as ever. He saw her at a party, which his old friend hosted just before the New Year. She had entered the room with a tall, dark, and Yory had to admit, rather handsome gentleman.

"So she is married," he thought. But because he had wanted to see her again for so long, he mustered his courage and approached her.

"Ola," he started but before he could say any more she interrupted him.

"Pedro," she said to the handsome man at her side, "this is Yory, I mean Jorge Martiniuk. He works in the agricultural agency with father's friend."

Yory was amazed that Oxana knew so much about him and had actually told this fine gentleman about his work.

"I have heard a lot about your efforts to improve farming in the region," the gentleman responded as he shook Yory's hand. "But, if you will excuse me…." and he was gone.

"I am sorry," Oxana said as the gentleman walked away. "My cousin finds the company here in Posadas a bit less than he is used to in Buenos Aries. But I am very happy to be back home."

The two young people talked about life in the big city and how it compared to life in Posadas and it soon became apparent to Yory that Oxana longed to return.

"So when will you be coming home to stay?" Yory finally asked her.

"I don't know," she replied. "My mother wants me to stay with my aunt until I find a suitable husband. The problem is that if I marry someone from Buenos Aries, I will never be more than a visitor here and I could not bear that. I love Misiones and would prefer to spend my life here even if I have to marry a plantation farmer."

Yory was amused by this last reference for he suspected she knew his father owned a plantation.

"Would you be happy living in Posadas as the wife of, perhaps, a petty government bureaucrat?" he asked a bit whimsically.

"Like my father?" she laughed, "Why not? It was good enough for my mother, although she seems to think I should aspire to something more grand!"

This was all very encouraging. It was clear Yory and Oxana were attracted to one another and had similar interests and aspirations. And so with the help of his friend, who had suspected Yory's interest in Oxana and had never missed an opportunity to promote him to her father, Yory was able to win the father's approval, if not the mother's. Oxana was able to marry Yory, the man she had loved since their first meeting and live in her beloved Posadas.

Myko

Myko's wife was an anomaly. She managed to get pregnant every time the previous child was just getting old enough to allow her to take an active role in the work of the plantation. Myko was very proud of his growing brood and his productive wife. They already had three fine sons, Fedir, Kyrylo, and Olek. Myko had visions of overwhelming the third generation of the plantation owners' families with his own offspring. At last he would be in charge and others would have to meet with his approval rather than the other way around.

As the decade continued, government bureaucracy grew, creating jobs for the middle class, while labourers turned more and more to unions to provide stability for their jobs. Attempts were made to monitor the activities of foreign investors and companies. Some Argentine resources, such as petroleum, were nationalized. Nationalization of natural resources and a general inward turning characterized the political climate in Argentina.

In 1934, the Iguazu Falls National Park was established and an effort was made to encourage a fledgling tourist industry. In addition to the park, a large military installation was established at Puerto Iguazu, primarily to provide local law and order, to protect the Argentine borders, and to put a stop to what had been the traditional smuggling of people and products into Argentina from the neighbouring Paraguay and Brazil. Of particular concern were the trafficking of humans and illegal drugs and tobacco.

In the fall of 1935, Taras and Ivan decided to take their extended families to see the magnificent Iguazu Falls in the newly created National Park. It was a long, dusty journey but both men felt having such a famous natural wonder in their own 'backyard' was definitely worth the trek. Not everyone went on the adventure, of course. Myko's family declined to participate citing the difficulty of travel with several small children but Taras suspected he simply didn't approve of the plan. Guillermo and Katya and their families joined the expedition. However, Yory and Oxana could not make the journey, which would have been twice as far from their starting point in Posadas. Ivan's eldest son stayed on the plantation but sent his own son along with his grandfather. It was an important trip, which confirmed for many of the participants how much they belonged to the new land in which they now lived.

On the evening before their departure, two plantation trucks were packed with tents, clothing, and food for the trip. Early the next morning the participants piled into the vehicles for the long, bumpy, dusty drive, northwest on the rough road along the Parana River. During the trip they took turns leading the company in songs and games designed to keep the younger children amused and to pass the time. At mid-day the company stopped along the road so the children could run about and the parents could prepare a meal. Temporary tents were pitched to shelter from the heat of the day and food was prepared. After everyone had eaten, many lay down on blankets for a short rest, while others cleared and repacked the food and utensils. By late afternoon the party was ready to resume the trek. It took two days for the plantation expedition to reach its goal. It was early evening when they finally arrived so the men pitched tents while the women prepared an evening meal. The children were excited to have finally reached their destination and ran boisterously about, playing noisy games. That evening the group gathered around a camp fire talking about all they had seen so far on the trip and anticipating what they would see the next day. It was difficult for the children to settle, so the adults remained gathered around the fire, talking in low tones long into the night.

The next morning was bright and clear. It would be a warm autumn day – perfect for their adventure. The group drove to the entrance of the new National Park, parked their vehicles, and followed a guide to view the spectacular Iguazu Falls. It was an awe-inspiring spectacle. Taras and the whole party would remember the magnificent sight for the rest of their days. Their adopted country truly was amazing!

At the age of fifty-seven, Taras continued to develop and implement the new ideas, which his son, Yory, suggested from the Agricultural Agency in Posadas. His partnership with Ivan, forged so many long years ago on the ship, which had brought him to this country, had been his life's work and he was proud of how successful it had been.

Taras was also proud of his family. A highly-educated son working for the government to improve farming in the region. Another son, who had given him three grandsons and two granddaughters! A third son, who more than anyone else, was the soul of the plantation. Guillermo continued to be the patient, empathetic partner, who everyone turned to for advice or comfort. Taras often wondered how he managed to help so many others and not ever be weighed down by their burdens. And his beautiful little Katya. He still thought fondly of his dear brother whenever he looked at her, she so much resembled Mykola. Taras now knew for sure that he would never see his favorite brother again in this lifetime and the thought saddened him.

Ushering in the era prior to the Second World War, an election in 1938 in Argentina was fraught with irregularities and fraud, which added to the political instability of the nation.

Taras could not help but be aware of the shifting political situation and was especially concerned about what these latest changes might mean for his son, Yory, serving as a bureaucrat in Posadas. Aside from these concerns, Taras tried to put the political problems facing his adopted country out of his mind and, instead, focus on his family and their efforts to make the family business successful.

9 THE SECOND GREAT WAR

The Great War. The war to end all wars. But it was not to be. Despite the death of millions on the battlefields, in occupied lands, and on the home fronts, the end of World War I (WWI) sowed the seeds for yet another world war. Just over twenty years later the world was at war once more. Will we ever learn?

Ukraine

In order to understand the start of the Second World War (WWII), it is necessary to realize that neither Nazi Germany nor Soviet Russia wanted the country of Poland to continue to exist. As a result of a secret agreement between these two powers known as the Molotov-Ribbentrop Pact, a few weeks after Germany invaded Poland on September 1, 1939, the Red Army occupied all of Galicia east of the San River. The San River flows to the west of Lviv. The common objective of the two invading forces was to totally destroy Poland and its people in order to access the territory for the expansion of their own peoples. Despite active fighting at the start of the war, the vast majority of casualties in the territory, which since the end of WWI had been Poland, were civilians.

The Polish government capitulated within a few weeks of the German invasion, fleeing west where it went underground for the duration of the war. The Nazis set about immediately clearing the area of occupants – be they Polish, Jewish, or Slavs - either through forced relocation, enslavement in labour camps, or murder. The purpose was to empty the territory for German settlers. The Soviet invaders used similar methods for the same purposes in the area they had invaded.

In order to prevent the wider world from condemning the Soviet invasion of Galicia as an act of aggression, the Bolshevik party claimed the purpose was to protect the 'Ukrainian brothers' of those living in the Soviet Socialist Republic of Ukraine. A Soviet-style election, in which only one name – that of the Bolshevik candidate – appeared on each ballot, was held. After the 'election', a 'request' was issued by the newly formed Bolshevik Government for the region to be joined with Soviet Ukraine, which was accomplished on November 1, 1939.

The Soviets had never declared war on Poland because they did not recognize the Polish Government. Soon after the invasion all Polish institutions were abolished, including churches and schools; large Polish landowners, referred to by the Soviets as 'Kulaks', were dispossessed of their property; and the Polish currency was withdrawn from circulation. The result of the latter was that the population lost its entire savings over night. Initially large Polish land holdings were redistributed to the peasants but the next step was to force those same peasants onto collective farms, called Kolkhoz. The peasants resisted as they were loath to hand over large portions of their crops for no pay, in order to meet state-required quotas.

The new regime with its collectivization of farms, nationalization of industry, and reorganization of education, did not target solely Polish inhabitants. Ukrainian institutions, periodicals, and church activities also were curtailed. Much of the Ukrainian intelligentsia escaped west into the German-held, former Polish lands but thousands were arrested, deported, or killed. Thus began the Second World War in the region, which was once Galicia.

Early on June 22, 1941 Germany broke its non-aggression pact with the Soviets in a 'Drive to the East' called Operation Barbarossa. The invasion came as three main army groups charged into Soviet Ukraine and Belarus. The objective was obliteration of the 'Untermensch' or subhuman inhabitants of the region, including Jews, Gypsies, and Slavs.

The southern section of German Army Group South marched in from Romania and overran Galicia by July as it pushed east toward Kiev. The retreating Red Army executed thousands of Ukrainians, who had been imprisoned for resistance to Sovietization.

Between June 30 and July 12, the Organization of Ukrainian Nationalists (OUN) established a sovereign Western Ukraine. The OUN had seen the Germans as allies against the Soviets. This autonomous state, however, was dismantled by the Germans who then arrested the OUN leaders. On August 1, 1941, Galicia was officially annexed by Germany despite protests of the Ukrainian National Council (UNC) in Lviv, which was then suppressed in March of the following year. At that point the Ukrainian Central Committee, under German control, was given responsibility for Ukrainian civic, cultural, and educational institutions in the region.

Under German occupation efforts toward political independence or any opposition to Nazi rule were brutally suppressed. The majority of Galician Jews, Gypsies, and many Ukrainians were deported, killed, or interned in concentration camps, as part of the Nazi plan to clear the region for expansion of German settlers.

Between June of 1943 and the German retreat in mid 1944, the Ukrainian Povstanska (Insurgent) Army (UPA) conducted a guerrilla war against both the Nazis and the Red Army.

The reoccupation of Galicia by the Soviets in the fall of 1944 saw the reestablishment of the former Soviet regime. Ukrainians, whether they had cooperated with the Nazis or had fought for political independence, were killed or shipped to far-off labour camps.

Metropolitan Sheptytsky died on November 1, 1944 and was replaced by Metropolitan Slipyj. On April 11, 1945, the entire Greek Catholic hierarchy was arrested and sent to labour camps where most died. This was the first step by the Soviets toward annihilation of the Greek Catholic Church in the region. The final blow was to come in the following year.

In August of 1945 after the war ended, a Soviet-Polish agreement set the border between Polish and Soviet-occupied Galicia along the Curzon Line, west of Lviv. Ethnic Poles were resettled in Polish territory to the west, while ethnic Ukrainians were resettled in Soviet Ukraine to the east. One of the goals of this forced resettlement was to destroy the basis of the Ukrainian Povstanska (Insurgent) Army but it continued its guerrilla warfare for another ten years.

Under Soviet rule historical Galicia ceased to exist and the region became known as Western Ukraine.

Mykola

Mykola at almost sixty years of age was crestfallen when he heard the news. In September of 1939, Germany had invaded Poland in the region to the northwest. The invasion had been so rapid that it was over almost as soon as it had started. Then a few weeks later the Soviet Army marched through the region of his small village and westward toward Lviv. This army was brutal, killing anything and everything in its path. Refugees streamed ahead of the army in an attempt to out run it and escape, but to little effect. The people lived in terror.

Then in November there had been the 'election'. And now the little village, where the two streams joined to form a tributary of the Dniester, was part of the Soviet Socialist Republic of Ukraine. This was not the long-dreamed of sovereign state of ethnic Ukrainian people. It was a Soviet satellite bent on the destruction of all that was Ukrainian. The people of the village had heard stories of how their 'brothers' in the east had suffered under Bolshevik rule. Life was no doubt going to get much harder than it had ever been.

Mykola thought about all the hardships he had seen in his lifetime and when he looked at his children and grandchildren he shuddered to think what their futures would hold.

Dora had married and now lived on the other side of the village with her husband's family. She had a fine family of three boys. Mykola loved to see Dora's children as often as possible and she had been good about bringing them to visit their aging Diedo and Baba. Mykola had formed an especially close bond with Dora's eldest son, Bohdan, who was now eleven years old. As he was his eldest grandson, Mykola often shared family stories with the boy. As often happens between two like-minded individuals a generation apart, a mutual love developed between the two.

Mykola's sons, Anton and Vasyli, and their families still lived in the family home and worked together to farm the family plot. Both grandparents loved the two little girls, Anton's Maria and Vasyli's Halia, who were now just old enough to begin helping in the kitchen and garden, as well as to begin their schooling. Mykola had taken it upon himself to be their teacher. So each day after the evening meal he would work patiently with the little girls to teach them to read and write, along with the basics of mathematics. Long ago, Mykola's father had sent him a book of poetry – his brother Andriy's first book, which was largely comprised of poems in his mother tongue. This was the only book the family owned and it had become a treasured possession. Mykola used the book to teach the girls to read. He never failed to tell them about his own brilliant brother, their Great Uncle Andriy living in Canada, who had written these beautiful poems. Andriy's early poems were filled with imagery from his homeland and his home village, as well as his growing love for the expanse of the Canadian Prairies. The little girls loved to hear Diedo read the poems and were anxious to be able to read them themselves. They dreamed, as only little girls can, of the far off land where the sky was so big and blue that you felt lost in the wonder of the world.

And then there were Mykola's young grandsons. Just as their first children had both been girls, the next children in the two brothers' families had been boys, Ivan and Taras. These two lively little fellows kept everyone in the household busy! They ran and jumped and played games, as little boys will do. Mykola had felt so blest by his bustling household. Sometimes he would think back to the days when it had been his own children rushing around the yard and the house and how old Uncle Vasyl had been so happy to be a part of the growing family. Mykola thought often of his Uncle Vasyl, who had been like a father to him from the time Mykola had returned from the army to find his family had emigrated. What a blessing Uncle Vasyl had been!

The years of the First World War had been horrific. The family had nearly starved but they had survived. The years under Polish rule had been difficult but the family had survived. And now they were to be ruled by the

Soviets. Mykola prayed that his wonderful family would continue to survive.

When the Polish currency was withdrawn Mykola couldn't help but think how strange it was. Uncle Vasyl had left him a small amount of savings but it had been in the coin of the old Austro-Hungarian Empire, which no longer existed. Now any Polish money the family had been able to save since the war was worthless as well.

"What good is money?" he thought.

There was still the little, soft, leather bag, which his brother's father-in-law had left with him. It contained a few pieces of jewelry, which had belonged to the gentleman's wife. It had been left with Mykola in case his brother ever returned. But it had been over twenty-five years since Mykhaylo had been conscripted. He wasn't coming back. Mykola knew that if it became necessary he would have to sell the bit of jewelry to keep his family from starvation. He would never let it get close to that again.

News was trickling into the village. The Soviets were starting to force farmers to work on collective farms. They said it was like the farm co-operatives, which had saved farmers during the depression. But everyone knew this was not true. On the collective Kolkhoz a large portion of the grain went to the state first and then, if there was anything left, it was divided among the farmers. Mykola feared this was a recipe for starvation. Villagers had heard stories brought west by the few people who had escaped Soviet Ukraine during the famine years of 1932-33. Their tales had been horrific. The famine had been caused by confiscation of all grain, all animals, all food, in order to starve the people into submission. Was this the fate awaiting his family and little village?

In addition to the changes in farming and industry, the Soviets had banned Ukrainian language publications. When Mykola heard this he told his family they must never speak of Andriy's book of poems and he hid it away with the soft leather pouch.

And then of course they had heard about the destruction of Polish Roman Catholic Churches. Would their beautiful Greek Catholic Church on the hill in the middle of their village also be destroyed? Mykola knew that

Father Mykhaylo was concerned. The two men spoke often about the coming changes. Father Mykhaylo always asked Mykola to pray for the protection of the church.

There had been disturbing stories about writers, musicians, teachers, doctors, and lawyers - all disappearing. Some may have travelled west. Some may have been imprisoned. But everyone knew some had been killed. It was not a good time to be a cultural or thought leader.

During that fall of 1939 and throughout the next year the people watched, worried, and prayed as they heard more and more stories about how their world was being destroyed by the Soviets.

And then when no one believed things could get worse – they did. In June of 1941 the German army rolled through Southern Galicia heading for Kiev. It was an odd time. Germany was attacking the Soviets, who they had worked with to dismantle Poland. Some Ukrainians, hoping for an autonomous nation and hating Soviet rule, welcomed the Nazi army as liberators. The brutal German Army had been ordered to treat Ukrainian inhabitants as sub-humans, just as they believed the Jews, Gypsies, and all Slavs to be. Everything was happening so quickly. Mykola had no idea what to make of all this. The world had truly gone mad.

The Soviet Army had been taken by surprise and as it retreated from the region, vented its frustration and anger on the local population, which had never welcomed or wanted them. Many thousands of peasant farmers were killed, just because they happened to be in the path of retreat. Many more were killed because they were believed to be collaborators of the attacking Germans. The German Army behaved in exactly the same way, killing civilians as they advanced. It was a blood bath.

And it wasn't just the German and Soviet Armies who the villagers feared. The Ukrainian nationalist guerilla forces also killed their own peasants, who were suspected of collaborating with either invading enemy. Everyone was suspicious of everyone else. Everyone lived in fear. Everyone just tried to stay out of harm's way.

And so for three years after the Nazis had steamrolled through the region on their way to Kiev, Leningrad, and Moscow, the people in the village on the tributary of the Dniester lived in fear under a new occupation. This rule was at least as brutal as the Soviet's had been. There was absolutely no tolerance for opposition of any kind. People were arrested, enslaved, imprisoned, or killed. Everyone else just tried to survive as best they could.

It was during those dark days that Mykola noticed how much Father Mykhaylo had changed. Both the Ukrainian Catholic and Ukrainian Orthodox Churches had been banned by the Germans. This would have been reason enough to change the priest but Mykola knew there was more. As his son's father-in-law, Father Mykhaylo had always been close to the family. He visited often. But now the family almost never saw him. Even his own daughter, Luba, didn't see or seek him out. Mykola was worried about the good Father and prayed often for him.

The tense, black days of Nazi occupation wore on and the people began to believe this would be their fate until the end of days. And then, as can happen in a war, everything changed again.

In 1944 the German Army was retreating, hotly pursued by the Red Army. The Soviet Army swept through the region once more.

"What will become of us?" Mykola thought and he prayed God would protect his family from further harm.

Father Mykhaylo

Father Mykhaylo was twenty-two years old when he came to the village in 1901 to assist the aging Father Borys. He had worked diligently through the years, often facing outside pressures on his beloved church. In the early days it was the pressure from Polish aristocrats, who had gained authority from the Austro-Hungarian rulers and who were bent on converting Ukrainian Catholics from their Eastern Rite. After the First World War, when the region had become part of reconstructed Poland, this pressure intensified. Through it all, Father Mykhaylo had walked a fine line of devotion to his church and the people it served, within the context of the political realities of the day.

He had faced many attacks both on the church and on himself because of his position as the Greek Catholic priest in the village. The fact that the church remained and continued to serve its people was a testament to the good Father's strength and intelligence.

But the world was changing once more. In November 1939 Galicia came under the rule of the Soviet Union. The Greek Catholic Church faced its greatest threat to date. The Soviets were openly hostile to the church and bent on its destruction once and for all and to replace it with the Russian Orthodox Church. While the two churches shared a distant past and similar rituals, there was a fundamental difference. The Ukrainian Church, since the Union of Brest in 1595, had been Catholic with the Pope in Rome as its head, while the Russian Orthodox Church was decidedly not Catholic.

Between 1939 and the middle of 1941 under Soviet rule, the church was under a great deal of scrutiny. It continued to exist but just barely. Seminaries were closed, publications ceased, and priests were forbidden to hear confessions or distribute communion in hospitals. In church-run schools, liturgical services were banned and crucifixes were removed. Church and monastery land was confiscated and monks and nuns were turned out. Parishes and priests were taxed huge sums of money. Priests were arrested, tortured, and deported. These actions against the Greek Catholic Church were only halted when war broke out with Germany.

Under the Germans from 1941 until the middle of 1944, nothing done in or through the church could be seen to be nationalistic or in opposition to the Nazi regime. Once again Father Mykhaylo walked the very fine line, trying to minister to his flock, while attempting to avoid unwanted attention from the authorities. This was very difficult for the good Father, because he was all too aware of the atrocities being committed against Jews and Gypsies, as well as Ukrainians, particularly those who were dedicated to political autonomy.

It was during those dark days of Nazi rule when Father Mykhaylo did the work, which would put himself and his beloved church in the most danger. The good Father developed a secret, under-ground system of like-minded volunteers to help persecuted individuals escape. At first his efforts were aimed at helping Ukrainians but when others sought his help, especially to save children, his conscience decreed that anyone who was in need would be aided. And so it was that the mild-mannered, supposedly rule-abiding priest in this little, out-of-the-way village, frequently received fugitives in the dead of night and helped them to find their way to the volunteers who would usher them to freedom. Occasionally he would hear of a group of fugitives, betrayed and killed as they attempted their escape, but with God's protection the trail had not yet lead back to the good Father, so he was able to continue his activities undiscovered.

Those had been stressful and difficult days for the priest, since he was now in his mid sixties. There had been no young priest sent to assist him and he had a dreadful premonition that he might be the last Ukrainian Catholic Priest in this parish. But Father Mykhaylo was fit for his age and worked tirelessly to maintain an outward appearance of cooperation, while secretly helping as many of those in need as was possible. How long could he continue this charade? He didn't know but he prayed God would give him the strength to continue until his efforts were no longer needed.

Father Mykhaylo's wife had died of influenza shortly after the First World War like so many in those difficult days. Their only daughter had married young Anton Martiniuk fifteen years ago. And so the good Father prayed that his activities would reflect on no one but himself.

But no matter how dark had been those days under Nazi occupation, no matter how black the deeds Father Mykhaylo had seen or heard of, no matter how difficult it had been to continue his life's work as a parish priest and his recent avocation as a smuggler of human refugees, worse was yet to come.

Young Bohdan

Bohdan was Mykola's first grandchild. He was Dora's first child born in 1928. Mykola loved all his grandchildren but Bohdan had captured his heart in a way that was almost overwhelming. Mykola had spent long hours with the boy as he grew, talking with him about his own youth, growing up with four brothers, a loving father, and a devoted uncle. Mykola wanted this grandson to know about his family.

Dora had always been close to her father and so it was no surprise that her father doted on her first-born son. She often brought the boy to see his grandparents and loved to watch the grandfather and grandson working together on some project and talking about the family. Dora had often heard these same stories when she was young and was glad her father continued to share them with her son.

Bohdan was a curious child and grew to be a thoughtful young man. He was always willing to help and had a high regard for and devotion to his extended family.

It was on a cold winter day in 1944. The young man, now nearly sixteen, had completed his chores and asked his mother if he might walk to his grandparents' home. He had something he wanted to show Diedo Mykola. Dora was happy to send the boy on his way along with her greetings to her parents.

Bohdan was walking with his hands thrust deep into his pockets and his collar turned up against the icy wind. His head was down as he tried to stay warm, despite the weather. He walked around a corner and right into a Soviet soldier. Both of them were caught by surprise but Bohdan didn't even have a chance to apologize. The soldier shot him. He fell to the ground, blood streaming from the wound in his chest. He was dead.

Bohdan's death had been a huge blow to the family. No one took it harder than Mykola. He grieved deeply for his lost grandson. He was sixty-four years old and for the first time in his long life he wondered why he was still alive.

It was very hard for Mykola not to dwell on all the people whom he had loved, who were dead or forever far away. In his grief for Bohdan, Mykola grieved once more for the mother he had lost so many long years ago. He had been sixteen years old – the same age as his beloved Bohdan - when his mother, Kateryna, had died. And after his long struggle to return home from the Emperor's Army he had lost his beloved brother, Taras, to an adventure in Argentine. The rest of his family had departed, as well, to Canada. And it had been just Uncle Vasyl who was left. Dear Uncle Vasyl. It had been over thirty years since he had died but still Mykola missed the old man, who had been a second father to him. And then there had been

Taras, his second son, who had died of influenza at the age of eight after the Great War. And now Bohdan.

There were times when Mykola didn't even want to go on. But his wife, Nadya, would take his hand and try to remind him of all the joy still filling their little house. They still had the rest of Dora's family and Anton's and Vasyli's families. There was much to be thankful for. And she would start to pray. Then, whether out of habit or true devotion, even she did not know, Mykola would begin to pray with her.

"This has really aged him," she thought of her husband.

Nadya had spent a lot of time and energy trying to help her daughter, Dora, after they first learned of Bohdan's death. Because she, too, had lost a young son, she was empathetic and along with Dora's husband and other children, the younger woman began to deal with the shock and overwhelming loss. But it had been different for Mykola. Perhaps it was his age. Nadya wasn't sure but she knew her husband was grieving for more than this most recent loss and it worried her.

Mykola had always been the steady force in their household. He was intelligent, strong, and always strived for righteousness. Now something seemed to have left him. She would have to do all she could to help him recover, for in these difficult times, the whole family needed his leadership and protection.

Anton also recognized the change in his father. It frightened him to think Tato was aging and losing the strength of character, which had always been the centre of their family. What frightened him even more was the prospect that he, at the age of thirty-seven, might have to take his father's place as head of the extended family in these difficult times.

Canada

Iryna

Ever since she had turned fourteen, two years ago, it had been an annual battle. Would Tato relent and let her go back to school? Every year Iryna worried that this would be her last year. But so far she had been able to return to school. This was in no small part due to Mama and brother George, who had taken up her cause.

In the fall of 1939 Iryna was sixteen. Tato thought she should be considering a nice local farm boy for a husband the way her older sister, Maria, had so sensibly done. It was time for her to have children of her own - not just spend time telling her nieces and nephews stories all the time.

Iryna had a wonderful imagination. She could tell story after story with little effort. Maria's children loved Auntie Iryna because she always kept them so well entertained. Maria welcomed frequent visits of her younger sister, because with five children and farm chores, she could use all the help she could get - and Iryna was so good with the children.

Iryna had completed grade nine in the previous spring. She had been fifteen, a year older than the others in grade nine, because the year before Tato had insisted she stay home to help her mother and sister. Iryna had been desolate. She so missed going to school that both Dariya and Pavlo noted the dramatic change in her bearing. She didn't sulk or become belligerent. She continued to work hard and help with all the chores. But when the day's work was done, she would go to her room and write. She wrote and wrote.

"Just like her Uncle Andriy," Dariya would comment.

"What on earth is she writing?" Pavlo wondered. But he knew that even if she ever decided to share her writing with him, he would not be able to appreciate it. And so Pavlo never asked his brilliant daughter to read her stories to him.

Dariya, who had never had the opportunity to learn to read and write, loved her brother Andriy's poems and would often ask Iryna to read them to her as they worked. Once Iryna asked her mother if she would like to hear something she had written.

"Is it a poem?" Dariya asked.

"Oh no, I am not as talented as Uncle Andriy!" her daughter replied. "It's just a story."

"Ok then," Dariya encouraged her daughter.

After Iryna finished reading the short story Dariya had to hide her face from the child. It had been a tender tale of lost love. It had been written so skillfully that Dariya thought it one of the most beautiful things she had ever heard. It had touched her heart and brought her to the brink of tears.

It was on that day that Dariya vowed she would do whatever was in her power to help her daughter continue going to school and writing beautiful stories.

So now in the fall of 1939, just as the world was erupting into war once more, Iryna was going to be able to go to school to take grade ten. She was elated. She knew it would continue to be a battle and nothing was certain but she hoped and prayed Tato would let her finish grade eleven, as well. That was the last year of schooling available in the two-roomed school in the hamlet near their farm.

The next year there was a new teacher for the junior students and Mr. Prytula would be teaching the senior students. When Iryna was allowed to attend the hamlet school for one final year, she was pleased to have Mr. Prytula as her teacher. She liked him and hoped to learn a great deal from him.

As the school year progressed Mr. Prytula became aware of Iryna's intelligence and writing skills. He encouraged her and spoke often of her completing grade twelve so she could go to university. Iryna would have liked to believe this would be possible but she doubted Tato would ever allow it.

And so it was painful but not surprising that in the following year, Tato would not hear of Iryna taking grade twelve by correspondence.

"Who will want to marry you if you have so much education. You don't need it to become a farmer's wife!"

Iryna was in despair. But she bore her fate with as much grace as she could muster and continued to write. All through the long winter of 1941 Iryna wrote. She wrote about the war and the boys who had gone off to fight. She wrote about the farmers who worked so hard to support the war effort. She wrote about anything and everything that sparked her imagination. That winter she submitted a short story to the Western Producer Newspaper. They had a policy of printing short stories of interest to their readers and anyone could submit a piece for consideration. The story was published and Iryna was thrilled.

At Christmas time Iryna saw Uncle Andriy. He had read her published story and praised her effort. A huge triumph indeed! Then Mr. Prytula had come to speak to Tato. They had gone to the barn for their talk and, of course, Iryna was very curious about what was being discussed. George volunteered to go to the barn to hear what might be said but Mama told him it was none of his business and if it were, he would know soon enough. Tato returned to the house alone and Mr. Prytula left in his car. Nothing of the conversation was shared.

Tato was quieter than usual following the visit. More than once Iryna thought she had seen him looking at her in a thoughtful way. She hoped he wasn't displeased with her. Perhaps he felt having a story published in the newspaper was improper for a young girl. She didn't want to displease Tato but she had to write and it was such a wonderful feeling to share her stories.

As spring approached Iryna submitted another story and once more it was published. This story was about a young soldier who went to fight in the war and was killed, leaving behind his grieving mother and father. It was skillfully written and struck a chord with many readers. A few weeks later Iryna received a letter from the editor of the newspaper. He wanted to commission a story and he would pay her for it! Amazing!

Maybe she didn't have to finish school. Maybe Iryna could write her stories and have them published in the newspaper. Could she be happy with that?

As the summer wore on, Iryna helped her mother in the garden and the house. She worked diligently. Her Mother bought her a new dress for every dance and George dutifully took his younger sister to all the community events.

Iryna knew the purpose was for her to find a husband but she really wasn't interested. She went to the dances and talked with the girls from town and the surrounding farms. She danced with the boys who asked her and she had a good time. It was a quirk of fate that her name brought her much attention from the boys, especially at the end of each evening. At that time it was a tradition for the last dance tune to be 'Good Night Irene' and so typically several boys would be vying to dance the final dance with her. And then the band would end the night by playing 'the King' ('God Save the King') and George would be protectively by her side, making sure none of the boys thought they might actually be escorting his sister home.

One night George had had a bit of horiwka to drink with his friends during the evening. This was not unusual but Tato would not have approved. They had taken the team, Dick and Dolly, hitched to a buggy to get to the dance. Iryna was a bit worried about George when it was time to go home but George just said, "Don't worry, Dick and Dolly know the way home, we'll be fine." And they were. And this was their little secret.

Iryna loved her older brother. He was good to her as he was to everyone. He had always taken her side and tried to help her whenever he could. She liked having a secret with him.

By fall Iryna was almost resigned to the fact that her school days were over. Then one day Mr. Prytula came to the farm again. This time he had a big brown envelope. He gave the envelope to Tato and was on his way again. A few days later Tato gave the envelope to Iryna. It was the application form to take grade twelve by correspondence. Iryna could have kissed her father but, of course, she knew that would not have been welcomed. So instead she ran out to the yard to find George, in order to share her good news with him.

In the spring of 1943 Iryna not only completed grade twelve by correspondence but also won a scholarship to attend university. This time, the only two things Tato said were "If you go to the city you must live with the nuns," and "Who will help your mother when you are away?"

Nick

Nick was the baby of Pavlo and Dariya's family. He grew up happy and content. He loved his parents and adored his older brother and sisters. There was nothing Nick wouldn't do for anyone in his family.

Nick had worked hard alongside his brother and father on the farm and had worked even harder in school. From the start he had owed a debt of gratitude to his big brother, George, who had taught him and Iryna to understand and speak English so they would be prepared for school. It was his brother, George, who began calling him Nick instead of Mykola. Nick didn't mind. He would answer to either name. To him they were both the same anyway.

Nick often saw the drama and conflict between Iryna and their father. In his heart he had to side with Iryna but he understood, perhaps better than anyone else in the family, just how difficult this had been for their father. Nick loved and respected his father and would have done anything to bring peace and understanding between Tato and Iryna.

So every chance he had, Nick would talk to his father about the world, about God, and about life. He would ask his father about how he thought God wanted to take care of us and what He wanted for us. Pavlo was deeply spiritual and he appreciated these conversations with his youngest son. Often, days after such a conversation, Pavlo would notice something that one of his children said or did and he would think, "God would be pleased by that; it is good."

And so as the battles continued to rage and Iryna managed, step-by-step, to continue going to school, there was a softening in Pavlo's heart. It wasn't because, as Iryna thought, he had been forced into it. It was instead, because Nick had helped him to see that all loving fathers, like God Himself, really did want what was best for their children. This was the greatest gift Nick had given to his family and it was especially beautiful to him, because he thought no one actually knew what he had done.

But he was wrong. Dariya knew her children very well. She knew each and every one of them and she knew Nick. She saw how Nick talked to his father and she loved that he was such a gentle and positive force in the family. Dariya thanked God every day for the gift of her youngest son.

So when it happened that Iryna got the news she had won a scholarship to attend the University, Dariya wondered how her husband would take the other news, which she knew was coming next. For Dariya had long suspected her youngest son had a religious vocation. And when she saw he often spoke to the priest, who came to the little church on the corner of their land, she knew the family must soon learn to live without Nick, as well as Iryna.

Nick and Iryna left together on the train in the fall of 1943, she to Saskatoon and the University, while he would go on to Roblin, Manitoba to St. Vladimir's Seminary.

Pavlo took his two youngest children to the train station in town, bid them farewell and good luck, turned around to head back to the farm, and thanked God for all his children. He had been very lucky in life and he was grateful.

"The two youngest are gone now. The house is so empty. This is not the peace I so often prayed for. How I will miss them. Iryna's youthful joy of life, her spirit, her stories. And my dear Mykola – Nick – he will be a good priest. But I am not ready to lose him, to share him with the world. It is so hard to believe he leaves us, his family, to become part of a bigger family. He is no longer ours. I wonder if those people he will serve can know just how much a mother gives up when her son decides to become a priest. Don't be so selfish! He will be a good priest. And we need priests. This is right. This is what must be. I will pray for both of them – my two youngest, gone off into the world. God go with you."

Lena and Lyudmyla

By the spring of 1940 Lena had been teaching in the little country school for five years. That year she finally convinced Baba Cione to let Lyudmyla spend the school year with her. Lyudmyla was thirteen and studying grade eight.

For a dance in the Christmas Concert that year, Lyudmyla was partnered with the most handsome boy in the school. Jaroslav was tall, with dark brown, wavy hair, and beautifully expressive grey-green eyes. He was an excellent dancer and had a lovely, deep singing voice. And when he laughed, which was often, his face and eyes sparkled with a mirth that melted the hearts of all those around him. From this event onward Lyudmyla felt Jaroslav would be the only man in the world for her.

For the start of the next school year Lena was asked to teach in a hamlet over fifteen miles to the southeast. There was a two-roomed school in the hamlet and she would teach the junior students, grades one to five. Previously an older, male teacher had been the Principal of this school, while a younger, bachelor teacher, who had been teaching there for two years, had taught the junior students. The former Principal had retired and gone to live with his son in the city, while the bachelor teacher, Mr. Prytula, would now be the Principal and teach the senior students, grades six to eleven. Students who wished to complete grade twelve did so either by correspondence or by attending a high school in the city. Because the bachelor teacher lived with his aged parents, who had retired from their homestead, the teacherage was to become a new home for Lena and Lyudmyla. Best of all, they would be living in a hamlet with a railway station, a grain elevator, two stores, two churches, and a community hall.

Lena was tired of living in the lonely wilderness surrounding her first school. The hamlet was further from home and Baba Cione but the offer was just too good to pass up. Lena accepted the position; she was twenty-six years old.

The teacherage was a spacious home for the two sisters. It sat mid-way along the northern edge of the large schoolyard, while the two-roomed school stretched across the eastern end of the yard. The teacherage was approximately square in shape. It had a porch all along the front of the house facing north. From the porch you entered into the kitchen on the left or the adjoining living room on the right. Behind each of these main rooms was a small bedroom; the slightly larger one behind the kitchen had a steep staircase up to the attic. The attic had a high, steep roof and a window at either end so it was a bright, spacious storage area.

Within a year, it became obvious that Lena and her fellow teacher were becoming very close. So Lyudmyla was not at all surprised when, in the spring of 1942, Lena married Mr. Prytula. Lyudmyla continued going to school in the two-roomed, hamlet school and live in the teacherage with the young teaching couple.

One of the great things about living with her sister and new brother-in-law was that he was a fun-loving man. He had a car and loved to go for a ride on Sunday afternoons. He also loved company and dancing, so whenever there was a community event or dance anywhere in the region, the trio would be in attendance. It was at one of these dances near Lena's first school, that Lyudmyla finally saw Jaroslav again. The two young people were virtually inseparable - something that did not escape the notice of Lena and her husband. Over the course of the next year Lyudmyla and Jaroslav saw more and more of each other.

Jaroslav was perfect for Lyudmyla, not just because he was handsome and fun to be with. It seemed to her that the only time she really felt 'worthy' was when she was with him. For most of her life she had harboured feelings of being not quite as good as others around her. She had first become aware of these feelings when her cousins had come to live with her and Baba Cione throughout the school week during the winter months. Although Lyudmyla had loved their company she had also felt a bit like an outsider. It was a feeling she was never quite able to shake. Then when she had lived with Lena in the remote teacherage, being new to the school and the teacher's sister besides, seemed to make the other students keep a bit of distance from her. She didn't develop close friendships during that year. But during the year she had met and fallen in love with Jaroslav.

Jaroslav always treated her as if she were the best girl in the world. He was more than kind and generous and always made her feel as though she were a part of whatever was happening among the students. That year would have been very uncomfortable for her if it had not been for Jaroslav. It was, she believed, entirely because of him that she began to feel more confident. And for that she loved him even more.

Canada declared war on Germany on September 10, 1939 one week after Great Britain and France. Within two months the first contingents of Canadian troops arrived in Britain to join the British Expeditionary Forces.

In the spring of 1940, the National Resources Mobilization Act (NRMA) was passed, providing for service registration of thousands of men, strictly for home defense. These recruits were trained for warfare; often along side the volunteers who were heading overseas. Throughout most of the war Canada sent only volunteer troops to fight overseas. And the country sent thousands of them. Volunteers enlisted from every province, from city and town, and from the hamlets and farms.

Canadian Troops played an active role in Dunkirk and Dieppe; Hong Kong and Burma; Italy; Normandy; and the Netherlands. The Canadian Navy escorted convoys and hunted U-boats while the Royal Canadian Air Force fought in the skies over Europe, North Africa, Italy, and in the Battle of Britain. Thousands of Canadian soldiers died and many more were wounded or taken prisoner. A World War II Cenotaph was raised in almost every town across the nation to honour its fallen heroes.

In June 1943 Jaroslav turned nineteen. He was three years older than Lyudmyla. Shortly after his birthday he was called up for national service under the NRMA. Jaroslav was more than willing to do his duty and reassured Lyudmyla he would not be sent to fight overseas. He was going to Camp Dundurn south of Saskatoon for training and would then be put into the reserves for national defense. Later that summer some NRMA troops, stationed in British Columbia, were sent to support 'Operation Greenlight' helping American forces re-occupy Kiska in Alaska after having expelled Japanese invaders. But this was still considered 'national defense'.

When mounting Canadian casualties and the lack of trained replacements further increased the pressure at home for new recruits, a plebiscite was held on April 27, 1942, which resulted in an overwhelming approval for overseas service conscription beginning late in 1944.

In November of 1944, just a few weeks after the start of conscription for overseas services, Jaroslav, as part of a twelve thousand NRMA contingent, was called up for active duty. Jaroslav prepared himself to leave for the war, as so many Saskatchewan boys had done before him but Lyudmyla was devastated. She had a sense of foreboding, which she could not shake. Jaroslav did his best to convince her he would be fine, they would write long letters to each other every day, he would tell her all about everything he was doing, and when he returned, they would marry and start a wonderful life together. Lyudmyla suggested they marry before his departure, as so many young couples were doing but Jaroslav was so convinced of his safe return he insisted they wait.

Jaroslav travelled east via a troop train and then on a troop ship to Southern England, where he was stationed at Aldershot Camp. It was reassuring for Lyudmyla to receive letters from him postmarked England and she prayed Jaroslav would not see active duty after all.

But the next letter told a different story. In February Jaroslav had crossed the English Channel. His infantry unit had been attached to the Second Canadian Division and, along with British Forces, was being deployed to push the Nazis out of Holland and back across the Rhine, in what would be called the Battle of Hochwald Gap. The desperate German forces were a formidable foe and, while the allied forces ultimately succeeded in crossing the Rhine at Xanten to open the way into Germany, the price in casualties was very high.

Toward the end of April Lyudmyla heard, not from Jaroslav, but from his father. Jaroslav was dead. Killed in action. Her world ended.

Lyudmyla grieved for the loss of Jaroslav, the loss of their planned life together, and the loss of her sense of being worthy of true happiness. Without Jaroslav she lost the self-confidence he had helped her to find. She had always been rather introverted but now she kept all of her thoughts and feelings to herself.

Even Lena was not able to reach her. Lena would have done anything for her 'baby' sister even if she had not made the promise to their dying mother to take care of her younger siblings. But because Lyudmyla had always kept her innermost feelings to herself, Lena didn't comprehend that the loss of Jaroslav was a tremendous blow to her sister's entire sense of self worth.

In May the war in Europe ended. By late summer Canadian troops were beginning to return triumphantly. Many families had been touched by the loss of a father, a son, a husband or fiancé, an uncle, a cousin, or a friend.

After two world wars, maybe now …. peace.

Pylyp

Pylyp had worked hard in Kirkland Lake. He had saved his money and was beginning to think about heading back home to Saskatchewan in 1939, seven long years since he had left. And then that fall war had broken out in Europe. Many of the men in town were volunteering to go over seas to fight. Pylyp wasn't sure he wanted to join them. Since so many men were leaving, better jobs were becoming available. Pylyp thought he might apply for a job with better hours and pay. It wasn't long before the honest, hard-working young man had a good paying job in the bank. And what was more - he had met someone.

Pylyp had gone to dances with the other fellows. He had talked to girls and danced with them but there hadn't been a special one.

Most of he girls in the rough mining town were from the region. Their fathers and brothers worked the mines and they, like their mothers, worked in the restaurants, laundries, and stores.

Then one day shortly after he started working at the bank, Pylyp noticed her. She seemed vaguely familiar but he couldn't place where he had seen her before. Then it struck him. He had seen her in church.

Pylyp had attended St. Vladimir Ukrainian Catholic Church since his arrival and knew many of his fellow parishioners. This girl though, might be new to town, for he could only remember seeing her once or twice.

Pylyp approached the young woman to ask if he could help. She seemed a bit taken aback.

"I was looking for Mr. Spencer," she replied.

"I am sorry," Pylyp responded, "he is not in right now. As his assistant may I help you?"

At first she hesitated. Perhaps she thought him too young or inexperienced. Perhaps she had a highly personal issue to discuss with the bank manager.

"I could take a message for Mr. Spencer," Pylyp added.

"Perhaps that would be best," she responded. "Please tell him I would like to see him about my father's affairs."

"And who shall I say was asking for him?" Pylyp politely inquired.

"Oh, of course," she responded. "Miss Ulianna Hryniuk. I can come back later this afternoon."

"Yes," Pylyp smiled, "he should be back by one thirty."

"Ulianna," he thought. What a pretty name.

As time went by, Pylyp began to think of Ulianna and watch for her in church and at the bank. He thought of her often.

Then one day, Mr. Spencer asked Pylyp to help him with some documents. To his surprise they were regarding Ulianna's father's estate. It seemed he had passed away and left some small amount of money and personal effects to Ulianna. Mr. Spencer had been asked by the lawyer to help Ulianna invest her funds until such time as she decided what she would do. Apparently father and daughter had come to Kirkland Lake just under a year ago. Her mother had been dead for a number of years and there were no other siblings. Ulianna had kept house for her father, who ran a business in town. Now that he was gone she was considering returning to the city.

Pylyp was distraught by the idea of this young woman, who had just barely entered his life, leaving town so very soon. Spurred on by this possibility, he determined to seek her out and speak with her.

When Pylyp saw Ulianna next it was in church. He waited patiently for her to come outside after the Liturgy and then approached her.

"I hope you won't be leaving town too soon," he said. "I would like to have a chance to take you for a walk or maybe to a movie."

This was bold indeed and Pylyp wasn't sure how she would respond.

"Actually," she replied, "I had hoped to be able to leave soon but it seems there are still a few details, which must be taken care of before I can go. When would you like to go to the movies?"

"On Saturday, perhaps?" he responded.

"That sounds good. I'll meet you at the theatre for the matinee."

And she was gone. He had a date. It had been easier than he thought it would be. He was overjoyed!

Pylyp and Ulianna enjoyed each other's company. They had much in common, including the fact that they were both far from any remaining family and both were now orphans. As they spent more time together, Pylyp told Ulianna about the hardships he had endured during the depression out west after his parents had died and on his fateful trip riding the rails to Kirkland Lake. He even told her about his mysterious encounters with 'Frenchie'. Ulianna saw in Pylyp a strength and maturity that belied his age. She liked and admired him.

While her father's estate was being settled, she told Pylyp about her desire to return to the city. Pylyp had never been to Toronto but she made it sound so wonderful.

"I wonder if I could get a job there," he said once.

"Of course you could!" she exclaimed. "My uncle could help. You should come back to the city with me and I will introduce you to him."

And so when Ulianna left Kirkland Lake, so did Pylyp. Her uncle did help the young man find a job and within a year the young couple were married.

Pylyp wrote a letter to his sisters to tell them the good news.

Throughout the war years Pylyp worked hard to be a good husband and, eventually, father to his growing family.

Argentina

Two cataclysmic events pushed Argentina into industrialization, the First World War and the Great Depression. In both cases, Argentines, who had previously depended on imported manufactured goods were deprived of these due to lack of availability, in the first case, and lack of ability to pay, in the latter. Throughout the thirties both the government and the military supported the burgeoning industrialization of Argentina. Despite efforts to increase Argentinian industrialization, by 1939 the economy was still behind the rest of the world in terms of trade and growth. Further encouragement of Argentine industrialization would result from the decreased availability of manufactured goods from foreign sources during the Second World War.

There were some who felt having remained neutral throughout the First World War had actually contributed to a shift away from foreign trade and investment in the country. After the First World War, Argentina's traditional, major trading partner, Great Britain, was in decline and had redirected its trade to largely within the British Commonwealth of Nations. Argentina sought to increase its trade with the newly emerging super power, the United States of America. However trade restrictions and tariffs imposed by that country, along with the Argentinian government's increasing desire to oversee foreign investment, made this an uneasy partnership at the best of times. By 1942, when Argentina alone among its Latin American neighbours had not declared war on Nazi Germany, tensions between the United States and Argentina escalated.

With the outbreak of World War II it became difficult to export Argentinian agricultural goods to continental Europe, so an attempt was made to reestablish trade ties with Britain. This was despite nationalist Argentine opposition, which was based on prior concessions having been granted to British meatpacking and railroad companies. At any rate, Great Britain had a mounting need for Argentinian meat and grain to support the war effort, so trade resumed.

Unfortunately Great Britain postponed payment for Argentine goods for the duration of the war, causing great dissatisfaction among Argentine producers. Because of the war Argentina could not even exchange its produce for manufactured goods, since all British industry had been converted to wartime production. The result was a huge Argentine gold reserve built up in Britain.

Growing dissatisfaction with the national government and concern that public unrest might lead to a communist revolution resulted in a military coup in June 1943. The group responsible was the Grupo de Oficiales Unidos (United Officer's Group or GOU). One of the leaders of this group was Colonel Juan Domingo Peron, an anticommunist nationalist with fascist tendencies. The new military government appointed Colonel Peron as Head of the Department of Labour.

As Head of the Department of Labour, Peron recognized the potential political power of the growing labour force. He dedicated himself to enforcing labour laws, negotiating collective agreements, raising wages, and improving working conditions. In addition, he lowered public transportation fares, froze rents, and introduced price controls on food. Through these efforts he was able to replace existing labour unions, some of which had communist roots, with state-controlled unions. All of this contributed to making Colonel Peron very popular among labourers and powerful within the military junta.

Myko

No matter how hard Myko worked on the plantation it seemed his efforts were not sufficiently appreciated. As a consequence he believed the share of profits he and his family received was never a true reflection of what he had contributed. So he became more and more discontented with the way the plantation was run and his position within it. He was ambitious and longed for a way to demonstrate to everyone, not least of all his wife, just how valuable his contributions were.

After almost ten years of marriage and childbearing, his wife had become discontented with her lot in the life on the plantation, as well. It had never really lived up to her initial expectations and for that she blamed, not her husband, but his father, Taras, and his father's partner, Ivan. She was loyal to her husband and empathized with his view that his input was often overlooked or undervalued.

Myko's eldest, his first-born son, was eight and his parents were determined their children have more to inherit than a common share in the plantation. Myko was not be content with the way things had been and was considering a plan to finally bring him the wealth he believed he deserved. He was going to enter the age-old trade of moving people and products from Paraguay across the Parana River and to the markets in central Argentina.

The location of the plantation on an arroyo of the Parana and the location of his home nearest the water, were perfect for his new enterprise. So one day Myko set off and was gone for almost a week. Taras was mystified by his son's absence but when he asked Myko's wife, she simply said he had business to conduct and would be home soon.

Myko travelled along the arroyo to the great river and then crossed it into neighbouring Paraguay. Not too far from the point of his crossing was a small village. In that village it was not at all difficult to find people who knew all about the business Myko planned to undertake. So with the limited funds Myko had been able to save he made his first investment in some tobacco. It wasn't much, it was easy to transport, and if by chance anyone stopped him to inquire about his load, he could convince them it was a lawful purchase for personal use by the workers on his father's plantation. Myko was a bit nervous about this undertaking but confident he could out smart any border guards who might challenge him.

The return trip went well and with no challenges. Myko stored the tobacco, which he had bought for a very small amount of cash in Paraguay, in a secret hiding place he had prepared in his home. Then the next time supplies were needed for the plantation, he would take the tobacco to Posadas to sell at a huge profit. It couldn't be simpler.

And so started Myko's career as a smuggler. As time went by he learned which products were easiest to transport and afforded the highest reward. As his sons grew up they, too, became involved in the family 'business', first as lookouts and decoys but eventually as traders in their own rights.

"There is always a way to make money," Myko told his sons, "if you are smart enough to do what it takes and willing to take some risks."

Taras and Ivan had noticed the decline in Myko's involvement in the work and running of the plantation, but in actual fact this had almost been a relief. Myko had never been easy to work with and his constant need for praise was wearing down everyone he interacted with. Myko worked less and less on the plantation but was always the first to volunteer to travel to Posadas for supplies. His sons worked but little on the plantation and always in tandem, so no more than one of them was working at any given time. This, too, seemed strange to Taras and Ivan, but since Myko's sons were as difficult to work with as their father, this was also seen as a blessing.

Yory

Yory Martiniuk, who was now referred to by many of those he worked with as Jorge Martín, continued to apply his intelligence and innovations within the context of his government position. He loved his job because he saw positive results from his efforts and he really believed he was making a difference for farmers in the region. New crops were slowly being adopted to help revitalize the land and making inroads in the markets in Britain, along with the traditional Argentine grains and citrus crops. The yerba mate market was growing but largely within the country and the rest of South America.

Yory loved living in Posadas with his cherished Oxana and now their two sons. Whenever possible, they would take their sons to visit Diedo Taras and Abuela Carmen. Yory was so grateful to both his parents. He had grown up in a multicultural home and truly believed he had been exposed to the best of both his father's and his mother's cultures. For one thing, he had learned both Ukrainian and Spanish as his first languages. This had been very helpful to him, since Spanish was the language of his schooling and now his workplace. He loved the rites and traditions of the Greek Catholic Church and equally the traditions of his Mother's Spanish culture.

Yory and Oxana were devout members of the San Vladimiro parish in Posadas. Yory had become a parish leader by giving generously of his time and talents to support the growth and success of the parish. He had served on the parish council and his many innovative ideas had contributed to a strong parish community. The vibrant parish hosted Ukrainian cultural concerts, fiestas, and religious celebrations. Oxana was also actively involved with the church and its activities, including teaching catechism to the younger children and working with the women to prepare for various religious and parish celebrations. The women played an important role in preserving Ukrainian traditions among the young of the parish, by teaching the Ukrainian language, songs, dances, customs, and crafts. It was becoming important to preserve the Ukrainian language and culture, because the language of work and school was the official national language,

Spanish. Liturgical services, which had been originally performed in Old Slavonic, shifted to the vernacular Spanish as the immigrant families assimilated into their new country.

Taras

Both Ivan and Taras had always seen the workers on their plantation as partners in the enterprise. From the start they had treated their workers fairly, paid them in cash - rather than in credits for a plantation store, as so many other plantation owners had done - and rewarded them according to the effort they contributed to the business. During the depression the two owners had done all they could to ensure their workers would survive the difficult economic times.

But times were changing. Some members of the younger generation were growing dissatisfied with the nature of the work on the plantation. Some felt they could do better in one of the many upcoming factories in the cities to the south. Others had heard of labour reforms to improve the lives of workers and supported the idea of government-sponsored workers' unions.

Ivan and Taras watched with dismay as some of the younger workers left the plantation. "It might become harder to replace them in the future," Taras thought.

But there was another threat to the future success of the plantation. The military coup in 1943 had ushered in a strong anti-communist policy. While neither Ivan nor Taras had ever been politically active nor did they support a particular political ideology, the way in which they had conceived and operated the plantation could be seen by some as being based on communist ideals. It was something that had never occurred to them until one day.

It had happened almost by accident. Taras had been in Posadas visiting Yory and Oxana. There had been another government official there at the same time. He was from the labour office. He had been talking to Yory about the serious threat of communism and gave the example of some of the large communes raising yerba to the north.

"These plantation owners mollify their workers with rhetoric about sharing in the profits, while they are not afforded the rights they are due under our labour laws," the fellow was blustering.

Yory had obviously heard such comments before but Taras was stunned. It was as if everything he and Ivan had believed in and worked for was being criticized by a bureaucrat, who knew nothing of their plantation and its workers.

The comments of the bureaucrat opened Taras' eyes. He would have to discuss this with Ivan. It was bad enough that some of the younger workers were leaving the plantation but if the government thought their plantation was a commune it could actually threaten their life's work. Perhaps it was time to start paying more attention to politics.

Myko

In Myko's line of work it was important to be aware of the way political winds were blowing. He had watched with interest when the military coup took over the government in far-away Buenos Aries. He had read some of what the new Labour Department Head, Peron, said about social change and worker's welfare. If these trends continued there might be an opportunity in all of this. He would have to continue being alert and watchful.

Then late in the year an opportunity did present itself. Myko was aware of the attitudes among many Argentines, especially among the German settlers. They had been vocal supporters of the Nazi Party and its leader in Germany. They had hoped Argentina would support the Axis more openly, but were proud that at least the country had not bowed to the pressure of Great Britain and the United States to support the Allies. They talked about the fascist leanings of the military junta with admiration. But now the war had ended and it had ended badly for Germany. There were rumors of high-ranking German officers being seen in the region.

Then one day when Myko was going about his usual business and preparing to cross to Paraguay, he was approached by a German farmer.

"Would you have room for two passengers?" the man asked.

“Where would they like to go?” Myko asked cautiously.

“Preferably to Brazil but if you are heading for Paraguay, that would be fine. I can pay you of course.”

Myko thought for a moment. This was a chance to make some real money. However he knew better than to be too greedy.

So after a bit of negotiation it was agreed that Myko would escort the two men across the Parana and take them to a settlement, just on the far side of the Paraguay-Brazil boarder.

Myko wondered why the man who had approached him had not taken the two travellers himself. But he flattered himself that it was likely because he was known as a successful and discreet ‘trader’.

10 POST WAR BOOM (AND BUST)

Canada

Lyudmyla

After learning of Jaroslav's death in the spring of 1945, Lyudmyla at the age of eighteen had lost all interest in life. She managed to complete grade twelve by correspondence but it was clear to all around her that she was just going through the motions. She mourned throughout the summer. Lena was very worried about her.

Finally one day toward the end of summer, after supper Lena asked her sister to take a walk with her. Lyudmyla was still in the depths of despair but she loved and respected her sister, who was more like a mother to her than an elder sister. She could not refuse such a simple request.

The two young women walked from the teacherage down the back alley, then north crossing the grid road, which served as the main street of the hamlet. From there they continued north across the train tracks and into the pasture, where the annual sports day was held. They walked on in silence to the base of one of the prominent hills in the region, referred to locally as 'Hoot's Peak' for the owls often seen there. Then they began to climb the hill. Near the crest Lena finally spoke.

"I must be getting old," she said. "I have to sit down for a minute."

Lena looked around and saw a fallen tree near the edge of the bush covering the hillside. She sat down with a sigh.

"Lyudmyla," she started, "most people could not truly say they know how you feel but I must tell you something so you will understand that I do. There was a young man who I had hoped to marry," and then she paused.

"Did he die in the war?" Lyudmyla asked half resentfully, although she was curious because she had no idea her sister had had a romantic thought before meeting her husband.

"No," Lena responded and paused again. "But he may just as well have been, for he was lost to me just the same."

Then slowly Lena relayed the story of a young man she had met while she was studying to become a teacher. It had been during the year after their mother's death. Pylyp had left for the east in the autumn and Lena had gone to Saskatoon to study. Lyudmyla had been only five years old when their mother died and Lena had made a promise to care for her siblings and to keep the family together. The 'loss' of Pylyp from her care had made Lena feel she had failed to keep her promise to their mother. She had re-doubled her resolve to take care of Lyudmyla.

The attraction between Lena and a fellow student had been mutual. They had studied together, gone for walks, and talked for hours. He knew of her family troubles and was sympathetic and supportive. They had even talked about trying to get teaching positions together. Lena was very much in love and thanked God for the happiness she had found.

After she returned from Normal School she waited and waited to hear from him. Finally she heard he had accepted a teaching position in the town near her school. She was so happy, believing her dream would soon come true. During the Christmas break she finally saw him at a community dance in her hometown. They danced and then he asked her to step outside for a moment. Lena was sure he was going to propose.

"I have missed you so much Lena," he started. "How have you found teaching?"

"Teaching is fun but living alone in the teacherage is hard. I am very lonely. And all the chores before and after school are very hard."

"I feel the same way. And we don't even know if we will be paid," he responded.

"Lena," he started and then paused. "I have something to tell you. I am to be married."

Lena wasn't sure she had heard him correctly. "Married?" she asked.

"Yes," was all he could say.

And Lena just stared at him.

"I am sorry," he added.

"But I thought …" she began. Then she saw the look in his eyes and stopped short. This was hard for him to do. He really did care for her. Why then?

Perhaps it was because she was poor but so was he. Perhaps it was because she had had the bad luck to lose both parents. Some people thought that sort of bad luck would follow a person throughout their lifetime. No he wasn't like that. Perhaps it was because she had a little sister she had promised to care for. Perhaps. Well there was nothing to be done about that.

So Lena forced a smile and wished him well. She couldn't face her friends and neighbours in the hall, so instead she ran home. Baba Cione had been horrified when Lena came home without her coat. Lena didn't care. She went to bed cold and cried herself to sleep. A friend brought her coat the next morning but Lena couldn't face her. Baba knew something had happened but didn't press the young woman. In a day or two she was herself again and soon she returned to her school and teaching.

When Lyudmyla heard the details of this story she was astounded. She had no idea of her sister's heartbreak. And then suddenly she realized she might well have been the cause. Did the young man change his mind about Lena because she had promised to care for a younger sister? Lyudmyla felt sorrow and guilt, but also extreme love and gratefulness. Lena had sacrificed her own happiness and Lyudmyla was the beneficiary. She gave her sister a hug and forced a smile.

"I will be alright," she said as cheerfully as she could manage.

Then Lena told her the most wonderful secret of all. She was pregnant!

At that moment Lyudmyla knew it was time to find her own way in the world. Lena had done everything she could for her and now it was time to take control of her own life.

And so as the dreary autumn approached, Lyudmyla decided to leave for Saskatoon. She planned to stay with the nuns in their new home on Spadina Crescent and get a job. Lena had suggested she go to Normal School to become a teacher but that had not appealed to Lyudmyla. Lena helped her pack and gave her a small amount of cash to help her get established. Then Lyudmyla was on her way to the railway station, heading for the city to start her new life. She left the teacherage and her sister and brother-in-law with a heavy heart but she knew this would be best for everyone concerned.

When Lyudmyla arrived at the Saskatoon train station her spirits lifted a bit. It was October and there were posters proclaiming a march of returning soldiers. It hurt her to think Jaroslav would not be among them but at the same time she thought it would be only fair for her to show her support. Who knows, some of these soldiers might have fought with him. One of them might have been the last person to see him alive. And so she noted the time and date of the march and vowed to attend.

Lyudmyla walked with the suitcase containing all her worldly possessions through the downtown streets to the Sister Servants of Mary Immaculate house across from the Roman Catholic St. Paul's Cathedral. Lena had written to Sister Superior, asking for room and board for her sister, so Lyudmyla was expected and, like her sister before her, was welcomed.

After she was shown her room and told when meals and morning prayers would be, she was left to unpack and get settled. "'Get settled', what a strange phrase," she reflected. "Would she ever feel settled again?" She had no idea but she would have to try.

And so Lyudmyla began to develop a routine. She rose early to attend Liturgy with the Sisters and then had breakfast with the other boarders. Then she would dress warmly, for the autumn weather was turning colder. She often had to trudge across the windy pedestrian bridge over the train tracks as she went in searched of work. Eventually she was lucky enough to find a job working in a restaurant on Twentieth Street. Once she had a bit of money she could pay the Sisters for room and board. As the winter progressed Lyudmyla occasionally even rode the streetcar to or from work. Some of the girls thought it rather extravagant that she spent money on riding the streetcar instead of walking but she had always hated the cold and had walked many, many miles in cold weather all her life. Now that she could afford the fare, she would occasionally treat herself to a ride rather spend her hard-earned cash on new clothing or movies, as the other girls did.

Lyudmyla knew what the other girls said about her 'extravagant ways' and, although she had no intention of changing her decision to suit them, it still hurt her that she was being criticized by others who had no idea of her reasons. This was just one of the small things preventing Lyudmyla from forming close ties with most of the other girls who boarded with the Sisters. As was her way, Lyudmyla was friendly but kept mostly to herself.

Sister Superior Eudoxia was a keen observer of human nature. She did not know everything about Lyudmyla but through her interactions with Lena, she knew how the girls had been orphaned at a young age and how Lena had taken care of her little sister. It was clear there was much more sorrow in the young girl's life and so the nun determined to do what she could to help.

It so happened that the physician who came to the house when one of the Sisters or girls was ill, was looking for someone to work with him in his office. His wife had, until recently, been his assistant but now that she had a child she no longer wanted to work. Sister Superior thought Lyudmyla would be perfect for the job. She had noted an empathy and a caring gentleness in Lyudmyla, which was uncommon among young girls and may have been the result of the hardships she had faced in her short lifetime. Sister was always on the look out for a girl who might have a religious vocation, so if Lyudmyla enjoyed working with the doctor perhaps some day she might become a nurse and even work in the hospital the Sisters had established in Mundare. But that was simply speculation and just a distant possibility. For now Sister simply saw a good potential job for a young girl, who could excel if given the opportunity.

So Sister spoke to the doctor and he agreed to give Lyudmyla a trial. Lyudmyla was grateful for the opportunity. She had found work in the restaurant physically demanding and hoped working with the doctor might be more to her liking. So Lyudmyla spent several days with the doctor's wife learning the office routine. It soon became evident that she had a winning way with patients and could become a real asset to the practice. So the wife left her position in favour of home and her child, while Lyudmyla provided the doctor with the help he needed to continue growing his practice.

Lyudmyla enjoyed working with the doctor and his patients. She soon got to know the regulars very well and they appreciated the way she helped them. She was earning a bit more money now, so she did begin to treat herself to a new dress or a Saturday afternoon matinee.

There was one girl who was also staying with the Sisters who Lyudmyla knew from the hamlet where she had lived with Lena. Her name was Iryna Dannyk. Iryna was a few years older than Lyudmyla, but hadn't been that far ahead of her in school. She remembered how Iryna had wanted to continue going to school but her father was always reluctant. So one fall Iryna might not return, but then a few months later - one time it was a whole year later - there she would be again. She was determined and Lyudmyla had really liked that about her.

One Saturday afternoon Lyudmyla happened to run into Iryna's brother, George. Although he was quite a few years older than Lyudmyla, she knew him from the Ukrainian Catholic Church situated on a corner of the Dannyk farm.

Lyudmyla had been feeling homesick that long winter, so when she saw George Dannyk she smiled and greeted him as an old friend. George recognized Lyudmyla, as well, and was happy to see a familiar face. He had come to the city to visit his sister, Iryna. She had finally finished high school a couple of years ago and had won a scholarship to attend university.

Tato had agreed, reluctantly, to let his daughter go to the city to continue her education. So Iryna was living with the Sisters and studying English Literature at the University.

George had been on his way to meet Iryna for lunch and asked Lyudmyla whether she would like to join them. Lyudmyla didn't usually make snap decisions, but for some reason, on that day she didn't even think twice and accepted the invitation immediately. George was glad, as he had always admired the young girl who had come to the hamlet with her sister, the teacher.

So the three young people walked down Twenty-first Street to the Commodore Café and found a booth. As they talked and ate Lyudmyla realized just how much she missed home and her sister. She had been back to the hamlet for Christmas, of course, and would be going again for Easter but these were always short visits and her sister's house was always so busy now with a baby and husband. It seemed the two sisters never really had much time together anymore. And Lyudmyla missed that. She missed having someone in her life with whom to share the day-to-day ups and downs. She wrote often to her sister and to her brother in far-off Ontario but it was not the same. At the age of nineteen she had lost her parents, was living apart from the only family she had, and had lost the love of her life. And she was so very, very lonely.

After a long and enjoyable lunch the trio walked back to the Sisters' house. Lyudmyla felt more alone than ever after parting with George and Iryna.

Several weeks later Iryna popped into Lyudmila's room and asked if she would be willing to walk to the University with her to pick up some books from the library. The two girls walked across the Twenty-fifth Street Bridge and down College Drive, enjoying the breezy, sunny, late March day. Iryna was preparing to write her final exams. She had wanted to stay in the city to work for the summer but her father was insisting she return to the farm. She had one more year of university classes to complete a Bachelor of Arts in Literature. She had been fortunate to earn scholarships throughout her university education. In addition she had been writing short stories and getting paid small sums when these were published. She loved the city and really did not want to go back to the farm. But Tato wanted her to come home to help Mama.

"My exams will be over before Easter this year. You *are* going home for Easter, aren't you?" Iryna asked. "We can go home together. George is coming for me in his car. I know George would love to see you again!"

"George?" Lyudmyla asked rather surprised.

"Of course," Iryna answered. "You must know he is smitten with you."

"No," responded Lyudmyla, "I had no idea."

"Well he is and if we leave it up to him he will never do anything about it. So come home with me. It will make it easier for me to go back. You can visit your sister and her family. We will have George take us to a dance after Easter and I am sure he would be happy to drive you back to the city after the break."

Lyudmyla felt very awkward about this proposal, but perhaps....

Iryna

Iryna had worked very hard to be able to complete high school and, largely because she had won a scholarship, Tato had been convinced to let her attend university. He, of course, thought that if she were going to study she should at least earn a certificate in teaching. By now he was beginning to worry his second daughter, who was long past the prime marriageable age - she was twenty-two - might never marry. So he thought she should at least be able to support herself.

But Iryna would have none of it. She loved to write and because she had been able to sell several of her short stories for publication, she believed she was good at writing. It seemed most people enjoyed her stories and she never tired of telling them. So Iryna had decided she would spend her life writing.

In the first months of university an astounding thing had happened. An older professor had noticed her carrying a book of poems. It happened to be her Uncle Andriy's first book of poetry. Iryna loved Uncle Andriy's poetry and had brought a copy of each of his books with her from home.

The professor stopped her in the hallway.

"Do you study poetry?" he asked, indicating the book.

"Not exactly," she replied, "this is just a very special book. I love this poetry and my uncle has inspired me to follow in his foot steps to become a writer, as well."

"Your uncle?" he asked in astonishment. "Do you mean Andriy Martiniuk?"

"Yes, he is my uncle," she replied, rather surprised that this aged professor would have known her uncle, since she knew he had never attended university.

"I knew your uncle many years ago," the professor replied. "I first met him when he came to the city to work for the winter. I helped him to learn English. And," he added with a great deal of pride, "I flatter myself that I encouraged him to write poetry in English, as well as in Ukrainian."

"How wonderful!" Iryna exclaimed. "I will have to tell him about meeting you."

"I would like that very much," replied the professor. "And I would like to learn about what your uncle has been doing all these years. Perhaps we could meet for coffee one morning?"

Iryna was flattered, so she agreed to meet the professor the following week.

It had been a fateful meeting, for the professor was one of a rare breed. He believed his job at the University was to encourage young intellect and talent and help aspiring poets and authors to meet their potential. Almost all of his students thought him to be the best teacher they had ever had.

And so after telling the professor all about Uncle Andriy and his life, Iryna was being asked about her own studies. It soon became obvious to the professor that this young woman had a spark of the same genius he had recognized, so long ago, in her uncle.

"What a remarkable family," he thought.

So Iryna registered in the professor's course and, although writing poetry was not her forte, she loved to learn and she found that, indeed, the professor was a very good teacher.

From that day forward, Professor Bill Elliott took a special interest in Iryna and her writing career.

Iryna loved the city. She loved the University. She loved to learn and she loved to write. She knew her parents worried that she was not married and she might not be able to support herself with her writing. But like many ambitious young people, she believed in her dream and in her ability to achieve it.

George

While Pavlo worried about his second daughter, he had no concerns about the fact that his eldest son was not yet married. There were plenty of bachelor farmers in the vicinity. Many of them eventually married. Even though George was already twenty-five years old, there was still plenty of time.

George had enjoyed school. If he had had his way, he would have gone to Normal School or University to become a teacher. He thought he would have been a good teacher. From the early days when he had taught his younger siblings to speak, read, and write in English so they would not suffer the same embarrassment in school he had, he knew he had a calling to be a teacher.

But it was not to be. Tato had put his heart and soul into the farm and it would have broken him if his son had not carried on. It was clear to George, long before his father realized it, that young Nick, the second son, would not be the farmer in the family. And so George had accepted his fate. He worked hard alongside his father. He *did* like farming; it just would not have been his preferred livelihood.

George had been a fun-loving teenager. He had enjoyed attending dances, fall suppers, and community celebrations. Later when he was asked to take his sister, Iryna, along wherever he went he didn't mind. She was an intelligent girl with lots of friends. Sometimes it had been helpful if he wanted to meet or dance with a certain girl – he would ask Iryna to introduce them. Sometimes, he would enjoy having a drink or two with his friends. On the rare occasion when he had had a little too much to drink, he knew Tato would never find out from Iryna, his secrets were always safe with her.

And so the dutiful son had a close relationship with his younger sister. He loved his older sister and his younger brother. He adored his mother. And he always wished to please his father.

If Pavlo ever commented to Dariya in a less than complimentary manner about George, her standard response was: "It's because you sold him when he was a baby!" It was a family joke referring to an event from shortly after George was born. Because his parents had lost their first two sons, a neighbour had taken baby George from his mother and given his father a two-bit coin as payment. This was to break the spell of bad luck the young parents had had with sons. Dariya's retort never failed to soften Pavlo's attitude toward his eldest son. His wife knew him so well.

Dariya had always had a special place in her heart for George. He had been the son God had allowed her to keep after losing her first two. Even later when Nick was born, he could not replace George in his mother's heart. Nick knew this instinctively but it did not bother him. He had always been wiser than his years. He knew his whole family loved him. He knew God loved him and what more could anyone want?

As George worked with his father on the farm there were many changes. The fields got bigger as they broke more and more brush. A tractor and a truck replaced the draught horses, Dick and Dolly. They even had a self-propelled combine now. And best of all, George had bought himself a car.

George had always wanted a car but it wasn't until the higher grain prices during the war years that he actually could save enough to buy one. Tato, of course, couldn't understand why George wanted a car when he could use the one-ton, farm truck any time he wanted. But George wanted a car and so, in 1945 he finally bought one. It wasn't brand new but it looked great and ran well. It was a 1940 Ford. George had bought it from a neighbour in the hamlet and he was on top of the world.

So now when he wanted to go to the city to see Iryna, he could drive his car rather than take the train. This was the height of freedom for him and he loved it! He loved it so much, he often drove to the city on a weekend to visit his sister. It was on one of those visits when they had met and had lunch with Lyudmyla Cione. He had known her since she arrived in the hamlet with her sister, the teacher. He knew she and her sister had been orphaned and had lived together ever since. He knew she had been in love with a fellow from a few miles away and he had died toward the end of the war. He knew all these things about her but it wasn't until their chance meeting and shared lunch that George knew he had fallen in love with her.

She was petite and quite pretty and George knew, when she was ready, there would be lots of fellows anxious to go out with her. George intended to be the one she would choose. So he tried to learn more about Lyudmyla. He arranged to take her and Iryna to dances and picnics and community events. And he bided his time hoping that one day she would recognize how he felt about her.

Pavlo

Pavlo turned fifty-seven in the year the war ended. He had still felt himself to be a strong man - stronger than his years would suggest. But this year he began to realize - perhaps his age was catching up with him. There had been days, not many of them but still a few, when he tried so hard to do all he had done in the past and somehow, he just couldn't manage to get everything done in one day. So he pushed himself. He worked harder and harder. Dariya had noticed this change in him and had been concerned. Eventually she felt she must speak to him.

"How are you feeling?" she asked him one day when he came into the house much later than usual.

"Tired," was his reply. "And I still have to milk the cows."

"I'll do it or we could send George, he'll be in from the field soon."

"No he's been working hard all day too, I'll do it, I just need to rest for a few minutes."

Now Darya was really concerned. For as long as she had known him, her husband had never said he had to rest. This was serious.

So she made him a cup of chai and without saying another word went out to the barn to milk the cows. When she returned the chai was only half drunk and Pavlo was stretched out on the kitchen floor next to the stove, fast asleep.

A few days later Pavlo came into the house with two buckets of milk and set them down in the pantry.

"Would you separate the milk? I need to rest."

"Of course," Darya replied and asked if he wanted a cup of chai.

"No I think I'll lie down."

"Lie down! Before supper?" Darya thought. Now she was really worried!

So the next chance she had she spoke to her son.

"I am worried about Tato," she told him. "He seems tired all the time. I know he is working very hard but sometimes I see he doesn't get everything done."

"I've noticed that too," replied George. "Should we take him to see a doctor?"

"Do you think we could persuade him to go?" Darya asked hopefully.

"Lyudmyla works for a good doctor in the city. She could make an appointment for Tato."

Dariya immediately saw the wisdom in her son's suggestion. Pavlo had warmed to Lyudmyla when she had visited the farm with Iryna over the Easter break in 1946.

Pavlo knew Lyudmyla had been orphaned at a young age, as he himself had been. There was something about Lyudmila's bearing, reminiscent of his two younger brothers after their parents had died. Pavlo had been too busy trying to help Baba Pelik provide for all the orphans in her care to be similarly affected. But his brothers, especially the youngest, had been transformed by the tragedy of their parents' deaths. Pavlo remembered how his brothers had become quiet and cautious. Pavlo sensed the same traits in Lyudmyla and his heart went out to her. He also noted his son's attraction to the young girl and saw her as an excellent choice of mate for George. The girl had enjoyed the farm. Her only sister lived in the hamlet just two miles away. What could be more perfect?

So the next day when George was working in the yard with his father he mentioned the idea of seeing the doctor Lyudmyla worked with in the city. At first Pavlo didn't say anything. It usually took him a while to consider a new idea. He was likely considering all the consequences of such an action. George knew better than to rush his father. Later that afternoon Pavlo told George to arrange an appointment but not until after harvest was complete.

"Tak, ok," George responded. "I'll set it up and drive you into the city."

"Why can't we take the train?" Pavlo asked.

"Driving will save time," was all George had to say and the matter was settled.

Pavlo knew his family was worried about him. He was a bit worried too. Unknown to them he had had to sit down to rest several times during the workday. It was only when he knew he could not continue working that he had gone into the house to rest. These required respites seemed to be increasing in frequency. Pavlo was annoyed by the fact that he was not as productive as he had once been but it seemed there was just nothing he could do about it.

One day during the height of the busy harvest season, Pavlo pushed himself to work through the whole long day without a rest. By the end of the day he had a throbbing headache and his muscles were so weak and shaky he wasn't sure he could even make it back to the house. When he did get into the house he walked straight into the bedroom and collapsed on the bed, fully clothed.

Dariya had no idea what to make of this but was grateful George would be taking her husband to see a doctor soon.

The next day Pavlo could not get out of bed. His head was pounding and, despite a long night of sleep, he still felt weak and shaky.

Dariya left some food out for him and went to drive the grain truck for George, who was combining in the field.

Pavlo stayed in bed for two days. On the third day he tried to resume his normal work schedule but by noon he was exhausted.

So it was with huge relief that, a week later, all three - father, mother, and son - bundled into George's car and headed for the city.

Lyudmyla greeted the family warmly and showed them in to see the doctor. He questioned Pavlo about his symptoms, took his temperature and blood pressure, and looked in his eyes and ears. Then he took the blood pressure reading again. They talked a bit more and then the doctor took Pavlo's blood pressure once more.

"Mr. Dannyk," the doctor said very seriously, "your blood pressure is very high. There are a few things we can do to help lower it. I will write a prescription for some pills. Lyudmyla will give you a list of the foods you must avoid. I will see you again in a month. If you don't take care of yourself you are in serious danger of having a heart attack and possibly dying."

Dariya was stunned. George hung his head. He couldn't imagine his father in danger of anything, let alone dying. Pavlo seemed to take the news with the same calm resignation with which he had faced all the trials in his lifetime. The drive home to the farm was very quiet.

When they got home Pavlo went straight to bed, while George and Dariya did the chores. After supper, George read to his mother the list of foods Tato was to avoid. Dariya was dumbstruck. What could she feed him if he had to avoid butter, cheese, cream, meat, and sweets - including pie! But she would have to try, for she couldn't imagine her life without her husband.

A month later the trio made a repeat visit to the doctor. Not much had changed, so the doctor told Pavlo to take two of the little white pills each day and to return in another month.

Throughout the winter of 1946-47, Pavlo saw the doctor on several occasions. Each time the doctor had the same thing to say. That winter George essentially took over the farm because his father had so little energy and stamina. Toward spring Pavlo began worrying about how George would manage the spring seeding.

"It will be fine, Tato," George tried to reassure him. "I will manage. Many farmers manage on their own and so will I."

"But you need a helper," Pavlo insisted.

Just then Dariya spoke up. "I will help George. You must rest and do what the doctor says. I am not ready to be a widow!"

George was astounded. His mother seldom spoke so forcefully. But it was clear she was not going to be gainsaid and so the conversation stopped there.

Immediately after seeding was completed, George had a long conversation with his parents. While they continued to live on the farm, Tato was tempted to do more than he should. During the seeding season he had tried desperately to do the daily chores in order to free George and Dariya to do the fieldwork.

"This won't do. Tato has to rest more."

"I agree," said Dariya.

By now Pavlo was beginning to accept how his condition was affecting them all. It was clear that despite what he wanted to do, he just didn't have the strength anymore. He would have to bend to his physical limitations.

And so it was decided that they would buy a little house in the hamlet and Mama and Tato would live there, away from the farm and the temptations for Tato to over do it. They would come to the farm regularly to see how farming was progressing but George would take full responsibility.

"He really needs a wife now," Pavlo said to Dariya.

"Yes a wife would be a big help to him," she replied, remembering their early days on the homestead.

Iryna

Iryna had completed her studies at the University, earning a bachelor's degree in English Literature in the spring of 1947. And now with the help of Professor Bill and Uncle Andriy, she was preparing a selection of her short stories, which she hoped would be published as a book. Her uncle had volunteered to write the 'Forward' and Professor Bill, she knew, had called in some personal favours, in order for her manuscript to be considered for publication. Iryna was more excited about her project than about earning a university degree.

Iryna had moved back from the city after completing her studies. George was busy seeding and arranging to move Mama and Tato, so she knew he would appreciate her help.

The little house in town would be perfect, Iryna thought. It had three rooms and a pantry and sat on the southwest corner of a large triple lot. There was an outhouse, of course, and a shed behind the house. There would be plenty of room for Mama to have a big garden and a few chickens.

Iryna fell back into the routine of farm life effortlessly, helping with the daily chores and cooking for her family. She took sandwiches and coffee in a thermos out to the field so George could take advantage of every moment of daylight to get the crop in. George was grateful for his sister's help and began realizing just how much more work there was to do if he had to do it all by himself. But perhaps that wouldn't be necessary.

In the evenings Iryna took supper out to the field for George, did the evening chores, and then during those long, glorious Saskatchewan spring days worked on her manuscript. Iryna had a sense that something of what passed when a writer was engaged in the craft found its way into the fabric of the work. She felt sure people who read the stories she was working on would feel the warmth and light of the lengthening Saskatchewan spring days.

As it happened, the University Convocation was scheduled just at the time when George was moving Mama and Tato into the little house in town. George was insistent Iryna attend convocation but she felt she needed to help Mama, because she knew the move would be hard on Tato. Besides it wouldn't be much fun going to her convocation without family there to be supportive and proud of you. She had considered inviting Uncle Andriy, but in the end decided it really wasn't that big a deal. So when the certificate from the University of Saskatchewan arrived by mail several weeks later it caught her by surprise just how moved she was. Iryna was the first person in her family to earn an academic degree.

After seeding was finished, Mama and Tato were moved into the little house in town but it became clear this was going to require considerable adjustment. The little house was too small for Iryna to live in with her parents, so she continued to live and work with her brother on the farm.

In early June George was driving Lyudmyla to the city. She was taking a train to Toronto to visit her brother. Iryna went along so she could meet with Professor Bill about her manuscript. George dropped her off at the University before continuing to the train station downtown. Iryna was grateful to have been dropped off first, since she sensed George really wanted to have some time alone with Lyudmyla before she departed.

Iryna went straight to the professor's office even though she was a bit early for their appointment. He was happy to see her, but had another student with him. So Iryna waited outside the office. After a brief moment, the professor called her to join the two men. It turned out the student was actually a schoolteacher. He was taking an intersession course to upgrade his teaching certificate. The professor had known him for several years and had mentioned why Iryna was waiting to meet with him. The teacher was very impressed that the young woman was actually preparing a manuscript for publication and asked if he could meet her.

After a brief introduction, the professor suggested the trio have coffee together and, if Iryna didn't mind, discuss her manuscript. He indicated the young teacher, Hrehori Danyluk, might be of some help, since he taught high school English and was himself an amateur writer. The professor had an inkling the two young people might have much in common.

So they walked and talked and had coffee and talked some more. Iryna got some excellent feedback and planned to leave a copy of her manuscript with the professor for more comments. Hrehori asked if he might read the manuscript after the professor. Iryna was usually guarded about letting anyone read her work before it was polished but the request was so genuine she agreed.

It wasn't until several weeks later that the professor returned her manuscript with some detailed suggestions. On a separate page were a few, well-thought-out suggestions in another hand. Hrehori had added his comments as well. Iryna wasn't sure what to think of this but as she read the comments she realized how insightful and helpful they were. At the bottom of the page the young man had written: "I very much enjoyed your stories and I hope to be able to read more of them. If you are coming back to the city, please let me know. I would like to take you for lunch and talk with you more about your work."

"How nice," Iryna thought, "I just might do that."

Lyudmyla

Lyudmyla had seen quite a lot of George during the long winter of 1946-7, as his father's health was failing. Not only had George brought his father into the city to see the doctor but he had come to visit Iryna and Lyudmyla, as well.

After the decision to move his parents into the hamlet had been made, George decided the time was right to ask Lyudmyla to marry him. The proposal was not altogether a surprise. Lyudmyla was now fully aware of George's affection for her and, to her surprise, she had become quite fond of him as well.

However Lyudmyla had not yet decided on what she really wanted in life. She didn't mind living in the city but by now she knew she could not work for the doctor all her life. He had been very good to her and she had learned and matured during her time working with him. She knew she didn't want to be a teacher. She didn't want to live in an isolated teacherage. She could see herself living in a hamlet or small village but could she enjoy living on a farm?

There was so much to think about and Lyudmyla needed time to think.

So she asked George if he would be patient with her for a few months, while she considered his proposal.

George would have waited for Lyudmyla forever and he hoped that giving her the time she asked for would produce the result he prayed for.

Lyudmyla was taking a trip down east to visit her brother. She hadn't seen him since he had left Baba Cione's care when he was fifteen. Lyudmyla had been six when he had left but she had fond memories of her only brother. In his Christmas letter he had suggested she take the train to Toronto to visit his family. The idea had been formulating ever since.

Lyudmyla had saved enough money to afford the trip. Lena had been very encouraging of the idea. Lyudmyla had been working long and hard and the doctor she worked for had actually suggested she take a vacation. And this would give her a chance to seriously consider her future and George's proposal.

So in June of 1947 at the age of twenty, Lyudmyla embarked on the adventure of her life up to that point. She boarded the train in Saskatoon and travelled for several days to Toronto. Pylyp was waiting for her at Union Station. He had come to pick her up in his brand new Buick. It was a huge car and it was obvious he was very proud of it.

Pylyp and his family lived in a rented house in a suburb of the big city. His wife was a pleasant woman, but very quiet. Lyudmyla thought her quite shy. The young mother had her hands full with three children, only one of whom was in school. Lyudmyla was fascinated by the children and did what she could to help with their care. This effort was much appreciated by their mother, so before long the two women were becoming fast friends.

Pylyp had to work every weekday but in the evenings he would take Lyudmyla for walks or drives to show her his home city. On the weekend the whole family piled into the big Buick and drove out into the countryside north of the city. Lyudmyla was amazed at how the landscape changed so quickly as they drove north and away from Lake Ontario. They picnicked among the trees. The children ran and played and got very dirty. The adults talked and laughed. It was so good for Lyudmyla to be reconnected with her brother and to be so warmly welcomed into his family.

Toward the end of her visit, on one of their evening walks, Pylyp asked Lyudmyla why she had finally decided to visit, six months after the invitation had been extended. He suspected his young sister was trying to make an important decision about her life. At first Lyudmyla was very reluctant to confide in this brother, whom she had not known for very long since she was a child. But he was a patient listener. He felt if there were anything he could do for his youngest sister, he would like to try. It had always bothered him that he had done so little for his sisters and this might be an opportunity to make up for the lapse - at least in a small way.

Lena, of course, had told Pylyp all about the tragic loss of Lyudmila's young love. When Pylyp had heard the story it broke his heart to think of her despair. So he was quite surprised when Lyudmyla began to speak, not as he suspected of a plan to go to school or to move far away from Lena, but of a farmer named 'George'.

So Lyudmyla talked about her meeting George's sister in Saskatoon when they both lived with the Sisters. How Iryna had loved writing and insisted on completing high school then earned scholarships to go to university. About how George worked with his father on the family farm but now the father was very sick and had to move into town.

"So George has asked me to marry him," she ended the story. "And I asked him to give me a few months to think about it. That is one of the reasons I am here. I wanted to be far away from everything I know to be able to think seriously about what I want in my life."

"And has it helped to be here?" Pylyp asked.

"Yes it has," Lyudmyla answered. "When I see you and your family, so happy, I think that is what I want too."

"And do you think you want it with George?" Pylyp asked.

He was so astute! That was the million-dollar question. And Lyudmyla was still asking herself the same question!

"I am not sure. He is a good man. I know he cares for me. I think I could enjoy living on his farm; after all it is close to Lena and her family. The problem is...." And then she fell silent.

After several minutes she picked up the thought hanging in the air between them.

"The problem is," she continued, "I did love someone once. And we were going to be married. And I thought he was the only man in the world for me because, with him I felt I was the best I could be. But he died in the war. I care about George but he isn't Jaroslav. But Jaroslav isn't here any more ..."

Then another long silence.

"Pylyp," she continued, "I have only ever spoken about this to Lena and Sister Superior. Sister told me she had wondered, when I first arrived, if I might have a vocation for the religious life but as she got to know me, she thought it was not the case. Lena encourages me to consider more education and says I am young and don't have to commit to anything until I am sure. I just don't know if I will ever be sure about anything again."

Lyudmila's lack of self-confidence had put her in the grip of indecision.

Pylyp felt helpless. He saw his sister's pain and he was at a loss as to how to ease it. So he put his arm around her shoulders and gave her a hug.

When she looked at him there were tears in his eyes.

"You look so much like our mother," he said trying to hold back the tears. And then he told her the story about how their mother had grieved for the little brother who died of diphtheria at such a young age. He told her how much he had wanted to help ease the pain of her loss and had prayed God send her something to smile about. He told her how a tiny, bright, yellow bird had landed on a branch of the tree just outside the kitchen window, and sang so loudly and sweetly that Mama had thought it was her lost little one, come to sing for her.

"I will pray that God send you a sign too," he finished.

"Thank you Pylyp for your prayers and for telling me the story about

Mama. I don't remember much about her and even less about Tato. I will always treasure that story."

That evening Lyudmyla prayed for guidance. She prayed for her long-lost mother and father and the little brother she had never known. And she prayed for Pylyp and his family.

When the time came for Pylyp to take her back to Union Station in the big Buick, Lyudmyla still wasn't sure what she would do but she was ready to return to Saskatchewan.

One of the many things she had learned on this trip was that she loved the prairies. She loved Saskatchewan. She knew it was where her heart was and where she was meant to live for the rest of her life.

Soon after returning to Saskatoon Lyudmyla told the doctor she would have to quit her job. He was sorry to see her go but he wanted what would be best for her. When her work was completed and her replacement trained, Lyudmyla packed her belongings and went back to the hamlet to spend some time with Lena and her family.

Iryna

The summer had been so busy. Mama and Tato needed help getting settled in the little house in town. Then Lyudmyla returned and, not too long afterwards, George announced they were to marry in the fall. Iryna was elated as were her parents. They decided to have a small family party for the couple in the little house in town, inviting Lyudmila's sister and her family to join them.

What started out as a family celebration soon turned into a community event. Because Mama had always helped everyone in the community with weddings, funerals, anniversaries, church events, etc., as soon as word got out that she was planning a celebration for her son and his future wife, everyone decided to join in. So women brought huge pots of soup, loaves of sandwiches, and cakes, squares, and pies. The little house was bursting at the seams with women preparing and serving food. The men set up long trestle tables and benches outside. Children ran everywhere through the yard. And then an impromptu band of neighbours started to play - a violin, a guitar, an accordion, and a cymbali. And everyone ate and drank and sang. Some even danced barefoot in the yard. It was a joyous event.

Iryna noted two consequences of the impromptu community celebration. First, Mama was in her element. It was clear, although leaving the farm had been difficult for her, she would soon enjoy living in town very much. Second, she had known Lyudmyla for some time now but she had never seen her young friend so joyful. Lyudmyla was overwhelmed by the fact that so many people were rejoicing for her happiness. On that day Lyudmyla opened her heart, not only to George and his family, but to the entire community.

Iryna wasn't back in the city until late summer. She had written to Hrehori and told him she would be in town. He had invited her for lunch in a down town café. As they ate and talked, Iryna realized how comfortable she was with this man she had only ever seen twice. When she mentioned the excitement in her family about the forthcoming wedding of her brother, he surprised her once more by asking whether he could attend. Iryna felt so comfortable with him that she invited him and gave him the details.

During the busy harvest time, Iryna often paused to wonder whether the young man would actually come all the way from the city to her brother's wedding. She needn't have wondered, for he was so enthralled with her he was counting the days.

George and Lyudmyla

Although it had not been his chosen occupation, after marrying Lyudmyla, George found his life as a farmer took on a new enjoyment, replacing his previous resignation. George loved to watch Lyudmyla carefully and thoughtfully take care of the old farmhouse and the yard. It occurred to him that she probably had never before had a home of her very own. It made George happy that he was the one who had been able to give her this source of joy and contentment.

Together the young couple worked to make the home a reflection of their own tastes. They worked together on the farmyard to make it tidy and efficient. They enjoyed working together and, because of their common goals, their efforts produced vast improvements.

Throughout the winter the pair cleaned the house from top to bottom, from the attic to the dugout, dirt cellar. Anything no longer of use or value was taken to the nuisance grounds or burned. Then the rooms were painted and new linoleum laid on the floors. The couple purchased a new bedroom suite, kitchen table and chairs, and best of all, a radio. Both George and Lyudmyla loved to have music in the house, especially when they worked.

In the spring, under Lyudmila's supervision, George trimmed the lilac and honeysuckle brushes along the front of the house. He built planters, which Lyudmyla filled with brightly coloured, fragrant, annual flowers. The small, old caboose, which had served as the chicken coop, was torn down and a new coop built a little further from the house and down the hill. The garden plot was rejuvenated and planted and a new well was dug. George was inspired by the improvements made in the house and yard and continued his efforts in the barn and workshop. Before long, the farm was transformed and the young couple was very pleased with their home.

George made a habit of regularly reading two farm newspapers, the Western Producer and the Winnipeg Free Press. In those pages he often came across articles about farm innovations. He had decided that if he were to be a farmer, he would be as good at it as he could be. And so it was not at all surprising that George was often the first in the neighbourhood to try something new. One year he planted a crop previously unknown in the region. It was called rapeseed (later known as canola). George had worried about how he would harvest the new crop, since the seeds were so very small compared to wheat or oats, but of course, as he continued to study the matter he learned how it could be done. As his first crop bloomed in early July, George was struck by the contrast of the radiant yellow field against the brilliant blue sky. "Tato and Mama would think this was the perfect representation of the Ukrainian flag," George thought. Then during the first harvest George could not get over the pungent smell of his new crop. It had been quite a departure from the norm but the success of that first innovation set George on the path to becoming a trailblazer in his farming community.

Lyudmyla had never had a pet. She loved to watch the barn cats scamper about when she went to milk the cows. That spring there was a new litter of kittens and Lyudmyla was determined to make one of them a house cat. It so happened that Dariya had come to visit the farm that day.

"Oh selecting a house cat takes care," she said. "You don't want one that will be wild or it will never come back to the house. You don't want one that just sleeps and eats, because what's the point of having such an animal anyway. You need the smartest one of the litter for a house cat."

"How do you know which kitten is the smartest?" Lyudmyla asked.

"I'll show you," Dariya responded as she walked out toward the barn.

So the two women found the nest in the hayloft. The mother cat was not in sight and the kittens were mewing softly as they tumbled over top of each other. Their eyes were opened but they were still quite small.

First Dariya set a shallow bowl of milk down near the kittens. They tumbled toward the bowl in a jumble of fur, small tails, and ears. One fell headlong into the bow, spilling some of the milk on the hay and getting its head soaked. One of its siblings began licking the milk from its milk-soaked fur. The next two were a little more successful in approaching the bowl and were actually lapping some of the milk.

"One of these two," Dariya indicated.

Then she took the two kittens that had managed to drink a bit of the milk and put them on the straw a short distance from the bowl. Then she did the most amazing thing. She took off the hat she had been wearing and placed it on top of the two kittens. Lyudmyla wasn't sure what to think of this.

Soon one of the two kittens fought its way out from under the hat and headed toward the bowl of milk. By now there wasn't much milk left in the bowl but the kitten persisted and was rewarded with the last few licks.

"That's your new house cat," Dariya proclaimed. "He is smart and resourceful; he will make a good mouser and a good companion in the house. Let's take him. You must keep him in the house long enough so he knows it is where his food will be. Then he may wander the yard and even the barn but he will always come back to the house."

Lyudmyla called the little, grey kitten 'Smokey'. Dariya had been right. He was a very affectionate and loyal pet and Lyudmyla loved him.

George and Lyudmyla had been married in October of 1947. In August of the following year, the young couple welcomed their first-born, a son. Lyudmyla asked George if they could call the baby Stephan, after her father. George, who would do anything for his wife, was happy to oblige.

Iryna

The young schoolteacher from the city had come to George and Lyudmila's wedding. He had met Iryna in the city several more times throughout the winter. He was fascinated by the young woman who was doing what he had always dreamed of doing himself – writing professionally. He could see she had the talent necessary to make her living by writing stories. He doubted he could be as successful. As a result, he decided he would like to be the one to encourage and support Iryna in her life's work.

It wasn't long before Iryna realized Hrehori was beginning to think of her as his life partner. She wasn't sure she felt the same way about him. He was intelligent, kind, and very supportive but she had worked so hard to earn her independence and she wasn't sure she wanted anyone else in her life at the moment. She wanted to write and she wanted to make a life for herself. She had to prove she could do it - at least to herself, if nothing else. And so to the world around them, they appeared as a young couple destined for the alter but Iryna resisted any attempts Hrehori made to even discuss such a future.

Hrehori was frustrated by the fact that Iryna seemed to like him and didn't seem interested in anyone else, yet was not at all interested in planning a future together. He wanted to get married. He wanted a wife and a family. He was happy to have a writer as his wife and would support her in her chosen career but what he wanted didn't seem to match Iryna's plans.

Pavlo tried one last time to have influence over his strong-willed daughter.

"You must marry Hrehori," he said. "You spend so much time with him. Everyone thinks you are engaged. You can't go on like this. People will talk. It's not proper for a young woman to see so much of a man and not marry him. I want to see you settled before I die. Please get married."

Iryna didn't agree with most of what her father said. The world was changing. A young woman didn't have to marry a man just because she spent a lot of time with him. But she knew her father was dying and she didn't want to worry him. On the other hand, it was her life and she was not going to sacrifice it for her father's wishes.

And so things continued as they were. Iryna and Hrehori went everywhere together. They spent most of their time together. But there was never any discussion of marriage.

"You'll lose him," Dariya warned. "He won't wait for you for ever."

How would she feel if Hrehori decided he wanted to get married more than he wanted to be with her? It could happen. She wasn't sure. She would miss him, of course. She thought they could always be close friends but if he married someone else would that be possible? Hrehori had become an integral part of her life. He had become an important supporter of her writing efforts. She relied on his input. Could she continue to be as good a writer as she had become if he were no longer in her life. She didn't know.

And then it happened. In the spring of 1949 Tato got very sick. The little white pills and resting in the little house in town away from the farm no longer helped. He lay listlessly in bed all day. Mama did what she could to keep him comfortable but it was clear to everyone he would not last long.

Maria brought her children to the little house in town to say goodbye to Diedo. Maria cried every time she saw Tato. She spent the days by her father's side while Dariya rested. Then Dariya sat beside her husband all night in case there was anything she could do for him. George, Lyudmyla, and baby Stephan came often to sit with Pavlo. He had always liked Lyudmyla and found her presence comforting. He had lost all interest in the farm and its activities but George didn't know what else to say to his father, so he told him about what was happening in the fields and pastures. Then he would walk around the yard while the women sat with the dying man. Nick had been ordained and sent to serve a parish in Winnipeg. He came home to comfort his family and dying father.

Iryna spent most of her time taking care of the house, meals, and her mother. She wanted to be close to her father but she didn't feel her presence was a comfort to him. She had come to believe she was the one source of discord in his life and she did not want to burden him now.

As the end drew inevitably nearer, the whole family gathered around his bed. Pavlo was still responding occasionally but it was difficult to know what he was saying and sometimes, what it meant.

Once he lifted his arm and put his hand over his face and said, "I'm sorry, the roads were rutted and I didn't mean to give her a rough ride."

The family looked at one another and shrugged, as no one knew what he was talking about.

Another time he seemed to be calling to some little boys. "Come back, you'll get wet and then you'll get sick. What will Baba do with sick kids. Come back!"

And still another time he held out his hand as if to someone who wasn't there. "Thank you, Father. Dyakuyu. I will repay you. Thank you."

This last made sense to Dariya. She knew of the good Father, back in the old country, who had sent Pavlo to Canada. The debt had been repaid long ago. It had not been easy but as soon as their little farm had produced a bit more than the family needed to survive, Pavlo had insisted on sending money back to Father Mykhaylo to repay him for the passage to Canada.

"It's ok," she whispered to her dying husband, "we sent Father Mykhaylo the money for your ticket. You have repaid him. It's ok."

At that Pavlo dropped his hand to the bed and he was silent. Then he opened his eyes and asked, "Where is Iryna?"

"I'm here Tato," she replied from the doorway.

"Come close so I can see you," he asked.

As Iryna approached, Pavlo lifted his hand once more and placed it on top of hers. "Be happy," he said with effort.

And then Pavlo's head fell gently to the side and he breathed his last.

The women cried softly. Nick prayed for his father's soul and for his whole family in its grief. George went out to the shed. He sat down on a bench and, with his head in his hands, he cried too. He had not always agreed with his father. He had always felt he had not lived up to his father's expectations but he had loved the old man and now he was gone. Life would be strange without him.

"'Be happy.' That's what Tato wanted for me, to be happy. What would it take for me to be happy?" Iryna thought long and hard about this for many weeks after Tato died. It was strange how his death had left a huge hole in her life. It seemed she had spent her life fighting against what he wanted her to do and now he was gone. There was nothing left to fight. 'Be happy'.

A few months later, Iryna and Hrehori paid a visit to Mama in the little house in town. "We want you to be the first to know," they said. "We are getting married."

Dariya threw her hands in the air and praised God. "Thank you, Dyakuyu," was all she said and in her heart she knew Pavlo was happy too. Their independent daughter would be married to a good man; a man who had proved he loved her and would stand by her no matter what. "There weren't many men who would have been right for you, Iryna," Dariya thought, "but this man must be the right one."

Dariya

In 1954 Dariya was fifty-six years old. She had been a widow for five years. She had seen her family grow and prosper. She had taken great pride in keeping the age-old traditions she had grown up with.

Every Christmas and Easter the whole family would descend on the little house in the hamlet. Dariya insisted, while she had the strength, her little home would be where the family celebrated these holy holidays together.

So before Christmas she cleaned her little house from top to bottom. Then George would bring a freshly cut evergreen tree and he and Lyudmyla, and later their children, would string festive lights and decorations on the fragrant branches. And on Christmas Eve, Dariya, with the help of Maria, Iryna, and Lyudmyla, would start cooking early in the morning to get everything ready for the special holy evening supper. They cooked the wheat, which came from the farm, in a huge pot, all day long on the back of the stove. They rolled cooked rice in cabbage leaves. They rolled out the pliable, soft pyrohi dough, to be cut into squares and filled with potatoes, cottage cheese, sauerkraut, or sardines. All the traditional dishes were prepared with love, in the time-honored ways. And when the youngest child announced the first star had been spied, high in the early darkening sky, the whole family gathered around the extended tables, which filled two rooms of the little house, to praise God for having sent His Son into the world. And then they ate and sang and enjoyed each other's company. Dariya always made sure there was an extra place set at the table, 'for those who cannot be with us tonight'.

Easter saw the little house, once again, scrubbed clean, bustling, and full of activity. It all started early on Good Friday morning. Dariya rose and covered all the holy pictures and mirrors hanging on the walls with clean tea towels. It was to be a quiet day of prayer and contemplation of the events leading up to the Great Day of Resurrection. There was much to do and little, if anything, to eat on that day. This was the day, like no other in the year, which would challenge the children, especially those who were too young to appreciate the graveness of the occasion.

On this day, Dariya baked the Paska (braided Easter bread), Babpka (yellow, sweet, tall bread, baked in a tin can), and the platsok (bannock). Then, just as the children were getting bored and impatient, she would bring out her equipment for writing the pysanky (decorated Easter Eggs). The children, from a young age, were each given a raw egg and a kistka (stylus). Dariya then patiently showed them how to draw the initial lines around the eggs for the time-honored designs. Step by step she showed the children how to complete the designs; to dip the eggs into successive dye baths, from the lightest colours to the darkest; and to cover the parts of the designs, which were to remain the current colour with bee's wax. As they worked, Dariya told the children the story and meaning behind each traditional design. And by late afternoon there would be a new batch of pysanky. By this time, only the older children were still engaged in the process. So Dariya helped them to carefully melt the wax off of their masterpieces. These lovely creations would be blessed, along with the Easter foods. It always amazed Dariya how the children progressed from year to year in their ability to write pysanky. This was a tradition she felt very strongly must be preserved for future generations and she felt blest that she could do so with her own grandchildren.

Holy Saturday was another busy day. The food for blessing was prepared: the ham and sausage were roasted, the eggs boiled and peeled, the ground beets mixed with horseradish – how Pavlo had always enjoyed his duty of finding the pungent root for the Easter feast. The baked platsok was cut into squares and mixed with butter and onions, eggs and cream, and then baked again as nachynka (dressing or casserole). This last was a traditional food but one which was not included in the basket with foods to be blessed.

Often the Easter services started in the early evening of Holy Saturday in the church on the corner of the Dannyk farm. The whole family went to the church along with their neighbours. Traditional, sacred service after service was performed. The hour grew late. The children fell asleep on coats, spread on the church floor. Eventually it was time for the Easter Matins. Children were roused so everyone could process around the outside of the church, as did the women who went early in the morning to Christ's tomb. And then the joyous Easter Anthem was sung and bells were rung and the Easter Liturgy was celebrated. The culmination was the blessing of the Easter baskets. By this time it was very late, or rather very early in the morning, and everyone was tired and hungry. The church was permeated with the smells of incense and all the Easter foods. And so with the knowledge of the Good News, the Resurrection of Christ, the Easter baskets were retrieved and everyone headed home to begin a joyous day of celebration.

Dariya's little home was also where the family gathered for birthday and anniversary celebrations. Dariya always baked the recipient's favourite cake and lovingly decorated it with icing and candles. And of course, she always had the recipient's favorites foods prepared for each celebration. She was in her element as the matriarch of her family.

And so as the post-war years produced a new generation of 'Baby Boomers', the first Ukrainian generation to be born in Canada contributed to the boom. George and Lyudmyla had three sons, Stephan, Philip, and Paul. When finally, their long-awaited daughter arrived, once more Lyudmyla asked George if he would mind if she picked the name for the baby. She had hoped to call her, Lesya, after her long-dead mother. Once more George happily agreed. Iryna and Hrehori had a son, Billy, named for the professor who had introduced his parents, and a daughter, Sonia. So from the birth of Philip in 1950 to the birth of Lesya in 1954, between George's and Iryna's families, there had been a new grandchild born every year. These five grandchildren virtually grew up together and were all very close – more like brothers and sisters than cousins. Dariya enjoyed all of her grandchildren and spent as much time with them as she could.

Dariya missed her husband but she managed to make the most of being a widow in town. She had a big garden and a shed full of chickens. She had several friends among the women of the town. She was still actively involved in the community and helped to prepare for annual celebrations. And although she was not called on anymore to help with the delivery of a baby, some of the older folk in town still came to her for advice and help with their ailments.

Often George and Lyudmyla brought their children to stay overnight with Baba, while they attended a wedding or went to shop in the city. Dariya found the boys lively and sometimes even a bit more than she could handle.

"I must be getting old," she thought when a particularly rambunctious game left her frazzled and cross. "I never used to be bothered by children's games." So then she would called the boys to her and sat them in a row on the couch to tell them a story about when she was a little girl in the old country. They would listen politely for a bit and then start tussling and pushing once more. "Ok, go outside and play. You need to burn off some steam." And out they went to climb trees along the back alley.

And at that instant Dariya knew. She knew the inevitable had happened. The dreaded, but inescapable thing had happened. She had become her mother! Not completely of course. Her mother had been an unhappy person most of her life and her inability to deal with Dariya's rambunctious children had resulted from that. Dariya, on the other hand, had been blessed with her own father's ability to be happy most of the time. In this case Dariya had simply lost patience with the boys. Perhaps it *was* her age. At any rate, she vowed she would not allow herself to become the baba her own mother had been to her children. She would be more patient and tolerant.

One night, George's middle boy, Philip, who was four years old at the time, awoke from a bad dream. Dariya carried him to the kitchen. She had a cure for bad dreams. So, she sat him on the kitchen table while she prepared the cure. The whole time she spoke to the boy in reassuring terms. "It was just a dream. You had so much fun playing with your brothers that your mind is too tired to sleep, so it made up a dream. Baba will fix it and then you will be able to sleep."

So Dariya took several hot coals from the kitchen stove and dropped them into a dipper of cold water. The little boy was fascinated by the steam and snapping sounds. She then took the cooled coals and used them to make the sign of the cross on the boy's forehead. Then she said a prayer over him. He was already showing signs of drowsiness. She carried him back to the bed and laid him next to his brothers. "Sleep well," she told him and kissed his forehead. It wasn't long before she heard the soft snoring sounds of a contented child.

Dariya was especially fond of George's youngest child, little Lesya. From a very early age, Lesya had spent a lot of time with Baba Dariya, her only grandparent, and had developed a very strong bond with her. Lesya had been at her baba's side, preparing for holy and family celebrations, baking traditional breads and cooking the traditional dishes, writing Easter eggs, and preparing the basket of special foods for blessing - all these things from the time she was very young. Dariya felt that of all her grandchildren, this little one would keep the traditions alive long after Dariya was gone. And so she spent as much time as she could telling the young girl stories about her own girlhood, stories about the old country, stories about coming to

Canada, stories about her parents and brothers, and stories about her beliefs and all the beautiful traditions, which had enriched her own life.

As the children grew it became clear that they would have more options in life than their parents or grandparents. George was anxious for his boys go to school and become whatever they wanted to be. He would not insist they be farmers but would have a choice in their future occupations.

One evening in 1957 after the chores were done, seven-year-old Philip was listening to the radio as he usually did. The most amazing story was being reported. But it wasn't science fiction - it was real. The Soviets had launched a satellite into space. They called it 'Sputnik 1'. Amazing! From that moment on, Philip would be fascinated with all things related to space. And he was living at exactly the right time, because the space race had just begun.

As time went by the farm got electricity and with that convenience came a host of electrical appliances, including a television set. Philip loved to wake up very early in the morning to watch the live broadcasts of the astronaut launches from Cape Canaveral. He was enthralled by what was happening in the world of science and exploration.

"How far we have come. From travelling halfway around the world on the ocean to men travelling into space. It's hard to believe. I look at my children and now they have their own children. Where did the time go? But of course .... I remember. There were weddings and funerals, hard work and good times, joys and sorrows. That's where the time went. It has been a good life. God has been very good to us. We have been blest."

Ukraine

Joseph Stalin had held power in the Soviet Union from the mid 1920's. He was a ruthless dictator whose reign of terror resulted in many millions of people being killed, starved, tortured, arrested, or deported to Siberia.

In 1946, the 1595 Union of Brest, which had created the Greek Catholic Church, was abolished and the Church was absorbed into the Russian

Orthodox Church. Priests who refused to accept the changes were imprisoned or deported.

Father Mykhaylo

When the Germans retreated in 1944, the Red Army advanced throughout the region. This time the Soviets would bring the Ukrainian people to heel. In April, Metropolitan Slipyj, along with other church leaders, was arrested and sent to a labour camp. The next year the Greek Catholic Church was abolished and all churches became Russian Orthodox. Father Mykhaylo was given a choice – convert and convert his flock - or face arrest.

The good Father prayed for guidance but it seemed no answer was forthcoming. He weighed the options. He could remain a priest, ministering to his parish, albeit in a different religion, or he could face personal defeat and probable death. If he were gone, who would the people have to lead them in worship? Would God care if they prayed in a Catholic or in an Orthodox Church? But there was even more at stake. It wasn't just Catholic or Orthodox; it was also Ukrainian or Russian. For centuries the Ukrainian people had resisted pressures to be something other than what they were. The pressures to be Russified were about to become monumental. So the good Father pondered the question - what would be best for his people?

Father Mykhaylo had seen the village synagogue converted to a pig barn. There were virtually no Jews left in the village, at least none who could be identified as such. The Polish Roman Catholic Church had been severely damaged by bombs and fire during the war and its ruins were being demolished. The potential fate of the lovely Ukrainian Catholic Church haunted the good Father.

He agonized over his decision. And then the time drew near for him to respond to the ultimatum. What would he do?

The day was bright and sunny, not unlike the day when he had first arrived in the village. He was struck by how little the village had actually changed in all those years, despite all the political and social turmoil swirling around it. He walked to the beautiful church on the hill, just where the two streams joined forces to rush headlong as a tributary toward the great Dniester River. There he donned his vestments and began to perform his very last Divine Liturgy.

There were only a couple of old women, huddled near the back of the church, for it was a week day and perhaps it was known that this was the day Father Mykhaylo must make his decision. Just as the Liturgy was to reach the climax, the consecration, four armed men burst into the church. Father Mykhaylo had failed to report to the authorities to submit to the new order. He was manhandled and arrested. The old women hung their heads in prayer for his soul. It was clear he would need all the prayers that could be mustered on his behalf.

Father Mykhaylo was taken to the police station where he was stripped, interrogated, and beaten. Then he was put in a dark, damp cell. Every day for a week the procedure was repeated. When it became clear that the man simply would not comply with orders, he was loaded with many other miscreants onto a cattle car and shipped east.

And that was the last anyone in the village ever saw or heard of Father Mykhaylo.

The people waited and wondered - what would happen next? Was an Orthodox priest to be sent to them? Were they to continue attending their beloved church on the hill, but worship in Russian? Weeks went by. Perhaps there weren't enough Orthodox priests to send one to this little village. Then months passed. People wanted to go to the church to pray but they were afraid. Even gathering in a neighbour's home to pray was punishable by arrest or worse. Armed men watched for people who might gather or approach the church and it was said that they would shoot on first sight.

So the people quietly and secretly prayed in their homes. Many had lost their beloved icons, prayer books, and rosaries but they prayed just the same.

Mykola

Since 1848 when serfdom was officially abolished in the old Austrian Empire, Mykola's grandfather and father before him had owned and worked their small strip of land. Uncle Vasyl had added to the small family holding in 1907, the year Anton had been born. So the family now owned two thin strips of land, totaling about eight morgs or twelve and a half acres. It was by no means a large farm, but perhaps a bit bigger than average among the Ukrainian peasants of the region.

It wasn't until 1948 that the combined efforts of the OUN and UPA were finally suppressed and the Soviet plans to enculturate the region began in earnest. The Soviets had dismantled the resistance movements through mass killings, arrests, and deportations. Now the real work of bringing the western region into the Ukrainian Soviet Socialist Republic and in line with Soviet policies could begin.

And so after the army and the dreaded NKVD, came the Russians and Russified Ukrainian settlers and the government propagandists. They claimed to be building on the popular and successful agricultural co-operatives, which Ukrainian farmers had organized during the depression. They claimed collectivization was the most efficient method of farming. They claimed kulaks, affluent farmers, and nationalistic bourgeoisie were enemies of the state and the peasant farmer. After the propaganda came the blackmail and threats, the arrests and deportations. The message was clear – participate or suffer the consequences. Collectivization was the trump card of sovietization.

Mykola, at the age of sixty-seven, listened to the speeches and read the pamphlets but he could see no good in the coming regime. He heard about the killings and arrests of nationalists and those who had collaborated with the Nazis, along with many innocents who were merely suspected of such 'crimes'. He knew the collectivization of farms, which had been started in 1939, would now be completed. From what he had heard of the formation of the kolkhozes, collective farms, he and his family would become surfs once more, not to wealthy landlords this time, but to the state.

Mykola prayed it would not be so but he knew there was no stopping this change. All but a small portion of the family land would become part of a kolkhoz. Most of their cows and pigs would go to communal barns. His family was allowed to keep a small private field and the garden plot but the majority of their work would be as part of a brigade, working alongside their neighbours, for a share of the remaining grain after and, indeed if, their kolkhoz met its state-mandated quotas. They would not be able to leave the land upon which they were required to work. And so, tied to the land; tied to working for a government overlord; having to pay taxes for everything they owned, which was not part of the kolkhoz; they would be again, nothing more than surfs.

The young people attended school and learned their lessons in Russian. Along with their lessons they learned about the October Revolution and its heroes. The people worked very hard on the new collective farm and many times had little to eat. It seemed the Soviet system hoped to keep the people tired and hungry so they would forget to pray. Sometimes this strategy seemed to work. When your mind is consumed with how your body will survive, it can be difficult to worry about the survival of your soul.

Khrushchev was a member of the collective leadership from Stalin's death in March 1953 until he consolidated his own power as Premier in 1958. During the 'Khrushchev Thaw' payments for crops grown on the collectives were increased and peasants were encouraged to grow more on their tiny private plots. Investment in agriculture increased. Some attempts at agricultural reform were less successful than others, such as the attempt to merge smaller collectives into larger units, which served only to cause confusion.

Mykola was seventy-three in 1953 when he received the letter from his beloved brother, Taras, in Argentina. It had been opened as usual. There had been fewer and fewer letters from either Argentina or Canada. Mykola wondered if his family had abandoned him or if their letters were simply being confiscated.

But somehow this letter had arrived. It was a joyous letter and it warmed the old man's heart. The most significant news in the letter was that Taras' grandson, Juan, was to become a priest. It was surprising that the censors had not blackened the passage – perhaps they had missed it. Or perhaps they had purposely left it in the letter to see how Mykola would respond. It might have been a trap. Mykola was tired of constantly wondering whether he and his family, as well as his neighbours, were being trapped into showing their true, anti-Soviet feelings.

Mykola praised God that there was still somewhere on earth where people could practice their religion and where a young man could become a priest. He thought of his old Uncle Vasyl, who had once told him of his dream of becoming a priest. Uncle Vasyl would have rejoiced at this news. Mykola would have liked to go to the cemetery beside the church to pray for Uncle Vasyl and tell him the news. But no one went near the cemetery any more except to bury the dead.

The beautiful Ukrainian Catholic Church had been turned into a granary and then, when production on the collective farm had dropped and there was less need of such a large granary, the building had been boarded up. No one was allowed to go near it. The armed guards made sure of that.

Tato, too, would certainly have been very proud of Taras' grandson. Mykola thought lovingly of the father he had last seen when he had left his family, on a bright, clear autumn day in 1901. He had been off to do his military duty for the Austrian Emperor. His return from service had been delayed and, as a consequence, he had missed the departure of his beloved brother, Taras, for Argentina and the departure of the rest of his family for Canada. That day seemed so very far away now – more than one lifetime ago!

So Mykola shared the letter with his family. It broke his heart when his grandson, eighteen-year-old Ivan, said he hoped priests in Argentina weren't jailed like his other grandfather, Father Mykhaylo. Ivan had been only nine when that had happened and it had been a painful experience for him, as well as for his whole family.

Mykola did not have to tell his family not to repeat what was in the letter. He wrote a short response, being very careful about what exactly he wrote. His daughter-in-law, Luba, had said the only thing about Juan's news, which Mykola thought he might dare write in the letter – "I'm glad there will be one in this world to replace my father." And then he burned the letter from Taras.

Things had changed since the collective farm was first established. In 1956 collective farms were first allowed to own tractors, but it wasn't until 1958 before there was one in the region. During this time the collective farms were also expected to build their own schools, hospitals, and roads. As a result, rural development suffered by comparison to the urban centres.

In 1958 the first Ukrainian mission to the United Nations was established. Although there was a steady increase in the number of Ukrainians in the Communist Party of Ukraine (CPU), in the region of the village on the Dniester Tributary the number of communist party members was never very great. A policy of partial Ukrainianization led to a brief cultural thaw.

Khrushchev's time in power was marked by shows of temper, as demonstrated by the infamous incident in which he used his shoe to bang on the podium during a speech to the United Nations. Other critical events included the erection of the Berlin Wall in August 1961; the Cuban Missile Crisis in October 1962; and a poor harvest in 1963. In 1964, Khrushchev was voted out of office and replaced with a collective leadership, spearheaded by Leonid Brezhnev. One of the principle goals during this time period was to forge a unified Soviet nationality, which in actuality was nothing more than the return of the former Russification policy.

Stripped of their land, language, religion, and as much of their culture as could be attacked, it was little wonder Mykola's family was slipping gradually, almost imperceptibly, away from their past.

Argentina

Peron

By 1945 the Argentine middle class was calling for the replacement of the military junta, of which Juan Peron had been a part, with an elected government. They were also calling for support of the Allies in the war. This served to increase the divisions among the Argentine population. In an attempt to appease the wealthy middle class, the military junta imprisoned Peron, who had served as a lightening rod because of his work in the Labour Department. A huge protest of the large working class forced his release on October 17, 1945 and it was this act, which would have a dramatic impact on the social and political foundations of the country, arguably for the rest of the century.

In June 1946 Juan Peron was elected as the President of Argentina. His platform had been to establish social justice and economic independence for the country. Together with his second wife, Eva (Evita), during his first term as President, Peron worked to legitimize trade unions, extend political rights to the working class and women, and make education available to anyone of ability. This latter was a bit of a contradiction, since during his presidency many university professors were fired or worse. Peron's first five-year plan was supposed to increase employment and wages, stimulate industrial growth, and improve infrastructure and social services, including universal health care and social security. To Peron, making Argentina independent meant making it less reliant upon imports and insulating the country from the effects of foreign events, such as the previous two world wars.

Peron's efforts to win workers' rights sparked massive strikes in 1945, alienating large employers but earning huge popularity for the President among the working class. He nationalized the Central Bank, railways, universities, public utilities, and transportation as well as created a single purchaser for grain and oil products. The initial result of these reforms was an increase in real wages and an apparent boom in the economy.

Peron's fascist leanings, his drive to make Argentina economically independent through nationalization of the oil and meatpacking industries, and American paranoia regarding communism in the Americas, put his regime in direct conflict with the United States. In the cold war era, the American response was to impose trade embargoes and, in 1948, exclude Argentine exports under the Marshall Plan, a post-war, European reconstruction effort. This latter action deprived Argentina of access to Western European markets, much to the benefit of Canada, and resulted in an Argentinian financial crisis and the halt to Peron's plans to transform his country.

The short-lived, initial boom of Peron's five-year plan eventually led to a dramatic increase, rather than the desired decrease, in imports; decreased exports; and ultimately, a financial crisis. Britain owed Argentina huge sums as a result of wartime exports of grain and beef but after the war impoverished Britain could not repay the debt. Ultimately a settlement took the form of repatriation of much of Argentina's British-built railways. Exports fell further still. The Central Bank devalued the Peso by seventy per cent between 1948 to 1950. Imports and industrial growth declined and recession struck. A better harvest in 1950 prompted a short-lived recovery but drought in the following three years and fifty per cent inflation by the end of 1951 led to an even deeper recession.

Peron reacted to the economic roller coaster by replacing the 1853 national constitution with one guaranteeing social reforms, nationalization of natural resources and public services, and the re-election of the President. Peron was re-elected in 1952, but later that year Evita died contributing to a decline in his popularity. While Peron had been hugely popular with much of the working class, expectations had risen to unattainable levels given the economy. Peron's popularity had never been without opposition from the wealthy, the large employers, and some elements of the military. And then opposition came from another source, the Catholic Church.

In July 1954 a rival political party was established by a group of Catholics. They organized their own labor union. Men who gain tremendous power are often threatened by those who might challenge that power. Peron responded by verbally attacking Catholic priests and accusing them of meddling in politics. Some priests were jailed, Catholic publications were shut down, and religious processions banned. Peron attempted to turn the people against the church and its meddlesome priests. In an attempt to garner liberal support he legalized divorce and prostitution, granted legitimacy to children born out of wedlock, and removed religious instruction from schools. The escalating confrontation led to Catholic demonstrations against Peron. Then Congress expelled two Argentine priests to Italy. The Vatican excommunicated those responsible for the expulsion. Finally on June 16, 1955 the Navy and Air Force launched a coup. The Plaza de Mayo, in front of Peron's residence was bombed leaving over three hundred civilians dead.

Peron went into exile, eventually settling in Spain where he married for a third time, a woman who would be known to the world as Isabel Peron. The Argentina Peron left behind was in financial difficulty and politically polarized. The military junta succeeding him tried to remove all traces of

Juan and Evita Peron from the country's consciousness. Although Peron was no longer in Argentina, he continued to influence the politics of the country.

Boom and Bust

When Juan Peron was elected as President of Argentina in 1946, many people of the working class rejoiced. They had seen what Peron had tried to do for them during his time as Head of the Labour Department and were optimistic as President he would make their lives much better.

Many things changed - some for better, some for worse. Social reform had less impact on those living and working on the isolated plantation on the arroyo of the Parana. During the time Peron had been Head of the Labour Department, some of the younger workers on the plantation had been tempted away for better opportunities in towns and cities. Those who remained were dedicated to the success of the plantation and by extension to the success of their families.

Myko had been one of those who had grown dissatisfied with his lot on the plantation. In 1944 he had approached his father with a request to purchase the land upon which he had built his home, next to the banks of the arroyo. Taras had insisted on discussing the request with his partner, Ivan. Myko was incensed that his father could not make even such a small decision on his own, for he feared Ivan would not be in favour of the plan.

"Why can't you do this one thing for me?" Myko raged at his father.

"It is not so simple," Taras had tried to explain. "If we sell a bit of the plantation to you, others may want to buy the bit of land that their homes are on. How could we say 'no' to others if we said 'yes' to you."

Myko was furious. He could not and would not see his father's concern. All he saw was that his father, as usual, would do anything to prevent Myko from getting what he deserved. Myko had long felt his efforts on the plantation had been undervalued and favor had always passed him by. He was done with the plantation … and his father… and Ivan! He would make his own way in the world.

"Don't even bother asking Ivan," Myko stormed. "It is clear that neither of you want me to have what I deserve. I will take my family away from this wretched place and we will never return."

This last comment was said intentionally to hurt his father and it did, very deeply.

Myko had always been difficult. As a young boy he had competed ruthlessly with his older brother, Yory. The elder son was so full of ideas and joy that he didn't see his brother's constant competition. The more Myko tried to better his brother the less he was noticed and that only served to further fuel the one-sided rivalry. Taras and Carmen had seen it all and they had worried about their second son. Now it seemed all the prayers and worry they had spent on Myko had come to no avail. There was little they could do. Myko was determined to leave the plantation.

In one last defiant act, Myko sold his house to a long-time, plantation worker. When Taras heard what the fellow had paid, he was embarrassed and ashamed of his son. It was clear Myko had taken advantage of the man. So after Myko left, Taras did the right thing, the only thing he could. He re-paid the man what he had spent on Myko's house.

Almost nothing was heard from Myko or his family for some time. It was Yory who eventually heard that Myko had taken his family to Buenos Aries. He had tried to get a job in the Labour Department and had used the fact that Yory was a bureaucrat in Posadas as a way to impress his potential employers. Yory had been contacted and asked what experience his brother had in labour issues. Yory felt he had been put on the spot. He told the official all he knew about his brother's abilities and work on the plantation. And then he heard no more.

Exports were declining dramatically. The precipitous drop impacted the plantation. Supply of what they produced was much higher than the demand for it, so prices fell. But worst of all, in 1950 the peso was devalued. It lost seventy per cent of its value in just two years. So whatever money had been saved and whatever could be earned was worth much less than it had been worth previously. This was a difficult time, financially, for everyone on the plantation.

Taras and Ivan watched and listened to the news of what was happening in Buenos Aries. The whole country was reeling as it sank deeper and deeper into recession. The plantation partners feared they might lose their life's work, their beloved dream, their plantation.

Taras

Taras had been growing a modest amount of black tea, in addition to the plantation's main crop of yerba, since 1924. In that year, the government had provided seeds to farmers to encourage this potential new crop. The small plot of foreign chai was lovingly and half-jokingly referred to on the plantation as Taras' Tetera (Taras' Teapot). Then in 1951 the Argentine government imposed a ban on imported tea. Since this non-native tea had become popular in the country, local demand created a new Argentine market for the crop. Many farmers who had given up on growing black tea back in the '20's now rushed to add it to their crops, while other farmers created tea plantations solely for this product.

Yory, who had been working in the Department of Agriculture in Posadas, was among the first to learn of the ban on imported black tea and anticipated the opportunity this could provide. He couldn't wait to tell his seventy-year-old father the good news. And so it was that Taras' innovation and perseverance and, perhaps a bit of luck, was about to pay off. It took little effort to expand Taras' Tetera, his modest plot of black tea, into a large field. While black tea remained a secondary crop to yerbe on the plantation it became a lucrative one.

The growing of black tea on a commercial scale had several positive consequences not the least of which was the building of the plantation's new, modern secadore or drying facility. Although the plantation had had its own primitive secadore and had not relied on others to dry their product, many of the other farmers in the region sold the yerbe they harvested as hoja verde (green plant material). It was then sent to large processing operations for finishing.

But few of the existing processors wanted or were equipped to handle the new crop of black tea. Being at the forefront of innovation often requires learning to do things differently than in the past. And so the plantation built its modern secadore, specifically for black tea. This decision would prove enormously valuable in the future, when the facility would continue to be used to process the plantation's yerbe, as well as its black tea, thus allowing them to retain more of the value of their crops.

In years to come, Argentina would be in the top ten, tea-producing countries of the world. Although Argentine black tea would be largely exported for blending with teas grown in other countries, for the plantation on the arroyo of the Parana River, it became an important source of income and growth.

An Unusual Visitor

In the summer of 1950 the plantation received an unusual visitor. The tall, athletic young man came riding up to Taras' house at the centre of the cluster of homes on the arroyo. The young man was dusty and weary as he hopped off his strange mode of transportation. It appeared to be a bicycle but it had been motorized.

The young man approached Taras, sitting on a bench just outside his home.

"Ola! Have you lived here long?" the young man asked.

"Almost fifty years," Taras answered.

"Then perhaps you remember Ernesto Guevara Lynch?" the young man asked hopefully.

"Yes I do," answered Taras. "He had a plantation north of here. They called it Caraguatai. But I think he sold in '47."

"Yes that's right," the young man answered. "I am his son, Ernesto. I spent the first few years of my life on that plantation. I am travelling in the area and wanted to see it again. Can you tell me how to get to it?"

"Of course," Taras responded and he indicated exactly how the young man could get to his former home.

"But you are tired. Perhaps you will rest for a bit and share some mate?"

"Thank you," the polite young man responded.

So the elderly man and the young man sat together in the shade, sharing mate. Taras was curious about the young man and his adventure on the strangely-adapted bicycle.

It seemed Ernesto was studying in Buenos Aries to become a physician. That made sense. Taras recalled his family had been well off and he thought he remembered one of the reasons they had left their plantation was that their eldest son had asthma.

"So besides coming to see your former home," Taras continued, "why have you come this far on that contraption?"

"I love to travel. I enjoy meeting people and talking to them about their lives. I plan to travel through the whole region this summer."

Just then one of the plantation workers approached Taras.

"We are ready to move to the next field. I just wanted to let you know of our progress," the labourer said.

"That's good. You got the job done quickly. Thank you for letting me know."

"Why do you sit here in the shade while that tarefero sweats in the sun for your benefit?" the young man asked with a touch of scorn.

"When I was younger," Taras answered evenly, "I spent a lot of time sweating in the sun alongside that man's father. Now both he and I sit in the shade. Our sons have taken our places."

"Did you really do the work of tareferos? That is unusual for a patron".

"Our plantation is different. My partner and I came from a land where our fathers owned very small farms, barely enough to feed their families. And to add to that hardship, they had to pay taxes or work for the large landowners. My partner came to this country as a labourer on a large estate before he decided to make his life here. He married the daughter of a

Guarani, who was also a labourer in the fields. We know all about the hard life of a labourer."

"When we decided to start this plantation, we knew we would need a lot of help. But we had seen how the patrons of large plantations mistreated their labourers. We did things differently. We paid our workers in cash, not in credits for a plantation store - just as your own father did. Everyone who works here can build a home and live here with us. They share in the profits based on their contributions."

"We don't refer to our workers as tareferos. They are part of our family. Their children play with our children. We even built a school here on the plantation so all the children could learn together."

The young man had listened intently, nodding as the elderly man continued with his story. "This is the way it should be," he thought. "And this old man has shown that it can work."

The two parted as friends, Taras glad to have shown the young man the way their plantation worked and the young man glad to have had the chance to see it.

He had seen a lot in his travels, so far, and much of what he saw had been abhorrent to him – people so poor they could not feed their children or themselves, while rich landowners had more of everything than they needed. As a physician, how would he be able to treat illness in people who were starving? No there had to be a change. A real change, not simply pandering to the working class as a way to get and keep political power the way Peron had done. In his heart, Ernesto knew that real change could only come about through revolution and he would dedicate himself to bringing about such change.

Years later, Taras was amused to hear that Ernesto Guevara, now called 'Che', with a comrade, Fidel, were causing quite a stir in the wider world.

Guillermo

There had been big changes on the plantation. Ivan, Guillermo's father-in-law, had died in 1948 at the age of seventy-four. He had been like an older brother as well as a partner to Tato. And Tato had grieved for the loss. It seemed to Guillermo the loss of his partner just emphasized how very deeply Tato had missed the beloved brother he had left behind in the old country and hadn't seen in forty-five years. "It must be hard to get old and even harder lose the ones you love, whether to death or to circumstance," he thought.

But there had been other changes as well – happy changes. In 1953 at the age of twenty, Juan, Guillermo's oldest son had gone off to Brazil to enter the seminary. They would have another priest in the family! How delighted Tato had been. He had written letters to his brothers - Mykola, in the old country, and Andriy, in Canada.

Andriy responded immediately. In his letter he had been urged to include the words of their half-sister, Dariya. Her youngest son, Nick, had been ordained a priest in 1948. She was elated that there now would be two priests in the family – their father Yuriy would have been so proud!

The response from Mykola had been much less exuberant. In the short letter of reply, which arrived several months after the original had been sent, there was little news of the family or what they were doing and only a single line regarding Juan's news. It simply read, "Luba is glad there will be one in the world to replace her father." Taras knew Luba was Father Mykhaylo's daughter and had married Mykola's eldest son, Anton. As he read the simple sentence a chill ran down his back. So Father Mykhaylo was dead. He wondered when and how it had happened. It was a strange response to the joyous news from Argentina and it had worried him.

In 1953, Andres, Guillermo's second son was eighteen and going off to study business. He had grown up on the plantation and loved the family enterprise. But the world was changing. Andres had often heard his father talking with the other men of the plantation about the various ups and downs they had faced in terms of the marketability and price of what they grew. Andres had become fascinated by economics, not just of the plantation but of his country, indeed of the world, for to him it was all interrelated. So he decided the best way he could make a meaningful contribution to the family business was to study economics and commerce.

Yory

Yory was at the height of his career, but working as a government bureaucrat was not always easy, especially during the Peron years. Mechanization had been one of the Peronistas goals and this movement was to be implemented on farms, as well as in factories. Yory, always the innovator, could see the value of mechanization of some farming tasks but he also recognized the limitations, particularly with regard to growing yerbe. Yory also anticipated the negative impact of mechanization on the size of the required work force in the farming industry. Mechanization would come but it would benefit the large plantation owners more than the massive work force. This, like many of Peron's policies, was in conflict with his touted support for the working class.

As with all government employees during difficult political times, Yory knew he must keep his observations on the impact of Peron's policies to himself. It was not wise to point out flaws in the President's plans. Yory had learned quickly and had become an astute bureaucrat. He had even learned to reign in his enthusiasm for innovative ideas and only share them when the time and place were right. This perhaps had been the most difficult lesson of his career, since it went against his natural inclination.

Myko

Myko had moved his family to Buenos Aries, but had not been successful in getting the type of job he thought he deserved. And so it was not long before he moved his family back to the banks of the Parana River. There he knew how to make money. And so Myko resumed his activity as a smuggler, this time unhampered by the demands of his father's plantation.

Myko's sons were growing up. They had been raised with their father's 'business'. It was all they knew and they had become good at it.

Myko had always been very competitive with his older brother. He had always thought himself better than those around him. So it was not surprising that his sons grew up thinking themselves superior to each other and everyone they met. They seldom worked together for a common goal, but rather competed with one another. At first this was in order to earn their father's favour, but over time it became their natural way of being.

By 1964 all three of Myko's sons were married and had developed their own businesses in direct competition with one another. Myko was fifty-five years old and very proud of his sons and their achievements.

As the post-war years rolled by, another wave of Ukrainian immigrants arrived in Argentina, some of them finding their way to the province of Misiones. These immigrants, however, were considerably different from their predecessors. They were teachers, engineers, doctors, and lawyers. They had been educated in the Soviet Ukraine. They spoke more Russian than Ukrainian and did not participate in the Greek Catholic Churches, which had been the central force for preserving Ukrainian culture in the province. Many of these immigrants were quick to learned Spanish and preferred to live and work in the urban areas.

11 TOWARD THE END OF A CENTURY

Ukraine

Mykola

In October of 1965, Mykola turned eighty-five. He had been lucky in that his health had been good most of his life. True, he had suffered from pain and aching, especially in his hands and feet as a result of frostbite he had suffered years ago when he had struggled to return home from his service in the Austrian Army. But over the years he had learned to cope with this relatively minor affliction. And, of course, as for most people in the region, there had been times of hunger, especially during the two world wars and all the conflict that had been the hallmark of those turbulent times. So perhaps his longevity was due to genetics or perhaps it was due to his positive attitude and striving to see the good in every situation, no matter how bleak. Perhaps it was his unfailing devotion to God. At any rate, Mykola had been very fortunate to have had such a long life.

Mykola's family was similar to many in the region with regard to their faith. Despite the fact that their church and their priest had been taken away from them, their faith persevered. The church had been used as a granary and then boarded up and guarded so no one could enter. It was dangerous to even cross yourself as you walked past the building, since you could be arrested for doing so. Father Mykhaylo had been arrested and sent to a work camp in Siberia. No Orthodox priest had ever been sent to replace him.

At first the people prayed in the privacy of their homes. But during the Stalin years, all shows of faith had been brutally censured. Holy icons, rosaries, and prayer books were confiscated and destroyed. The raids on people's homes to find and remove all such items came so swiftly there hadn't been time to hide or bury them. Many people, especially the older ones, were deeply shaken by these events. But Mykola knew he could continue to pray and keep his faith alive without the physical items he had used and loved. So despite the danger and fear, the faithful people continued to pray.

As time went by and it seemed there would be no reprieve from the ban on their faith, people began to become defiant. Repression often spawns resistance; this is a hallmark of human nature. And so over time, the faithful slowly and very carefully built an underground or 'catacomb' church. Priests were trained and secretly ordained, even in prison cells and labour camps, and a few bishops were secretly consecrated. Then in the late 1950's and early 1960's another wave of persecution resulted in the arrests of underground priests and faithful laymen. In 1963 Pope John XXIII persuaded Khrushchev to finally release Archbishop-Metropolitan Slipyj, after eighteen years of imprisonment in Lviv. At the age of seventy he was allowed to live out his final years in Rome. Thus he became the leader of the Greek Catholic Church in Exile.

It was only toward the end of the summer of 1965 that Mykola's family recognized a noticeable decline in the family patriarch. Nadya, his wife, was the first to notice the change in her husband. She was just a few years younger than her husband and had been aware of her own decline, so it was not surprising to see it in Mykola as well. What was surprising, however, was how quickly his condition was changing. Anton and Vasyli were next to recognize their father's decline.

"Is Tato ok?" Anton asked his mother one bright August morning when he saw his father was still in bed, while the rest of the household was up and bustling.

"He's just tired," Nadya responded. "After all he's almost eighty-five! Who would have thought we'd live this long?"

Both Anton and Vasyli were worried and wanted their father to see a doctor, but of course, he refused.

"I am just old," Mykola said. "A doctor can't do anything about that."

And so Mykola stayed in bed later and later each morning. He spent more and more time sitting in the sunshine on the bench in front of the house.

The brothers told their sister, Dora, that they were worried about Tato so she began to come more and more frequently to visit her beloved father. The visits could not be very long because of her work and family commitments. At the age of sixty she still had workdays on the collective farm and when she wasn't working, she helped tend her grandchildren so their parents could work. However, she tried to spend as much time with Tato as she could.

Soon even his grandchildren realized that Diedo was in decline. The eldest girls, Maria and Halia, were married with families of their own and they, too, were very busy with home and work commitments but each made an effort to visit Diedo when they could. Fortunately the grandsons, Ivan and Taras, still lived near the original family home, so they and their families were more frequent visitors to the old man.

Throughout all of this, Nadya, lavished her attention and care on her ailing husband. Everyone's attention was focused on Mykola and so no one even noticed that Nadya, too, was failing.

So as Mykola's birthday approached, the whole family saved rations and planned to gather in celebration of the patriarch's birthday. It was a joyous occasion. The younger great-grandchildren ran through the house and yard and played noisy games. They all loved these rare occasions when they could be together at Baba and Diedo's house. The adults prepared a meal and visited with each other, getting caught up on the latest news of the various families. Mykola and Nadya were very happy to see their extended family all together in one place. This had not been possible for some time and that made it a very special occasion, indeed.

The family talked and laughed and enjoyed each other's company all afternoon and well into the evening. At one point Anton whispered to his mother that he thought Tato had drifted off to sleep.

"Should we put him to bed?" Anton asked.

"No, he wouldn't want to miss any of this. He'll wake up and want to still be surrounded by his family."

So Mykola dozed in the midst of his loved ones. The sound of the children's laughter and the others chattering was the sweetest music he had ever remembered hearing.

It was only a few weeks later that Nadya woke to find Mykola had died in his sleep. She prayed for his soul and then she cried for the loss of her husband of almost sixty years. Then a thought flitted through her mind. She wished she, too, could die so peacefully and be reunited with Mykola.

"Shame on you, staryi baba (old grandma). Your time will come soon enough. It is not up to you, but to God, when you will come and when you will go!"

Nadya was a widow for only one year. After Mykola was gone, her health declined rapidly. Her children thought she must have used all her strength to care for their father and now that he was gone, she had no reason to continue. She had been ill with a nasty cold. She had recovered briefly and then the illness had returned with vengeance. A high fever, congested lungs, and a cough wracking her fragile, old body was the end of her. She was gone.

The old house just wasn't the same after Mykola and Nadya were gone and their passing left a huge hole in the family and in the hearts of all who had loved them throughout a lifetime.

When his father died, Anton had written to Taras, in Argentina, and Andriy, in Canada. A year later he wrote almost the same letter about his mother.

In 1968 when the Greek Catholic Church in Czechoslovakia was restored, yet another round of raids and arrests of underground priests and faithful ensued in the region of the village on the Dniester Tributary.

Brezhnev succeeded Khurschchev in 1964 and died in 1982. He was succeeded by two, short-lived rulers, Yuri Andropov and Konstantin Chernenko.

In 1984 Major-Archbishop Lubachivsky from Philadelphia, succeeded Cardinal Slipyj as Metropolitan in Exile of the Greek Catholic Church. Attempts by religious and human rights activists to legalize the Church fell on deaf ears and, instead, more of the closed churches in the west of the Ukrainian Republic were re-opened as Russian Orthodox Churches.

Then in 1985 Mikhail Gorbachev was elected General Secretary by the Politburo. He was the first Soviet leader to have been born after the October Revolution. He had been born into a Ukrainian-Russian family in the Caucasus region and had lived and worked on a collective farm. He had survived the Great Famine of 1932-33, although other members of his family had not. Over the course of six years under his leadership, the Soviet Union as it had existed in one form or another since the 1917 Revolution, ceased to be.

Gorbachev's policy was based on four principles designed to reform the stagnating Communist Party and the state economy. These principles were glasnost (openness), perestroika (restructuring), demokratizatsiya (democratization), and uskoreniye (acceleration of economic development). Under his leadership the constitutional role of the Communist Party in governing the state came to an end. The introduction of glasnost in 1988 gave the Soviet people here-to-fore unheard of freedoms, including greater freedom of speech. There was less control of the press and thousands of political prisoners and many dissidents were freed. The 1988 Law of Co-operatives permitted private ownership of service, manufacturing, and foreign-trade businesses.

Hope for religious freedom and the return of the Greek Catholic Church to the faithful, especially in the west of the Soviet Socialist Republic of Ukraine, was sparked in 1988 when Gorbachev actually allowed a celebration of the millennium commemoration of the baptism of the Kievan Rus. The celebration was to be controlled by the Russian Orthodox Church but it seemed a miracle that the milestone would be celebrated at all in the atheistic Soviet Union.

In the same year two momentous decisions reoriented Soviet goals, contributing to the end of the cold war. First, the agreement with the United States to eliminate all nuclear weapons by 1996 and the full withdrawal of Soviet forces from Afghanistan. The second was the stance that Eastern Bloc Countries were free to determine their internal affairs without interference. The latter immediately opened the door for elections in Poland, toppling the communist government followed by similar popular upheavals across Eastern European Countries.

Early in 1989 elections to the Congress of People's Deputies were held throughout the Soviet Union; these were the first free election since 1917. In May of 1989 Gorbachev became Chairman of the Supreme Soviet. Late in 1989 people were allowed to freely cross the Berlin Wall, opening the way for reunification of Germany.

On January 23, 1990 the first Greek Catholic Synod held in Ukraine since the Second World War, took place in Lviv. It declared 'invalid' the 1946 Synod, which had revoked the 1595 Union of Brest, and called on the Soviet government to legalize and rehabilitate the church.

In October, 1990 Ukraine declared its laws to be sovereign over Soviet Laws. On August 24, 1991 Ukraine declared its independence. Then on December 1, 1991 in a national referendum, the Ukrainian population voted overwhelmingly for the Act of Declaration of Independence. The countries of Poland and Canada were the first to recognize the Ukrainian Nation. As the second most powerful republic in the former Soviet Union, this independence put the final nail in the coffin of the old union.

Ultimately the result of the reforms, unintended though they may have been, was the rise of long-suppressed nationalism and anti-Russian feelings and the collapse of the Soviet Union in 1991, when republic after republic declared independence. While political reforms may have been a triumph, particularly for Eastern Bloc Countries, the economic reforms resulted in a huge Soviet deficit and shortages of basic foodstuffs.

Vasyli

In 1991 when the whole world changed, Vasyli was seventy-eight years old.

He praised God that he had lived to see this momentous day. The Ukrainian people finally had a sovereign nation. How he wished his father, Mykola, and especially his brother, Anton, could have seen this day. As it was, he was the only remaining member of his generation of the family still alive to celebrate the great event.

Vasyli wanted to do two things now. He wanted to tell to his children and grandchildren the history of his family and all they had lived through to get to this day. The second thing he wanted to do was to let his father's brothers' families, in far-off Argentina and Canada, know about the miracle.

To address his first goal, Vasyli set about writing a letter to his family. He wrote about his great-grandfather, Ivan, who had been only the second generation, no longer a surf. He had owned a tiny plot of family land, left to him by his father. That had been in the days of the old Austrian Empire. He wrote of his grandfather, Yuriy, who had taken most of his family half way around the world to Canada, in search of a better life for generations to come. He wrote of his father's brother, Taras, who had gone to Argentina in search of a better future. He wrote about his father, Mykola, who had chosen to stay. He wrote of all the hard work and hardships, which his father had endured - during his time in the Austrian Emperor's army; during the First World War; during the depression, which had followed the Great War and the time under Polish rule after the reconstruction of that nation; during the Second World War; and most recently, during the time of the Republic of the Soviet Union. These were the stories his own children and grandchildren and generations to come must hear, in order to understand just how important it was that the country they now lived in was, indeed, their very own. He felt they had truly be blest by God.

With regard to Vasyli's second goal there was a problem. While he knew that his father, Mykola, maintained a correspondence with brothers in Argentina and Canada and his own brother, Anton, had written final letters to tell his uncles of the deaths of their father and mother, Vasyli himself had not been a part of writing these letters. Vasyli searched the little family house for the information he needed to pick up the correspondence he now felt duty-bound to continue. There were no old letters, no evidence of directions or addresses anywhere in the house. Anton, like his father, had been cautious. He had likely destroyed all evidence of the family correspondence. Vasyli grieved that he could not share his joyful news with his far-flung, distant family.

Argentina

Taras

Toward the end of 1965 Taras received the letter he had been dreading. Anton, Mykola's eldest son, had written from the old country. Mykola was dead. Taras was not ordinarily disposed to depression but this news was a tremendous blow to him. He prayed for his beloved brother. Carmen found her husband in tears as he sat reading and re-reading the letter. She tried to comfort her husband but she knew this was something he would have to come to terms with on his own.

Taras took to walking through the untamed jungle areas on their plantation. He tried to rekindle the initial wonder and joy for the birds and vegetation, he had felt during his early days in the region. He spent hours thinking about his boyhood growing up with his beloved brother, Mykola, in his father's house in the village on the Dniester Tributary. They were all gone now, his father and long-dead mother, his beloved Uncle Vasyl, his partner, Ivan, and now his favorite brother.

"This is just the start," he thought, "I guess I will be next."

But Taras felt well. He was still fairly strong and he had only a few aches and pains. He knew he was doing very well for a man of his age, for he would be eighty-four at his next birthday in September. Eighty-four! Imagine!

Taras sat on a bench in the early morning sun. "It would be hot today," he thought. It suddenly struck him as odd that when he was young, his September birthday had been in the cool autumn of the old country. Here, where he had celebrated so many birthdays since his arrival sixty-three years ago, his birthday was in spring.

He had seen so many changes since he and Ivan had first started the plantation. Now, so few people were needed to do much of the work. He remembered those long, backbreaking days when he had worked alongside his partner and the hordes of labourers they had employed, in order to clear the land and establish the yerba bushes. Now, with all the technology and machinery, production was much higher and the profits greater. And there were so many fewer people on the plantation. He missed the community of workers who they had once established. The plantation seemed so empty now, so impersonal. But then so many of their workers, especially the young ones, had left in the days when there were more jobs in the cities.

The world was changing. "It must be a sign of growing old," he thought. "I am sure the world was changing when I was young but somehow, I didn't notice it as much then. Or maybe I did notice and actually enjoyed the change." And at that thought he smiled to himself.

Taras had been following regional events he had found strange and somewhat distressing. It seemed everyone wanted higher prices for their yerbe. They were calling for more government regulations and the protection of producers' rights. There was even an organization that had formed to fight for these things. It was called the Movimento Agrario Misionero (MAM) and fight they did. They advocated strikes and roadblocks to get what they wanted. "That is not for an old man," Taras thought as he slowly shook his head.

"These young ones talk of diversifying crops and protecting the environment as if these were new ideas, which they just invented! Why even he had diversified the crops on this plantation. Wasn't it he who had started growing black tea before anyone else in the region? And Yory had been working on diversifying crops for years. And the environment! Ivan's wife's old father, the Guarani, had always shown the way to help keep the land productive by taking care of it."

Carmen first noticed the changes in her husband a few months after he had received Anton's letter. At first she thought he was just grieving for his lost brother. But then she realized it was more than that.

It started with forgetting simple words. He'd be talking about something very familiar and suddenly the word he wanted would not be there.

"It's normal for someone of his age," she thought.

Then she noticed occasionally they would be talking and he would switch into Ukrainian. She had learned his mother tongue when they had married, just as he had learned Spanish, but for many years now their conversations, indeed all conversations on the plantation, had been in Spanish. It had been years since Taras had spoken to her in Ukrainian. She thought this was rather strange. She mentioned it to their son, Guillermo. Though he agreed it was, indeed strange, he didn't seem concerned.

Then Taras started doing unusual things. He would misplace something and go in search of it but when Carmen asked what he was looking for, he suddenly didn't know. He became frustrated and sometimes even angry. This was highly unusual. In all the time she had known him, Taras had seldom lost his temper. This latest development did concern Guillermo.

So Guillermo wrote to his brother, Yory, in Posadas and asked that he make an appointment for their father with a doctor.

Guillermo and Carmen accompanied Taras to Posadas to see the doctor. The news was not good. The doctor said many older people can have memory problems. There was nothing to be done. And, they must prepare themselves, for it would get worse.

And so over the next several months Taras suffered the most dreadful thing that could have befallen him. This man, who had always been intelligent, creative, and innovative, came to the disastrous realization that his mind no longer worked the way it had in the past. He felt like he was losing himself and it terrified him.

Carmen and Guillermo tried very hard to comfort Taras but his forgetfulness and frustration continued to increase. They tried to be patient with him but even that was becoming difficult. Carmen was almost at her wits end, as living with Taras had become very difficult.

Then one day he was gone. Carmen woke up and Taras was not in their house. She searched everywhere and could not find him. She had Guillermo come to help her search. When still they couldn't find Taras, they called together the entire workforce of the plantation to search for him. They searched for a whole day with no success. Guillermo contacted Yory, who arrived the next morning to help with the search. Finally, in the evening of the second day they found him. He had wandered into the untamed jungle and had gotten lost. He could not find his way home. When they found him he was scratched and dirty, hungry and dehydrated. Carmen was beside herself.

Taras was brought home and tended to but it was clear this had been a close call. From now on Taras would have to be watched closely to prevent a repeat of the near-disastrous event.

The days in the jungle had worked on Taras' mind. He had known he was lost and had feared for his life but there was nothing he could do to help himself. His sense of self-worth had been shattered.

He hated the fact that everyone was so careful around him. He was never left alone anymore. He could not go anywhere by himself. He felt himself dying from the inside. In the depths of despair he began to think it would be better if he were dead.

"No, I can't think that way. It is a sin. I must pray. God has his reasons."

But as the autumn approached Taras' condition declined rapidly. Now he got lost in the compound unable to find his own house among the several huts clustered together on the plantation plaza. Katya tried to spend as much time with her ailing father as she could. One day her father's conversation became very distressing.

"Who are you?" Taras asked her as she sat beside him on his favorite bench.

"I'm Katya," she responded.

He looked carefully at her.

"Oh," he said. "You must be Mykola's daughter. You look so much like him. He's dead you know. I miss him so much. We were close growing up and then he left me. I don't know why, maybe he didn't love me anymore."

"Oh Tato," Katya responded in tears. "Mykola didn't leave you, you left the old country to come here, to Argentina. Your brother stayed in the old country."

"Really?" he asked. And he shook his head. Then a tear rolled down his check.

"They used to say, 'you can't get just one Martiniuk boy – they come as a pair.' We were always together."

It was that evening. Carmen, who had been so worried about Taras, found him in the bedroom. He was lying face down on the bed, fully clothed. He was dead.

She ran to call Guillermo and Katya. They didn't know what had happened but Carmen believed Taras had just lost the will to go on.

They gathered around the corpse and prayed for his soul. It had been such a sad end for such a brilliant man. He and his innovative ideas would be terribly missed on the plantation. Soon word spread and all the workers came drifting into the house to pray and say good-bye to the man to whom they owed everything they had. He had been a good man. A kind and generous man. He and Ivan had created the plantation out of nothing. They all owed him a great debt for his ambition, hard work, and insight. The plantation would never be the same without him.

Guillermo notified Yory that they were bringing Tato's body to town for burial. After the funeral, together the two brothers tried to track down Myko to let him know of their father's passing. It was as if their wayward brother had vanished from the face of the earth – they could not find any trace of him.

In 1973 Peron returned to Argentina after a 'stand in' member of the political party that bore his name, Peronist, was elected as President. When that President stepped down, Peron with his third wife as his running mate, was elected in a special election that fall. He died the following summer and Isabel Peron succeeded to the Presidency. Her Presidency was marked by chaos and ended with her arrest in 1976.

Once again a military junta followed and attempted to remove all traces of Peron. Their ruthless efforts resulted in over five thousand people being killed and many more jailed and tortured. Between 1975 and 1979, it was estimated that six to fifteen thousand antigovernment activists 'disappeared'. Economic reforms, including privatization of the banks and industry, could not control the rampant inflation gripping Argentina.

Myko

Economically and politically, Argentina had become a difficult place in which to live. In 1975, Myko was an old man of sixty-six. His wife had died a few years before. Their last years together had been tumultuous. While they had lived on his father's plantation she had always supported him and shared their common belief that his contributions were undervalued. But when they had left the plantation and Myko couldn't get the job he thought he deserved in Buenos Aries, things began to change. His wife would have liked to continue living in the national capital but Myko could not find a way to earn enough money there. So the family had returned to the north. They had squatted on land on the banks of the Parana, further north than his father's plantation. Myko had selected the spot for its isolation and convenience to resume his smuggling business.

Things had gone reasonably well for a while. The boys had grown and in the spirit of sibling competition, which Myko had always encouraged, each had set up a business and moved further afield. The daughters had married and moved away as well. Occasionally one or the other of the brothers would return to their parents' home, usually to brag about some major endeavor or to ask for a loan. On the rare occasion when more than one brother came home at the same time there was always rivalry and heated arguments. Myko's wife had grown tired of these exchanges and had even told her sons to avoid descending on her home, except one at a time.

But now she was gone. Myko was surprised just how lonely he had been since her passing. The boys had come less and less frequently and eventually stopped coming altogether. Myko had a lot of time to think.

One day he was thinking about the stories his father had told about growing up in the old country. He especially remembered his father gushing about how close he had been to his older brother, Mykola. How on earth could two brothers be so close? It must not have been true. No doubt the old man's recollection was shaped by the fact that he missed his family.

Then Myko's mind wandered and he wondered what it would have been like if he and Yory had been close. That of course could never have been. Yory was always flaunting his great ideas and their father was always so impressed with whatever Yory's next great plan for the plantation was.

Myko was tired. He lay down in his shack. He watched the sunlight filtering through leaves on the trees, gently blowing in the breeze and listened to the birds and insects twittering and buzzing. He had never paid much attention to nature but now he had a lot of time on his hands. And then an idea struck him. Harmony. That's what he saw in nature, harmony. Everything seemed to work together. Peace and harmony. That would have been a nice way for him and his wife to have spent their last days together. It would have been a nice way for his sons to have been together. He wondered why it had not been so.

But Myko had missed an important life lesson - if you sow discord you cannot reap harmony.

Myko died alone in his shack in the far northern reaches of Misiones on the banks of the Parana.

In April 1982 in an attempt to gain the support of the people of the nation, the Argentine military invaded and claimed possession of the Falkland Islands, which had previously been claimed by the United Kingdom. The British Forces defeated the Argentines quickly. It was a national disgrace.

In 1983 a human rights activist, Raul Alfonsin, was elected as President. He attempted to prosecute members of the former government, who had been in power during the time of the disappearances. In addition, he attempted to halt inflation by replacing the peso with the austral. Renewed inflation and increasing wage demands overcame these efforts.

In 1989, Carlos Menem of the Peronist Party was elected as President and then re-elected in 1994. He reduced government spending and the role of government in the economy, along with introducing capitalist reforms.

Despite economic success, allegations of corruption toppled this government in 1997.

In 1991 the Regulatory Commission of Yerba Mate (CRYM) was replaced with reduced trade barriers and the elimination of quotas on yerba production. This deregulation benefited large producers, who increased plantation size and increased mechanization to further increase yields.

In 1999, Fernando de la Rua Bruno was elected as President and tried to dramatically decrease the country's deficit. Provincial spending could not be controlled and economic growth stagnated, resulting in the currency, again, being devalued. Social and political chaos ensued as the economy fell into another massive recession. Violence, looting, and police repression culminated in the resignation of the President and replacement with his prior opponent, Eduardo Duhalde.

Andres

By the end of the century, Taras' grandson, Guillermo's second son, Andres, was in his early sixties and largely in charge of the plantation. He had studied business and economics and he had shepherded the plantation through difficult and changing economic times. His two grandfathers, Taras and Ivan, had built the plantation out of nothing, almost a hundred years ago. They would have been proud of the operation today.

Andres had developed a brand for the plantation's yerba mate, as well as several flavoured varieties of the product. He had established an international distribution chain. Now the operation was largely mechanized and they were able to capture more of the value of their product by controlling production from plant to the final packaging, thus avoiding middlemen. Therefore it was possible to compete on price with other large producers. But Andres had not lost sight of his grandfathers' guiding principles of fairness. He offered the services of the plantation's secadero (drying facility) to smaller producers at a reasonable rate. He also bought their hoja verde (green plant material) at competitive prices so they, too, could continue to make a living. He was a good businessman and a fair one.

Andres loved the plantation. He felt proud and privileged to be a part of it and the family who had founded it. He thanked God for the many blessing his family had received. They had, indeed, been blest!

Canada

Dariya

In 1967, Dariya was sixty-nine years old. She had been a widow for eighteen long years. She had suffered from arthritis for many years. The remedies her mother had always used for such aches and pains no longer seemed to help. Dariya didn't mind the pain as much as she minded the fact that she could no longer do what she wanted to do. She wanted to plant, tend, and harvest her garden but that had become just too difficult. George and Lyudmyla had been good to come in spring to cultivate her large garden plot and help her plant it. In recent years, Lyudmyla and her teenaged daughter, Lesya, had done almost all of the work, while Dariya told them what to plant and where. They helped weed and tend the garden and then they helped pick the produce and process it. It had become their garden. Dariya knew they did it for her, because they had a large garden of their own on the farm. She was grateful to them for the pretense.

There was another problem with Dariya's health. Several years ago she had noticed some strange things beginning to happen. It had come on gradually and she thought it was just because she was aging. She had, of course, been tired a lot of the time but that was nothing unexpected. Then she started having to go to the bathroom more and more frequently. It was annoying at best. She couldn't last through the Divine Liturgy without having to rush to relieve herself, even if she had just done so before hand! And she was thirsty all the time - it seemed she just couldn't drink enough water.

George had insisted on taking her to see a doctor. The man told her she had to start taking little white pills and stop eating all her favorite foods. "Is that all doctors know? That's exactly what they told Pavlo to do?" she thought and yet she didn't have the same thing he had had, she knew that much. And then the doctor had told her she had to do the strangest thing. She was supposed to pee in a bowl instead of the toilet and dip a tiny piece of paper into the bowl to see what colour the paper turned. Ridiculous!

Dariya's mother had known a lot about many ailments and if she had been alive, she would likely have had a remedy for this strange problem. But as it was, Dariya had never known anyone who had had the same symptoms. The doctor called it diabetes. He said there was no cure and if she didn't do as she was told she would have more problems. Dariya wondered whether the doctor's orders weren't worse than the disease.

"It's so hard getting old. My Pavlo is gone and I am alone almost all the time now. I still see my friends at church but I can't walk down town or to their homes any more. And there aren't that many friends left, fewer and fewer every year. You silly woman. Why do you dwell on negative things? You are alive. You have children who love you and come to visit you – when they can… and one is a priest! They are all so busy with their own lives... And then there are the grandchildren, especially my little Lesya. Not so little any more. She is growing up too. How I love it when she comes to visit and even stay over night with me in my little house. And then there are the great-grandchildren. Such smart little ones. But here I sit, barely able to take care of myself. I can find something to eat but I don't cook as much as I used to and what I want to eat the doctor says is bad for me. There you go, feeling sorry for yourself again. Better pray, that will help. Where is my rosary?"

Father Nick

Nick had been ordained in 1948. He had served in several parishes across the Prairie Provinces after his ordination. By 1967, he had been a priest for almost twenty years. Now finally, he had an opportunity to visit Ukraine. As the youngest in the family, his mother Dariya had often told him stories of the village where she had spent the first seven years of her life. These stories, which Nick had grown up with, had planted within him a deep desire to see the village for himself.

So in 1967, when the opportunity came for him to attend a religious conference in Lviv, he was thrilled to finally get the chance to see the village of his mother's birth. He had talked for long hours with her, trying to get as much information about the village as he could.

"It's too bad your Uncle Andriy is no longer with us," she said to her son. "He's the one who kept in touch with Mykola in the old country. He could have told you more than I can. I was only seven when we left. I can't remember much, I'm sorry."

When Father Nick asked his mother about the church and where it was in the village she proudly told him, "On a hill, just where the two streams meet to form a tributary of the Dniester River. The cemetery is behind the church. My brother Mykola is buried there. If you get there, you must pray for him and take a picture of his grave for me."

"I will Mama," he promised.

And then she laughed out loud.

"What is it Mama?" Nick asked.

So then she told him the story.

"I was born in the village but I wasn't baptized in that church. When my father went to see the old priest to arrange for my baptism, he was told my name would be Petronilla, because I was born on her saint day. Tato didn't like the name the priest was going to give me, so he took me to the next village to be baptized. The old priest never forgave him!" And she laughed some more. It was her favorite story about her father.

After the conference in Lviv a fellow priest, whose family had come from a neighbouring village of what had been Galicia, decided to join Father Nick in an expedition to visit the two villages. First they travelled to Ivano Frankivsk (formerly Stanyslaviv) and from there they took a rented car to the remote villages. They had been warned about the rough condition of the roads but nothing could have prepared them for the reality.

The two priests had dressed as western tourists for the excursion. It had taken them more than twice as long as they had anticipated to reach the first village. As they approached, Nick spotted what had been the church, high up on the hill in the center of the village. His heart leapt at the sight.

After parking as near to the building as possible, they immediately noticed two uniformed men. They approached the men with caution.

"Ty poteryalsya? (Are you lost?)" the first man called out to them in Russian when they were still some distance from the building.

"No," Father Nick's companion responded in Ukrainian. "We were hoping to take a look at the cemetery."

"Why would you want to do that?" the man responded, this time in Ukrainian. It was clear he understood and spoke both languages.

"My mother's brother is buried there," Nick responded this time.

"Many people are buried there," the man retorted.

Then the second uniformed man leaned over to the first and they had a quiet conversation.

"You wouldn't be here to say a prayer at the grave of your uncle?" the first man asked Nick.

"I'd like to be able to tell my mother I saw her brother's grave," was all Nick responded, avoiding a direct answer to the question.

The second man smiled slightly. He recognized the clever response for what it was.

The first man, who had done most of the talking, motioned for the two tourists to come closer.

When Nick and his companion reached the two uniformed men, the first man said in a low voice, "We are going over to that tree to have a smoke. If you go near the cemetery just keep walking, don't linger in any one spot. We should not see you when we get back from our break."

As the two uniformed men walked toward the tree, Nick and his companion walked quickly toward the cemetery. It was old and in poor repair. Many head stones were decayed or toppled. Nick scanned the names on the headstones as they walked slightly slower along the edge of the closest row of graves. He thought he saw the name 'Martiniuk' on one, but couldn't pause long enough to be sure. He saw many familiar names. It was not surprising, as many of the settlers in the area of Canada where he had grown up, had come from this region - from this very village, in fact.

As the two men walked slowly past the edge of the graveyard, Nick realized they could not see the two uniformed men by the tree. If he could not see them - they could not see him, so he pulled his Kodak Instamatic Camera out of his pocket and took a quick picture of the graveyard. Then he turned around and quickly took a picture of the church. It was boarded up, unpainted, and desolate. It was clear it had not been used as a church for some time. Nick quickly hid his camera back in his pocket and continued to walk. The two tourists walked in a wide arch past the graveyard and the church and back to their rented car. They got in and drove away. Nick hoped and prayed his two quick shots would actually turn out when developed. He would love to be able to show them to his mother.

The two tourists were seen in the village as they stopped to speak with a few people. They were asking for the house of the Martiniuk family. One old baba stood in the street and pointed at one house after another and said the same phrase over and over again: "pishov v Kanadu (gone to Canada)". It wasn't long after, that the village policeman appeared.

"Vy b krashche zalshyty (You'd better leave)", he told them.

And so the two disheartened tourists got back into their rented car and drove away from the village.

Dariya

Nick got home safely from his adventure in Ukraine. He was so excited to get his films developed. He had planned to take the pictures to show his mother for her birthday in June.

But things got busy on his return and it wasn't until almost the end of summer before Father Nick could make the trip to visit his mother.

"Mama," he said, "how are you?"

"Much better now that you are home," she replied.

So he made some tea. She wanted to put sugar in it but Nick found the Saccharin instead. Then they sat side by side on the couch as he told her all about his trip and showed her his pictures. When he told her about his visit to the cemetery and church, she was very quiet. She didn't realize how much things had changed in the old country. "Uniformed men, speaking Russian, telling her son not to linger in the graveyard? And the church! The beautiful church … all boarded up. How could that be?"

When she saw the picture of the graveyard, neglected and in disarray, she could hardly hide her distress. And when she saw the one picture he had of the church it broke her heart. Her memories of the church had been of a beautiful, grand building, with golden banias and tall windows. The building in the picture bore almost no resemblance to what she remembered.

Nick knew it would be a shock for his mother to see what had become of her village since she had left but he had underestimated the impact it would have on her. He stayed several days. He talked with her and prayed with her. By the time he had to go, he was hoping she had gotten over the shock of the pictures he had taken for her. He had asked whether she wanted to keep them. She said "no".

Later that year, Dariya was really not feeling well. George took her to the doctor and the news was not good. In addition to diabetes, which had not been properly controlled, she had a heart condition. So she had to take more pills.

It wasn't too long after that, Dariya fell in her house. Luckily a neighbour had come by to bring her some milk and found her on the floor of her bedroom. George came and insisted Dariya move back to the farm, where he and Lyudmyla could keep an eye on her. Dariya didn't want to leave her house. She didn't want to upset George's family. She remembered when her mother, Anna, had moved into the same farmhouse and the disruption it had caused with her own family. True, Stephan had just left home to start university but she knew if she returned to the farm she would be sharing her granddaughter, Lesya's room, while the two younger boys shared the middle bedroom. But George insisted and Lesya didn't seem to mind sharing her room with Baba.

The new living arrangement didn't last long. Dariya's condition worsened and she was taken back to the doctor. This time he put her in the hospital.

It was a strange place full of strange sounds and smells. She didn't like it one bit. And, although George and Lyudmyla and Maria and her husband took turns coming to see her, the hospital was twenty miles away and it was an inconvenience for them. Soon Iryna came from the city to see her mother in hospital and before the week was out, Nick had arrived as well.

"I must be dying," Dariya thought. "Why else would they all be coming to see me?"

So after a long, Sunday afternoon visit in the hospital, George and his siblings decided to go downtown to get a bite to eat at the café. They had just ordered their food when the waitress came back to their table.

"It's the hospital, Mr. Dannyk, they are calling about your mother."

George went over to the phone on the counter next to the cash register.

"Hello, this is George Dannyk," he said.

"It happened just a few minutes ago," the nurse said, "she's gone."

"Please hold our order," George asked the waitress and the party returned to the hospital. Nick prayed over his mother's body and his siblings joined in. Maria, Iryna, and Lyudmyla cried quietly. Dariya had been the closest thing to a mother, other than her older sister Lena, that Lyudmyla had ever known.

The funeral was held a few days later. Prayers were said in the little house in the hamlet. The funeral service was held in the church on the corner of the Dannyk farm. Dariya was laid to rest in the graveyard on the outskirts of the hamlet, on the hill overlooking a large slough. She was buried next to Pavlo and just two rows ahead of where her own mother, Anna, rested. A short distance to the west, in one of the first rows of graves were two small crosses surrounded by lilac bushes. These were the graves of the 'little brothers', Dariya's first two sons. They were all together now in peace. Vichnya Pamyat. Eternal Memory.

Paul

All three of George and Lyudmila's boys were bright and enjoyed school, which pleased their parents very much. Stephan completed high school in 1966. After high school he attended the University of Saskatchewan. He studied long and hard and became a physician, graduating in 1973.

Philip, who had spent his boyhood immersed in every detail of space exploration, followed his brother to the University and studied engineering, earning a bachelor's degree in 1972. He was then accepted to continue his studies in aerospace engineering at a university in California.

By the time Paul, the youngest son, was in grade nine, he had had to take the bus to a central high school in a larger, neighbouring town. So many farmers had sold or rented their land and moved into towns or the city. The hamlet had lost over half of its population. The number of active farmers had declined dramatically. As a consequence, the hamlet's two-roomed school only had students from grade one to nine. In just a few more years it would close altogether, due to the decline in student numbers.

After graduation, Paul wasn't sure he really wanted to go to university but his brothers had gone and were happy with their life choices, so in the fall of 1970 he set out for Saskatoon as well. He enrolled in courses he was interested in and did well, academically, but he really didn't know what kind of work he wanted to do for the rest of his life.

Paul had been a thoughtful and well-adjusted teenager. He had many friends, both boys and girls, but he had never had a girlfriend. He had gone to dances and parties and had enjoyed the company of many of his female schoolmates but he had never really preferred one of them to all the others. As a result, while many of the boys of his age were going steady with one or another of the girls in school, Paul preferred to keep company with many of them, usually within the context of a group rather than on dates, as such.

Part of the problem was there had been a girl who had sparked his romantic interest. She was the daughter of a local farmer. Her parents were among the French contingent of the community surrounding the hamlet. She was the prettiest girl Paul had ever known. She had dark hair and sparkling eyes. Her name was Annette Beaulieu. She had been in his class throughout school in the hamlet, but then had gone to a girl's boarding school run by French Nuns, rather than to the central high school in the larger, neighbouring town. Paul had had a crush on her since the first day he had seen her when they were both in grade one.

During his first year at university Paul had made many new friends. Some were from small Saskatchewan towns. Some had grown up on farms. A few had grown up in the city. Paul enjoyed hearing about how members of his generation had grown up and how their experiences compared with his own.

Paul, like his brothers before him, attended Ss. Peter and Paul Ukrainian Catholic Church on Munroe Ave., not far from the University. But the cafeteria at St. Thomas Moore College on campus was a good place to eat a reasonably priced lunch and meet other students who shared his faith. One day he had been playing cards in the cafeteria between classes, when someone he hadn't met before joined the group. As they talked, about where they were from and what it had been like where they had grown up, the new fellow became curious about Paul.

"Are you sure you are Catholic?" the fellow asked.

"Yes of course I am Catholic," Paul responded.

"Then you must be Polish not Ukrainian," the fellow retorted.

"I am Ukrainian Catholic, it is the Byzantine Rite," Paul answered.

"There is no such thing as a Ukrainian Catholic," the student answered. "You are either Roman Catholic and a Pole or you are Ukrainian and Orthodox."

Paul was angry with the young man for his uninformed comments, but held his tongue. His faith had never before been questioned. He couldn't believe how ignorant this guy was.

Not long after that episode Paul had run into the Annette, the object of his long-held crush. She had been with several friends, but seemed happy to see someone from home. She invited him to a party she and her roommate were having the following weekend. Paul eagerly accepted the invitation and anticipated seeing her again. The party had been a crowded affair with hordes of students spilling out of the tiny, rented house and into the yard and even onto the street. By the time Paul had arrived, many of the partiers had clearly had far too much to drink. Paul drank one of the six bottles of beer he had brought to the party and watched for a chance to speak to the hostess. It was clear she was preoccupied with her guests and what appeared to be her boyfriend. "Well that's that," Paul thought. So he finished his beer and didn't even bother to retrieve the other five he had brought, but simply left for home.

Paul happened to run into the Annette just once more during his first two years of university. Again it was at St. Thomas Moore College, but this time in the library. He had found the library a convenient spot to study between classes. He spotted her across the room and watched as she and a young man - Paul couldn't tell whether it was the same one he had seen her with at the party - studying from the same book.

During the summer of 1972, following Paul's second year of university studies, George developed a case of Shingles. It became clear Dad and Mom needed help on the farm. All three boys had grown up helping on the farm from an early age and all three had enjoyed the farm life, although none had actually considered it for their own occupation. Stephan was in the final, grueling year of medical residency and Philip, while about to convocate, had already accepted a position at a university in California. Lesya had just finished high school and was preparing to attend the University in fall. Paul gladly volunteered to return to the farm to help for as long as was needed.

Lesya

During the summer of 1972 Lesya was preparing to follow in her brothers' footsteps and enrolled as a student at the University of Saskatchewan. In prior years the Sheptytsky Institute at the corner of Wiggins and College Drive had been the University home to the Dannyk brothers. However, Stephan was now in his final year and would be away from the city a lot for practical training to become a doctor, so it was decided that a basement suite within walking distance of the University, would be a comfortable temporary home for Stephan, Paul, and Lesya. Then later that summer, their father, George, became ill and Paul decided to remain at home to help on the farm. So it was that during her first year of university, Lesya resided in the basement suite in the city, alone much of the time.

Lesya hadn't been quite sure what exactly she wanted to study. She had thought about teaching. Her father, George, had been very pleased when she mentioned that idea. Lesya knew it was because he had wanted to become a teacher himself. She didn't want to disappoint her father but by the same token, it was her life and she had to make her own choice. Her reluctance was not based on a lack of affinity for teaching; she knew she could be a good teacher and would likely enjoy that profession. The problem was she just couldn't see herself in a classroom, year after year, teaching the same lessons to successive cohorts of students. She thought the repetition would drive her mad. She knew herself and knew she thrived on change and new challenges.

So in her first year of university, Lesya took the usual courses in the College of Arts and Sciences. The elective course she chose was art. It was a basic drawing class. Lesya had always liked to draw and she thought this would be an enjoyable course. It was in this class that she had met her new friend, Mary. Mary had lived in the city all her life and had had the opportunity to take all sorts of classes and be involved in many activities while she was growing up. Mary's diverse interests and talents amazed Lesya.

It was Mary who introduced Lesya to Ukrainian Dance as an art form. Mary's mother taught traditional dance and had established a local dance troupe. Mary, of course, had been dancing under her mother's instruction since she was very young. Lesya, who had learned the basics of traditional Ukrainian dance for Christmas concerts in school, was fascinated by the level of professionalism of Mary's mother's dance troupe. It wasn't long before Lesya joined the dance troupe.

Dancing became Lesya's avocation and obsession. She loved the practices and the performances. Mary's mother was a wonderful instructor and had seen the natural talent in Lesya and had nurtured it. Before long Lesya was on the road to becoming a very accomplished dancer, in her own right. She sought her instructor's advice about how to make dance her life's work.

"You are very talented and there is no doubt you enjoy dance and can do so for many years. But there will come a time, sooner than you like, when you will not be able to continue. You must have a back-up plan. Continue your university education. Get a degree. Then dance as long as you can but when the time comes, you will have your education to fall back on."

So Lesya continued, year after year, and eventually earned a degree in education. She did teacher training and that experience confirmed her suspicions that she would not be content teaching in a classroom for the rest of her life. It was then that her dance instructor, and now mentor and friend, asked if she would like a position as assistant choreographer for the dance troupe. Lesya was ecstatic. This was her dream come true.

Paul

Being back on the farm after two years of city life had made Paul realize just how much he had enjoyed living on the farm. And so it was soon agreed he would become the farmer in the family. George recovered and continued to work with Paul to make the farm a profitable and comfortable place to live and work.

Father and son spent long hours talking about the future of the farm. Things were changing. Farming had been greatly influenced by new technologies regarding seed, fertilizer, and machinery. Furthermore, for a farmer to be successful now-a-days, he needed to have a much bigger farm than just two sections of land. So eventually the pair decided they had to formulate a plan, in order to ensure the future success of the farm. It was decided that Paul would go back to the University and earn a degree in agriculture. He would, of course, continue to work on the farm with his father between school terms. George would talk to the banker about expanding the farm. There was no shortage of farmland available for sale or rent but what they needed was a strategic plan.

Over the course of the next few years, George and Paul increased the size of the family farm, invested in the necessary machinery, and with his knowledge of new agricultural methods, Paul helped to prepare the Dannyk farm for the coming millennium. The farm was no longer a 'mixed' farm with both grain and animals. The raising of farm animals, which had been critical for providing much needed food for the early settlers, had become very specialized and now, there were dairy farms, cattle ranches, and pig farms. Some grain farmers still kept chickens and maybe a milk cow or two, but just for their own use. The Dannyk farm had become a grain farm. And it wasn't just oats and wheat or even canola being grown in the fields. They had devised a complicated rotation of various crops, including field peas, lentils, and flax, in addition to the all-important wheat and other grains.

Paul was on his way to becoming a successful farmer. But there was still something missing in his life.

There is a saying: 'when a door closes, God opens a window'. Perhaps that's true. It is rather strange how some things in life happen. It had been over five years since Paul had seen Annette, the girl he had so admired most of his life. One day he had taken a part from the seeder into town to have repaired and, while he was waiting for the job, he strolled into the café on Main Street. He couldn't believe his eyes, for there she was.

"I heard you were back on the farm," she commented after they had exchanged greetings. "How do you like farm life?"

"It's great," Paul responded. It was clear he really meant it.

"What have you been doing?" Paul asked, almost dreading that he would hear a story of a successful husband and a house full of children.

"Well," she said slowly, "I earned my degree in nursing back in '74 and then took a job in a big hospital in Toronto. I lived there for a couple of years and decided I really wasn't cut out for big-city life. So now I am just visiting the folks and looking for another job – probably closer to home."

Paul really wanted to ask her if she was married and had a family, but didn't think he could. He wanted to see her again but once more, that seemed highly unlikely.

"How long will you be around?" he asked.

"Oh, probably just another week. Mom needs some help and I haven't heard anything yet about the jobs I've applied for. We should do something together," she said.

Paul couldn't believe his ears.

"Sure," he responded. "Do you want to take in a movie or something?"

"Where?" she asked half laughing, "in Humboldt!" indicating the closest town big enough to have a movie theatre.

"No, no, we could drive into the city," he responded.

"That would be nice – maybe on Sunday?"

Paul was walking on air as he returned to the shop to pick up the repaired part. He couldn't believe he had a date and with the girl of his dreams, no less. How had it happened? Many years later he would still be mystified by whatever alignment of the stars, stroke of sheer luck, or grace of God had afforded him the opportunity but he was eternally grateful!

After a short time, Paul and Annette realized how very much they had in common. They had grown up together. Their parents had been neighbouring farmers and members of the same community. They had many shared experiences and memories. They became close friends.

Eventually Paul learned that Annette had had a very serious relationship with a fellow university student but she had learned, too late, that he was more interested in conquests than a long-term relationship. It had broken her heart. That was why she had taken a job in far-off Toronto. But after two years in the big city she had been homesick, so had returned to the prairies.

She was in the process of looking for a nursing position in either Saskatoon or Regina. Paul hoped she would get a job in Saskatoon so they could continue to see each other often. Then she heard about a position as a travelling public health nurse based in a town not far from home. It meant doing a bit of travel in the area but she thought she might prefer that to shift work in a hospital. Paul was delighted.

And so, as Paul established his position as a farmer and Annette took on the role of public health nurse, it suddenly became obvious to the two young people that they might actually build a life together. It's funny how some things work out.

Lesya

Lesya danced and taught dance. She developed innovative renditions of traditional dances. Eventually, she took over as the artistic director of the dance troupe Mary's mother had created. The dance troupe became famous in Western Canada performing at many Ukrainian festivals. Their fame spread and soon the troupe was performing throughout the country, throughout North America, then in Europe, and eventually in Ukraine.

Although Lesya had always wanted to visit Baba Dariya's home village, travelling with the dance troupe never afforded an opportunity.

During their performances in Ukraine, Lesya was always fascinated by the response of the people. The old women cried and wiped their tears on the corners of their aprons as they remembered by-gone days. The older men tapped their toes and sang the words to the traditional songs, as they marveled at the precision steps and choreography. The young people just couldn't believe what they were seeing because it was something so different, so old fashioned, and yet so energetic and modern at the same time. Lesya enjoyed being able to bring home this tiny bit of their common culture.

And there was something else, which made Lesya happy about what she was doing. In her heart, she just knew Baba Dariya would have been very proud of her for doing her part to keep the traditions of their culture alive. Lesya thanked God for her baba and all she had learned from her, as well as the opportunities she had been afforded to do the work which meant so much to her.

Father Nick

In 1988 the Greek Catholic Church around the world celebrated a thousand years of Christianity for the Ukrainian people. In 988, Vladimir the Great, ruler of the Kievan Rus, converted to Christianity and decreed his subjects be baptized and accept the new religion, as well. The millennium was a momentous occasion for the church.

After the millennium celebrations, the Greek Catholic diaspora became even more proactive in supporting, in any way possible, the underground church in Ukraine. In Canada in 1989 the Synod of Diaspora of the Ukrainian Catholic Hierarchs created a special commission to collect and send religious literature to Ukraine. Two priests were among the many who had contributed to the efforts to do what could be done for the people of Ukraine, as they struggled to re-gain their church.

Father Nick Dannyk from Canada, now in his early sixties, and Father Juan Martiniuk from Argentina, in his late fifties, both had strong family reasons for being committed to this effort. Back in 1967, Father Dannyk had visited the village his mother had been born in. There were certainly still descendants of his long-lost uncles living in that part of the world. Father Martiniuk's grandfather had left behind a favorite brother in western Ukraine back at the turn of the century.

It was a coincidence that the two priests, both working for a common goal, finally met at a Sobor in Chicago in 1989.

Father Dannyk had just arrived and was scanning the list of attendees, when he spotted a familiar name. Intrigued, he sought out his fellow priest from Argentina.

"Hello, I am Father Nick Dannyk from Canada. I noticed your name because it was my mother's maiden name. She was Dariya Martiniuk and she had a half brother who went to Argentina before the rest of her family came to Canada."

"Really! My grandfather had a sister and two brothers who went to Canada. Maybe we are related!"

After just a brief exchange of information it suddenly became clear that Juan's grandfather was Dariya's brother, Taras.

"My mother would have been so happy that we have found each other!"

So the two became fast friends dedicated to working together to support the church in Ukraine.

The two priests who had met in 1989 kept in contact and apprised of what each was doing for the church in the land of their forefathers. Then in 1990 they both decided to travel to Lviv to attend the 'Ukrainian Youth for Christ' week. Both priests wanted to see what more they could do to support the cause. Both had the secondary goal of visiting the home village.

And so it was that in 1990, when so much political change was happening so quickly, Father Dannyk and Father Martiniuk 'came home'. This time, Father Dannyk was determined to find any long-lost relatives who might still be living in the village. Shortly after his first trip to Ukraine he had paid a visit to his cousin, Vasyl (Bill), Uncle Andriy's son. From him, he learned that the precious letters between Uncle Andriy and the two brothers, in Argentina and Ukraine, had been carefully preserved. The two cousins poured over the creased and aged documents. Soon they discovered the vital clues, the house number of the original family home in the village and the names of children and grandchildren. Father Dannyk was sure he would be more successful on his next trip than he had been on his first visit.

It wasn't hard to find the house with the correct number but it looked nothing like the description his mother had given him, so many years before. Father Nick speculated that it might have been because his mother had been so young when she had left the old country. Perhaps the house had looked bigger to a seven-year-old than it actually was. Also, she had described a typical two-roomed house and this house seemed to have an additional room to the back. Nick Dannyk and Juan Martiniuk, dressed as civilians, knocked on the door. No one answered. They looked around the outside of the house. There was no one around. They called out. No one answered. The next day they returned. This time there was a woman working in the garden next to the house.

"Is your name Martiniuk?" Nick asked her in Ukrainian.

At first he thought she hadn't heard him. So he repeated the question, this time in Russian.

Slowly, she looked up. "Who wants to know?" she asked in Ukrainian.

"I am from Canada and my friend is from Argentina. We are looking for someone who is related to the Martiniuk family who used to live here."

"Talk to my husband. He will be in from the field tonight."

So Nick and Juan returned to the house that evening. Once more, they knocked on the door. This time a man in his mid-fifties opened it. Nick was amazed. Perhaps his eyes were playing a trick on him. This man looked so much like his Uncle Andriy had!

Nick introduced himself and Juan and told the man why they were there, all the time wanting to know if this man was related. The man looked at Nick and Juan very carefully. He didn't smile or show any signs of recognition as Nick recited the potential family link.

"Come in," the man finally said.

Nick and Juan entered the house. They were shown chairs and sat down.

"Dovesty horiwka," the man called out to his wife as he too sat down. Then and only then did the stony faced slowly melt into a subtle smile. "You are the son of my grandfather's sister," he said pointing to Nick. "And you, you must be the son of my grandfather's brother."

Juan told the man he was actually the grandson of Taras, Mykola's brother.

"We must drink to family," Ivan Martiniuk said, as he filled three kalishicks (shot glasses).

And so began the friendship between three, long-lost relatives. Ivan Martiniuk was pleased to have two Ukrainian Catholic priests visiting his home and best of all, they were his relatives, his own flesh and blood. As the evening wore on his wife brought bread and pork fat for the men, who she fully expected to continue talking and drinking into the wee hours of the morning. The three men talked of their common ancestors and told the family stories each had heard over the years.

When Father Nick mentioned the collection of letters his Uncle Andriy had saved, Ivan's eyes lit up.

"Andriy, he was a poet!" Ivan exclaimed. "I know because that is how I learned to read. My grandfather and father loved his book of poetry and they used it to teach us how to read. We had to keep the book hidden but I memorized the poems. I always knew the book was there. And even if it had been found and taken, they couldn't take away the beautiful words from my mind. Those beautiful words .... There were so many times when those beautiful words were all that kept us going."

Father Nick marveled at the reverence with which Ivan held Uncle Andriy's words. He had felt the same way all his life. It was an unbreakable bond between the two men. And then he knew what he had to do for this long-lost relative. He vowed to send Ivan a copy of each of Uncle Andriy's books as well as those of his sister, Iryna. This was a man who would appreciate these books, even those written in English. He would find a way to hear and understand the words, Father Nick was sure of it.

Before the end of the year, the new Soviet law on freedom of religion was passed and seminary education in Ukraine was reestablished. There was so much that could be done to support the Church in Ukraine.

During the 1994 Winter Olympics, Oksana Baiul, won the gold medal in the women's singles figure skating competition. The world watched as the Olympic organizers scrambled to find the Ukrainian National Anthem to play as she stood on the highest podium. The anthem is called 'Shche ne vmerly Ukrainy ni slava ni volya' ('The Glory and Freedom of Ukraine Has Not Yet Died'). The lyrics, originally a poem written in 1862, was set to music, written in 1863 - a testament to the long-held dreams of freedom of a people.

12 THE NEW MILENNIUM

Argentina

In June 2001, small yerbe producers rallied with their little old tractors in the central plaza of Posadas to protest ('el Tractorazo') against the reforms of the 1990's, which had lead to low prices. This and similar demonstrations resulted in a new regulatory organization called the Instituto Nacional de la Yerba Mate (INYM). This organization was to set the annual selling price for yerbe, in order to create stability in times of price fluctuation. However, its efforts were not always successful. Some large processing companies used several means to lower their costs, in order to preserve their profits. Practices such as paying small producers much less than the INYM price or giving advances on the coming crop at a fraction of the actual value, contributed to the reduction in numbers of small producers and their continued demand for better regulations.

In April 2003 Nestor Kirchner was elected President. The country was in the midst of economic, social, and political crisis. By renegotiating the country's foreign debt and promoting foreign investment, along with a strong export rate, the economy began to recover and unemployment decreased. Cristina Kirchner, Nestor's wife, won the October 2007 Presidential election as the first woman President of Argentina.

In 2009 seventy-five per cent of yerba producers in Misiones were small farmers who had fewer than ten hectares of land. The ten largest producers were supplying eighty per cent of the product. Larger operations, which were more efficient due to economies of scale, continued to put pressure on the small producers.

In 2003 the yerba plantation started by Ivan and Taras, was one hundred years old. It had expanded over time and was among the largest in the region. It specialized in two crops, the traditional yerba, which was the mainstay of its production, and a secondary crop of black tea. At the age of sixty-eight, Taras' grandson, Andres, was still firmly in control of the operation. He was, however, grooming his own two sons to eventually take over the plantation and its business interests. Jorge Martiniuk, the eldest, was his father's right-hand man. He, like his father, had studied business at the University and had developed many innovative and cost-saving methods to make the production of the plantation's products efficient and profitable. Juan Martiniuk, Andres' second son, also had a business degree and was in charge of international marketing and distribution. He had had a tremendous success in introducing yerba mate into the United Sates of America, a potentially huge market.

Despite the cyclical nature of the Argentinian market for mate the plantation on the arroyo had learned how to weather the storms of over supply in the early years of the new millennium. Oversupply and the devalued peso had resulted in most small producers giving up the growing of yerba. Many actually abandoned their family farms and moved to urban areas. But the Martiniuk Plantation had become large enough to survive the ups and downs of the local market. Having access to the international market was a huge part of their survival and success.

In 2013 yerba mate was officially declared the national infusion of Argentina.

Ukraine

Although Ukraine became a sovereign nation in 1991, progress in the political and economic arenas was slow and frustrating for the people.

At the start of the new millennium the country was lead by President

Leonid Kuchma and Prime Minister Viktor Yanukovych. Kuchma had been a long-standing member of the Communist Party of the Soviet Union until 1991, after which he declared himself to be an Independent. In the 2004 Presidential campaign Yanukovych was running for President, as Kuchma had served two terms and could not run again. His main opponent was Viktor Yushchenko of the Our Ukraine Party. The campaign was highly charged and controversial, due to claims of intimidation by government forces against its opponents. A climax was reached when, in September 2004 Yushchenko was mysteriously poisoned with dioxin. He recovered sufficiently to complete the campaign and the election was held on October 31, 2004. No one candidate won more than fifty per cent of the ballots cast and so a run-off election, between the two leading candidates, was held the following month.

When Yanukovych won the run-off election, nation-wide protests erupted, because people believed the election had been marred by corruption, intimidation, and fraud. The protests were known as the 'Orange Revolution' for the colour Yushchenko had chosen for his party. The protests continued until the results of the November run-off were annulled and a re-vote was held in December of 2004. This time, under intense domestic and international scrutiny, Yushchenko won fifty-two per cent of the vote.

In 2010 Yanukovych beat Yushchenko to become President. He worked to repair the relationship between Ukraine and Russia, which had suffered under Yushchenko. However, he was ousted in February 2014, as a result of violent and deadly clashes in Kiev's Independence Square.

The year 2011 marked the twentieth anniversary of Ukrainian independence but the young country still had a long road ahead of it.

In 2013 Lesya Kovelenko and her husband, Roman, travelled to Ukraine. It was not Lesya's first visit, as she had travelled to the area with her dance troupe several times in the past. However, it was her first visit to the Independent country of Ukraine. The purpose of this visit was to see the church in the village where Baba Dariya had been born one hundred and fifteen years before. It was very important that the trip coincide with

Easter celebrations, as Baba had always told the story of how her family had celebrated one last Easter in the old country and then left for Canada on Bright Monday, 1905.

When they arrived in the village, Lesya couldn't wait to see the church. She had seen the picture her uncle, Father Nick, had taken back in 1967 but she knew the church had been restored since then. It was beautiful! It was painted white and had a large central drum topped with a dome. The four small banias and the dome were all painted gold and each was crowned with a golden cross, just as Baba Dariya had described. Inside, the tall windows in the alcoves and the windows around the drum bathed the whole interior in a heavenly light.

Lesya and Roman attended the early morning Easter Martins and Divine Liturgy. Lesya lit a candle for her great-grandfather, Yuriy, her Baba, Dariya, and her father, George. Lesya was overwhelmed by the beauty and joy of the centuries-old celebration. She heartily joined in the singing of the Easter anthem. On this Great Day, it was impossible not to believe in resurrection and salvation! Afterwards, the people laid their baskets of Easter foods out on the courtyard before the church for the priest to bless. Lesya had prepared her basket, just as she had learned to do from her baba, and as she had done in her own home since she had married. This had been the trip of a lifetime and she had enjoyed every second of it!

Lesya visited and celebrated Easter with Ivan Martiniuk, the long-lost relative first discovered by her uncle, Father Nick, back in 1990. It was a blessed and joyful family reunion.

In 2014 Ivan Martiniuk, at the age of seventy-nine, died peacefully in his home in the little village where the two streams meet to form a tributary of the mighty Dniester River.

Canada

In 2012 the farm Pavlo had homesteaded from the time two years before he married Dariya, earned the designation of 'century farm' – farms, which had been in existence and farmed by the same family in Saskatchewan for one hundred years. Paul Dannyk, at the age of sixty, was still farming the original homestead with his own son, George.

Yuriy's homestead had become a 'century farm' in 2005 and it too was still being farmed by one of his descendants. Andriy and Elena's grandson, Terry, had grown up loving visits to his grandfather's farm. His own father, Bill, had had no interest in the occupation but Terry couldn't see himself being happy anywhere else. He had willingly spent long summers working with Grandpa Andriy and learning what was necessary to be a good farmer as times and methods changed.

In 1960, at the age of seventy-five, Grandpa Andriy had actually increased the size of his farm holdings. He and his brother, Petro, had jointly inherited the original quarter section of land, which their father had homesteaded when they arrived in Canada. His brother's dreams of creating a large family farm with and for his three sons had evaporated. The boys had grown up working very hard alongside their father but one by one they had tired of the challenges and uncertainties of farm life. Each, in turn, had drifted to jobs away from the farm, initially to supplement their share of the farm income, but eventually as their permanent vocations. One had become a mechanic in the nearby town, but had tried to continue to help his father especially as the old man aged. Another had gone to the city to train and eventually managed a retail store. The third had married into a family of daughters and had become involved in his father-in-law's business. So when Petro died in 1960, Grandpa Andriy had bought his brother's land.

Six years later, Grandpa Andriy was gone as well and at the age of twenty, Terry Martiniuk inherited the family farm. It was only three-quarters of a section of land, by no means a huge farm. Terry felt himself to be the luckiest man in the world and he was eternally grateful to his grandfather, who had provided him with such a magnificent start in life. He felt truly blest!

Lost and Found

Lesya Kovelenko had always loved history. She had grown up inspired by the stories told by Baba Dariya, her father George, and Auntie Irene, who was by this time a famous author. So it was only natural that as she reached a certain age, Lesya would become obsessed with tracing her family's roots. She began by sorting through the documents and letters, which had accumulated over the years and which she lovingly referred to as the 'archives'. Her father, when he saw her interest, suggested she contact his uncle's grandson, Terry. Terry was less than a decade her senior and they shared a passion for family history. More importantly, Terry had inherited all the family correspondence, which his grandfather had preserved along with his books of his poetry. Together, the two re-created the family tree, all the way back to Yuriy and Vasyl, who had been born in the mid-1800's.

When they had exhausted the information available from family documents, the pair began searching for more information using the internet. As in most families there were some mysteries. For instance, whatever happened to the middle of Baba Dariya's five stepbrothers, Mykhaylo? They knew he had married and had a son and then was drafted to fight in the First World War, but there the story ended.

And so the search continued. Then one day Terry phoned Lesya with an amazing bit of news. He had located a family in upstate New York. He was fairly certain they were the descendants of Mykhaylo Martiniuk, the long-lost, missing brother. Together, they planned how best to approach this possible, distantly-related family. They didn't want to bother them. They didn't want to be thought of as 'crack pots' or 'schemers'. After all, not everyone was interested in or wanted to know about past family ties. So carefully they drafted a letter. They thought that a written letter would be seen as more serious than an email and less intrusive than a phone call. They included a brief description of the initial part of the family tree and where they believed the possible link might be. Then they mailed the letter and waited.

It was some time later before a reply arrived. Terry couldn't wait to share it with Lesya. They had indeed found the descendants of the lost brother! Baba Dariya and Grandpa Andriy would have been so pleased. So the next step was to share more information. Then someday, hopefully soon, they could plan a family reunion.

EPILOG

It was two in the morning and she couldn't sleep. When she was young, she had often had problems getting to sleep but while she was working it hadn't happened often. Now that she was retired the old problem had returned. Her knees and legs were aching.

She got up and went to the bathroom. Maybe an ibuprophen? No that upset her stomach when she took it at night. Maybe she'd just read for a bit.

Returning to bed, she switched on the bedside lamp and picked up the book she was reading. It was by one of her favorite authors, Edward Rutherford, and was called 'London'. Lesya had bought it because she was planning a trip to that great city. She also admired the author's writing style and the way he incorporated history as he told his stories.

After a few minutes, she decided to get up. She wandered to the kitchen. Maybe something to eat? Or maybe a bit of vodka. She took the bottle from the fridge freezer and poured a small amount into a kalishick, then went to the living room. The city was covered in snow. The South Saskatchewan River was frozen. The city lights sparkled below her as she gazed through the big window of her riverside condo. "It's a cold one out there tonight," she thought as she wrapped herself in an afghan and began to sip the vodka. Gazing at the city lights her mind wandered.

She had been so lucky, so privileged. What would her life have been like if great-grandfather hadn't come to Canada? Or, as her father had often said to them when they were young, if great-grandfather had gone to Argentina? Through all the many years, some filled with hardship and pain, she knew her extended family, whether they had stayed in Ukraine or made Argentina or Canada their home, had been blest - thrice blest!

She walked back to the bedroom and her gaze fell on the ancient icon, which hung on the eastern wall. She had known this icon all her life. Baba Dariya had left it to her father and mother, who in turn had left it to her. Along with Baba's coral necklace, this icon had always been her most prized possession. And at this moment it seemed she must say a fervent prayer before the holy relic.

She would sleep now. She had to, because her grandchildren would be coming in the morning to bake cookies for Christmas!

ABOUT THE AUTHOR

Marianne Greer grew up in a small community on the Saskatchewan prairies near the family farm, which had been homesteaded by her Ukrainian grandparents. She earned a bachelor's degree and a master's degree from the University of Saskatchewan and a Ph.D. from the University of Texas at Austin. Marianne is a retired pharmacist and an accredited gemmologist. She lives in Saskatoon with her husband of forty-four years.

49475151R00248

Made in the USA
San Bernardino, CA
25 May 2017